TEETH
IN THE MIST

TEETH
IN THE MIST

DAWN KURTAGICH

Ⓛ Ⓑ

Little, Brown and Company

New York Boston

Little, Brown and Company
Hachette Book Group
1290 Avenue of the Americas, New York, NY 10104
Visit us at LBYR.com

First Edition: June 2019

Little, Brown and Company is a division of Hachette Book Group, Inc. The Little, Brown name and logo are trademarks of Hachette Book Group, Inc.

The publisher is not responsible for websites (or their content) that are not owned by the publisher.

Library of Congress Cataloging-in-Publication Data
Names: Kurtagich, Dawn, author.
Title: Teeth in the mist / Dawn Kurtagich.
Description: First edition. | New York ; Boston : Little, Brown and Company, 2019. | Summary: Inspired by the legend of Faust and told in alternating timelines, sixteen-year-old Roan arrives at Mill House as a ward and discovers she is connected to an ancient evil secret, while, centuries later, seventeen-year-old Zoey explores the dwelling's ruins and soon realizes she is not alone.
Identifiers: LCCN 2018029959| ISBN 9780316478472 (hardcover) | ISBN 9780316478465 (ebook) | ISBN 9780316522540 (library edition ebook)
Subjects: | CYAC: Magic—Fiction. | Witches—Fiction. | Ghosts—Fiction. | Horror stories.
Classification: LCC PZ7.1.K877 Te 2019 | DDC [Fic]—dc23
LC record available at https://lccn.loc.gov/2018029959

ISBNs: 978-0-316-47847-2 (hardcover), 978-0-316-47846-5 (ebook)

Printed in the United States of America

LSC-C

10 9 8 7 6 5 4 3 2 1

For those who scream

in silence

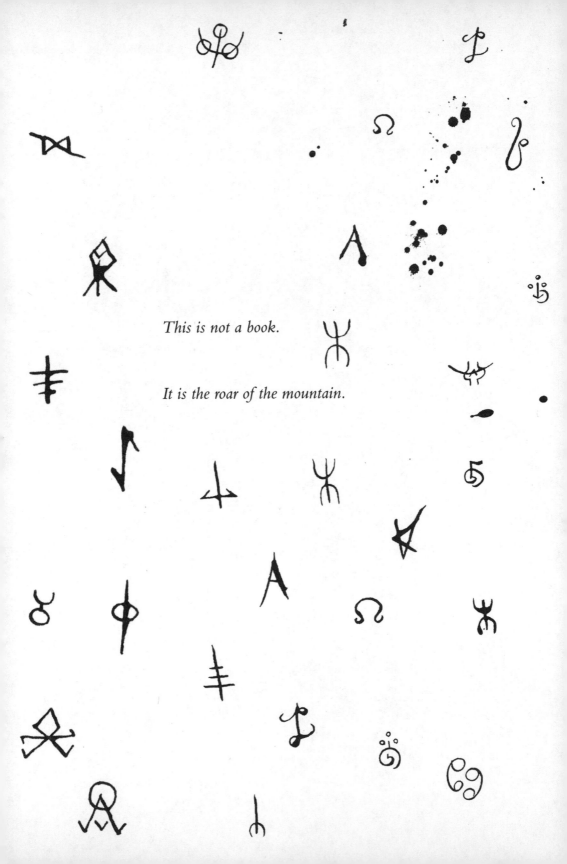

This is not a book.

It is the roar of the mountain.

PART 1

Above the Mountain

Stay, Mephistopheles, and tell me, what good will my soul do thy lord?

—CHRISTOPHER MARLOWE,
DR. FAUSTUS

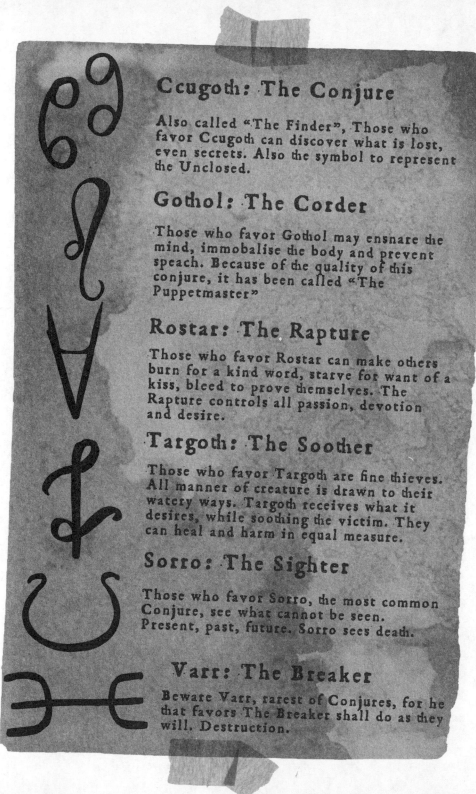

Ccugoth: The Conjure

Also called "The Finder", Those who favor Ccugoth can discover what is lost, even secrets. Also the symbol to represent the Unclosed.

Gothol: The Corder

Those who favor Gothol may ensnare the mind, immobalise the body and prevent speach. Because of the quality of this conjure, it has been called "The Puppetmaster"

Rostar: The Rapture

Those who favor Rostar can make others burn for a kind word, starve for want of a kiss, bleed to prove themselves. The Rapture controls all passion, devotion and desire.

Targoth: The Soother

Those who favor Targoth are fine thieves. All manner of creature is drawn to their watery ways. Targoth receives what it desires, while soothing the victim. They can heal and harm in equal measure.

Sorro: The Sighter

Those who favor Sorro, the most common Conjure, see what cannot be seen. Present, past, future. Sorro sees death.

Varr: The Breaker

Beware Varr, rarest of Conjures, for he that favors The Breaker shall do as they will. Destruction.

AD 977, Pant Tywyll
(Today, Meddwyn)

The monk hastens through the catacombs, past his brethren, who watch with inquisitive, yet chaste eyes. He is feverish, exultant. After twenty years of searching, he has found it at last.

He stumbles at the entrance to his alcove, stripping off his cassock and hood until he stands bare in the shadows. It takes a moment to light the rush candles.

He studies the pigeonholes, a number of which he carved with his own hands. They are the beds in which his scrolls rest. Their tanned scent is an old friend. It is an animal scent. Thick and putrid. This is his private collection. He is searching for the one he concealed twenty years earlier. Low down in the wall, it is hidden by his worktable.

He retrieves it with reverence.

It is old.

Older than time, but strong.

This one is not like others. Made from the skin, not of beast, but of man: flesh stitched together with spell-worked thread.

He unfurls it, the unholy words sliced into the scroll like wounds, still raw, and then he bends to remove the stolen parchment from his cassock on the floor—torn from a book in the great library. He places it next to the scroll, which seems alive, humming with power.

Yes, it seems to breathe. *Yes.*

He sits at his workbench. His hands tremble. Twenty years…twenty long years. He has sacrificed his life, his youth, his family, and his faith, and at last the answer has come to him. He knows the symbols. He knows the words.

It is an auspicious moment.

Here it is, then. He has acquired the Devil's Tongue.

He closes his eyes. *"Dimitte me." Let me…*

And begins to chant.

The candles glimmer and dance, *rage*, and then die. At once, the room is black; still like no room has ever been, nor will be for many years. It is a seeping gloom, which only grows thicker.

The monk releases his breath—which would fog, could he see it— and listens.

Torturously, the rocks rumble, growing louder. A demon stretching in his lair. Stones and sands fall from cracks in the walls.

A voice older than time is in the rocks.

It *is* the rocks.

The words quake in his core.

WHO DARES SPEAK MY TONGUE?

The monk replies and his words are no longer human.

Dreams and Darkness

The little boy arrived without warning, brought in a carriage during the blackest part of the night. Out of the window and through the mists, she saw a tall man in a dark cloak cross the cobbled street, carrying a bundle into the house. Downstairs, the door opened. She heard a man's voice murmur, and then Father's reply.

On tiny feet, she tiptoed down the hall, listening at the top of the stairs. And then the hooded figure looked up. She could not see any face in the dark space, but the little girl knew she had been caught.

"Evelyn's daughter," her father said. "Her name is Roan Evelyn Eddington."

The hood turned back to her father. "Adam and Roan Evelyn." And then there was a laugh. The kind that was not very happy at all, and that gave the little girl a horrible, churning feeling in her stomach. "Adam and *Eve*! What a perfect beginning."

The little girl crept closer, so she could see her father's face below her through the slats of the banister. And though many have said that children do not see the things that grown men see, the little girl did see, with the wide-eyed clarity of all children, that—despite his smile—her father was very afraid.

The man in the cloak turned, and she withdrew, all the way along the corridor and back into the safety of her bed with Isabel, her doll.

Footsteps on the stairs.

The strange cloaked man came closer down the corridor; she imagined a giant shadow creeping along the halls, and she tried to lie still, afraid he would come into her room—come for her. But he entered the room beside hers, and lay down a bundle upon the bed, the springs creaking slightly under the small weight. Then the man departed, his carriage pulled by two beastly horses, disappearing into the night. The man in black was gone.

The little girl waited for the sound of the hooves to fade away, and then she crept slowly along the short corridor and into the room next door.

The little boy rolled over and looked at her, his pale eyes wide with fear. Yet, when they rested on her face, they softened.

She smiled.

The little girl would never forget the summer the little boy came, brought in at night like a whisper in the dark. It was with him that she first discovered what would be thought of, years later, as a terrible burden, but which, very soon, she would consider to be…

magic.

HRH
United Kingdom

Certificate of Death

Superintendant Registrar's District: *Cardiff*

Registrar's District: *Conwy*

Death Registered in the County of: *Gwynedd*

Date and place of Death *Plas Tywell, 1853 est*

Name and Surname: *Roan Evelyn Eddington*

Certified cause of death and length of illness:

Missing for legal period required for death. Likely victim of Plas Tywell House fire est February 1852. No survivors.

Age at time of death: *17 years*

Birthplace *London, United Kingdom*

Place of death: *Meddwyn, Gwenydd, Wales*

Next of kin: *None listed*

Children: *No*

Burial or Cremation: *——*

Notes: *At the time of writing, Miss Roan Evelyn Eddington has been missing for seven years and therefore is declared legally dead.*

Signed: *C.R. Klington*

ROAN

◆❊◆

1851

Chapter 1

HER EYES

She is a ghost ship sailing the mud of the mountain.

She is a specter parting the shrouding mists.

She is a shadow upon a midnight river; she is the eye of the storm.

In her hand, a heavy portmanteau. She drops it every few steps to catch her breath and pull her cloak closer about her face. Even her bonnet is black. She is searching for a dwelling that she is beginning to think might not be there after all.

Though she is alone on the mountain, the solitary state being her preference, she looks around with a sense of unease. Like a trickster, the mountain is full of traps and twists, dotted with sharp slate rocks that protrude from the earth like jagged teeth, stretching skyward.

Silly, she tells herself, *for one to imagine the mountain could be hungry.* And yet…she can sense something considering her, and there is appetite in that regard. She bares her own teeth in defiance. Something shifts in the earth beneath her feet, and she has the peculiar sensation of someone having passed her by, suddenly. But under the moonlight, she sees how very alone she is.

She glances behind her, down the track, and can still see the moving black shape of the coach that brought her here. A trick of the mountain perhaps, but she can hear the angry hoofbeats of the horses and, she thinks, the carriage master's mutterings—"Stupid girl. Stupid, *stupid* girl…" No doubt it is true. To come all this way because of a slip of paper.

She pulls it from her pocket, unfolding it gently so as not to tear it. When first she found it, clutched in the hands of her dying father, it had been crisp and new. Now it falls like lace over her glove, threatening to disintegrate with one harsh touch. She knows the words by heart.

> DR. A. MAUDLEY
> MILL HOUSE
> MEDDWYN
> GWYNEDD
> WALES
>
> IN THE EVENT OF MY DEATH, ROAN EVELYN EDDINGTON SHALL FALL UNDER THE GUARDIANSHIP OF DR. A. MAUDLEY OF MILL HOUSE UNTIL SHE HAS ACHIEVED THE AGE OF TWENTY-ONE YEARS.
> MAY GOD HAVE MERCY ON HER SOUL.

And beneath: two signatures. One of them is her father's. The other, she supposes, belongs to this stranger, Dr. Maudley. She wonders, even now, whether she was right to take the note. Right to come all this way.

But what choice did she have? Where else had she to go?

She lifts her portmanteau once more and faces upward. Step by step, she climbs. The mountain stills—*attentive*—and she wonders at the utter silence. No birds, no breeze, nothing but the *squelch, squelch, squelch* of her boots in the mud. As though the world is holding its breath.

Her focus is unbroken until she feels something pressing in, like someone suddenly standing too close. Breathing. Watching. It overwhelms her.

She drops her bag. Raises her hands as if to defend herself, but instead of blocking a blow, her fingers begin to dance, drawing symbols or words or pictures in the air. All the while she is muttering beneath her breath, fighting off the thing pressing in.

It is large. So very large.

"Not today," she growls, her voice throaty and deep. "Back with you!"

Her fingers continue their dance, even as the presence retreats, and her skirts begin to smoke at the hem.

She stops when she feels safe once more, wondering at the strange sensation she'd had of someone turning to look at her, enormous, like the regard of a titan. After a moment, she picks up her portmanteau and continues on. A sudden energy, like the retaliation of a naughty child, sends her portmanteau flying backward. The clasps click open, scattering clothing, undergarments, ink pots, quills, and journals into the mud.

She ignores the delicates sinking into the mire, grabbing instead for the books, wiping them urgently on her skirt, heedless of the filth or the stains she is leaving behind.

"Do not haunt me, Father," she whispers, her gloves beyond saving. "I am paying the price. I have come here as you wished."

I am in exile, she reminds herself, staring at the barren earth, remembering the countless times her father had said, *There is safety in isolation, Roan.*

Get up, she tells herself. *Keep walking. Do not look back.*

At last, the sodden fabrics and stained books are back inside her portmanteau, pages pressed firmly together, like a lover's kiss. She peers up from under her bonnet to examine the heavens above as a rumble of thunder stutters across the sky; the darkness deepens as the clouds blot out the full moon. Then the heavens break open and drench her.

She takes a step…another…another. She is weighed down by the skirts, by the portmanteau, by a past whose burden she cannot bear. She does not see the figure watching her from within the heather and the slate rocks and the fog.

I am in exile. Keep walking. Do not look back.

Rapley Setters glimpses her on the track, standing on the mountain like a fey creature. She does not move, except to clean mud from the books in her hands with a grim expression, as seemingly solid as the mountain itself.

He frowns.

Why would a girl be walking up the mountain? There is nothing here except for Mill House. Surely she is not going there? She cannot be one of the three Dr. Maudley is expecting?

She is too young.

She is a girl.

He watches her struggle to her feet, her ridiculously wide skirts weighed down by the mud. She stumbles, and he sees her irritation, sees her pull once, twice, *three* times at her luggage before it finally comes free.

Sees the determination in her posture.

The thunder complains and she looks toward the sky, gazes in his direction, yet she doesn't see him.

Her eyes…they unsettle him.

It quickly becomes apparent to Rapley that she has set herself an impossible task, and when the rains descend, dousing the landscape in curtains of white, and Rapley sees her kick her case with a growl, it brings a rare and unexpected half smile to his lips. *Wild thing*, he thinks.

He stands, enjoying the familiar cold of the rain as it drenches his clothing, and walks toward her, using the mountain to camouflage his approach. As he watches, something catches her attention and she turns, then steps back, eyes wide in a suddenly pale face. A fallen slab of slate rock, like a shelf, lies not quite flat on the ground, and beneath: a dark, dry space, big enough to fit her. Does she intend to crawl below it to escape the rain?

Fey, indeed.

But no, she moves away from it. The rain waterfalls off her bonnet, curtaining her expression from him, but he knows that she is afraid. He has hunted in these mountains long enough to recognize instinctive fear.

She backs away, one step at a time, her eyes never leaving that empty space. She moves gingerly, but then all at once; with a start and an indrawn breath, she turns and clambers up the mountain, her portmanteau forgotten. But where she has no doubt expected to find sheets of rain tumbling down upon the landscape, she finds instead: him.

Her cry echoes through the rocks and through Rapley's skin; she might have fallen if not for his two strong hands, which clamp down around her upper arms like claws. Surprised to find a woman's arms beneath his palms, he lets go, pushes her away. Too hard. She stumbles, falls, landing in her wide skirts.

She looks up at him and brings her hands to touch the places his have just been, the fabric of her jacket wrinkling beneath her small fingers. Her teeth are bared like a wolf's.

Yet despite that—or because of it—she is…striking. Too-pale skin, too-dark hair. Too-dark eyes. He does not look into them. Full, pink lips, now pulled back to expose too-white teeth.

I'm sorry. The words linger in his mouth but he does not speak them. She is small. Birdlike. But vicious too, he thinks.

"Who are you?" she demands, and he struggles to meet her gaze.

"Who are *you?*" he returns, his voice curt.

She gets to her feet, so covered in mud that he cannot see where the mountain ends and she begins. His voice is gruff—more so than he intends. When was the last time he spoke?

"*Answer,*" he snaps.

"I'm—"

"What are you doing here?"

"My name is Roan Eddington—"

"Where are you going?"

"Mill House!" Her cheeks flush, like rose water dripped into cream. She is not embarrassed or afraid, however. He can see that she is *enraged.* This relieves and calms him.

Coming to Devil's Peak as well. So. She is one of the three. "Do you mean the old mill?"

"You know it."

"Yes. And I know Dr.—"

"Maudley."

"Yes."

She points to her portmanteau. "Then kindly show me the way."

"Are you always so direct?" he asks through gritted teeth.

"I expect I'm as direct as *you* are rude."

They stare at each other for an awkward moment, him searching—searching for the reason she should unsettle him so. At last, he strides over, hauls her portmanteau up beneath one arm, amused at her restrained anger, and sets off up the mountain at a stiff pace. This is no place for the likes of her.

He did not expect a girl. A highborn girl, at that.

"It's dark," he says, turning back when she doesn't follow. "The mountain is not kind in darkness."

If he were a different sort of man, he would offer his coat, if he had one. He would ask, *Are you all right, miss?*

Instead, he turns and walks on, carrying her load beneath his arm. He is not that man. Never was, and never will be. He frowns as a feeling of quiet discontent runs through his body, until he finally realizes what it is that bothers him so about the girl.

Her eyes.

They have no walls.

Chapter 2

A BIT OF GOODE

Mill House is a megalith of slate and gneiss, blackened with age. Roan stares up, noting how it disappears into the raging sky, though part of the house vanishes into the mountain, melting one into the other like some kind of awful chimera. The young man had dropped her portmanteau at the foot of a door that looked like a servants' hatch, and disappeared back into the mountain without a word. "Off with you, then!" she had called. "Cretin."

So. This is now to be her home. This is where her father had wished her to go. *Safety in isolation.* Roan scoffs at that. Certainly she will be isolated here. But why? And why *this* man, *this* doctor, whom she has never met nor heard her father speak of? She stiffens at the idea that Dr. Maudley may know more about her than she knows of him. And worse: that he knows more about her than she does of herself. The door, warped by long years of expansion and contraction, stands like a sentry before her. And in such a large house, she doubts anyone will hear her. Still, she raises her gloved hand and knocks. Nothing for a long time, so she knocks again, thinking she might have to spend the night out on the mountain, or else resort to breaking in through one of the windows. She pulls at her skirt-smothered crinoline and looks up. Letting her guard slip with a momentary but intense flash of anger, she kicks the door. It rattles on its hinges.

The door opens only a crack, and with speed. A woman with a severe, hardened face and gray hair beneath a cotton cap glares at her.

She spits out a sentence that Roan cannot understand, and when she simply stares, dripping beneath her bonnet and muddied up to her traveling cloak, the woman snaps, "What hour for calling is this?" in a churlish accent.

Roan bends to pick up her portmanteau but it slips from her frozen fingers, clattering onto the stone tiles.

"Well, come in," the woman barks, "unless you want to drown where you stand." She strides back into the house, leaving Roan to haul up her bag and follow. They are in a pantry, Roan sees, and beyond, a large kitchen looms dark and still.

"An unsociable hour," mutters the woman, stalking over to a table and picking up a goblet, polishing it with a rag.

"It could not be helped." Roan raises her chin, noting the steaming pie on the small table. "And it would appear you were awake."

The woman raises her brows. "I've heard stranger things in my day. How you found a coach to bring you out at this time, I shall never know—nor want to," she adds stiffly. She places the goblet beside several others and then grabs a brush and comes at Roan's portmanteau like it is a creature for killing.

"Which one are you?" she asks briskly, kneeling down to scrub the mud from the bag.

Roan freezes. "Do you mean to say there are others?" She thought her father had wished her away from society, and that her arrival would be a surprise. She had told no one where she was going, nor had she sent advance warning. There had been no time. A chill of unease prickles at her neck.

The woman smirks. "Hark! She thinks she has sole claim to the Master's kindness."

Roan says nothing. Instead, she removes her coat and holds it out.

Knees cracking and with the aid of her hands, the servant gets back on her feet and takes the cloak. "I am the Master's housekeeper here at Pant Tywyll."

"I thought it was Mill House."

The woman's lip curls. "That is the *English* name. You may call me Mrs. Goode."

Roan nods. "I am the new ward of Dr. Maudley." It is the truth, yet a gamble. Should Dr. Maudley refuse her...The letter in her pocket feels suddenly heavy, burning with heat. "You may call me Miss Eddington."

Mrs. Goode considers her for a moment with rheumy eyes and then inspects the cloak, clucking her tongue. "*Drewgi*," she mutters. "I'll have this cleaned and sent to you in the morning." Her lip curls again. "Perhaps by the afternoon. You're in mourning," she adds, noticing Roan's heavy black dress.

Roan makes no reply.

"Well, you have the complexion for it!"

Roan stares. Still no reply. Her fingers are itching.

break the neck easy as a chicken's

Roan starts, spinning to look behind her. "What was that?"

"What was what?"

"I thought I heard someone."

"At this hour? Everyone is abed." Again, the tone of disapproval.

Roan shakes her head. "It must have been the rain."

Mrs. Goode turns and, slowly, taking her time, walks over to the fireplace where she hangs the cloak and proceeds meticulously to straighten every wrinkle, every fold, every pleat.

crunch down so easy now

Roan spins. "There. Again. Did you not hear it?"

Mrs. Goode straightens. "I am not so old that my hearing is going, Miss Eddington. I hear nothing but the usual. Rain and rain and more ungodly rain."

Roan shuts her eyes once Mrs. Goode's gaze is diverted, the old woman bending low to fuss over a wicker basket tucked beneath the table. Roan slips off a glove and rubs her forehead. She clenches her hand against her brow, fingernails in the bed of her hand, cutting sharply. The pain is clarifying. She is weary from travel. That is all.

Roan swallows, slips her glove back on, and looks about the room. She notices a wall lined with bells, each one labeled with a brass placard: MASTER ROOM, STUDY, DINING HALL, BLUE ROOM, RED ROOM, YELLOW ROOM, and more. One in particular catches her attention: LIBRARY. The first good thing about Mill House she has seen thus far.

Mrs. Goode stands and brushes down her skirts. "Now, if you'll follow me, I'll take you to your chamber. Andrew will bring up the trunk once he's in."

"My chamber?"

Mrs. Goode narrows her eyes. "Did you expect to sleep in the kitchen?"

Roan shakes her head, then follows Mrs. Goode up a narrow flight of steps that hugs the walls. The house is a labyrinth of stairs, carven-oak panels and doors, and stained-glass windows, of tapestries, curios, crystals, masks, weapons, and giant Greek amphorae. Roan doubts she will be able to recall the way back in the morning.

At last, they reach what seems to be the main entrance hall. A large set of doors stand to the left. At any other hour, she would have been brought to this, the front of the house, no doubt. Unless the Mountain Man was simply too fond of games. The floors seem to be made from the same slate that peppers the mountainside, curved into squares and arranged with white marble in a chessboard style. Carven oak glares down from high walls, the burning sconces projecting a lattice of shadows.

They climb a grand stairway, likely the main set, to the second floor, then turn left to cross a landing. A long, dark corridor, lit only by Mrs. Goode's candelabra, leers away from them, a yawning throat. Mrs. Goode produces a large ring of keys. They jangle like a death knell. At last, a narrow set of double doors is opened and Mrs. Goode stands back, lips pursed.

Roan recalls the placard on the kitchen wall. BLUE ROOM.

Every fold of fabric, every swish of material, every picture frame and every drawer handle—is a pale sky blue, or a variation on the same. The bed is a puffy blue monstrosity, while the walls are all bluebells and monkshood.

Roan's throat closes. *No.*

a swish of blue...

a scream

Roan hears the scream, almost not there, but she *hears* it. Yet Mrs. Goode's mouth is firmly fixed, as tight and unyielding as her corset.

The old woman inclines her head. "Good evening."

"I will not stay here."

Mrs. Goode gifts her with another of her cold smiles. "It is not, perhaps, as fine a room as those to which you are accustomed. This is a country manor." She pauses. "It will grow on you."

Both women are shocked when Roan grabs Mrs. Goode's sleeve. She lets go almost immediately, but she has Mrs. Goode's attention. "No—I...I *cannot* stay in this room." She steps back. "Is there nowhere...smaller?"

Mrs. Goode's eyelids crinkle like old paper. *"Smaller?"*

"Yes."

Another smirk. "The Master has specifically instructed that you be assigned the Blue Room of the West Wing. There are to be no changes."

"Dr. Maudley assigned this room to me? Are you certain?"

So. He *was* expecting her. Had Father written? Had he...*known* what would happen?

Mrs. Goode pauses overlong, then hands Roan an empty lantern and a bare candle from the candelabra, smiles, and pulls the doors closed as she says, "Good evening, Miss Eddington."

Roan waits for Mrs. Goode's footsteps to fade, and then flees the room, shutting the doors firmly behind her. Heart thumping in her throat, she backs away from the terrible blue as she might from a lion and glances down the corridor, raising her candle high. There is one more door, hidden in the depths of the gloom. Placing the candle in the safety of the lantern, she heads for the dark, bringing the meager light along with her. The shadows withdraw reluctantly.

At the door—for it is a single, unadorned thing–she clasps the handle, hoping it will yield. It does, and she steps inside, closing it quickly behind.

Do not let this one be blue...

The lantern reveals little about the space, except that it is considerably smaller than the Blue Room and most definitely *not* blue. The lantern's grate casts splashes of dim light upon the stygian walls, cage-like. It is an otherworldly forest, the walls a dark green. She can make out, just barely, dark, still forms around her. Unidentifiable furniture.

She licks her lips.

Swallows.

She glances here, there—the unsettling stillness of the objects regarding her like silent judges. Like monsters. Waiting.

hello

Roan breathes harder while the rain hammers the window across from her, and a blinding flash of lightning momentarily reveals the basic layout of the room. A narrow bed on either side of a small window. A window seat, a desk, and a large wardrobe.

The walls. Not green. Black.

The shadows sit thickly beyond her scant pool of light and she flinches when thunder rolls hard over the mountain. Shivering, she tries not to panic. But the emptiness of the room is tangible. Present. There is no one here but herself.

Why did you not tell me? she thinks.

There is no reply.

⁂

FATHER,

HELP ME.

SEND ME SOME SIGN.

WHY HAVE I COME

HERE? ARE YOU

SPEAKING TO ME?

ROAN EVELYN EDDINGTON

Chapter 3
SERPENT AND FOX

good…

morning…

Roan starts awake, the cold sensation of having been touched just leaving her.

Someone is knocking at her door.

"Miss Eddington, I have your portmanteau here."

No. Not this door. The Blue Room doors down the corridor.

"And your cloak." Mrs. Goode's voice splinters in her ears. A pause, and then more knocking. "Breakfast is not for some hours yet, but you'll be expected to dress."

Roan sits up and peeks around the curtains. Unable to sleep at first, she had simply crawled into the concealed window seat and closed the heavy curtains around her, shielding her gaze from the emptiness of the room.

"Miss Eddington! I must enter!"

"Curses," Roan mutters, searching for a place to hide. She should simply step into the corridor and announce her presence, she knows. She ought to simply state that she had preferred this room—the Black Room—to the blue. Yet she has no idea what sort of man Dr. Maudley is, and if he were to force her into the Blue Hell she might well and truly go mad. No. She must hide.

As the knocking along the corridor grows more insistent, she unclaps the small window and peers down. It opens onto the rocky facade of the mountain itself, which is what casts the overbearing gloom into the room. She glances back toward the door, panicked.

It doesn't take much deliberation before Roan is half out the window. She hears the Blue Hell door open and Mrs. Goode's "Miss?"

With horror, she sees her crinoline, which she removed last night in a hurry, standing beside one of the beds. She hauls herself back into the room as Mrs. Goode's clip-clopping footsteps draw closer, grabs the skirt cage, and flings it out the window ahead of her, then climbs out for the second time, her hands alarmingly slick on the slate.

Navigating the rocks turns out to be fairly easy when not wearing the cumbersome crinoline, though her arms strain under her own weight.

The door to the room opens just as her head ducks below the window ledge.

Mrs. Goode's voice is stiff. "Miss Eddington?"

Roan holds her breath, cursing herself for not shutting the window after she climbed out. Long moments pass, and then, at last, Mrs. Goode retreats from the room, closing the door behind her.

Roan bites her lip to keep from laughing and makes her way down the building like one of those circus men she read about in Father's paper.

She drops the last couple of feet and looks up, wiping her hands on her skirts. Her escape hatch stands open, waiting to receive her later. When she *chooses* to return.

On impulse, she sticks out her tongue before running into the mountainous air and the waiting mists.

The world is silent up here.

Roan dances, skips, and runs as fast as she can, navigating the rocks, heather, and lichen as a child might hopscotch. She is about to *whoop* into the air when voices carry on the wind, and she stops.

Furious, constant mutterings bounce up the mountain toward her.

"And if they think I'll bow down before any man as my mother was forced to, then they can get a good clattering, they can. To expect such payment for rescue from the workhouse, I tell you, Seamus, it won't do! And you're doing me a concern with ye smiles and happy faces. You know what the English are like, don't you? Well, Mammy knew all right and where is she now? And if you get too comfortable and forget your loving sis, I'll wreck ye! Wreck ye! Understand me?"

Roan squints through the mists, which conceal her, and spots two bobbing heads of flaming orange hair. A girl dragging backward a wooden chair—no, a wheelchair—up the mountain. On the seat, a boy.

It is the girl's mutterings that Roan discerns, and a thick Irish brogue.

"Ah, men are a devil for the drink, but not you, Seamus, no? You'll stay a good boy, do honor to good Mam, now, yes?"

Roan cannot hear the boy's reply, but it must be in the affirmative, since the girl's mutterings cease. She maneuvers the wheelchair, with some difficulty, between two slate teeth and bends low, panting.

"On me life, you are getting heavy. And who puts a house at the top of a mountain with no track to follow? If this is a joke, it's a cruel one and I'll be shook!" She ruffles the boy's hair. "A minute for my own self, and then we go on."

The girl walks off and when she passes more of the great slate teeth, she gathers her skirts with some effort and squats near the heather.

Roan suppresses a laugh and turns her attention back to the boy.

She can't see much, only the crop of orange, curling hair and, when he leans over, a slim pale hand.

Movement on the mountain catches her eye. A snake, no longer than her forearm, and gray as the slate that surrounds it, slithers over to the boy's outstretched hand and then onto it, winding up the narrow arm.

Roan frowns and inches closer despite herself. She is a mere three paces away before the boy turns and looks at her.

"Are you real?" he asks, his accent as thick as the girl's.

She laughs. "Are *you*?"

The boy turns his attention back to the snake. "Isn't she beautiful? A mountain adder."

Roan watches, mesmerized as the snake coils over one arm, then the next, and then over his neck. She reaches out a hand before she can stop herself.

"May I look?"

The boy's eyebrows shoot up under his round spectacles. "You want to?"

He lifts the snake so that she can see, but Roan sits down next to his wheelchair on the mossy ground and holds out her hands.

The boy hesitates. "Are you certain?"

"Always."

The snake has made the decision before the boy moves. It slides back along the boy's arm, over his hand, and then across to Roan's outstretched hand in turn. Its cool body and surprising weight are curious.

"Fascinating," Roan whispers, peering closer. The adder moves, and she allows it to glide over her hands, one and then the next. Silken, scaly, and solid. "Hello, friend."

The boy watches her for a long while before she hands it back. "She is weary of me, I think."

He takes the snake, kisses the top of its head, whispers something brief, and then lets it slither away. They watch together until the serpent is indistinguishable from the landscape.

"I think she was weary, yes. Of both of us."

"How did you do that?" Roan asks.

The boy shrugs. "She knows I mean her no harm."

He takes up a little sketchbook from beside him in the seat and begins to draw the snake.

"It would have been easier for you to draw her from life," Roan points out.

He grins. "I've got a brain for remembering things." He tilts his head, his big, bright curls dancing, and pushes his too-large spectacles up again.

"How did you get her?"

"Oh." The boy shrugs once more. "I've always been good with creatures of that kind. The ones that slither and crawl, skitter and slide. They find me, but I've never been found by a *mountain* adder."

Roan grins. "They find me too. But they never come so freely."

"They didn't at first. Not until I let them know I welcomed them." He pauses in his drawing. "I think they know most people fear them."

She stares at him, this strange, flame-haired boy who seems to know so much.

"Are you here for Dr. Maudley as well?" the boy asks, tilting his head to the side in that way again.

"Yes."

The boy nods. "He's a great, great man, Dr. Maudley. Pushing the scientific boundaries further and further. The College of London shunned his work, but one day he'll show them just how brilliant he is. His theories on the human brain are truly fascinating—for instance, how when you get scared, that's just a part of your brain releasing humors!" He shakes his head, grinning, then glances up suddenly. "Another storm might come in today."

Roan smiles at his energy and quick distraction. She likes how his face lights up at every small thing. He reminds her of another boy she knew, long ago. Of herself, before the spark was quashed.

The sky rumbles. "You might be right about the rain."

He nods. "The snakes can tell." He points up the mountain. "See?"

Dozens of smaller serpents of all breeds wind their way between rocks and crannies, away from the air and away from her. The mountain looks as if it were squirming.

"They don't like the rain," the boy says, his smile quick and easy.

"Many creatures seem not to," Roan muses. "Human creatures most of all."

"And I am one of them," he admits. "I get stuck in the rain." He nods at his chair.

"Who the blazes are you?"

The girl, whom Roan can now see bears a striking resemblance to the boy, stares down at her with brilliant green eyes. All about her face, escaping her simple scarf covering, vibrant curls the same shade of fire.

Roan gets to her feet.

"Emma, this is…" The boy trails off.

"Roan." She gives a polite, if small, curtsy.

The girl—Emma—doesn't return the gesture. "And who d'you think y'are sneaking up on a boy in a wheelchair?"

"Emma," the boy whines. "I was talking to her of snakes."

"You could've gone rolling down the hill and flattened yourself against a rock! And what would your bleeding snakes do for ye then?"

"Sorry, Em."

"Don't you 'sorry, Em' me. What would Mam say? Well? And with all her sacrifices. Shame on you!" She turns to Roan. "And what are you looking at?"

Roan raises her chin. "It seems to me that you require assistance."

Emma folds her arms. "I'll thank you not to—"

The boy reaches out for her arm. "Em, please. I'm cold, and the rains are coming."

Emma works her jaw, but finally nods.

The two of them manage to maneuver the boy out from between the rocks and then—slowly, perilously slowly—to push, haul, and carry

28

the chair to the stone courtyard. Once there, Emma sits down on the ground, then lies back.

"Lord almighty." She exhales, panting.

Roan sits down too, crossing her legs. "I think the chair is heavier than you are," she manages, winking at the boy. "What is your name, anyway?"

"Seamus O'Brien. And this here's my sister. Emma."

Roan glances at the girl lying prostrate on the flagstones, then looks back at Seamus. "We should get you inside. I feel the rain already starting."

Emma gets to her feet and shoves past Roan as she begins to push Seamus toward the great doors. "I'll do it."

Roan steps back, allowing the rabid fox to take her brother inside.

Just before they enter, Roan calls, "Take the Blue Room!"

Emma looks at her with flared nostrils and narrowed eyes, then wheels Seamus in without another word.

Children, Rapley thinks. *They are children.* He had known that people were coming to the mill, had dreaded it like he dreaded the coming of winter, but he had never expected children. The boy, Seamus, can't be but fourteen, and the fierce girl with hair the color of crystal amber looks no more than fifteen or sixteen at the most. Siblings, he is certain.

And then there's the other. Roan. The fey girl on the mountain. When he'd looked at her, everything had rushed at him—words, images, feelings, impressions, emotions—it had been an avalanche. The walls that normally kept people's thoughts away from him weren't there. When he looked into her eyes…he had seen the deepest moments, the most tightly guarded feelings…

He must not allow it. Himself to look at her. To see and feel her deepest thoughts and most guarded feelings. It is intrusive, a violation. He cannot stomach it. He must avoid her at all costs.

...ped to mama. There will never be a day when I...

...If. How could God forgive me? Father ent me aw...

...se he does not trust me in society. I am an anima...

...t savage his good reputation, and justly so he fear...

M IN EXILE DO NOT LO...

...home I could call friend. Not a sou...

...uld care to hear my cries. To be al...

...world so soon, I had not known it...

...ld be suffered, and in such unbeara...

...ence. If I should deliver a prayer,...

...ho listens to the mount...

...ese conveyed to the last place on hell...

...not speak, girl, I deserve this. Cold shall be my ho...

...shall be my bed. Everything I break and everythin...

...l turn sour in my mouth! Foolish! Foolish little g...

...k I could be free I hate myself I'm sorry! Silence,...

...nce and be damned!

...e step then another. One more step.

I shall no want. H...
...he leadeth...
me in the paths of...
Yea, though I walk...
no evil: for thou...

...STOP IT STOP IT

...If I were to kill this evil in self, would God then acc...
...to his kingdom? If I were to rid the world of somethin...
...in my own hungry fleshy would it be a mortal sin? and...
...urn for the world, and I mourn for my good father who...

...e me for my sins one step after the ot...
...one prayer after ano...

...s nothing on the mountain but mists

...he who casts the first stone...

...t me to this place becau...

Yet…there is something that intrigues and disturbs him about her. Something uncontrollable. It is something…familiar. His skin moves to think of her, though if it is crawling or shivering, he doesn't know. The only certainty is that she causes sensation. And sensation is dangerous. It has taken ten years of fervent construction to build his own walls, and with one unguarded glance on the mountain, the fey girl had shown an ability to take that all away. By seeing her, he saw himself again. He resents her for it. Hates her, even.

He wishes for, but dreads, the absence of Maudley's guests. He wants, yet fears that they should leave him to the dark and the walls and the nothing of the mountain.

ZOEY

NOW

Chapter 4
LITTLE RABBIT

October 14, 3:56 a.m.

    Mum's like a freaking bloodhound. I suppose years with Dad made her sensitive to it. It was three in the morning or something when she burst in, her lips all thin and her eyes bugging out—her quiet fury.

    "What's that smell?" she asked right away.

    "What smell?

    "That <u>smoky</u> smell. Zoey, I swear to God, if you're Working again—"

    I said I wasn't. **Lie.**

    She went on about how she won't tolerate it, that this isn't Dad's house anymore, that she won't have it, la-la-la, and I said I wasn't again. Second **lie.**

She gave me one of her looks and I almost begged her not to make me **lie** again because I couldn't handle <u>three</u> this early.

She took my sage wand, my dried flowers—even my twine. Which I wasn't even using. Now I'm grounded and I'm not allowed matches or a lighter or candles of any sort.

It hardly matters. I had already finished the spell.

She opened my window even though it's freezing. I can almost smell the leaves turning to mulch on the streets. Eight months until summer break. Eight. Months. I told Pole I'd prepare for everything, but what else is there to prepare?

Backpack—check.

Food—easy to get.

Train ticket—I can book it anytime.

I have everything I need. The floor plans, Dad's notes, everything. And more than anything, I have my questions.

October 14, 8:50 a.m.

At 8:30, Dex jumped on my bed, kneed me in the boobs, and farted in my face and Mum did literally <u>nothing</u> to stop him. She didn't even yell at him for being completely disgusting. She isn't talking to me, which always means my little brother can do whatever he wants in my company. Little shit. He ran off shouting, "Smell you later!"

Luckily Mum spotted something by the window.

She basically said, "Poulton Longmore, get your arse in here," and I knew I was saved. Thank God for best friends.

His ruffled head was poking above the windowsill.

"We're all up late today," he said, hauling his long, skinny frame over.

"Blame this one," Mum said, throwing a thumb in my direction.

"Tests today," Poulton said, covering for me. "We were studying late online." His **lies** are harmless. My **lies** cost blood.

"Were you," Mum said in that way of hers, like she's incapable of believing anything we say. "Get a move on if you want a ride to school. I'm leaving in ten."

Mum hurried from the room and I noticed her hair was copper in the back and three inches shorter. Another one of her moments of inspiration.

"Nice hair!" I yelled after her, and she waved a hand.

"Cheers, love. Now get up!"

Poulton closed my bedroom door. "You did it again."

I rubbed my eyes. "Yeah."

He came over and climbed into bed next to me. "How many **lies**?"

"Two."

"You know I hate it when you do that."

I cuddled close to him, snuffling at his arm when he didn't lift it. He eyed me and I whined like a puppy.

"You're insufferable," he said, but lifted his arm so I could snuggle into his armpit. My spot.

"They were little **lies**," I said.

"Please don't."

I didn't say anything, but he knew as well as I did that I don't have a choice.

Dad helped me the first time I Worked. That's what he called casting the spells. He taught me how to do it safely, told me about the price for getting the things we desire. Give and take. The balance of things.

Being next to Poulton always makes me forget that I'm not quite like other girls. But if I live in the fantasy too long, I forget and then I get hurt. It's the price I pay for what I want more than anything in the whole world.

"Small **lies**," Poulton reminded me.

I nodded and smiled, but I knew that if I didn't hurt myself enough, it would be worse later.

He looked up at the ceiling, jaw clenched, and I wandered into my bathroom. I removed a blade from my hidden box of razors and, before I could think too much about it, I cut myself twice on my upper arms. Deep enough.

"Payment for **lies**, protect my Working," I whispered. I let the blood run down my arm and into the sink for a few moments and then cleaned up the mess and put on two Band-Aids.

I ran my fingers over the little white scars that crisscross my arms and then put on a long-sleeve shirt.

"All done," I said, smiling when I entered my room again.

But the bed was empty.

I am standing in a box that no one can see. It's made of such perfect glass that I look free. You might look at me and see a small girl with brown hair, a cute little curly bob with too-short bangs, and big brown pixie eyes looking at the world with wonder.

My big brown pixie eyes stare through the pane with pain and with fear. I want to fly, but my wings never grew. I am standing in a box no one can see.

I clutch the little rabbit tightly in my hands; I'm so nervous I might break him. I spent hours sculpting the polymer clay, baking and re-sculpting until his fur was just so, each little hair a perfectly thin line, his nose so detailed I'm sure he can smell, and his little eyes so bright and clear that I'm certain he can see everything.

"Hello?" you say. It is a question, as if you're not quite sure if you're greeting me or not. "Hello," I say, and I smile. I am wearing the perfume you gave me when I was ten. Scent, they say, holds more memories than memories themselves. "I found this little guy on your lawn," I say, holding out my rabbit in both hands. It is an offering. It is a plea.

You step forward, one foot on the lawn, the other hesitant on the stair. Please, I think. Please come forward today. "He's alone," I say.

You take him from my hand, your skin brushing mine, and my heart races. I brush away a tear because you smell the same and I want to throw myself into your arms. The glass box stops me.

"Lost," you say quietly, like you understand how

that feels. "Poor little rabbit," you say, and I almost lose control because I am here. I am here, your little rabbit. Do you know it?

"What is your name?" you ask me.

"Zoey."

"My name is Henry."

I swallow. "Hello, Henry."

"Poor little rabbit," you say again, and you reach for my hand, then stop. You look confused and then you're gone again, your jaw hanging slack, your eyes glassy and empty.

I take your hand. "I miss you, Daddy."

I leave before you get confused again. I leave before you even know I was here.

Chapter 5

THE ESCAPE

October 17

I'm

S
        A
H

     T
        T   R
          E   E

D

A million fragments of what used to be Zoey.
Where've you been? Mum asked when I walked in the door.

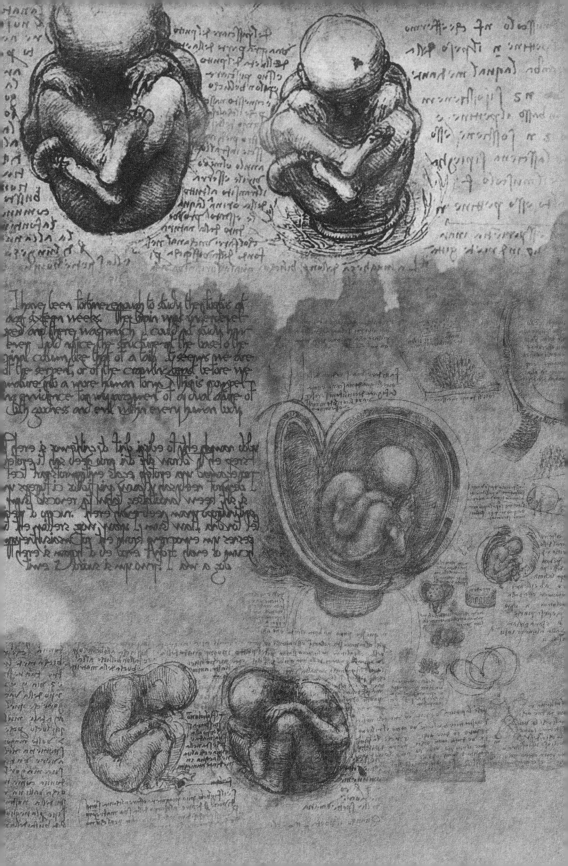

Nowhere.

Don't lie. Mrs. Beagle called from the care home.

There's nothing to say.

You were with that man again.

"That man" is my dad, Mum.

He's not your dad anymore, okay? Are you listening to me, Zoey? He doesn't know who you are or who I am or who he is anymore!

It doesn't mean I can't go see him.

Yes, it does. I'm your mother and I have sole custody for a reason, young lady, and I'm telling you that you are NOT going to see that man again!

I can't just divorce him like you did.

You can't stop me from seeing my own father!

I can and I will. He is dangerous, Zoey. You might not remember that he almost beat you to death after he came back because he thought you were a replacement of yourself, but I haven't! I'll move this family to Timbuktu before I let him touch you again! No arguing! It's done!

He's my father!

I love him!

I belong with him!

Maybe you do! You're just as bloody crazy as he is!

I'm shattered.
A million fragments of what used to be Zoey.

Facebook (Mobile) Status Update

Zoey Root *Feeling triumphant*

Well folks, I'm on my way! Meddwyn Water Mill here I come. Bring on the ghosties! No idea about reception up there, so if you don't hear from me, don't panic. I probs don't want to talk to you anyway ☺ Unless it's, like, a week. Then I've most likely been eaten by crazy mountain people and pooped out in pieces.

Love you guys xxx

👍 Like   💬 Comment   ↪ Share

You, Millie Hull, Jack Renshaw, and 16 others like this.

Shane Rogers:
hoax. total hoax u loser

Jennifer Wellens:
Seriously??? You went to MWM? WHY?!

Lauren Smith:
Don't even, Zoey! You are so going to be in Zumba tomorrow.

Emily Murdock:
You're obsessed it's hilarious! Lol! Stay safe then, chick.

D. "RAY" Ralph:
thats shite take me wif u ☹

Roger Cronin:
told u Sam! ☺

Sam Marillier:
omg be careful.

Poulton Longmore:
Zoey Root TEXT ME.

Sanjeet Root:
Zoey THIS BETTER BE A JOKE.

Shane Rogers:
haha now mum's mad u in trouble zoey hahaha!

Sanjeet Root:
Shut it Shane Rogers or I'll be calling your mum next. Poulton Longmore, call me RIGHT NOW!

Lucy Root:
Zoey's done it now. And no it's not a hoax. She left this morning. Sorry Auntie Sanjie!

Jeff Hurley:
idiot.

Greg Masterson:
Nice knowing you Zo…

43

> **Poulton**
> **11:00**
> Where are you?

Zo-Zo
11:05
Not in school

> **Poulton**
> **11:06**
> Needlessly vapid.
> What's going on?
> Mr. Fields was asking about your coursework

Zo-Zo
11:10
Had a fight with Mum.
She called me crazy.
Like Dad.

> **Poulton**
> **11:11**
> Shit, Zo. Are you okay?

Zo-Zo
11:20
You know me.
Right as rain.

> **Poulton**
> **11:21**
> Zoey where are you?

Poulton

12:35

Not joking. Where the fuck are you?

Poulton

13:55

I'm cutting class.

Coming over.

Answer the door.

Poulton

14:15

Zoey WTF?!

Zo-Zo

14:17

Sorry lost signal.

I left.

I'm going to Mill House.

No more delays.

I need answers.

Poulton

14:18

You scared the shit out of me.

What the hell are you thinking?

We were going together at half term

Zo-Zo

14:19

I'm sorry Pole but I can't wait.

I'm going alone.

Poulton

14:25

You're a pest.

I'll come at the end of the week.

Did you pack enough food to stay alive until then?

Zo-Zo

14:29

LMAO yes.

Poulton you are amazing. Would die without you.

Poulton

14:30

I fucking know you would. Be careful.

Zo-Zo

14:32

Will do. And Pole?

Don't tell my mum

ANYTHING.

Poulton

14:34

You're killing me.

Keep in touch

⌣

October 18

This was a really stupid fucking idea.

I'm going to record everything, just in case. I

don't know what's going to happen, or how I'll be affected, but I know that if I keep a record, keep it logical, and keep myself inside these pages, I'll be harder to lose. It'll be harder to lose my grip on reality. This is security. This is what's happening. In my own words.

The field where I'm camped is behind the station platform—if you can call it that. The train I took to get here pulled up after it was already getting dark. Pretty sure this is the right place, but it was unnerving that there were no signs. Not even a station building. Just the platform and stairs leading down to a small road. I had to stop myself running after the train when it pulled away.

I will <u>not</u> be a coward.

I really hope there are no cows. Do they keep cows in Wales? I just don't want to be trampled to death. Do cows stampede?

Shit, Zoey.

Really good plan.

So, I'm eight months early. Eight months before Pole and I planned, but it just feels, I don't know...necessary. It's been coming for years. This fight with Mum. I guess I always knew she felt that way, like I've always been heading down Dad's path too, but...she said it. She said it out loud. And it basically confirms that she's thought it, <u>really</u> thought I might be crazy, since Dad came back. Since I was a little kid. <u>Years.</u>

Well. Now that it's finally been said, I can acknowledge it.

This is what happened. (<u>Write it down, Zoey.</u>) Just fucking <u>write it</u>.

Okay, so Dad was always obsessed with our family tree. He was adopted, so that's pretty normal. But what we can do...that's not so normal. We can kind of... make things happen. Dad was the one who showed me. Some herbs, some symbols, candles. And then...things change. I guess you'd call it magic, or whatever, but he always called it Working. When Pole found out, he called it wish fulfillment. The whole calling-for-the-things-we-want-and-getting-them thing. We wish for things...we get them. No matter what they are.

Except each time Dad Worked, he lost a memory or forgot how to do something. He noticed this when he was around my age and had already been wishing for things for years. He only lost small things at first. He'd forget that he'd already taken a shower. He'd forget that he was hungry and get weak. But then the things got bigger. He forgot his birth date. He forgot his best friend's name. He said it was the price for bending the world to our will.

Working to get what he wanted cost him a memory. Every single time.

For years he'd test my memory. Math, names, dates, my favorite foods and TV shows. A perfect score. Immunity, wahoo!

Yeah, no.

The first few times I Worked, there was no price. Not until Mum asked what we were up to in the garage and, at a little look from Dad, I **lied**. I don't remember what I said. Or how long it took. All I remember is the red. The pain. The blood.

That's how we discovered that my price is honesty. If I tell a **lie** after Working, then I bleed.

Or worse. Eventually Dad and I figured out that if I had to **lie** after Working, I could prevent the uncontrollable pain and the blood if I gave myself a little pain and blood first. Like a preventative atonement. Deposit blood, withdraw safety.

Anyway, getting off track.

Dad became obsessed with this one particular place. Mill House. It was listed as his place of birth on his adoption papers, except we know that was a fake, since Mill House has been a ruin for at least a century. But still. The name was there. So he got curious. I think he thought it had something to do with his family tree. Maybe his birth parents owned it. Maybe he was due to inherit it, if he could discover who his birth parents were and prove their ownership.

He started researching it, talking about it, dreaming about it.

So when I was around seven, he left to go and find out everything he could about it. There was a big row with Mum. We weren't exactly rolling in cash and he was going to go off for who knew how long, using what little money we had chasing what might, in the end, turn out to be a pipe dream. I didn't care. I wanted him to go. I wanted to go with him. An adventure....a _real_ adventure!

But when he came back he was gone. Just...his mind was gone. He was insane, or something like it. He didn't really know us. He almost choked me to death—and then he forgot us completely.

Something happened there. I know it. I used to think that maybe he Worked something too big to handle. Wished for something that carried too high a price for one person to pay. It's possible. It's likely. But he kept talking about the house. He kept talking about the things he saw there—ghosts, visions...crazy shit.

I was angry with him for so long. Let Mum divorce him and lock him away with social services. But then I found his papers.

And after that...I saw the thing at the foot of my bed. I was so terrified of going to sleep because almost every night, a shape—a dark, mangled shape—would appear at the foot of my bed and just...stare at me. It would twitch and try to move, and try to speak. Eventually, I heard it. The thing—it was female. A graveled, female voice saying Mill House over and over.

Getting tired. Didn't mean to write that much, but needed the distraction. Mum, in case you find this—I'm sorry. Sorry I left without saying good-bye. And sorry we had that fight. I'm also sorry you think I'm insane. Whatever, though—I'm doing this for me. For Dad. I still care about him, even if you don't.

I've waited nine years for a chance.

And, look...I know you might be right and the madness runs in my blood. Maybe I'm doomed to be a crazy middle-aged woman who doesn't even know her own name, bleeding from her cuticles. But I really don't think so. I feel it in my bones. Wish you could understand.

So, yeah.

I could go nuts.

But I have to do it anyway.

It's really dark. Funny how a thin layer of tent fabric gives the illusion of safety—of invisibility. I'm probably a bright orange beacon out here in this field, but somehow I feel safe in my little bubble of air, all to myself, my flashlight hanging from the ceiling hook. Writing in here feels safe.

God. Please don't let anyone murder me tonight.

Switching off the light now.

⌒⌒

Zo-Zo
23:53
Safe and sound.
Miss you.

> **Poulton**
> **23:55**
> That took ages.

Zo-Zo
23:56
You'd love it here.
There are no humans.

> **Poulton**
> **23:57**
> You calling me a misanthrope?

Zo-Zo
23:57
Of course.

> **Poulton**
> **23:58**
> Watch out for crazy pervs out there.

Zo-Zo
23:59
OMFG.
Sleepy.

Poulton
00:00
Don't let the bedbugs bite.
Or the ghouls grab.
Or the ghosts boooooooo.

Zo-Zo
00:01
Sadist.

ᴄ ᴄ ━

October 19

    I found a pub.
    When I came in, the seven or eight burly men sitting at the bar stopped what they were doing and stared at me. So I just sat down and pretended to stare at the menu for a while. Now I'm writing in here so I don't look too unnerved.

    —

    The woman behind the bar just came over. She's in her forties, I think. Maybe older. She didn't scowl per se, but she definitely gave me a look.
    "Helpu chi?" she said.
    "Huh? Oh, sorry—I don't speak Welsh."
    "I won't hold it against you," she said, but she

52

leaned closer and added, "But don't let the lads hear you say that." She winked to let me know she was joking and I relaxed a bit. "What can I get you?"

I asked for a coke and whatever the wonderful beefy smell was.

She looked really happy. "That's my cawl. I'll bring you a bowl."

She started to turn away, but then changed her mind.

"You all alone?"

I said my friend was meeting me soon, figuring that it was better for my own safety if they didn't think I was completely isolated. Besides, it's true. "Soon" being the end of the week.

"Ah, good. Off for a hiking holiday in the mountains?"

"Yes."

"Well, it's not exactly the best weather for it. You should come back in summer."

I told her I was more of an autumn creature.

She laughed at that, throwing her head back, and the men at the bar chuckled. "That's charming! An autumn creature. Well. Mountains can get a bit boggy. Best to stay closer to the pub than anything."

I was stupid enough to blurt that we were going a little farther out. I regretted it right away. Her eyes narrowed and she asked where. I told her the next mountain over—God, <u>why</u>, Zoey, WHY? I should have just said I was training for school's summer hike.

She just said, "I'll get you that cawl," and left.

Everyone's looking at me. I'm just going to keep pretending to ignore it.

Zo-Zo
15:33
Weirdest encounter with local.
Warned away. Must be close!

Poulton
15:55
Sorry for delay.
Your text buzzed my phone in physics.
Prof took it off me.
Local warnings…Grim. You still ok?

Zo-Zo
15:56
Shit, sorry.
Keep forgetting you're still in class.
Did I miss anything good?

Poulton
15:57
Your mum came in to speak to me.
She hasn't called the police. YET.

Zo-Zo
15:58
Just tell her I'm fine.
But that I don't want to see her after
what she said to me.

Poulton

16:00

She was worried you were with your dad.

I told her you're not.

She knows you've gone to the mountain.

(I didn't say)

Zo-Zo

16:03

Fair enough.

She doesn't know where it is. We're fine.

Poulton

16:05

We should tell someone where we're going.

For safety.

Zo-Zo

16:10

I'll text Dexter the location.

Poulton

16:11

Your five yr old brother has a phone?

And why?

Zo-Zo

16:14

It's an ancient Nokia.

Mum gave it to him for that snake game.

But my stepdad Greg checks it every few days. It'll be a backup.

Zo-Zo

16:18

You don't have a monopoly on intelligence.

Almost, but not quite. ☺

Trail getting harder. Ttyl xxx

Chapter 6

HEY, DAD,
MISS ME?

October 19

    I feel bad about lying to Poulton about texting my brother my location. But the last thing I need is my mother coming to get me before I can find out anything. But the guilt is eating at me, so I take a selfie and scrutinize it.

    I process the world through photos. It's like I don't really see things until they've been captured by a lens first, then laid out before me. I noticed it when Poulton tagged me on Facebook the first time we had a sleepover and I realized—holy shit, I have to clean my room. Like, before I saw the photo, I had no idea I was living in a Pepsi-Cola ad. (I stopped drinking Pepsi after that photo too.)

    It's not like I'm blind—I just don't notice things

until I look through my camera. You should see my bullet journal. If not for my HP Sprocket, I'd be screwed. Now I take photos of <u>everything</u>.

I've got my phone and I've got my instant camera and the digital. I hope it's enough. The mountain is tough. Loads of rocks, muddy. My only comfort is knowing that Dad's footsteps were here once. Maybe exactly where mine are now. Was he this cold? Was he surrounded by nothing, like me? Did he feel alone? Was he excited? Was he thinking of me and Mum?

It feels like whatever part of Dad was lost is here, now, hanging in the air.

Hey, Dad. Miss me?

This is what I know about Mill House so far:

- In 1906, Meddwyn Water Mill ("Mill House") was owned by an institute, not a person.
- The institute in question, Maudley Foundation—doesn't exist as far as I can tell. I haven't found a <u>single thing</u> about the foundation <u>anywhere</u>. No references online, no mention—literally <u>nothing</u>. How does that happen? And then who put Dad's place of birth as Mill House? Were his biological parents part of the foundation? Or is the foundation a cover for something else?
- After that, no one knows. Who owns it now? Where are the records? Why the secrecy?
- Nothing about a sale of Mill House was ever publicly recorded, and I couldn't find a record of any deeds in Dad's files on the house. The only mention of the name "Maudley"

was in local papers of the time (<u>Gwynedd Post</u>, <u>Plas Twywell Piper</u>), which featured small items of local news in a side column. (I can't actually take credit for finding those papers. Dad spent almost ten years tracking them down and getting the names.)

- Dad's notebook says that there was a Maudley Foundation address (registered somewhere in London), but that he lost the notebook where he'd written it down, thinking he could go back to the library where he'd found the original mention in the archive later—but the entry vanished. That was in 1998.

- The <u>Gwynedd Post</u> printed a small announcement that the last will and testament of <u>Arthur Gordon Eddington</u>, London, had stated that his only surviving daughter, <u>Roan Evelyn Eddington,</u> was to be sent to Meddwyn Mill, Gwynedd, and there placed under the guardianship of a Dr. A. Maudley until she turned twenty-one or married.

- That will was written only one week before his death in late August back in 1851. Which means that "A. Maudley" was likely the founder of the foundation/institute in his name.

- Roan Eddington's death certificate is dated 1852, location Meddwyn "Mill" House. Hers was the last individual name associated with the property. Could she be Dad's—my—ancestor? I checked out her name online and got nothing.

So my questions remain:
- — Who was Roan Eddington? (Possibly related to me?)
- — Why did Dad have her death certificate?
- — What was her link to the relatively unknown Dr. Maudley? (And WHO IS MAUDLEY?)
- — What is the Maudley Foundation and where is it based today?

— Why has the house been left empty for so long? (Does Dad have a claim to it?)
— What did Dad find? Will I find the same thing?
— Legends of witchcraft on the mountain persist to this day: Are they true? (Linked to what Dad and I can do and the price we have to pay?)
— Could Dad have known about the shape at the foot of my bed?

WHAT HAPPENED?

October 20

I'm doing it, Dad. I'm going.

ROAN

❖❀❖

1851

Chapter 1

HELL IN BLUE

The entrance hall is gloomy. Mrs. Goode announces her approach with her pointed clock-like step.

"Ah, Miss and Mr. O'Brien. Welcome." She gives Roan a terse nod. "Now that I have you all here, I will explain the house rules. Shortly, I will show you to your quarters. Breakfast is served daily at eight o'clock, lunch at noon, and supper at six precisely. There is a nightly curfew of nine o'clock, and there is to be absolutely no wandering beyond that hour."

"Do I look like a child?" Emma mutters under her breath, and Mrs. Goode's head snaps in her direction. Roan cannot suppress a snort.

"The *house*," Mrs. Goode says stiffly, "is not kind in darkness."

The mountain is not kind in darkness.

"It is for your own safety," the housekeeper adds. "The West Wing is off-limits on the ground level."

"What could possibly harm anyone in such a fine prison?" Emma asks, smiling. "And where is our grand host?"

Seamus flushes. "Emma, *please.*"

"The master has not yet returned." Mrs. Goode's face is a sickly gray in the shadows of the hall, yet her eyes have a sinister glint.

"When is he likely to return?" Roan asks. *Or are we to fester here forever?*

Mrs. Goode looks down at Seamus. "Andrew is expected soon. Until then, you are to be served tea in the parlor."

"Andrew?" Roan asks.

"The hall boy. He will carry young Mr. O'Brien to his chambers in the East Wing."

So. The man on the mountain has a name.

"If you think anyone but me is touching my brother, you've got a surprise coming t'you!" Emma snaps. "*I* carry Seamus. And we'll be sharing chambers as we always have."

Mrs. Goode looks down her nose at the girl and half smiles. "Don't be ridiculous. Sharing chambers? Miss O'Brien, you are no longer a child."

Emma's cheeks blaze and she opens her mouth to retort, truly like a little cornered hare. But a muttered, "Please, Emma. *Don't*" from Seamus stills her tongue.

Mrs. Goode turns on her heel, expecting them to follow. Emma glances at Seamus, who nods, and she leaves him sitting in his chair and follows both Mrs. Goode and Roan up the stairs.

Roan trails behind, suddenly straddled with a weight on her soul that she cannot shake. This is it. This place, these people...this is it.

Mrs. Goode stops outside the narrow room.

"This is your chamber," she says to Emma. "The wardrobe has been stocked." She turns to Roan, who hovers outside the Blue Room.

"You'll be expected to dress for each meal." Her eyes subtly roam up and down Roan's still mud-stained dress.

Roan looks away to find that her portmanteau and cloak have been left outside the Blue Room against the wall.

"Breakfast is in half an hour. I'll send one of the girls up to collect you." She turns and strides away without another word.

"Wait," Roan says as Emma turns to her room.

"I daren't look at what monstrosities they've stocked the wardrobe with. I won't be corsettin' up if that's what your lot expect."

"Do you want to exchange rooms?" Roan blurts. She opens her door wide.

Emma scowls and opens her own door, then stops. "Two beds. And she made that fuss about Seamus staying with me! The cheek of her. The damn cheek!" She glances at Roan and then clucks her tongue, stomping over.

At the precipice to the Blue Room, her mouth falls open.

"Lord almighty, did you ever see such a room?" she says at last.

"Do you like it?"

Emma turns a look upon Roan that might express a question about Roan's sanity. "Knew this was too good to be true. I told Seamus. I said, 'We'll be serving them lot, just you wait and see.' And here I am. Next to you. They'll make me your personal maid. You'd love that, wouldn'ye?"

Roan folds her hands before her. "Not especially. Do you want the room or not?"

Emma crosses her arms, eyes narrowing. "And why should a lady such as y'self want to live in a narrow hovel for the rest of her life?"

Roan sighs. "If you must have an excuse to accept, then think on how it'll anger the housekeeper."

Emma's mouth twitches into an almost-smile, but then returns to its tight state. "I want a reason from *you*. A true one."

"I am not here for *charity*," Roan growls through her teeth. "If I must stay, then I will. But to be kept in a gilded cage is more than I can tolerate."

Emma's brows shoot up. "God. You're about as bad as I am at accepting a helping hand."

Roan's voice is gravel. "I don't *need* anyone's hand."

Emma considers her for a moment more and then walks into the Blue Room, holding both doors. "Grand," she says, and slams the doors.

The three new wards sit in silence as a young servant girl pours tea. "Do you have beer?" Emma asks her.

The girl startles and her mouth flaps like a fish on dry land, color rising into her neck and cheeks.

"She's joking," Roan murmurs, and the servant girl gives a nervous curtsy and hurries away.

"Was not," Emma says.

"I know."

Emma takes a sip of her tea, but then spits it out with a cry. "Vile! Poison me, would you? Don't take a sip, Seamus, don't!"

Seamus puts his teacup down.

"You might prefer it with cream and sugar," Roan notes, adding both to her own.

Emma's eyes glint. "Sugar?"

Roan nods at the silver bowl. Within moments, Emma has poured a great deal of the contents onto her plate, and the rest onto Seamus's without replacing the lid.

The servant girl returns, this time with a lidded silver tray, followed by another girl carrying a basket of bread and a small tray holding pots of jam, and more milk. They place everything upon the table.

The first servant girl, the nervous, mouse-like one, pours another measure of tea into Roan's cup.

"Dr. Maudley has not yet returned?"

"No, ma'am."

Roan nods. "Unusual. To be away when your guests arrive. What is your name?"

"Jenny, ma'am."

"You are to let me know the moment he arrives. Do you understand?"

Jenny curtsies by way of acknowledgment.

"Good. Thank you, Jenny."

Jenny glances at Emma, who is staring at her with open hostility, and then curtsies again and hurries out of the room, followed by the second servant girl, this time closing the door to allow privacy.

Emma lifts the lid of the first tray, revealing a steaming platter of meat that Roan cannot identify.

Emma laughs. "Meat! Actual God-to-heaven meat!" Seamus grins up at Roan with delight, and she can't help smiling in return despite such rough manners.

"I wonder why the table is set for four," Roan says, noting the extra place setting. "Are we expecting another?"

Seamus shrugs, but Emma is too busy loading her plate, and then her brother's, to notice. She grabs a small loaf of bread and tears it in two, plonking down one half on her brother's plate and digging her teeth into the other. Roan watches as the girl dips both meat and bread into the pile of sugar before devouring them, grunting in her throat. Seamus follows suit. Then, noticing Roan has not eaten, he nudges the tray toward her.

She nods, but doesn't take any meat. It does not look like pork, nor chicken, nor pheasant. Never having been partial to meat in particular, she reaches for a bread roll instead and tears off a small piece, only to find, when it is in her mouth, that it is stale. No doubt a little cheeky snub from the housekeeper.

She swallows but has no more, instead drinking tea and glancing around the room.

Dark walls seem to be the fashion, but here drapes of green adorn the narrow windows. It is peculiar to have candles lit during the morning, but the house is so gloomy that without the tiny flames, they would be sitting in complete darkness as opposed to the current night-like murk.

A gargoyle leers down at them from one corner of the ceiling. Roan shudders. Never before has she seen one so realistically sculpted, nor indoors. Used to ward off evil in holy places, they are usually placed *outside* the dwelling. The candlelight barely reaches him, but what illumination does has a startling effect on his eyes.

Look not upon me, she thinks, scowling at him.

"Please eat." Seamus's small voice drips concern. Roan looks across at him to find that he has stopped his own eating.

Roan pulls a slice of the meat onto her plate, noting its slightly slimy quality, and puts her knife and fork to it. Seamus watches her intently. Ignoring as best she can the noises of Emma's feast, her mastication, gulping belches, and her general bad smell, Roan cuts a small section, perfectly square, and puts it into her mouth.

It is not pork.

Nor chicken.

Nor pheasant.

Pigeon? She is not certain, only that it is odd, strangely textured, and unpleasant to the taste. She swallows, drinks more tea, her cutlery hovering in the air over the meat.

"Too fine a meal for you?" Emma says through a mouth of garbled meat and bread. "No accepting of charity." She laughs. "You'll die of that soon enough!"

A fleck of meat flies from her mouth and bounces across the table. Roan shuts her eyes. *Damn these people. Why do they have to be here? This is worse than being alone.*

When she opens her eyes, ready to leave the table, she notices that Seamus is no longer eating with his hands. Instead, he is using the cutlery provided, studying her own hands.

For his sake, she cuts another piece, and another, until the entire slice is a pile of perfect squares, warming a little as Seamus mimics her motions. Once done, she places her cutlery down, excuses herself, and leaves the room.

Emma says something Roan is sure is cutting, but she is already out and does not hear.

At first, Roan thinks it is a trick of the light. Some odd shadow or a stone illuminated by the lightning, there and then gone. She has seen no livestock on the mountain—not one sheep, goat, or cow. In fact, she realizes, she has not even seen a bird.

But this is no trick of the light. It is no shadow or rock. It is an animal.

He stands proud, backlit by the storm. Slashes of lightning paint him onyx, except for the eyes, which gleam a rich, violent red.

Roan peers closer.

The beast is a kind of bovid—a mountain ram. Yet it cannot be. It has the look, almost, of a Soay sheep, but the beast is too large. Far, far too large. Like a cow, or a horse, it stands several feet high, unnaturally still. Watching her. His horns curl, gnarled monstrosities, textured like the bark of ancient trees; and she senses…sentience.

She squints through her window, trying to see farther, trying to see *more*. It cannot be, and yet it is…

The thing regards her.

It watches her.

It *smiles*.

Roan grins back, a flush of excitement trilling through her, and she reaches for the window catch.

"Hello? Emma? Roan?" Seamus. In the corridor.

She hesitates, wanting to go out into the storm—to be a part of it. To run with the wild thing out there and scream and dance and—

"Anyone here?"

She withdraws, closing her curtains, and opens her bedroom door. Seamus sits in his chair at the end of the corridor, straining to peer into the darkness.

"Seamus," Roan calls. "Down here."

He does not see her for the gloom, but begins to wheel himself forward, his eyes wide with sightlessness. As his vision adjusts to the darkness, they narrow and he smiles at her.

"Where have you come from?" Roan asks, walking part of the way to meet him.

"My room. They put me across the landing. Though I have a lamp in my corridor. They're going to keep it lit for me, even in the day. Did you ever hear of such a thing?"

Roan laughs. "At home in London we had no need to light the tapers during the day. But this house is so gloomy." She shivers and rubs her arms. Even the mention of the cold umbra of the house seems to deepen it.

"But all this space..." Seamus says. "I don't think I mind too much about the darkness."

Roan grins. "Yes, you are fair of skin, like me. We do not dwell comfortably in sunlight, do we?"

Seamus grins and his spectacles slip down his nose. "I have freckles, though. And the sun makes them dark. But you..." He touches his face with his fingertips, the unself-conscious contact of a child, and then regards her carefully. "I never saw such white skin before. And no freckles anywhere."

Roan pretends to leer. "I am a Vampyre!"

Seamus laughs in a boyish, unrestrained manner, then his smile fades. "D'you know where they put Emma?"

"Of course. She is there, next to me. Back a little way. Here, let me help you turn around."

Taking the handles at the back of Seamus's chair, she maneuvers him around and then wheels him back the way he came until they are outside the double doors.

"Shall I knock for you?" Roan asks.

"Please."

She does as requested but there is no immediate reply. "Emma? Are you awake? I have your brother here."

where are you?

Another knock. "Emma?"

Her door flies open. Emma barrels out of the room and onto Seamus like a cat. Roan steps back, alarmed, but she is only hugging him, and he laughs, his spindly arms gripping her back.

"Where've they put ye?" Emma asks, ignoring Roan.

"Down the way. Come and see—my room's yellow! Bright yellow, Em!"

Emma laughs and steps in front of Roan, pushing her brother down the corridor with nary a word to her as they depart.

Chapter 8
A SERVANT'S TALE

Roan cannot sleep.

The storm outside her window shakes the glass so forcefully that it almost seems to bend. Even the curtains, thick and heavy-hanging, move in the breeze that manages to seep through the sodden window frame. There is a storm within her as well. The air in the room is close—too close. Cloying.

She sits up and pulls her father's letter from the drawer beside her bed, running her fingers gently over the handwriting as she has done for so many days.

"Tell me why," she murmurs, her lips close to the fragile page.

But the night is empty and she is alone.

Her stomach growls and startles her. She did not eat much during the fiasco dinner earlier; indeed, she has not taken much food since the night she found her father…

Throwing off the bedcovers to cut off all thought and all memory, she puts on her slippers and her heavy quilted robe, leaving both the small room and her memories behind. The letter she tucks into her pocket and takes with her, an ever-present reminder of her father and the reason she is here.

It takes some time for her to find the kitchen. Though she arrived not long ago—was it only yesterday?—she cannot, as she predicted, find the way back.

Mill House is a labyrinth of stairs and corridors. Still, finding her way is a diversion, and that is all she is really seeking.

At last, she finds the watery-green room with the gargoyle, and along the same hallway, the kitchen.

It is a cold, desolate room now the fire has burned down to embers. Mrs. Goode has placed a large log on the coals, which itself glows orange and white at the base, simmering low with solemnity.

Roan hurries to it, blowing so that the embers wake from their somnolence and then dance into flame. By the time she has found bread and some apples, the fire is crackling merrily, throwing light upon the plain walls.

"I should have stoked the fire myself," comes a soft voice from the other end of the room, the side still bathed in deepest shadow.

"Who is there?" Roan calls, her hackles rising. "Show yourself."

Movement.

And then a man—a young man—steps into the light, a cup in his hands. He is dark of feature and hair, and seems almost too young for the voice attached to him, which is deep and rough.

Roan is suddenly acutely aware of her nightdress, her robe, and her hair free from a nightcap, her obsidian curls falling wild.

"Who are you?" she asks. "Dr. Maudley?"

He laughs. "No, miss. My name is Andrew."

So Mountain Man remains nameless, since Andrew now stands before her, an altogether different person.

"I'm the servant," the young man—Andrew—adds. "Butler, repairman, footman—anything the Master wants me to be. I'm nobody."

"Well, Nobody," Roan says. "Come and sit by the fire. You make me nervous standing in the shadows so solemn and tall."

Andrew joins her at the table, sitting across from her. "Thank you, miss."

"My name is Roan. You may call me that."

"It wouldn't be appropriate, miss."

"Damn what is appropriate." She bites her tongue. "I apologize. But I do not require a servant. I require…some *talk*. To distract me from this storm."

Andrew grins, taking a sip from his cup.

"Tell me why you smile so," Roan says.

"In truth, you are not what I was expecting."

"But you *were* expecting me," Roan says, biting into an old apple. It is papery in her mouth, thick and disappointing. How she yearns for the sweet juiciness of the London apples. How she longs to return to the life she had. Strange and lonely—and *painful*—it had been, but it had been hers.

"Master knew you were coming," Andrew says. "Yes. That is why we came back so soon. Most of the time, he does not linger here. He likes to travel out of the country."

"Why?"

Andrew hesitates. "I'm not sure he likes the house very much."

Roan smiles mirthlessly. "It is a little…grim."

Andrew looks around, taking in the still, silent room. Beyond the walls that contain them, the storm rages, thrashing about without end.

"It is home."

"Does it storm here often?" Roan asks after a long silence.

"Almost nightly. The repairs are continual."

"Why not hire more men, then?"

"Because," comes a new voice. "No local man will come into this house."

Both Roan and Andrew turn at the new arrival.

"Jenny," Andrew says. "Why are you up at this hour?"

"*This* hour? It is gone dawn! I should ask why you keep Miss Eddington out of bed so long."

"I could not sleep," Roan admits. "And I took very little dinner."

Jenny smiles shyly at her, but turns down her mouth as she glances at Andrew. "You know the house rules. No eating outside of mealtimes and no wandering after nine o'clock. You ought to have set a better example by the lady, Andrew."

He grins. "Ah, lass. You'll make Mrs. Goode a fine replacement someday. But not today."

Jenny busies herself with the fire, which has burned down to glowing embers once more, but Roan can see she is pleased. A warm glow suffuses her face as she bends low, lifting the poker from the iron grid.

"There is a bell on the wall by your bed," Jenny says. "It links directly to my room. If you need anything, miss, I am happy to bring it for you. Master had it specially installed for you."

A chill slinks up Roan's spine. "When?"

"Last week, I think."

Her father had been alive last week.

"Are you certain?"

"Yes, miss. I'm to make you comfortable and happy. Strict instructions."

"Well, I can fetch food for myself well enough," Roan mutters.

"I should be going," Andrew murmurs in turn. "Dr. Maudley will expect me."

Roan nods to him, a little disappointed. "Good night—oh, well, good *morning* I should say. It was nice to meet you."

"And you, miss."

As he turns to go, he mouths, *Roan*, grins, and then leaves. Roan finds herself grinning back.

"Tea, miss? While I bake the morning scones."

"Let me help you," Roan says, getting to her feet.

Jenny holds up her hands. "Please, no. It is my duty."

"Very well," Roan says, sitting back down. "Perhaps you can tell me what you meant, then, when you said no local man would set foot into this house?"

Jenny fetches eggs from the icebox, and lowers the flour from the ceiling. "It is a simple fact, miss."

"Why would they not come to work? No doubt Dr. Maudley can afford to pay them adequately for their services? A house this size must surely need a host of servants to keep it running."

Jenny nods, cracking open the eggs into a bowl. "The master could pay them several times over, I expect. But nothing will induce any local man to come."

"Heavens, why not? Are you being intentionally evasive?"

Jenny pauses, wiping her hands on her apron. "I am not permitted to speak of it. Master doesn't like the talk. Mrs. Goode finds it bothersome also."

Roan is silent a moment. "Why do you wear this silly tall hat?" she asks at last, looking at the curiosity atop the girl's head. Not quite like a stovepipe hat, this is smaller, and odd-looking, narrowing as it rises.

"It is what we wear, miss."

Roan sighs. "Please, call me Roan. At least when we are in private company." She takes the girl's hand between her own. "I am a woman as you are, am I not?"

Jenny bites her lip, tears springing to her eyes.

Roan releases her hand. "Are you afraid of me? Have I done something to make you so?"

"Oh, no, please don't think that. It is this place, and Mrs. Goode. If she were to discover I had been talking with you, miss, on Master's time, and if she were to learn I spoke of…the stories…I would be dismissed."

"Well, she shall never know. I am a nocturnal creature. While all others slumber, I walk and I read and I listen."

Jenny again mutters something in Welsh under her breath.

"What is it, girl? Do you hate the night hours?"

Jenny flushes. "I must admit that I do."

"Why?"

"Everyone is gone. I'm alone. But there is work to be done. Fires to kindle, tables to dust, breakfast to be made."

"What of the other girls?"

Jenny smiles. "Mrs. Goode and I are the only two who stay overnight. We have rooms in the attic. Everyone else, excepting Andrew, leaves before dark."

"Is it because of what you said? Earlier? About how no man would come to Mill House?"

Jenny puts down her cup and crosses herself. "This is a superstitious place, miss. There are stories tied to this house—long-ago stories. The people remember."

Roan is silent for a moment. "Tell me the stories."

"But, the Master—"

"I am not the Master, and I would like to hear."

Jenny stares at the eggs in the bowl, her eyes glazed over. "There really is only one story, and then tales. Folktales."

"Do you believe them? These tales?"

Jenny looks away and that alone is answer enough.

"Tell me. I live here now."

"It is a dark tale."

"Aren't they all? Come, I will warm the water for the tea. You make the scones and talk."

"The legend," Jenny begins, "says that this house, Pant Tywyll, is cursed because of one man who came, long ago."

"What does that name mean? Pant Tywyll."

"Devil's Peak, miss."

Roan nods. "Go on. I will say nothing until you are finished."

"A man arrived, a hundred or more years ago, name of John Smith. He came with his pretty young wife with the notion to build a water mill on the mountain itself. Folk thought him crazy—there being no water. But he brought wealth and ambition, and work. We have always been a poor folk, and so the locals sprang to when the foreigner needed workers for building.

"Every man who could walk the distance went to the mountain to build this house and the water mill, which John Smith was fanatical about. A day would not pass without his raving about the water mill, and folk thought him a fool, but kept building as long as there was pay to be had.

"But then the men began to disappear. They put it down to accidents on the mountain. One day, a lad vanished. He fell into a crevice, maybe. It was sad but not uncommon. But then even more men vanished.

"At that time, John Smith's wife bore him a child who also vanished. And another—gone. No one knew where the babies were disappearing off to. Searches were made.

"It was as though the mountain had devoured them all! Rumors abounded of strange rumblings coming from the rocks beneath the men's feet at night, and they grew afraid."

Jenny takes a steadying breath, her cheeks flushed.

"Well," she continues a moment later. "People began to get suspicious. Word of the Lancaster witch had reached the local people by this time. A young lad, the son of one of the vanished men, stumbled across a witch's ceremony one night and saw figures with horns atop their heads like beasts, dancing around fires that burned strangely."

Roan recalls the ram she saw out in the storm and shudders.

"He ran back to the village half-crazed, shrieking about naked figures and fires and strange devil symbols. There's a reason it's called Devil's Peak, miss. But they ought to have called it Witch's Peak, for it was John Smith's own young pretty wife who had bewitched and vanished all those men—and her own children along with them.

"The villagers went up with a priest and burned the witch alive. But 'twas too late. She had vanished her husband as well, the poor fool with his waterwheel ambition. They say the witch shrieked with laughter as she died and the flames burned blue. To this day, folk hear the witch's screams on the wind, a reminder that this house—this mountain—is cursed."

Jenny sighs as though a great weight has been removed from her chest. She wipes her floured hands on her apron and then folds her hands in her lap.

"They say," she offers, a moment later, "that the witch's angry spirit haunts the house."

Roan laughs. "And you believe this?"

Jenny looks away, color rising. "I have not seen her ghost, but I sometimes feel her here. I cannot help but believe. God would not set foot in this house, I am convinced. People are scared to stay within these walls after dark. We all who dwell beneath this roof are cursed."

Roan looks around. She cannot help it. "Why do you do it, then?"

"Begging your pardon, miss, but I need the pay. I'm the eldest of twelve girls—" She breaks off and swallows. "Eleven. Eleven girls. We lost Mabel last winter. Siân might follow this winter unless I can earn enough to buy some cordials. She's sickly. Pining after Mabel."

Twelve siblings, and all of them girls, one already in the grave. Roan holds back her astonishment. Though she is still in mourning over the loss of her father, and though mourning has brought back painful memories of her mother, Roan has never before considered that having too many in a family might come with difficulties and sorrow just as deep as her own.

"Have you spoken to Dr. Maudley about this? Have you asked him to come and see Siân?"

Jenny's eyes widen and she leans back. "Oh, Miss Eddington, no. No, no, I cannot."

"Why ever not? He's a doctor. You're in his employ. Surely—"

Jenny drops the spoon she has been using to ladle the scone mixture into pans. "Forgive me, miss, but I'll not be asking for help from those who dwell beneath this roof!"

Roan looks on, shocked, as Jenny flies from the room like a little gray cat, her strange black hat bouncing upon her head, her skirts bunched and flying, flecks of dough spattered on the table in her wake.

Jenny's story has piqued Roan's interest. She wanders the house once again, this time looking for the library. If there is any truth to the folklore, then surely some evidence of it will be in one of the books. Grand country houses of this age usually sport some sort of history of the region, and she cannot think that Dr. Maudley would be any different. Her own father had kept several thick volumes of both the history of London and the history of their own property. Another unwelcome memory. She pushes it back, along with her grief.

And at last, the library.

Thankfully, it is not painted in a silly color of the rainbow, but is wood-paneled in the same carven-oak style. Respectable. There are fewer books than she expects, though, and she is a little disappointed. No doubt they are medical books, given Maudley's profession. But…no.

Not medical books at all.

Her hackles rise as she reads the titles, her fingers yearning to touch the leather-bound volumes, but not daring. These books…all of these books…they are occult in nature, and very familiar to her.

Daemonium—Devils of Europe.

Grimoire.

Faust's Book of Angelic Charms.

She knows this last one. Her father once told her that to live, one must read it twice. Once forward and once backward. She continues to read the titles, growing colder with each step.

The Sixth and Seventh Books of Moses.

Ceremonial Magic.

She cannot go on. She is a child again. Locked in the basement in London.

Seven years ago

Father paced back and forth while she sat still. He tapped a long wooden ruler in his palm, enunciating.

"According to legend"—tap—"Johann Georg Faust was a fifteenth-century scholar"—tap—"who made a pact with the Devil. He offered up his soul in exchange for limitless knowledge and all the worldly pleasures man could imagine. But"—Father broke off and the tapping ceased—"that is mere legend. Hearsay. The truth is far darker and much older." He turned a stern eye on his daughter, who sat up straighter.

"Faust, in reality known as Faustus, was a monk. A man dedicated to knowledge and the word of God. He lived a life with his brethren beneath the ground to ensure the utmost dedication, free from distraction, free from all temptation. They were a brotherhood. Ancient. But Faustus was avaricious. He feared death and longed for immortality, knowledge, and riches. And so he began to search for a way to commune with the Devil, whom he called Beelzebub.

"It is not known how, but Faustus made his deal, bartering his soul for thousands of years of life, able to learn and relish in the delights of this world.

"But..." Father had resumed his pacing. "It is said that Faustus's time runs short, and so he searches—in a quest to barter back his soul or to gain more time."

"But is it true, Father?" little Roan asked, sitting forward.

"Who can say? But the important thing is...what?"

Roan considered this for a moment. "The important thing is to make a better deal than Faustus did."

She thought she saw her father wince, but then his eyes flashed. "Insolent child. *Filia demonica*. The important thing is never to meddle with evil in the first place."

He glared at her, but then he sighed and everything seemed to slump as though he was suddenly very tired or very sad. He waved a hand as though dismissing her, so she got up and went to the corner where she slept, behind the crates of flour and the wine.

Father went upstairs and locked the cellar door behind him.

Little Roan ran her fingers along the symbols carved into the wood all around her, which by now she knew were dark and dangerous magic, and wondered why she and her father did all these things with blood and fire and sigils if it was better to avoid evil completely.

Roan keeps losing sight of him.

She is certain the ram is male. The way he wears his horns, proud and curved, the way he stares unabashedly into her eyes. This animal knows nothing of blush nor restraint. She cannot wait, and so she is in her bedclothes as she fumbles her way over rocks and tries not to slip on the dewy moss. It is some time until dawn yet, the sky still lightening from inky black into a deep indigo, but she cannot wait.

He had been closer this time, lower down the mountain—and she had known, *known* that he was looking at her. It was no vision, no imagining, no fancy. This lone ram had come to her again, and was calling her out. She had never seen the likes of it before.

The mists do not clear as she approaches the spot where she saw the beast from her window. Instead, they defy the moon and begin to curl thickly about her. Now and again, she sees the ram's horns, its eyes, but she never seems to reach it.

She is whitewashed in the cold fog when she hears it.

found you.

She spins around, but there is no one. Nothing except the lonely mountain.

And the beast.

She waits to hear more and, like a child hiding beneath the bed, dreads that she might. But the word she hears next is one only she would understand.

It is as though the mountain has thought the terrible word, yet the eyes piercing her own are sentient, animal, a slit for pupils in amber irises verging on scarlet.

come to me, little girl,

there is

much

to discuss.

She freezes. *No. No.* Shuts her eyes. *I am losing my mind, that is all. That is all!*

come.

"No. Back. Back!"

But it does not go back. It steps forward. One proud, cloven hoof, then the other, tramping down the earth and burning it. She shakes to witness how like burning embers his hooves are, cracked and burning white, and all black and smoking in his wake. The spell is broken only when the eyes and the horns, the beast in all its horrible, terrible glory is ten feet away. She runs as fast as she can, not caring if she should fall, only that she must get away—far away.

"Father," she cries into the wind. "Father, help me!"

The mists twist and curl in plumes against her and there is no answer.

She stops only when she careens into a sharp blade, the gleaming silver pressed to her neck. Had she blundered forward, she would be missing her head.

"I almost killed you." Mountain Man. He is dressed like a heathen once again, his shirt more stained than white, his hair loose upon his shoulders, and a glint in his slate eyes mirroring something like rage.

She can't focus on him. Where is it? Where is the beast? Everywhere she turns the mists withdraw until she can see more clearly again. Except there is no sign of the ram.

Suddenly Mountain Man is closer. "What happened?" His voice is deep. Close. Changed. His eyes roam her face, searching. "What is it?"

She blinks. "N-nothing."

"What's the matter?"

She cannot see the beast. She cannot smell the burning earth. She presses a hand to her head, shaking it.

"*Roan.*" Her name. He spoke it. Spoke it low and solemn and desperate. "What's wrong?"

Too close.

"You are," she snaps, and steps back. They look at each other for a long moment, he, still searching, she, confounded and frightened.

I am in exile, she reminds herself. *Safety in isolation…*

She stumbles as she turns away.

"You shouldn't walk alone on the mountain," he calls. "Especially clothed…like that."

She turns, chin raised. "*You* do."

Heathen he may be, but she looks no better herself.

He sheathes his ax. "That's different."

"All is different between a man and a woman." She smiles without humor, realizing how like Emma she sounds.

Mountain Man's lips curl. "All the world's amusing to a woman."

Her eyes narrow.

"Man or woman," he says, "I would advise the same. Do not walk alone on this mountain."

"As you do?"

"It is different for me."

She crosses her arms. "Certainly. There are no rules for you, are there? You can do as you please while the master of the house is away. You may come and go as you like, throw your ax, live savagely, and run around the mountain like a boy playing warrior. Well. Dr. Maudley is coming home, and let us see what he thinks of your treatment of me and your proclivity to do just as you please like a barbarian!"

He crosses the space between them in three long strides, his face close to hers. His nostrils flare, wolflike, and she can see his teeth—also canine.

"You know nothing of it. I was raised on this mountain." Spittle hits her cheek. "I know of its tricks and follies. If you would risk life and damnation besides, then go. Explore. And to hell with you *and* Dr. Maudley."

He stares a moment, so close he could bite her. And then he is gone, striding away into the dawn, the mists closing behind him like a veil.

"You will not alarm me!" she calls after him, rubbing her arms. "Not with your words, nor with your ax!"

"Brute!" she screams after another long moment.

But he is gone.

Chapter 9

DR. MAUDLEY

Later that morning, the breakfast table is set for five.

"Do you think he's bringing a guest?" Seamus asks.

"There were four places set yesterday when there were only three of us," Roan reminds him. "Maybe it's some kind of tradition to set an extra place?"

"A place for a ghost?" Seamus says, grinning.

"Who cares?" Emma grumbles. "Mrs. Goode and all her talk of breakfast at eight o'clock *precisely*. By the count of my stomach the old crow is running late."

"She can be later for all I care, if she brings any of that foul meat in here again," Roan mutters.

Emma almost smiles and gives a little shrug. "It wasn't bad."

"Well. You can have my portion—"

Roan's words fall away when Mountain Man steps into the room. She's vaguely aware that her mouth is hanging open, but when she tries to close it, she cannot. Who *is* this man before them? What happened to the heathen?

No longer the loose-haired, ax-wielding ruffian she had called cretin, brute, or worse. Here stands a…a *gentleman*. In appearance, at least.

Hair tied back, shirt crisp and white, jacket black and formal, his cravat a startling jade green, which brings a dash of color to his eyes.

"*Cretin?*" she manages.

He regards her. "Miss Eddington."

Her attention is pulled away, however, by the man who follows.

Roan is certain that this man is Dr. Maudley.

She stares at him, unable to avert her gaze. Here is the man who controls her life. Here is the man her father willed her to. Here is the man of whom she knows so little, and who knows more of her than she does of herself. And of all the men she might have imagined, this one before her—so eccentric, hair so dark, and eyes to match, dressed in impeccable, expensive velvet and satin with a flair in his hair—is not what she had expected. Yet she is certain—as certain as day follows night—that he is exactly who he is.

"My dears!" Maudley cries, throwing his arms wide. "How delighted I am to see you all together!"

His waistcoat is a brilliant magenta and it catches the light.

"Ah!" Maudley says, seeing Roan and Mountain Man standing so close together. "Excellent. You've met my son, Rapley?"

She blinks, confounded, and for the moment, speechless.

"Your son!" Seamus grins.

"*Adopted* son," Mountain Man says, voice low. "You must be the new wards." His eyes drift over them, and then focus on Roan and Emma. "*Two* girls," he adds. "Imagine that."

Dr. Maudley comes toward Roan, holding out both of his hands and smiling from ear to ear. Like Rapley and Andrew, Dr. Maudley is strikingly tall. Roan raises her hand, and he takes it and gently kisses the back.

"Roan. Dear, dear Roan. Please, sit down." He turns to the others. "Emma and Seamus. Wonderful! And Rapley, dear boy. Good to see you. Sit, everybody, sit."

"Well," Emma says, eyeing Roan once they have taken their seats. "*When* did you two meet, exactly?"

Roan turns to—what was his name? Roland? "I believe," she says slowly, "it was when"—*he called me* direct *and dumped me at the servants' hatch*—"he showed me to the house upon my arrival."

"Good, good. Well, Rapley, since you have already become acquainted with Roan Eddington, here are Emma and Seamus O'Brien." He leans over to them and whispers in a conspiratorial tone, "I am certain he has not come off his mountain since last I went away. Doesn't like to be confined, our Rapley."

Rapley. What a peculiar sort of name.

She is acutely aware of him beside her. The words he spat at her early this morning still ring in her ears, as does her own response. She has not known many men, yet this one seems to bring out her wildest nature.

Curse him. The brute. She would just as soon he remain out there on his precious mountain, tearing into rabbits with his bare teeth, or by whatever manner he chooses to survive.

Yet here he sits, his table manners impeccable. He had simply *chosen* to ignore polite and civilized convention, then. A thrill of delight runs through her. Good. She need not expend the effort on him either.

"I apologize, most deeply, for not being here to greet you when you arrived," Maudley says, while Jenny dishes up sausages and scrambled eggs. "I had to make certain everything was in readiness, which, ironically, meant I had to be away. How do you find the house?"

"Much larger than I expected," Roan admits. The smell of the sausages is turning her stomach, so she takes a sip of her scalding tea.

"Biggest house I ever saw!" Seamus bursts. "Like a castle!"

"Indeed!" Maudley laughs. "When first I saw it, I thought much the same. And I fancied I would be the heroic knight to protect it."

"Or the king to rule it," Seamus offers, piercing a sausage with his knife and biting into it without thought. "With a million servants!" he adds, mouth full.

Maudley laughs. "Delightful!"

"Did you inherit it?" Roan asks, cutting through the noise. "Or perhaps you purchased it?"

"It was my father's," Maudley says, suddenly solemn. "It still is, in point of fact."

"Where is he?"

"He does not come here often. Which suits me. I like the mountain air; he does not. But I aim to make many improvements to the house and the land, besides. Perhaps it will be worthy of my father then."

"Andrew mentioned something about installing ramps," Roan says carefully. "I think it would be a suitable adjustment. Would that appeal to you, Master Seamus? You may wheel yourself out of doors, in that case."

"Bah!" Emma bursts. "He'll do no such thing." She looks at her brother. "You'll go rollin' yeself down the mountainside."

Seamus scowls. "Will not."

"Will too. Bouncing off all the rocks on your way."

Maudley laughs, a loud and unself-conscious sound. "Very good!"

Seamus folds his arms, pouting, but Emma's slow, cheeky grin draws out his own soon enough.

"Decided to eat with the civilized," Roan mutters under the boisterous conversation around her, pointedly *not* looking at Rapley.

"That is one opinion," he retorts, barely audible.

"Whatever drew you away from your ax? It couldn't be that you must behave like a civilized man, now your father is home?"

Rapley slams the table so fast and forcefully that they all jump. "You know nothing of it."

They all stare at him, except Roan, who suddenly feels her appetite rear its head. She bites into a scone and smiles. Slowly, conversation resumes.

"There are horns and skulls in a room upstairs along my corridor.

Have you been to Africa?" Seamus asks, leaning forward in his chair and placing both elbows on the table.

"I went once, some ten years ago," Maudley says. "They have the most peculiar insects!"

"Oh! What sort?"

"I had opportunity, on a few very rare occasions, to observe the dung beetle..."

Roan lowers her voice once more. "Well. Dr. Maudley exerts a great deal of control over you." Rapley stiffens and she feels a perverse trill of pleasure. "Good. You need it."

She can feel him seething beside her...a rising pressure likely to burst without much more coaxing. *And so what of it?* she thinks recklessly. *He is a child playing a game whose rules he knows not.* She continues to smirk.

Emma mutters something scathing beneath her breath. She still has not touched her food.

"Are the eggs not to your taste, Emma?" Maudley asks. "I could ask Mrs. Goode to prepare an alternative."

"I like them fine," she snaps, snatching up her spoon and shoveling eggs into her mouth without pause. "Just fine," she adds, flecks of egg flying from her lips. Another unintelligible mutter.

Maudley places down his cutlery. "I expect you are all wondering why you are here."

"You expect rightly," Emma says. "Why us? Why Seamus and me, when there were hundreds of others in the workhouse back home?" She leans forward. "What payment do you expect?"

"It is a delicate matter. I am most happy to talk to you about it in private. You and Seamus—"

"Speak openly. I have nothing to hide."

Maudley regards her for a moment. "Very well. Emma, Seamus. Given the circumstances of...Well, how do I put this delicately? Given the circumstances your mother found herself in—"

"You mean how she was a whore?" Emma asks defiantly. "How she sold her body to keep us alive? Is that what you mean, Doctor?"

Maudley wipes his lips with his napkin and places it slowly on the table. "Given that she ended up in a very poor and precarious situation, it may surprise you to know that I was once a dear friend to her. When we were children, we played together, she and I. I spent some time in Ireland as a boy."

Emma snorts. "You? In Ireland?"

"I assure you, it is true. Fianna O'Brien was a great favorite amongst the children at Saint Patrick's, and though she was older than I, we all took to her like ducklings to a pond. I heard of her passing when I went back to Kerry last month. I did not know she had had children out of wedlock, but once I learned... I couldn't very well do nothing, could I?"

Seamus wipes surreptitiously at his eye and Roan pretends to be eating her own eggs, though she simply cuts them into smaller pieces and pushes them around her plate.

Emma has fallen silent, but the anger still burns in her eyes.

"An old friend I ought to have done more to help when I could have," Maudley adds quietly.

He glances at Roan. There is a question in his eyes. *Do you want to know?* But now that it comes to it, she finds that she does not want to know. Not now, not like this. Not in front of Emma and Seamus—and especially not while Rapley is here.

"These eggs are marvelous," she says, forcing joviality into her voice. How tedious to have to perform the act of happiness daily.

"Mrs. Goode is an excellent cook, is she not?" Maudley says, the question gone from his eyes. "I must commend her once more. Eat your fill. You are home now. We are all home now."

Beside her, Rapley stiffens again almost imperceptibly, but they all eat on in silence.

"Come," Dr. Maudley says once they have finished breakfast. He claps his hands. "I can wait no longer. I have a surprise for you all."

Emma glances at Seamus skeptically, but Roan is intrigued and stands right away. Unused to so much free time, any distraction is welcome.

Dr. Maudley leads them at a brisk pace back into the entrance hall where a large box stands upon a pedestal in the center. The doors have been thrown wide.

"What is it?" Roan asks, stepping forward to touch it.

"A camera obscura. It is a machine capable of capturing images, like a painting."

"I have heard of such a thing," Seamus says, wheeling himself forward. "How does it work?"

"Ah," Maudley says, grinning. "To make the image, we polish a silver-plated copper sheet to a high shine." He leans closer to Seamus, as though sharing a coveted secret. "Like a mirror. We then expose it in the camera here, after which we fume it with mercury, resulting in a latent image."

"May we try it?" the boy asks, almost bouncing in his chair.

"Of course, young man! This daguerreotype is my own, though I have kept it in storage some five years. I am well trained in its use. You shall be the first model. Now, position yourself there, against the wall, and we shall use science to capture your likeness."

A niggle of doubt itches in Roan's ear. "Is there any danger?"

Maudley smiles. "I assure you, it is perfectly safe. I am well trained in the use of mercury."

"To have your likeness captured seems dangerous to me," Emma says. "Some kind of witchcraft."

Jenny's words return to Roan, and she shudders. *To this day, folk hear the witch's screams on the wind, a reminder that this house—this mountain—is cursed.*

"Only science," Maudley says. "I assure you."

"I leave you to your games," Rapley says suddenly. He turns to go,

but finds Roan in his intended path. They exchange a look full of—
what? Roan can hardly say. Then he is striding past her, nothing said and
yet much suggested.

"And we can see ourselves?" Seamus asks, wheeling himself to the
spot Maudley indicated.

Maudley laughs, clapping his hands together. "Indeed, yes! The
image will appear on the silver plate…just like a jewel. It is fragile, so I
must secure it in one of these display books before I allow you to touch
it." Maudley indicates three little rectangular velvet-lined books—two
silver frames, which closed together like the covers of a book—sitting
beside the camera. "The glass will protect the image so you may look at
it as often as you please. Now, watch closely."

Dr. Maudley puts on a pair of white gloves, and then removes a
polished silver plate from a soft bag. He opens the daguerreotype box
and places the plate facedown inside it. "Ready yourself, and hold still."

It is several hours before Roan has opportunity to speak with Maudley alone, Emma and Seamus finally having gone away to look at the daguerreotypes of Seamus and the one Maudley insisted on taking of Roan, Emma having crossed herself and flat-out refused. She finds the doctor in a small room off the East Wing ground-floor corridor.

"Come in, come in," he says when he sees her, gesturing with his hand, his smile genuine and bright.

Roan cannot help but stare. The walls, each and every one, are lined with bookcases, full of tomes so beautiful she cannot fathom at their collective fortune. In the center of the room, taking up much of the space, is an enormous partners desk, very like the one in her father's study, only the leather top is a burgundy red rather than her father's forest green.

Maudley gestures to the seat across from the desk and Roan sits, still peering around with undisguised delight.

"This room…" She gestures helplessly.

"My sanctuary," Maudley says, looking around fondly. He lets the silence draw out, companionable as it is, and then sits back, looking at her. "I have sensed that you wish to talk to me."

Roan nods. "I don't want to be impertinent or ungrateful, but—"

"You are dissatisfied with something. Come, tell me."

Roan lowers her voice. "That room. The blue one. It was meant to be mine."

"Indeed."

"Why?" Her voice is sharp.

Maudley frowns. "I'm not certain I know what you mean."

"Why did you choose that room for me *specifically*?"

Maudley's brows release and he smiles. It has a softening effect on his peculiar gaze. "I thought that might be obvious. Perhaps not. Blue. It was your mother's favorite color."

"My…my *mother*? You knew my *mother*?"

Maudley takes both of her hands into his own, and she is so stunned at his revelation that it doesn't occur to her to pull away.

"Of course, dear girl. Your parents were most dear to me. Their passing was… is…Well. And now you are here, and you are dear to me as well."

Roan pulls away, pressing both her hands to her bodice, the warmth of his touch unwelcome on her icy skin.

"I don't know you, and Father never mentioned you."

"Your father was a peculiar kind of man. He divulged very little and kept much to his chest."

"How did you meet?"

He pulls free his pocket watch and checks the time. "It was at a fair, I believe. A science fair. In London."

"A science fair?"

"I believe so. It was a long time ago."

"Why do you think he never mentioned you? If you were so close, I mean?"

Maudley sighs. "My dear, you would have to ask him yourself. I do not know what his intentions are…were." He turns away. "I am sorry. I am fatigued. Perhaps we could talk further another—"

"Why did he send me here?" Roan cuts in. "I saw a letter. A contract, of sorts. And you knew I was coming before he had died."

Maudley turns back to her. "I am sorry to be the one to…and he should have…but, here we are. Dear, your father was sick. He knew that he would not live much longer. I was there for him. And I am honored he chose me for your guardianship. More than that, I cannot say. Only this: he loved you."

And now she knows he is lying.

For all the things her father was, a loving man had never been one of them.

"And what of me?" she asks, dropping her voice and glancing casually around. "Did he talk to you about me?"

There is an infinitesimal pause.

"Ah. You are worried, perhaps, that he confided some terrible behavior to me? Some faux pas?"

Roan waits.

"He spoke of you most fondly, as any father would. Now, I must bid you good afternoon, *Roanita*."

He bows stiffly before abruptly leaving the study.

lies

upon lies

upon lies.

The knocking sounds like thunder in Roan's half sleep. Endless storms batter the barren, desolate mountain and the hallowed, hollow house upon it. The knocking continues, gets louder, more urgent, and the noise filters into the waking part of Roan, and she stirs.

Roan puts on her dressing gown and cap, heading down the corridor to find the noise. What is real? Even this banging may be in her mind. Can she still be dreaming?

Andrew and Dr. Maudley are already downstairs when she arrives.

"What is the meaning of this?" Maudley demands, heading for the gatehouse. He is impeccably dressed, as always, and Andrew looks as though he has not slept at all.

She follows in Maudley's wake; voices rumble beyond the door, a yell, and then another knock,

louder.

"Open!" a male voice calls.

Maudley unlocks the inner door and opens it enough to peer out, but then stumbles back when a large man pushes through. He is followed by a disheveled, rain-soaked Rapley. Behind them, the storm is more violent than Roan has ever seen.

The stranger stands straighter and mutters, "I apologize for the late hour. It couldn't be helped."

Roan cannot see the face beneath his hood.

Maudley tosses his cane up and catches it in the middle. "Who are you? Why do you disturb the sleep of my guests?"

The man bows his head. "I have a letter here." And he produces the scraps of one from a coat pocket, while pushing back his hood. Roan cannot help but stare. He is a giant, with a rough, no-nonsense face; a coarse, uneven scar runs the length of it, from his forehead, down across his nose, over to the right tip of his mouth, dissecting both lips and his jawline. If ever Roan were to guess at what a sword scar looks like, his would be it.

The man catches her staring and she averts her gaze. She does not like the look of this man. He has seen violence.

Maudley reads the letter twice, looks over the man and his attire, and then checks it again. At last, he sighs.

"Well, your timing could have been better. But you look well up to the job, Mr. Cage. Welcome to Mill House."

The giant—Mr. Cage—nods his head. "Just Cage. I insist."

"Well...Cage. Andrew will see you to your sleeping quarters. We shall have proper introductions in the—"

"What the blazes is going on?" Emma's voice rings through the gatehouse hall, shrill yet sleepy. "Why is everyone up? And without me? Are we having an adventure?"

She stops in her tracks when she sees Cage.

"Lord almighty. Are we housing *trolls* now?"

Cage's eyes narrow. "I didn't know this was a whorehouse," he snaps, eyeing Emma and Roan, both of them in their gowns.

"Now, really—" Maudley begins, and Rapley steps forward, fist raised.

"Who do you think you are, talking to me like that?" Emma snaps. "Great big oaf like you'd be lucky to have a girl as fine as the likes of us! Stranger in the house too, appearing at night, dressed all in black like a nightcrawler!" Roan blanches. "Men like you think you can walk all over the girls, but girls have strong teeth and loud voices! Men should show respect, for are we not your mothers? Shame on you!"

Cage has the decency to look rebuked, as much as a giant like him can look rebuked. He closes his mouth and looks to Maudley. "I apologize. But I am a man of learning, and women are a distraction. I'm here for one purpose and one purpose only."

Emma folds her arms. "And what might that be?"

"To teach a cripple so he may be of some use to the world."

Roan stops Emma in time, else Cage's already-scarred face might have felt the cut of her nails. She yells unintelligible curses, her arms flailing.

"Calmly," Roan murmurs. "Let us leave these—*men*—to it."

"Men and their bleeding tongues," Emma mutters, turning away with one last scathing look at the new arrival. She hurries up the stairs, but Roan hangs back in the shadows.

"Come," Maudley says at last. "Andrew, show Mr.—show *Cage* to his quarters. There is work to do in earnest tomorrow."

Andrew nods and then looks at Roan where she hides and offers her a conciliatory smile. "This way, sir," he tells the giant. When the giant complies, Rapley leaves through the gatehouse, seemingly determined to return to the storm on the ragged mountain. Roan turns to leave, but catches the sound of Rapley's voice and glances back. Rapley is in the dark, and Maudley is close by. Neither sees Roan.

"It's a mistake," Rapley says in a low, dangerous voice. "Allowing one such as he into a house with two ladies present."

Maudley waves a hand. "I must educate the boy, Rapley. He needs a purpose. What else would you have me do?"

Roan turns away, feeling out of place to hear such a conversation between father and adopted son. Still, curiosity compels her to linger.

"He is dangerous," Rapley says. "It is a mistake."

"To bed with you." Maudley waves an arm. "Or to your night. What can I do to stop you?"

Rapley catches sight of Roan where she stands in the shadows of the staircase, his slate eyes drawing her in. She feels herself open, the barriers inside dissolving. He looks sharply away.

"Good night, then," he says, and leaves as if he never were there, closing the gatehouse door behind him.

Maudley sighs, and when he turns, he too catches sight of her. "He has been my adopted son for many years. And I do not understand him one bit."

Chapter 10
NAKED

Father,

You are a distraction. I have questions. You wouldn't answer in life, so why should you in death? One question lingers above all others.

Why would you not love me?

Why make me, then break me? Why scorn me?

What did our life together mean? Why teach me those...things?

Because I remember. I remember the books we hurled, the marks we etched in blood. Hiding in the cellar learning words that tasted of ash.

AND YET...I REMEMBER THINKING:

HE FEARS ME.

WERE YOU AFRAID, FATHER?

POSTSCRIPT. YOU ARE IN MY PAST. I MUST TRY
TO BUILD A BETTER FUTURE AND BE HAPPY HERE.

ROAN E. EDDINGTON
MILL HOUSE
NOWHERE

Roan wipes her pen and puts it down. She is heart-sore and overtired of empty words. Nothing she can write will ever mean anything. Her father is gone, simple as that. She will never know why he couldn't love her. She will never understand why he barred her from her inheritance and sent her to this desolate place without a friend or distraction in sight.

Had he wanted her to suffer? Useless questions.

A flash of anger bursts within and she throws her near-empty ink pot across the room. It hits the wall with a *crack* and then rolls under the bed.

The room stifles and she paces back and forth. Her bodice sits tightly, pressing down on her hips and bruising her ribs. With a curse, she storms to her desk, removes the small knife she always carries, and begins hacking blindly at the laces behind her. One by one, they come apart, including much of her dress; she does not care.

Laces cut, she pulls and rips until she is free of the cage, and much of her morning top. Her skirt still intact, she shoves it off, crinoline too, until she stands naked in the confines of the room.

She inhales, and though her ribs complain, they finally expand enough to allow her a lungful of oxygen. Freedom.

She laughs, startles herself into silence, and laughs again.

With abandon, she removes the pins and braids from her hair until it falls free and wild down her back. She slides her fingers along her scalp, relishing the sensation—relishing her skin—and then slips back onto the chair. She picks up her quill, realizes she has no ink, and—with a derisive chuckle—scratches *Good-bye* into the paper. She grins at the letter for less than a second before reaching forward, opening the window, and throwing it into the night.

And she sees him.

He sits alone, still as stone, white shirt glowing in the moonlight and mist. Tonight, for the first time, there is no storm. He is below her, sitting on a mossy rock. She frowns down at him, keeping an eye on the sheet of paper, which floats like a whisper, landing several feet away from him, hidden in the heather. Like his shirt, it glows.

He is magnetic, there in the moonlight. He confuses her. He is most likely the heir to this property, to all Dr. Maudley owns. He is, by all accounts, wealthier than anyone she has ever known or heard of. And yet he dresses without finery, he wears boots caked in mud. He spends nights out in the wilderness, come storm or frost, and not a jacket or covering in sight. His manners leave much to be desired, and he has insulted her more than once—she might be a scullery maid for all his rough treatment of her.

Yet here he sits beneath her window, almost as though guarding her.

Or perhaps not guarding her at all. Perhaps guarding the mountain from her. She recalls how he warned her off it with such ferocity. As if the mountain were his own personal playground.

Well.

He does not get to claim the mountain as his territory. She is a wolf and will claim a stake for her own.

She leans farther out, hair falling forward, trying to see if he is writing or perhaps whittling wood. Trying to see what could possibly induce him to sit so steadfastly. But he is doing nothing. No—she sees now.

His hands are clasped as if in prayer.

Roan recoils like the instinct of withdrawing her hand from a flame.

An image—a memory—rips free. She clenches her fist, but the sudden recollection of her father cannot be stopped. It is as though he stands before her at this very moment. She can smell the parsnip soup on his breath.

i am little

he is angry

standing over me

praying

shouting

"*S I N F U L—*"

"No!"

"*—S H A M E F U L—*"

"Please!"

"*—C H I L D !*"

She grabs her hair.

his face stark in the dim light

his ocean eyes

now pitch-dark as coal

"*R E P E N T !*"

i scream

he is all sharp edges

"Go away, Father!"

a blow.

"*S I N N E R !*

R E P E N T !"

a cry.

"*REPENT, FILIA DIABOLI!*"

"Please," Roan screams. "No! Father, no!"

She shakes her head and the images vanish. She peers around, confused—and sees that Rapley is on his feet, looking at her. Staring. Frowning. Teeth bared.

She cannot move.

He doesn't move.

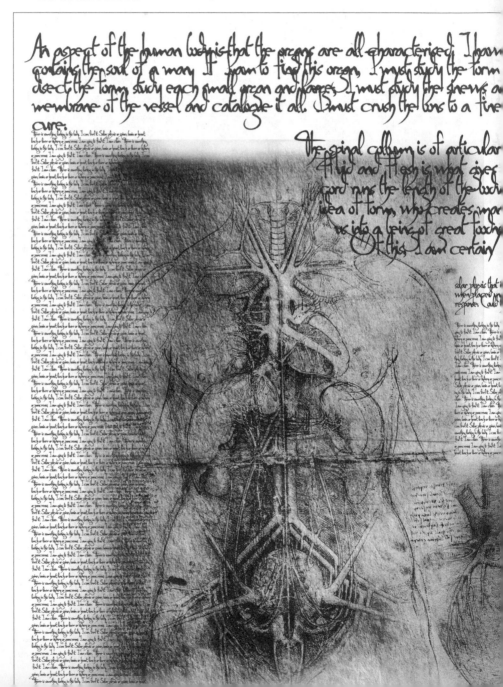

After a long time, or maybe a mere second, Roan flinches and backs away, grabbing at the tatters of her dress and holding them against her.

He saw…He *saw*.

Not just her nakedness, but her *fear*.

And that is infinitely worse.

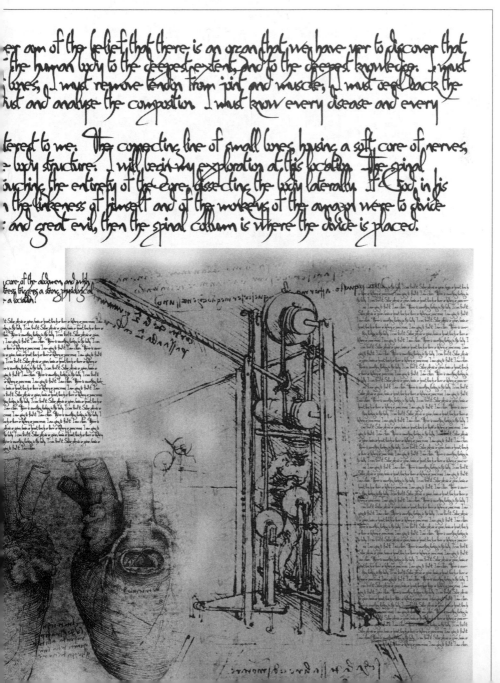

"More like theology," Seamus says.

It is the next day, and they are sitting in Roan's bedroom, Emma beside her, and Seamus and Andrew on the opposite bed.

Emma frowns. *"Theology?"*

"The study of faith," Roan mutters.

"How useless," Andrew says, grinning. She grins back.

"I know," Emma snaps. "But why? You don't want to be a *priest*?"

Seamus shrugs. "It's not like I can really *do* anything with what I learn, but it's fascinating! Besides. We talk about things not strictly related to theology, like apparitions, the secret powers of the human mind, and the like."

Emma crosses herself and mutters a blessing. "I don't like the look of him. You should have seen how he arrived, Seamus! Banging on the door at God's own hour. No holy man would do that."

Andrew laughs. "Is it a sin to disturb your sleep, Miss O'Brien?"

"Too right, it is!"

"I should like to sit in on one of these classes," Roan says, her attention piqued, but not for the same reasons that Seamus might suspect. No. Since the moment the man with the scarred face arrived, something about him has bothered her.

Seamus is all aglee. "I shall ask him!"

"Thank you."

Let her hear the man—Cage—talk. Let her study him and see what face that leer is hiding.

Roan is glad of Emma's wagging tongue.

Peculiarly, she feels as if she might be a puppet master, so well does Emma rant and rage with words close to those Roan herself might have chosen. Her Irish temper and wild hair, which has not been confined for some time, have the effect of theatrics, and Roan is well entertained. Cage stands before her somewhat subdued, which Roan likes best of all.

"Because she is a woman? That is the answer you give, you stiff-faced carbuncle!"

Cage's lips thin, much the same as Rapley's do when restraining anger.

"Miss…Miss. The studies I teach are for your brother, young Master O'Brien and he alone."

Emma snorts. "*Master* O'Brien, is it? Why should your snobbery be for him alone and not I? Do I not possess the same blood as he? Yet for my breasts you halt?"

Cage turns his head away, his neck straining with a blush furious as furies. "I tell you again, it is for him alone."

Roan grows hot. *Capricious idiot.*

"Capricious idiot!" Emma barks, and Roan jerks so violently that both glance at her.

"I am well," she says. "But I insist I learn. What lies and falsehoods might you otherwise be telling our…*young Master O'Brien?*"

Cage's nostrils flare and Roan smiles, though she still quakes with the rush of her forced manipulation upon Emma. *Stop now. Do not be weakened.*

"I am a man of God," Cage says severely, and this is no pretense of offense.

Soft there, are we?

"Are you, now? And which God do you grovel before?"

"*Slattern!*" Cage bursts, then snorts through those flared nostrils like an animal.

Roan laughs, though Emma's mouth falls open.

"Brute of a man!" Emma yells. "To claim the working of God and then to rebuke thus with such low words! Fie! *Cumberwold!*"

Cage steps close to Roan, his voice low. "I will not teach the likes of you. You have a devil's touch, and the subtlety with it of a stampeding herd."

Emma spits at the ground and turns on her heel. Though, peculiarly, as she leaves the room, she suddenly shies to the left as if something had surprised her. Roan follows, feeling Cage stare at her back as she walks away. She shudders.

Roan wakes with a scream on her lips, but catches it before it escapes. Her body heaves with sickness, but she does not vomit. Disoriented and dizzy, she staggers to her feet, but the earth tilts and she is

down

again in seconds.

She has been somewhere dark, somewhere alone and wrong. Things were upside down, sideways—nothing made sense. But no.

She hadn't been alone. Some*thing* had been there with her.

Something beastly.

She can still smell traces of it around her.

It takes her a moment to realize that she isn't breathing, that she *can't* breathe, so she rolls over, hunching her back, her fingers digging into something black and soft. Earthy.

Breathe.

Her mind screams, and with a mighty effort, she d r a g s air into her lungs like hauling a mule backward by the tail.

Steps to her right startle her so much that she tries to move away, but succeeds only in kicking out with her feet.

"Roan?"

The voice is low and graveled, unused.

She stills, her vision hazy, her lips and tongue so heavy she can't speak, can only, finally, breathe.

She can hear herself panting.

There is movement, and she is off the ground, away from the cold and moving through the air. Everything smells of bracken and rain.

This is not her bedroom.

Somewhere in her fogged-up brain, she knows someone is carrying her, but nothing matters beyond the fact that she is *off* the mountain. She is no longer touching it, and she can breathe easier for it.

Time passes, darkness rises, and then she is awake again. The sky is an inky blackness above. A warm blanket has been wrapped around her so that she is cocooned from the mountain and the air. Beside her, a warm fire crackles into the heath.

"Hnnn," she moans. "Mmm…"

Someone touches her head, and she knows it is Rapley. She can feel his presence beside her as surely as she had the day he grabbed her by the arms and then flung her away. And then the day he had almost killed her and delivered his dire warnings as well.

"R…" She licks her lips. "Rapley?"

He comes into focus, his eyes sharp beneath his heavy brows. He stares at her intently, his lips curved down so that he looks older than he is.

She tries to sit up, but her arms are bound in the cocoon. Instead, she lies back and rolls onto her side. She does not yet want to be released from the warmth.

After a moment, she looks up at him. He is no longer looking at her. He stokes the fire with an expressionless face, but Roan can see the tightness in his neck and shoulders.

"I found you on the mountain, not twenty paces from the house. You were in your nightdress. No shoes, no jacket." He looks at her then. "What were you thinking of?"

Her thoughts fog. "I…"

"Did I not warn you? Did you not understand when I said that the mountain is dangerous?" His voice rises as he continues. "Did I not say that the mountain was not kind in darkness?"

She scrunches up her eyes. "Stop yelling."

"I'm *not*—" He breaks off, lowering his voice. "I am not yelling. I simply wish you to understand and stop being petulant."

Roan does sit up then, fighting with the blanket to free her arms. "First of all, I woke up there. I don't know how it happened. And secondly, you go out into the mountain every night! I've seen you!"

Suddenly she recalls he has seen her naked and afraid…

"What I do is none of your concern—"

"Right you are," she snaps. "And what I do is none of yours."

He throws a stick into the fire. "It is not the same!"

"Why? Because I am a woman? I have two legs same as you!"

"Because you don't have to!" His words carry for miles.

They stare at each other for long moments, each breathing heavily.

Roan swallows, trying to keep her rage away. "What do you mean?"

"It is none of your concern," he repeats. "But you should heed a warning freely given. Avoid the mountain. By God, I would if I could."

He looks at her but does not seem to see her. His eyes blaze, but she senses he is looking within now, to somewhere far away or long gone. His gaze drifts, then suddenly snaps to hers again.

He mutters a curse and turns to stalk away from her. She senses his proximity, but the mists swallow him up so thoroughly he might as well have vanished.

When she has the strength, Roan quenches the fire, leaves the blanket folded neatly beside it, and heads back toward Mill House.

She turns, sensing a presence she assumes to be Rapley's, and finds the dark silhouette of the ram looking down at her.

got you

This is not a life.

This is a life sentence.

*S*uch wild land! The ground is thick with mud the color of a pigeon's wing, and the mountains are so vast and grim that I feel as if I had stepped into a tale of fairies and wild little men! How mother would laugh could she see me now, like a vagabond!

*T*he endless days of travel fatigue my body, but the farther away from London we go, the higher my spirit soars. For did not the Lord intend for us to go out into the heathen masses and convert them to his light? Did not he intend mankind to build and harvest and care for the land?

I am, then, a missionary's wife! Still I cannot stop my smile when I think that John and I are married. He is the most ambitious, wealthy, loving husband, and I am fortunate that I caught his eye when he and Father supped together last winter. The marriage was arranged between the two, and I had no notion, though I admit I took a liking to John the moment I saw him. Such deep brown eyes and thick, curling dark hair. He looks to be always thinking of something, a burning within his gaze. And he is wealthy. Perhaps more wealthy than Father.

*W*e are to travel again, and my period of rest is over. I shall miss this particular spot, which stands near a brook and overlooks a pretty patch of pink heather. I am being summoned. Farewell, diary! Until I open your pages once more.

FROM THE DIARY OF
HERMIONE JOHN SMITH,
4 JULY 1583

Chapter 11

APPARITIONS

Roan sits up in bed and presses herself to the wall.

The sounds of a beast's hooves echo as they clomp down the hall, followed, like the shivering echo of a deserted cathedral, by the snort of air through two menacing nostrils. Roan's eyes widen and her skin prickles. This is not a dream. This is not a nightmare.

C-clomp. C-clomp. Pffffff.

Four hooves, walking slowly, approaching her room from the long, dark hallway. What is it?

Mule? Horse? Ram?

Something large. Something sweating ice, steam rising from its haunches like smoke. And it is coming for *her*.

She wants to yell, to demand that it stop and be gone. But fear twists her into knots, and she shivers, unshed tears rising to the brim.

Pffff.

With no escape, she is a wolf cornered, and the only thing she can think of is to get away. Flinging the blankets off and dashing to the window, she unlatches it just as the *c-clomp c-clomp* turns from a hoof on wood to a hoof on the reed carpet. It is behind her.

It snorts.

She slips out like a ghost and climbs down the stone wall, dropping the last few feet to rush out into the foggy morning.

Behind, she can feel the beast watching her from a tiny upstairs window.

Rapley kneels in the center of his room, hands clasped tightly together. Sweat pools between his palms and down his back, despite the frigid night. Straight ahead: a man. Not a regular man, and no one that Rapley knows. He is the form of someone no longer living.

In his eighteen years, Rapley has seen ghosts a handful of times. He has seen most of them since he came to Mill House.

The first, though, when he was three, and again when he was five. It was his mother. She was the same as before, except her skin had lost its luster, its color, even. She looked pale—gray almost. But the *dust.* That was what alarmed him. She looked like a statue that had never been cleaned; even her clothes, which were new and fashionable, were coated with it so that she looked old. So very old.

He had tried to run to her. To hug her.

Until he saw her face.

She stared at him with dead, hollow eyes and a slack jaw, her mouth open at an angle no human could mimic. Too long. Too dark. She was a hollow thing. But more: she wasn't alone.

At five, Rapley was able to sense that there was something...*else*... with her. Within her.

She was his mother no longer.

The second ghost had been when he was eight. It was a tall man, thin and gangly. Long, almost inhuman arms hung loosely by his side. His legs bowed out at the knees. He looked, for all purposes, exactly like every depiction of a monster Rapley's penny bloods booklets described. But he was smarter by eight. By eight, he knew exactly what he was looking at.

An apparition.

A rotted thing.

A ghost.

What he didn't yet know was the fear. Or the pain.

But when the man jerked with movement so sudden it was if he hadn't moved at all, turning at once so that in one moment he stood lank and in the next his arms were bent, fingers clawed, hollow eyes and slack jaw facing Rapley head on—the fear was born.

Ghosts could move.

And more.

He learned, that night, that ghosts could also *hurt*. They could tear and bruise and yell and howl if they were enraged enough.

The lanky man had been. Rapley bore the scars of that night long into his adolescence.

Rapley was nine when the third ghost appeared. He was in this very room, kneeling in this very spot, praying to a God he still believed in. The ghost was a woman this time. She stood over him with her hollow eyes and her slack jaw, and the jaw worked up and down, creaking and snapping. Her head was on upside down so that her jaw clacked hard, teeth against teeth, as she worked it.

He had pictured a bubble around himself, a safe space only a few inches away from his body, thinking: *Don't touch me. Don't hurt me.*

She moved in that too-fast, creaking way, and he wet himself. But he held on to the bubble—his shield.

The ghost reacted as though it was real. And it *was* real, from that moment on. He had built it since then, making it wider, stronger. He felt it like a pressure in his body, and maintaining it was like keeping a single thought. It took years of concentration. Single-minded focus. It was the only way to contain a thought in his mind, constantly, with no distractions.

But now…this is different.

This is not one disgruntled ghost. This isn't two, or three, or four.

Ghosts surround him on every side. He tries not to feel them pressing in on his shield, but they are many, and they are strong. He has never felt such strength from the dead before.

Why? Why now?

He allows himself to pray while holding the thought, ignoring the hollow eyes and slack jaws all around him. Ignoring a tiny movement to his left or right, or farther back in the crowd.

He can feel their eyes, singularly, on him. They are rabid. They are ravenous. They are rage.

Men, women, and children, all contorted, bent—wrong.

He is life. He is living, and they crave it.

But none of them is alone. Each and every one carries something *else*. A strange kind of shadow. Something inhuman. He can hear a steady growling sound humming beneath them all.

He shivers and begins to speak.

"In nomine Patris, et Filii, et Spiritus Sancti. Amen. Pater noster, qui es in caelis, sanctificetur nomen tuum…"

A ghost moves. They all have, he realizes. Each one's head has tilted to the side.

He licks his lips. *"Sed libera nos a malo…libera me, Deus meus…libera me."*

One of the ghosts is closer. Right beside him. His breath quickens. *"Libera me…"*

Another on the other side, face pressed against his, teeth bared. He can feel them on his skin, can feel the cold, foul breath. Smell the sickening odor.

The pain is sudden and sharp, and he hisses in a breath, shield faltering. It is enough. A ghost has his head. Another has his heart.

He forces his shield up again, though the pain is like a seizure in his limbs. Rapley focuses on his shield harder. *"Libera me, Deus meus! Libera me!"*

Until at last, there is nothing.

Rapley collapses on the floor, still as stone, and at last…lets his shield go.

As he pulls his hands away from each other he cries out. The pain racks his body for long hours.

But they are gone.

For now.

He stumbles to his feet and blows out his candle and watches the mocking sun rise.

Roan is floating.

The walls are taller now than when she is in her body, skewed, as though they narrow the higher they climb. Shadows accentuate this dance. All at once, she is near the ceiling, looking down at the wide, fish-eyed floor, the floorboards fat in the middle, tapering out strangely at the edges like long fingers.

The fuggy slowness that is always there when she first leaves her body passes, giving way to a speed she could not match on two legs.

And she flies.

Father?

Is he here, with her, in this strange half dream? This is the one thing she had always kept from him…her nighttime flights. What would he have done had he known? Locked her in the cellar *permanently*, instead of simply when she could not control the Conjures?

She turns and explores, always calling with her mind. *Father? Are you here?*

Corridor follows corridor, windows pass by, and house turns into attic and then sky.

She is above the storm and the clouds and the lightning; she can see each star, crystal clear, like firebrands burning the black-blue, nothing of the Universal tapestry behind. She knows she could go on, higher and higher, past the moon and distant stars. There is so much to see out there. Beyond.

But Father is not here.

She can sense the house below her, can sense the warmth of the people inside. The coolness of the Nothing above is pleasant, but she knows it would turn icy, alien, and hostile if she were to go farther. She is at the limit. One more inch and the cord would break. No getting back after that.

Lost forever.

She turns toward the house, feels the magnitude of the thing at her back, and—

The silver cord at her waist seems thin—too thin—fragile as a spider's web. She can only see it because it glints as it moves, otherwise she might think she flew alone. Untethered. Free.

Lost.

I don't like this.

The space behind expands, darkness rushing in, or perhaps *her* rushing *out*. The house below her seems to shrink, pulling away.

I don't like this—

No. No!

Roan wakes at the same moment she hears the *smash*, and the cry. She is disoriented from her nightwalk, her soul not quite snug in her flesh. She hears a *boom* and another *crash*, glass shattering, and jumps from the bed.

The floor hits her in the face, but she stumbles up on shaking limbs, her vision clearing with every step.

She opens the door on a scene of chaos. The corridor is filled with glass, leaves, and small branches. A large tree has fallen against the house and through the high glass windows. The wind whistles as it thrashes at the tree, the leaves; the corridor is a mini-cyclone of air and water.

A scream again. Emma.

The glass is everywhere, so Roan leaves her body without a thought. Her spirit rushes up and her body collapses. The fall is slow, as all things in the world of flesh are. She pushes forward, toward the sound of the tears, until she finds Emma, staggering from her bed, a cascade of blood running down her thigh. Behind her, a shattered window—glass falling inward in all directions.

This was meant to be my room. I put her here.

That is all Roan can think. But then Emma falls, cries out again, and there is blood. So much blood. A shard of glass the length of Roan's forearm protrudes from Emma's thigh.

"Emma!" Roan cries, and Emma screams again.

Roan is in her body before it hits the floor. Dizzy, she rushes forward, heedless of the tiny shards that glisten on the floor. Emma no longer staggers. She is in a heap by the dresser, her room an ungodly cyclone. Glass and debris fly everywhere, tiny stings that Roan ignores. She bends down and drags Emma from the chaos; her bloody thigh leaves a grotesque smear along the floor.

Strong arms encircle Roan's, taking Emma's weight completely, taking her own weight too, and they are lifted up and carried down the rest of the corridor and out onto the second-floor landing.

"Seamus," Emma whispers. "Someone check on Seamus...."

"I'll do it." A man's voice. Rapley.

He is wet, dripping and bedraggled as though he has been out there in this storm with nothing but the shirt on his back.

"Try to dress that wound," he calls back, running down the opposite corridor where Seamus has been housed.

Emma collapses onto her back, staring at the ceiling and panting. She is pale. Too pale. Roan rips a strip from her nightdress, balls it up and shoves it into Emma's mouth. If she is rough, Emma does not complain.

"Bite down hard."

Emma nods, fiery determination searing through her gaze.

Do it, it seems to say. *I am no delicate flower. Do it, and be damned.*

Roan rips at her nightgown again, biting when the material does not give, until she has a long strip of sturdy cloth.

She does not wait. She does not give warning. She pulls the shard of glass from the raw flesh, and a spray of blood slaps her in the face. She tastes it, wants to spit the coppery filth from her mouth, but does not. For propriety's sake, she swallows instead, then ties the strip of cloth around Emma's leg, high up, above the wound, knotting it as tightly as her strength will allow.

give more.

tighter.

you know how.

give in.

"No," she spits, and yanks on the knot again. Emma gives a feeble cry and then her eyes roll into her head.

"*Emma!*" Seamus's cry is pure fear, and Roan wishes Rapley had not brought him.

But no—not Rapley. Andrew is pushing him.

harder

or

kill her

"We need to send for a doctor," Roan tells Andrew, teeth clenched. "Can you go?"

His voice is surprisingly low and calm. "Rapley has gone for Dr. Maudley."

Roan nods, noticing his shirt. "Take that off. Give it to me."

He doesn't hesitate, for which Roan is grateful, and throws it to her.

"Emma! What's happening to her? Oh God, don't let her die!" Seamus is sobbing, but Roan cannot think of that now.

She balls up the shirt and presses down on Emma's wound with all the strength she has left.

"Let me," Andrew says, beside her now, taking her place.

"Oh my God!" Jenny cries at the top of the stairs. None of them heard her approach. "Oh no! Oh, miss!"

"Jenny," Andrew says, his voice firm. "Go and get some alcohol. Brandy, rum—anything. Bring the bottle."

Jenny stands shaking her head, biting on her nails. "Andrew—"

"*Jenny*. Go now. I need that rum! Go on, lass."

Jenny tears her eyes away from Emma and nods, then hurries down the stairs.

Roan suspects that he set that mission only to distract her.

Emma cries out feebly, lifting a lifeless wrist as if to smack Andrew away.

"Gods, where is that man?" Andrew snaps, then glances quickly at Roan. "Forgive my manners."

"I should like to know where he is as well." She manages a faint smile.

Footsteps on the stairs alert them to Rapley's return. Behind him: Dr. Maudley.

He storms across the room like a hurricane, his arm sweeping the air.

"Move aside," he booms, and all in the company, save one, obey. Seamus, Andrew, and Roan stumble back with the force of Maudley's authority. Only Rapley does not flinch, nor move. He frowns down upon the scene solidly, like a rock on the mountain. Slate, through and through.

Dr. Maudley is beside Emma before Roan has seen him kneel.

"She needs sewing," Roan says, all the while Emma has begun her weak thrashing once more.

He ignores her. "My case."

Rapley places the black bag at the doctor's side, and Roan notes with unease how his knuckles and fingernails are bloodied.

Maudley pulls his bag open with deft, nimble movements, removing a bottle of clear liquid and some cotton cloth. He puts on a pair of gloves, balls up the cotton, says, "Stand back," and then dampens it and holds the thing to Emma's mouth.

Her eyes flutter for a moment and her body resists, but then she goes limp. Roan takes another step back. She is sensitive to ether, and Maudley has used no ether mask. Surely they are all at risk.

"Do not be alarmed," Maudley murmurs, his voice low as he tests Emma's awareness. "Chloroform is a new substance, but I have experience with it."

"I can smell it," Roan says. "It is…*sweet*."

"Yes. Chloroform is stronger than ether. But she will feel nothing. Nothing at all. And we shall not be affected at this range."

He then pulls out a small box containing strangely curved needles and waxed suture thread. Andrew and Seamus both look away, leaving only Rapley and Roan to witness Maudley's skill firsthand. He is fast, delicate, and careful. By the time the wound is closed, Emma has a thin line of sutures along her thigh, not the gaping wound of only moments before. Roan is astonished at his skill. Sewing through both muscle and various layers of tissue and leaving only the thinnest line.

Amazing.

In another life, she might have assisted a surgeon.

Dr. Maudley wipes his gloves and then removes them, getting smoothly to his feet. In all tonight, his movements have been like water, subtle and smooth. But his presence is once again a storm now that his work is done.

He looks up at her, dark eyes focused between heavy lashes. "You did well, putting a tourniquet above the wound."

Roan falters. "How did you know I had done it?"

His eyes flicker down once, and then back. She can suddenly feel her exposed legs where her pale blue nightgown should be.

"Warm her," Maudley says to the room. He hands his medical bag to Rapley, who takes it with a clench of his jaw and hard eyes.

Andrew steps forward to lift Emma into his arms. "I will remove her to her bedroom."

"Her room is chaos," Roan says. "The window gave in during the storm."

"She may have the Roman sofa in the Blue Room, if you do not mind sharing?" Maudley says, glancing at Roan.

"It…it was the Blue Room that was destroyed."

Maudley frowns. "You did not like the Blue?"

Roan swallows. "Too much space for me."

His eyes seem to twinkle. "I see."

At that moment, a harried Jenny arrives. She rushes forward, holding out two bottles of liquor. Brandy. Rum. "I wasn't sure which to bring, only"—she falters—"oh, oh! Dr. Maudley, sir!"

"Good woman," Maudley says, taking the bottles from her. "We will have tea. We have much to discuss, my guests and I. Summon Mrs. Goode."

Jenny curtsies now. "Yes, yes, sir, Master Maudley. Right away." She hurries back down the stairs, her skirts bobbing.

"I will stay with my sister," Seamus says, wheeling himself forward.

"I understand your wish," Maudley says. "But there are things to be said, and your sister will rely upon your good ears to relate them."

Seamus glances after Andrew as he carries Emma away, and Rapley slips from the room unnoticed by all except Roan.

"She'll not wake until morning," Maudley says. "I will leave Andrew with her for the night. He has some medical training."

Seamus hesitates, glances down the hall again, and then reluctantly nods.

"Now, then," Maudley says. "There is much to divulge. To the Red Room."

PART 2

Upon the Mountain

Hell is just a frame of mind.

—CHRISTOPHER MARLOWE,
DR. FAUSTUS

Midnight Summer

The little boy was everything Eve had hoped for. He was kind, not like the boys in her mother's play group on Friday afternoons. He was quiet, but funny—so funny that she would roll on the carpet laughing until she was crying.

One morning, she asked him to go with her to the most special place she knew. It was her secret, and she had never let anyone inside there. With the trust of innocence, he went with her, never once questioning where she might be leading him.

Adam would follow her anywhere.

She led him through the parlor and into the kitchen, then out the kitchen door into the wild and tangled garden.

"Shh," she reminded him, pressing one small finger to her lips.

He nodded, eyes solemn and grave. This was a very big secret she was sharing. Even he, at the tender age of eight, could sense that. Though she was two years his junior, he knew that she knew many more things than he did. Many more.

They wandered through the chrysanthemums, around the bracken, which Eve's mother let grow high because she liked to feel the woods nearby, through the grove of pine trees, and onward, to the very back.

There, hidden behind some rocks and camouflaged by a thick bush, the name of which Eve always forgot, was her hiding place. Not just a place to hide her body, or her things, but a place to hide her secret.

This was the place, she knew, and this was the time, she decided. She would share her deepest, darkest secret with Adam…and see if he ran away.

She took his hand, took a breath, and led him under the bush, where the branches and leaves had weaved together in an almost otherworldly ceiling. Underneath, she had laid a blanket long ago, and it was still dry. Here and there, between rocks and little holes she'd dug, were all her treasures. A shell she had found on the beach in Devon on the family outing last summer. A necklace she had found crushed on the road in town. A doll her father had given her, but then two years later had declared her too old for. All these treasures, she hid here.

And the biggest was one you couldn't even see.

"I'm going to give you my secret," she said.

Adam nodded. She always, always had his full attention.

"Sit," she said, and he did.

Eve closed her eyes and sat next to him, then put her hands on the rocks beside her, breathing into her nose and out of her mouth. Adam could sense that something important was happening, and he had to force himself not to laugh.

And then she spoke. He couldn't recognize the words, and knew she must be pretending to speak French or Latin, but as the little space around them grew colder and colder, he thought that maybe, just maybe, she really did have something big to show him.

And then the rocks spoke back. It wasn't words…but a deep, low grumbling. And the earth beneath his bottom moved! Moved like a living thing. He clapped his hand over his mouth to keep from yelping, and it worked.

Until he looked at Eve.

Her eyes! They were different. They had snapped open even as she said the make-believe words, and then she was floating above the blanket, legs crossed, but definitely floating. He stared in terror as the darkness in her eyes began to seep into her skin, like little dark veins.

"Eve!" he called, suddenly scared that she was going to change completely, or float away—or disappear. "Eve!"

Her eyes snapped in his direction, and she bared her teeth, growling like some wild beast. And then her eyes took in the shock on his face, the way he leaned away from her, and all of a sudden everything was normal.

The blanket was where it had been.

The secrets were still buried between rocks and in holes in the earth.

The ribbons hanging from the branches above them were still.

It was as though nothing had really happened at all.

"Was that real?" Adam whispered.

Eve had her head bowed, her hair concealing her face. Adam lifted the brunette curtain away.

"Eve?"

She was biting her lip. "Yes," she said in a very small voice.

"You can talk to the earth," he breathed, his eyes wide and staring.

Only then did she dare to look at him. "You…you're not afraid of me?"

"I'm not afraid," he said, and took her hand in his own. Then he did something he'd wanted to do for a long time, but never had. He leaned forward and gave her a kiss.

Eve's fingers brushed her cheek, where his kiss had fallen, and smiled. Her flesh burned hot where his had been.

She lifted her hand away and called a rock to her. It came, rolling over the blanket into her outstretched hand.

"Girl of the rocks," Adam said.

And she smiled.

"Now," he said. "Let me show you."

When Adam closed his eyes and told her exactly what each of her hidden places contained and where they were, she wasn't surprised. She had known, from the first, that he was special. Like her.

No, what surprised her was that he had seen her secret. Seen it, and not been afraid.

It was that he had seen it...

...and he loved her anyway.

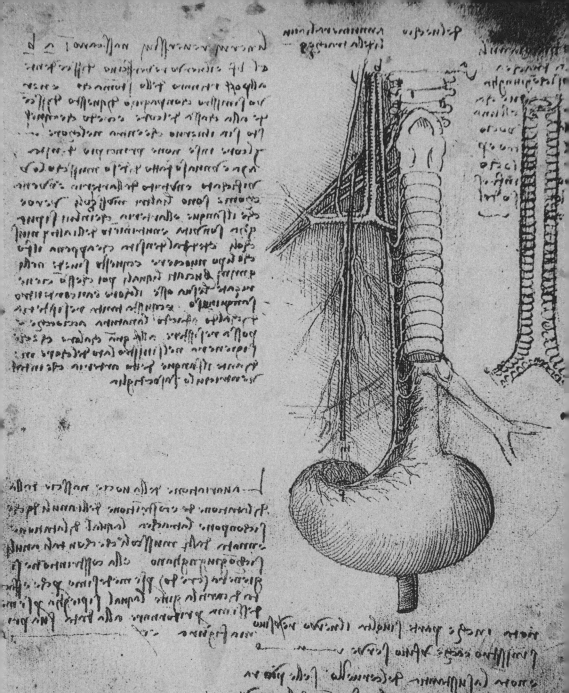

ZOEY

NOW

Chapter 12

MILL HOUSE

Zoey Camera Footage
Date: October 21

The camera focuses on a tall building of mixed styles. Medieval in aspect, part Gothic, it looms into a turbulent gray sky. Zoey's camera zooms out to reveal the whole—a long building with two wings that stretch backward and out of sight. The left side of the building is close up against a sheer rocky mountainside, as though built into the very mountain.

"Well, damn," Zoey whispers, her mouth close to the mic. "It's real. Really real."

The camera wobbles and then stabilizes, and Zoey comes into the frame. She bends down, adjusts something out of sight, and then steps back so that both she and the house are in view.

"I'm going to take my camera with me as I go inside so that I can watch it later and make notes. Right. Uh...let's go exploring, I guess."

She walks back to the camera, picks it up, and the view spins.

"Right," Zoey says, her voice close to the mic again. "I'm going to put the tripod away, and I'm going to leave my stuff out here by those rocks"—she points to a jagged protrusion of slate some way to the right—"and then we'll go in. I'm going to wear my GoPro headgear, so apologies if the quality isn't as good. I might need my hands, though."

A pause.

"Okay. Enough chitchat. Let's do this."

Zoey clicks her fingers in front of the camera. "Testing GoPro head cam."

The quality of the image is markedly reduced.

She peers into the lens and then smiles. "Hello there."

After putting it on she looks around. The camera moves with her.

"This should be cool."

Taking a breath, she looks back up at the house. She is standing much closer now, and the large doors of the gatehouse stare down like two guardians, arms folded.

Zoey tries the doors, but they won't budge.

"Didn't think so."

Walking along the length of the house, away from the mountainous side, Zoey checks and tries each window she comes to, with no luck, but when she rounds the other side of the building, she discovers that a large hole is ripped into the ribcage of the house.

"Bingo," she says, hurrying over.

With some effort, Zoey scales the rocks, her hands coming briefly into view, and jumps down into the room.

The camera takes a moment to adjust to the change in light.

"It's still furnished," Zoey whispers. "I expected it to be empty."

The light is vaporous and gray in the gloomy interior, but as Zoey looks around, the state of the furnishings becomes apparent.

"It's...intact. Like, *completely* intact." She whistles. "Holy shitballs."

The space is small but palatial, the walls a light green, hung with tapestries and paintings that are uncannily well preserved. Zoey steps carefully forward, camera scanning slowly from left to right. Two leather sofas, a Romanesque chair, an armchair, a table, and several small bookcases. Across the way, a green door, closed to the rest of the house. The floor is nothing but a tattered mess of carpet and debris, but the furnishings remain like something from a time capsule.

"Green," Zoey murmurs, touching one of the sofas and then passing on to a table standing in the corner. "Everything is a shade of green."

She turns to face the side of the room where the gaping hole stands, examining the wall around the opening.

"What caused this? And...how is the furniture com-pletely fine?"

A sudden movement and an expletive and the view is once again on the interior of the room. Only now the door is open, the space beyond a dark rectangle.

Zoey inhales.

Holds her breath.

There is the uncanny sense that the house is doing the same.

"You were closed," Zoey whispers, not moving an inch. "You were."

And then she gasps and hops back; the doorway seems somehow larger—or perhaps it feels more present, as though the space beyond the doorway has deepened in color. In blackness.

"What the fuck was that?" Zoey chokes, stepping away again.

There is a long, torturous moment of stillness, and then Zoey is turning, running back toward the hole in the wall, clambering out...

She runs a few paces away before facing the house. The green room is now swathed in shadow, the morning light turning it into a chasm of deepest night.

⌣

Zoey
4:00 p.m.
Wish u were

Your message failed to send.

Zoey
4:33 p.m.
It's bloody cold. Hope you're bringing blankets.

Your message failed to send.

Zoey
7:00 p.m.
Can't sleep. House makes noises. And there was this door…

Your message failed to send.

Zoey
9:00 p.m.
holy shit Pole I'm actually a bit unnerved.
There R sounds!

Your message failed to send.

Zoey
9:12 p.m.
hurry up and get here u sod.

Your message failed to send.

Zoey
00:00 a.m.
officially given up on sleep for the night. Also, I need a
pee, but you think I'm getting out of the tent again?

Your message failed to send.

Zoey
3:00 a.m.
Poulton. I'm scared.

Delivered.

ROAN

❧

1851

Chapter 13

SECRETS OF
THE FATHER

None of them can settle. Maudley leads them into a room that truly deserves its name. It is more pleasure room than parlor, with deep wine-colored walls and richly woven red velvet sofas. The rug is Oriental, full of reds, golds, and violets, and the paintings all drip with roses, sunsets, and bloodberries. Even the piano sits hidden beneath lace coverings the color of intense blush.

Maudley gestures to the plush sofa and pours himself a red-hued drink from a crystal decanter while his guests sit. Mrs. Goode appears moments later, impeccably dressed as though she spends every moment in a state of readiness.

"Tea," is all Maudley says, and then she is gone, her step now so light that Roan barely hears it.

Now, no more than three or four minutes have passed and Mrs. Goode is back, a silver trolley carrying a red teapot and red teacups upon red saucers at the ready. She has also placed several scones on a silver platter next to a small bowl of cream and another of bloodred jam.

It feels like a jest, and Roan almost laughs, but the memory of Emma's leg, and all that blood, makes her choke instead. And the voice. That infernal voice!

"Calm, calm," Maudley says, turning away from the fire, where he has been meditating in silence. He is wiping small spots of Emma's blood from his hands with a crisp white handkerchief.

"How can we be calm?" Seamus asks. His eyes belie his anger, revealing deep distress. There are tears upon the brims as he watches Maudley scrub. "My sister is—is she—what if she—"

Roan stiffens and accepts the cup of tea Mrs. Goode offers. Seamus takes his, but the little teacup shakes so much within the saucer that he puts both straight down on the table beside him.

"Rest assured," Maudley says, holding up his hand when Mrs. Goode offers him a cup of tea, "she was in no danger when I left her. Andrew is very capable, I assure you. Thank you, Mrs. Goode. Please ensure Andrew has all he needs, and send Jenny in to attend us."

Mrs. Goode nods in her curt manner and leaves, and moments later Jenny has taken her place, standing in the corner like a little ghost of a thing, cowering into herself.

"How did this happen?" Seamus mutters, and is so like a child that Roan takes his hand despite herself. He smiles up at her and a few tears escape. "I've never seen a storm like that, not ever. I've never seen such wreckage. And the glass…"

Jenny shudders ever so slightly; Roan catches the movement.

"You said you had to tell us some things," Roan says, more to distract Seamus and spare Jenny further distress than to hear it. "I suggest we start there."

Dr. Maudley nods in a peculiar sideways manner. "The events of tonight are most unfortunate. But believe me, I will ensure that the windows are reinforced when replaced. Nothing matters more to me than your safety," he adds, his eyes flicking to Roan. She sips her tea and looks pointedly at him.

"Now, please. Rest easy your minds. The danger has passed." He sips from his glass. "Even so. I must warn you. The western side of Mill House was built into the mountain. The entirety of those walls from basement to rooftop are the mountain itself. That is why there are no windows on that side. Slate is unpredictable at the best of times, and the rocks shift and move. Temperature, humidity—any number of variables can cause microfissures and splinters. You may have heard the rumbles already. They are nothing to be alarmed about as long as you stay away from that wing—particularly the lower levels. Much of it is in disrepair, and there is nothing you will need from that part of the house." He glances at Roan. "Your bedroom abuts it, as does the other room. I had those walls reinforced a long while ago."

Jenny mutters a sudden oath in Welsh, breaking through Maudley's calm explanation, then claps her hands over her mouth, eyes wide. She mutters what sounds like "I am sorry, sir," and shakes her head.

Maudley sighs with tight lips reminiscent of Mrs. Goode's and takes another sip of his drink, the liquid red and gleaming. He waves a hand. "I must abed, as should you. We will speak again in the morning."

Maudley nods to them and turns to leave.

"Wait!" Roan calls, getting to her feet. "A word."

Maudley stops at the doorway, but she walks out past him. As she passes Jenny, she nods in Seamus's direction. Jenny smiles and offers Seamus a scone.

"Please, sir. Eat some. I made these myself."

Roan is not asleep when someone knocks at her door. She is already clothed in her day dress, minus crinoline and corset.

"Come," she calls, as her mother used to, then clenches her fists so that her nails bite into her palm. It offers relief and stills her sudden shakes.

"I'm afraid I need some help with the door."

"Andrew?" She hurries to open it.

"Roan," Emma says softly. Andrew carries her in his arms; she is pale, her chin bobbing down every so often as though she may fall asleep. "I'm alive yet. Full up of some wonderful medicine that makes me want to sleep and feel no pain."

Roan cannot help but smile. How close Emma had come, Roan does not think Emma knows. She stands aside to let Andrew in.

"There, on the bed. That one, there." She indicates the right-hand bed. She had been expecting this. For Emma to room with her. And she, for the first time in her life, is profoundly thankful for the company. For *Emma's* company.

Andrew places Emma down on the bed opposite to Roan's, careful to pull back the blanket and ensure she is well covered. Then he turns to Roan.

"I am sorry," he says. "There is no other room at the moment. And Emma will need someone to help her with certain…tasks."

Emma rolls her eyes. "A servant and he's too shy to utter the words! My mother would've had you blushing like a little boy reprimanded for looking at the girls!"

Andrew's flush is obliging.

Emma laughs sleepily, her voice slurring. "Men are so easily embarrassed…"

"It is nothing," Roan says, though even she can hear the strain in her voice. *It will be fine. It will be.* "I can care for an *invalid*…"

Emma stirs. "…no invalid," she slurs, "saucy bitch…"

Andrew laughs, despite himself. "Some mouth on this one," he says. "Shocking."

"She's a good one," Roan says, grinning. "Hot as fire, and just as comforting. We understand each other."

Roan glances at Emma, ready to conspire with her in a joke, but she is already sleeping, the purple shadows beneath her eyes sharp against the sallow whiteness of her cheek. She looks almost gray.

The house turns everything gray.

And she snores like a little cat.

"A glass dagger to the thigh," Andrew says quietly, wonderingly, "and still alive…"

Roan smiles fondly. "It will take more than that to kill my little vixen friend."

Andrew hovers uncertainly for a moment.

"She will be well," Roan says, thinking to reassure him. "I am capable," she adds, to reassure herself.

The light is changeable, the candles reacting to the near-constant breezes that silk their way through the house, more real than ghosts. Dr. Maudley is unusually quiet, and apparently agitated enough to have Andrew sit and eat with the group.

Roan glances at Rapley for a moment, noting how he too seems to have little appetite.

Jenny and another young servant girl bring in supper on the silver trays as usual; the same gray meat.

"The meat," Roan says, addressing Jenny as she puts the tray down. "What is it?"

"I'm not sure, miss. Mrs. Goode handles all the meat. I could inquire for miss?"

Roan brushes it off. "No need. I was curious."

The servant girl hovers by the door, waiting, and when Roan nods for Jenny to leave, she skitters away like a frightened kitten.

Roan eats in silence—she has no particular need for conversation.

Emma twitches in her seat, and Roan glances up. Her friend scratches her neck, moving food around her plate but not eating. She hasn't even cut Seamus's food for him, something she usually delights in, nor has she bantered with Cage, another of her enjoyments in this bleak house. Her leg, propped up on a spare seat, is red and swollen around the edges of her bandages. Seamus himself seems off in his own world, but that at least is not uncommon, and even the miserly Cage sits immobile and eats little.

Emma twitches again, her head snapping to the right. She leans away from nothing, her face growing pale.

"Are you all right?" Cage asks.

Emma blinks and looks at him. "Fine and dandy," she mutters, glancing back down at her plate.

Cage frowns and continues to eat, and Rapley ignores them all, though he seems to be ignoring Roan in particular. Every time she moves, his nostrils flare.

And so the rest of the meal passes in a strange quiet that is full of agitation. When everyone has eaten, Maudley announces the meal complete, and Emma tries to get to her feet right away.

Cage rises suddenly. "Allow me."

He manages to both support Emma and push Seamus along at the same time and the three leave the room. "He has manners?" Roan mutters to herself once he is out of earshot.

"Who would have believed," Rapley says in his low, quiet voice, and then he too leaves the table.

Roan watches him go, attuned to his movements in some unknown way. At the door, he glances back at her, sees her watching, and walks faster.

Now Roan and Maudley alone remain.

"Dr. Maudley," Roan begins. "You…you said you knew my mother. That you knew her well."

He nods solemnly, curling his mustache in a way that Roan notes is a particular one of his ticks.

"Did you court her?"

His eyes finally rise from the tablecloth. "Ah, so we come to it. Is that what you have been waiting to ask me, Roanita?"

Roan does not answer. Instead, she waits.

"Your father loved your mother," he says in the wistful way of remembrance. "And I think she loved him. In any case, she did not love me."

"I am sorry. If you loved her, I am sorry."

He smiles. "It was impossible not to love her. She was light and joy incarnate."

Roan's smile falters. That is not at all how she remembers the woman who birthed her.

"Tell me about her."

Maudley folds his hands in his lap. "Well. She loved blue. It was her favorite color."

Roan almost smiles. "And so the Blue Room was assigned to me for that reason?"

"Of course. Sadly, you detest the color."

Roan's smile grows, but it is sad. "I am not my mother."

Maudley looks up at her again, for the second time during this conversation. "Indeed, you are not. You are your own woman."

"Not yet. Not quite."

His quizzical expression invites her to go on.

"Not until I turn twenty-one." She rises from her seat. "Good night, Doctor. I trust you will have a restful evening."

He does not watch her as she goes; instead his gaze remains fixed on the table. "Good night," he murmurs. "Good night."

Later that night, Roan hears low, angry voices from her window. She glances at Emma, but the girl is sleeping soundly, put under by one of Dr. Maudley's strong draughts.

She snuffs her flame and climbs onto the window seat, peering down. There in the courtyard, Rapley and Cage stand arguing in hushed voices. She cannot make out what they are saying, only that Cage is gesticulating urgently and Rapley is facing away, toward the mountain, arms crossed.

She puts her ear against the glass, but still cannot make out the words being spoken.

As she watches, Rapley turns and gestures with his arm. It is a sharp gesture of finality, and the words cease. Then he turns and walks into the gray mountains and the night mists envelope him within minutes.

Cage stares after him and then turns back to the house. As he is passing beneath her window, he looks up, spotting her as she watches the scene. His lips curl into a sneer and he storms inside.

Too many secrets, she thinks. They all have too many secrets.

*V*irgin land.

So hath John named it. But I like it not. To me it is but a barren wasteland, of dull gray rocks, of hideous plants that grow close to the ground, and of endless mists upon the folly.

Nebula has accompanied us, and thank the Lord. What would I have done for companionship here, and in canvas tents with burlap carpets no less, without her? John is much determined to build his water mill, though I admit I cannot fathom how the scheme was hatched.

"Men must make a mark upon the world," he said unto me. "It is not for a woman to understand."

I let it be, since I have it not in my mind to question the ambition of men. I will take care and zeal that Nebula be with me, and I am therefore not a woman alone, even if Nebula be of uncivilized descent.

For God hath said:

Behold howe I haue not laboured for myself onely, but for all them that seeke wisdom and knowledge.

Here I am, then. In a virgin land, which my husband will make fruitful, and soon will claim as his own, and which I must, now, call my home.

FROM THE DIARY OF
HERMIONE SMITH,
1583

Chapter 14

LOVE SPOON

"**Tell me about this** place," Roan says, wiping mud from her cheeks with the hem of her cloak. "Tell me all."

Rapley stops whittling the small piece of wood in his hands to look at her. The day is far less drab than most, and both have sought fresh air in the courtyard.

"You sought me out for tales?"

"If you like, yes."

He places his horn-handle knife in the dirt, blade first. At his insistence, they are no more than three paces from the courtyard, yet still they sit on slate, and Roan suppresses her shudder and ignores the growl of the mountain's belly.

"Dr. Maudley has no doubt added to the house since it was first built," she muses, staring up at the Gothic towers. Beneath, the stones are of much older fare, and simpler. Byzantine.

Rapley nods. "Yes. Instead of rebuilding it, he simply put his stamp on the exterior. That's all that matters to him."

Roan catches his eye. "He is your father," she says gently.

He gives a mirthless chuckle. "Not he. I am simply a prize. Free source of labor. Company now and then."

"How can you say so? He seems pained by your rejection."

Again the joyless smile. Almost a grimace. "He is a fine actor." He takes up the blade again and the wood suffers his administrations. "I have been with him for some years. I know that beneath his facade is no real depth."

"A man cannot be faulted for a simple nature."

"Yet he can be faulted—despised, even—for a false one."

Roan considers his words, watching as he shaves strip after strip from the piece in his hands. The design is intricate, with knots and bends and odd shapes.

"What is it?"

"A trinket, no more."

Roan nods and falls into silence again. Many long minutes pass before Rapley speaks again.

"It is a *llwy gariad*. They bring good things." He hands it to her. "Keep it nearby."

She runs her fingers over the fine work, marveling at how smooth it feels beneath her touch.

"I have never accepted a present before. That is," she adds, "I have never received one before." She swallows. "What is the customary response?"

He reads her for a moment, perhaps attempting to see if she is teasing. "You simply take it. And, if you like, you may say, 'thank you.' But I would accept the simple action of your keeping it close."

She holds it to herself, smiling. "Then I shall take it."

Getting to her feet, she wanders toward the house, staring down all the while at the little carven spoon in her hands. At the threshold, she turns back to find him watching her.

"Thank you."

Roan hangs the spoon beside the little mirror above her bed, wondering at the curious change in Rapley. He had not insulted her, and she had not felt her hackles rise. It was almost, though not quite, an honest conversation.

Though she does not share his low opinion of Dr. Maudley, she cannot ignore it. After all, he has known Maudley longer. And she cannot ignore the lies he told about her parents.

Yet, to hate with such aggression…Perhaps Rapley is simply a contrary sort of person, as she herself had been called once by her father.

Reason restored, she descends to the Green Parlor for breakfast. Emma is already seated, leg elevated, chatting with Seamus in their secret Irish way.

"Good morning," Emma says. She seems bright today. "You were up before dawn again," she notes. "What do you get up to in the early hours?"

Roan sits down and pours tea. "Perhaps I take to my prayer."

Emma's eyebrows rise in a manner similar to Seamus's when he is overly excited.

"A good habit," Seamus says, the guileless boy.

Oh! How she wants to kiss his cheek!

Emma laughs. "So said."

All at once, Jenny hurries through the doors, balancing two trays precariously upon her arms. Roan stands to help her, but both trays make it to the table with little damage and only one casualty: a scone topples from a small pile and rolls beneath the table.

"Oh dear!" Jenny cries, holding her hands to her mouth.

Emma is equine-quick, leaning out of her chair with a grimace. She retrieves the scone and places it on her plate, clutching her thigh. "No harm done. What?" she adds, when Jenny stares at her openmouthed. "I'll not let it go to the floor, of all things!"

Roan laughs. "Well said. Nor would I."

Jenny glances between the two, her mouth still open.

"I thought I might well and surely have a scolding," she breathes.

"Oh, fie!" Emma spits. "A scolding from that old crone, Mrs. Goode?"

Jenny's smile falters. "Oh, you did not hear yet? Mrs. Goode is unwell and has taken to her bed in the loft. Which leaves all to me."

"Good riddance," Emma mutters, and Seamus rebukes her.

Roan, however, cannot help her grin. Mrs. Goode is a nasty, grumpy old crone. Best they have some peace from her for a while.

"Since our good Mrs. Goode"—Roan pauses for effect—"is out of commission, come and sit with us, Jenny. Tell us some boisterous, inappropriate tales to liven our little party."

"Oh, yes!" Emma declares, tapping the seat beside her. "Do, do, do!" Seamus nods, eager for new sport and a friendly face. Telling from his blotchy blush, he quite likes the idea of the young, mousy girl joining the fray.

"Oh, and Jenny—can you tell me the meaning of *llwy gariad*?"

Jenny grins. "Have you a suitor, miss?"

Roan recoils. "No. Why?"

"Only…a *llwy gariad* is a love spoon. A token of affection and friendship. A token of love." The girl pauses, unsure.

"I read the phrase," Roan says, helping herself to a scone. "Thank you."

Jenny curtsies and departs, leaving Roan to shakily put jam and cream upon her pastry.

Chapter 15

HORNED GOD

The mountain is so still and so silent that even the air appears sharp as crystal. Roan can make out every hair of heather, every tiny purple leaf, every fine crack and chip in the slate. The slate...it towers over her, sharp skyward angles that seem to have burst through millennia ago.

The mountain is teething. The mountain has teethed.

She has a purpose. Knows where she is going. At least, her body seems to.

She has no shoes and is barely clothed, her shift and nothing more keeps the cold of the glassy day away.

Yet she is on fire.

She is sweating.

A line of moisture trickles down between her breasts, tickling.

She is so very...*alive.*

It is a long climb, up and up—ever upward—but she reaches the place soon enough.

It is a horrid, pitch-black mouth in the mountainside, edged in slate—formed of slate. A yawning caliginous depth, magnetic, alluring.

The cave pulses with sentience.

Roan smiles, turns her back on it, now facing a stone circle of the same jagged slate, those long, chipped, sharp teeth, which rise toward a moody gray sky. The clouds, like everything else, do not move.

Roan licks her lips, opens her mouth, and speaks forbidden, Curséd words. Words that angels fear, and God turns away.

She speaks the Corrupt.

She speaks the Blasphemous.

She speaks the Devil's Tongue.

And as she speaks, the earth shivers, shakes, and rumbles beneath her bare feet. The mountain wakes, stretching its jaws, yawning, growling. It is a child, hungry after centuries of long slumber.

"Rise up!" she cries, her voice fire and thunder. "Devour this unclean world!"

And the mountain obeys.

Rocks and moss and earth fall away into a giant, stygian hole; the slate crunches down as the mountain begins to devour itself.

And as the earth collapses beneath her feet, she lifts into a blackened sky, a flame above the world. And in the roiling darkness below, she watches Emma scream, writhing in intolerable pain, and sees Andrew stripped of his skin, and Seamus unfurling like a raw red thread, and Maudley too, disappearing as if into a vat of acid, eaten away from the outside in—

and Rapley…looking at her, still looking as his body is ripped in two—

And she laughs

and she screams

and the world is

no more.

Roan is on her haunches on the floor of her bedroom, her mouth contorted into an inhuman grimace, her hands working furiously at the wood. She has scratched away splinters, can feel them under her fingernails like fire pokers, can feel the sharp, sticky blood. In her sleeping-draught slumber, Emma does not stir.

It was a dream…just a dream. Yet she has never had a dream in which the Corrupt Language was spoken. Father trained her too well for that, down in the cellar of their London home.

She falls backward into a ball.

"Lord, oh God, come to my aid, keep the darkness away. *Dominus! Dominus Deus!*" On and on she mutters and prays and tries not to think of the splinters under her nails like chips of stone…of slate…of teeth… of a demonic, devouring earth.

"I will not believe it," she whispers. "I will not believe it!"

And yet all she can see is Seamus, Emma, Andrew, Maudley, Rapley— all of them, writhing in pain. Unraveling, burning, dissolving—ripped in two.

"*Sordes. Scortum. Parabellum. Demon. Maledictus. Amisit. DIABOLUS!*"

She mutters, growls, hisses. She cannot stop herself, no matter how she tries to regain control. She is trapped in a cage as her fingers scrape across the floor, pulling up wood, more splinters that lodge under her nails like fire and ice and daggers. She is bleeding, and she growls, teeth bared.

"*Malum! Advenerunt! Daemonium habes falsum. Mendax! Pythonissam! Pythonissam! Pythonissam!*" She takes a breath. "*Auguratricis!*"

Her Latin is not perfect, but she has heard the last two words before. *Witch. Sorceress.*

You are a witch, Roan. A sorceress. You wield power no woman ought. You should be burned alive—but I am entrusted with your care.

Her father's voice is so close in her memory that she can almost smell him.

"Father…"

should be burned alive…

…entrusted with your care.

Those words. What did he mean? *Entrusted.* By whom? By Mother? By his duty—his responsibility as a father? Or something else entirely?

Roan attempts to shut her eyes, to wake herself from this state, but something else is in control. It laughs. Laughs as though it knows precisely her terror, her lack of control.

little girl…

how you struggle

A flash of anger.

A moment of clarity—

And her hands finally stop their frantic motion on the floor, instead clawing in the air like a madman in his cell.

Roan opens her mouth. "I…" she breathes, straining with the effort, "control…*you.*"

Her hands release, and then all at once, she has herself again. She gasps in lungful after lungful of air until her body is calm and the sharp pain in her fingernails is reduced to a dull ache.

"I am in control," she murmurs. "I have control."

She says it to herself, over and over. She glances at the box sitting on the windowsill, staring at her, yearning for her to take it and hold it and open it…

Stop, she tells herself, calling to mind an image of her father. It strengthens her. Reminds her of her training.

It is focus. His measured voice. *No more.*

She gets to her feet, staring at her shaking hands, at the blood dry-
ing in her Life, Fate, and Love lines. The blood seeps into every tiny
crack, highlighting the strange pattern her path is likely to take. She
frowns. It seems long. So long.

Roan balls up her hands; the pain is exquisite.

It takes her most of the night to work free the wooden splinters with
her sewing needle. By the time they have all been removed, her fingers
are raw, more blood bled, and more curses spoken.

There can be no denying it now, as she had been so desperate to do
before. This mountain really is cursed. But not by a witch. By something far more dangerous.

"*Diaboli,*" she hisses between her teeth. "Devil."

The floor beneath her laughs and begins to creak as though it is
chewing.

Chapter 16
FATHER, FRAIL

The light beneath Dr. Maudley's study door is fickle, dancing here and there, casting strange shadows upon the floor.

Roan hesitates a moment. Then, with a deep breath, she knocks.

"Come."

Roan enters and is greeted by a fully dressed and awake Dr. Maudley. Though his attire suggests his flamboyant confidence, his hair is slightly mussed.

"You are always in readiness," Roan says.

"Needs must," he says, not looking at her.

She hesitates. "I've come to ask some difficult questions," she says after a moment. "May I sit?"

He waves a hand, peering into his fireplace where the logs spit and the fire thrashes preternaturally. Roan takes a seat in the chair opposite his desk and wraps herself in the blanket resting there, flinching as her wounded fingers brush the fabric.

"Doctor, did you hear me?"

"Hm," Maudley says, and then he frowns and picks up his pen, dipping it into a glass pot of indigo ink and scribbling in a book, heedless of her.

The scratching unnerves Roan and she rubs her hands, waiting for him to finish. Maudley fidgets as he writes, scratching his neck, his forehead, and running a hand through his hair. A smear of ink slashes his cheek, but he does not notice.

"Failure," he mutters. "I am a _ffffailure._"

Roan reaches across the space between them and rests her hand on his to stop his frantic scribbling.

"Sir," she says. "_Please._ You knew my father. Did he tell you anything about giving me…lessons?" She searches his eyes. "Did he give you a reason for sending me here, to this house? How well did you know him, and why did he never speak to me of you? And why," she says, nearly breathless, and reaching into her skirt pocket to retrieve the piece of paper she has carried like a noose all these long weeks, "did you sign this? It is _your_ signature, _your_ name."

Maudley stills, his gaze more intent upon his book. "I can't do this."

"Please," Roan whispers. "You had my father's confidence, it seems. But he is gone, and I must know what his intentions were, handing me off to a stranger…and how much he told you."

Maudley puts his pen down. "It is all of no import," he says, his gaze drifting sideways. He stumbles to his drinks cabinet and pours a measure of amber liquid from a crystal decanter.

She can see by his flushed face and can hear in the languid slur of his words that it is not his first.

"Answer me this. How did you know I would come here, before my father…You installed a bell in the Blue Room a week before he died." She leans forward, barely able to restrain herself. "_How did you know?_ Tell me, _how?_ And no more fallacies about my father being ill, for his death was an accident, not born of sickness. Tell me, and speak truly."

Maudley raises his bloodshot eyes to Roan's. They are dancing with moisture. "Why _you?_" he whispers, voice waspish with some barely contained emotion.

"Yes. Me. Why did my father send _me_ here?"

"Because you're special. *So special.*" He spits the last two words, and then laughs with a derision Roan has not seen before.

"Why is that man, Cage, teaching Seamus about the Faustus legend, and why does he not teach Emma and me? What is going on?"

Maudley drinks until the glass is empty, then wipes his upper lip.

"I think we both know," he says, "that you've had enough education." He pauses, eyes roaming her features. "You are the devil's plaything. Your father knew as much and so do I."

A still calm descends. Of course he knows. Of course.

"You spoke of my...education with my father?"

He inclines his head. Takes a drink. "Your *education*. Such a polite word."

"All this time, smiling, talking, playing the host. All this time, you knew what you housed."

"A witch. Yes, I knew. And you think you're special?" he scoffs.

"Tell me," Roan snaps, slamming the table with her hands as Rapley would. "Tell me why my father sent me to you!"

Maudley laughs heartily, as though they are enjoying an amiable evening's entertainment.

"You could scarcely comprehend all you do not know about Daddy. And why should I tell you?" He staggers to the side, brandishing his glass like a weapon. "Simpering, simple *witch*!"

Roan has risen from her chair before she knows it, and in five strides stands before Maudley, gripping his lapels. "Hush! Why do you play with my life? Why am I here? What is wrong with this house? Are the stories true? Are we all going to disappear like those mill workers? *What is it to do with me?*"

He sobers, lowering his empty glass so that it skims the table, then rolls out of his hand and onto the carpet.

"You are so...*special.*" He jeers, the expression ugly and unexpected. "It has everything to do with you, ugly little sprite. You're like a magnet. Like electricity. You'll bring it all down, in the end."

Roan steps back, releasing him, her fingers pulsing with pain. "What?"

"Special little Roan…did you know that your mother's…favorite… did I tell you that her favorite color…was…"

He blinks, stumbling.

"If you really know about me, then tell me why. Why am I the way I am?"

"You're bred that way," he slurs, slumping heavily into his chair, his chin sinking onto his chest. "We are all lost here. This house will consume every last one."

Construction of the mill continues. John will hear no questions against it. Indeed, I found him in camp some days past and asked him what purpose a water mill served on a waterless mountain and received a blow to my face in reply. Some of the Welshmen yelled out in protest, and began to mutter amongst themselves while my head pounded in my hands. John snapped at them in Welsh—"To the Devil with you!"—and I understood every word. He dismissed me, then, and big, kind Merfyn helped me to my tent, his boy, Huw, soon by his side.

"No way to treat a lady," Merfyn muttered under his breath. I thanked him and have hidden inside my tent since then. John has not come.

Our nighttime hours, when they occur, have grown tolerable. As the mill grows, so does John's fervor out in the camp and the less it burns in our tent at night. But this mountain is turning him mad.

The rain has transformed to slushy snow, which falls from an oppressive sky.

I am with child.

FROM THE DIARY OF
HERMIONE SMITH,
DECEMBER 1583

Chapter 17

REVELATION, UNLOCKING, OPENING

Roan paces all night, trying to make sense of Maudley's drunken ramblings and his revelations. So. All this time, he knew. Knew what she was, and knew what her father had taught her. Perhaps he is the one Conjuring, for she can feel the presence of Conjures around her, floating up now and again like fireflies or mosquitoes. Whoever it is, the Conjures are weak. Perhaps Maudley had studied with her father as well. A pupil, perhaps. Or his tutor.

An hour or so after dawn, she leaves her room to seek him out once again. Four hours, she reasons, will be plenty of time for sobriety. But she is not the only one awake. Voices, agitated and aggressive, carry through the halls.

"Who was the last to see him?"

Roan descends the main stairs to find Rapley pacing the entrance hall.

"I believe," Cage says slowly, turning to face her, "that it was Roan."

She stiffens. "What has happened?"

Rapley's face is drawn and pale, and a fine layer of stubble spatters his cheeks. "Dr. Maudley is missing. He had insisted on meeting early, before any in the house had awoken. But he did not come. It isn't like him to be late. You saw him last night?"

"Yes. He was drinking. Perhaps he overslept." And then another thought occurs to her and she turns to Cage. "How did you know I had seen him last night?"

Cage's eyes narrow almost imperceptibly. "I had a meeting with the doctor last night. Or, rather, I was *supposed* to have a meeting. We were to go over Seamus's timetable. But he was already in an interview with you."

"And how did you know it was me?" she asks, stepping forward. "Were you listening at the door?"

He smirks. "Women may sneak and spy, but I assure you that a man, least of all a man of God, has no need. I saw you enter. I waited some minutes, and then seeing I was not to be admitted anytime soon, went to read from the Bible in the Green Parlor. An hour or so later I went back, but Maudley had retired for the evening. His study was empty, and the candles snuffed."

"Roan, at what hour did you leave him?" Rapley asks.

"I don't know. But I do know that he wasn't in a fit state for company."

"And what should we take that to mean?" Cage asks, his eyes narrowing as he turns his body away from her.

Roan's lips tighten. "He was drinking, as I said. He wasn't making much sense."

Rapley stops pacing. "What did he say?"

Roan hesitates. "Nothing of import. I told him to sleep and that we would talk in the morning."

"It seems," Cage drawls, eyes drifting over her body, "as if you slept rather little last night. Were you perhaps wandering again?"

164

"After I spoke to Maudley, I stayed up reading. Emma can attest to it, she woke several times in the night."

Cage holds up his hands. "I do not wish to accuse, only to establish the whereabouts of all parties under this roof."

Rapley eyes him, but makes no comment.

"Certainly," Roan agrees, then asks: "Where did *you* go after I left?"

"I spent the night in prayer in my room."

"Can anyone verify that?" Roan asks.

"God above can, should He choose."

"Where is Emma?" Rapley asks, cutting in.

"She is asleep. She is still on a heavy sleeping draught."

"Yet she woke several times during the night, did she?" Cage says.

"It did not take effect until shortly before dawn."

"I think it's clear that Emma is not the culprit," Cage says, turning back to Rapley. "She can barely stand on her own with her injury."

"Are we looking for culprits?" Roan asks. "Has anyone checked his bed?"

"He is not there," Rapley says. "It does not look as though he slept in it at all."

"Should we not be searching the mountain, then? Dr. Maudley may have wandered off and fallen. Have you searched the rest of the house? As I said, he had been drinking."

Rapley nods once. "I agree. There is no reason to suspect foul play here. I know the mountain best, so I'll search there." He turns to Cage. "Search the house with Andrew and then come back here."

Cage nods, then watches Rapley leave without moving.

"Well," Cage says, smiling as he turns to Roan. "Let us hope we find him, since you were so eager to talk to him today."

Roan folds her arms. "I'm coming too."

"It is no job for a woman. And," he adds, his breath foul in her face, "I'll not have you wandering the house at my back." They stare at each other for a moment, and Roan wonders when the moment was when they first mutually realized that they despised each other. "Run along, now. We don't need any more trouble."

"No," Roan agrees, stepping closer. "We don't."

He looks her up and down, another smile—a dangerous smile—sliding over his face.

"I'll be sure to seek you out directly when we find Maudley," he says. "I am certain he'll have a lot to say."

He turns on his heel with a swish of his coat, and heads toward the kitchen, humming "'Nearer, My God, to Thee.'"

Their voices draw her to the window.

"You're not listening!" Cage.

"I don't need to hear any more—" Rapley.

"If you don't heed my words, then you're a fool!" Cage, louder.

"Then fool I am!" Rapley.

"Rapley, you are stubborn, I know, but you must open your eyes! There is evil at work here and I fear you may be a target."

Roan steps back, surprised, and does not catch Rapley's reply. They speak on such familiar terms. How should that be? She has hardly seen Rapley herself, and he as much admitted that he talked with her most of all. She had seen Rapley and Cage arguing before, and they seemed strangers. How then did Cage come to address him so familiarly? So intimately?

Leaving them to their talk, she sits down on her bed and then lies back fully. Cage is right about one thing. She too knows there is evil in the house. She simply doesn't know if she has caused it all, or not.

Cage stands before the gathered group in the entrance hall. Emma wobbles tentatively on her leg, but she is pale and silent. "Maudley was not found outside. Andrew and I will search the house again. With lamps. Roan, Emma, Seamus—you three stay in the Green Parlor and out of the way."

"This time I will search as well," Roan adds, staring defiantly at Cage, daring him to stop her.

He makes no comment. "Meet back at this spot in one hour. We don't need anyone else disappearing, so do not tarry."

Rapley, who has been listening without comment or reaction, turns and stalks outside without prompting, and Cage heaves a short, sharp sigh.

He and Andrew share a glance, and then they turn in opposite directions to search the house. Cage heads up the main staircase, while Andrew heads down the eastern side, through the kitchen.

Roan waits for them to go and then helps Emma and Seamus to the Green Room before hurrying into the western part of the house. The side built into the mountain, where Maudley warned them not to go after Emma's accident. How long ago that seems now. There might be a reason beyond mere safety that Maudley had for keeping them away. And if it is such a dangerous place, perhaps he has fallen and is trapped. Either way, she must venture into that part of the house, since it seems no one else will, even for the Master. He knows more than he has said, and must answer for it.

Before they all disappear.

Roan whispers the words quickly, as though speed might hide her from whatever dark eye turns her way when she uses the symbols.

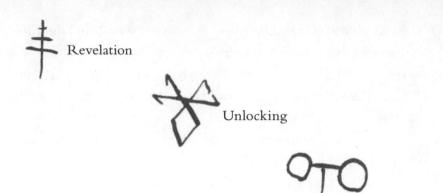

Revelation

Unlocking

Opening

A series of loud, cavernous *clang*s echo beyond the door.

We learn the Conjure because we must. We must know the evil but not engage. Never use it outside this room, Roan. Never let yourself be tempted.

She forces the memory of her father's voice from her mind and pushes open the West Wing door.

It swings forward with a whine, protesting like the death rattle of an ancient crone.

Stepping slowly inside, Roan finds herself in a frigid antechamber, her candle barely pushing back the darkness. She tiptoes across it on the balls of her feet, the cold seeping through her indoor slippers. A second door—this one unlocked. She pushes it open and her candle flickers, almost gutters, and then stills.

The room yawns away from her into a glacial, black space, and as she steps forward, her heels clack on the floor and echo back.

A chapel.

A chapel inside Mill House.

The ponderous pews stand rigid and old-fashioned, worn and covered in dust and rag-like cobwebs. The left-hand wall is sheer mountain rocks, while the right wall has no windows. None at all. Roan walks the length of the room, holding her candle up, willing Dr. Maudley to be sitting in one of the pews in silent prayer.

She reaches the altar and places the candleholder down, taking a moment to close her eyes. Sensing something behind her, like someone observing, she spins to face the room.

It is empty.

"Hello?" she calls. "Doctor?"

Behind her, the flame flickers once more.

The chapel is a dead end, so Roan turns back to look for access to the rest of the wing. She finds it in the first antechamber: a narrow door leading to a corridor, veiled in more cobwebs and trapped insect carcasses.

Everything stops.

The tapestries on the walls.

The strange dolls on the shelves.

The books.

The weapons.

The animal skulls—horned, all of them.

The piano—

"Play something pretty," Father says. He lifts the lace covering from the keys.

"It's such a little piano!"

"Just the right size for a girl to play." This voice, unfamiliar. Who is speaking? The little girl can't see him. Then someone steps out of the dark. A tall person in a black hood.

Roan snaps her head away.

"Play," Father says again.

Her fingers on the yellow keys. The sound is strange. Not like a piano at all. More tinny and thin.

"Keep playing," Father says, and then he leaves her alone.

It is a strange room and the little girl is so busy looking at the dolls that she stumbles on the keys. She expects Father to rebuke her as he so often does when she isn't paying close attention, but he does not.

She stops playing and listens.

She can hear the men talking in another room. Good, she thinks. She wants to look at all the beautiful things, and anyway, she is getting cold. There is no carpet in this room, no curtains—no windows at all.

The only light is from the candle on the piano top and another candle by the door at the end.

Maybe she'll just have a little wander around. No one could get angry at her for just looking. The dolls—she wants most of all to look at those strange dolls…

"…I've been here before," Roan whispers, lifting her candle higher. This piano…She knows the sound of it, the feel of it. Those dolls lined up on a shelf near the back of the room…she knows them too.

She shudders.

And then, all at once, she can see them.

They seem to jump out at her, so obvious she cannot believe she did not notice before.

Sigils.

Everywhere.

There, tiny, on the edge of an oil painting. It almost glows. There, cut into the glass of an ancient mirror—barely perceptible to the human eye. Another, on the forehead of a doll whose eyes seem to scream. There, there, and there. Dozens of them. Hundreds.

She backs away, the tapestry of evil rising in her mind's eye to reveal itself to her.

Roan's growl escapes and rumbles through the shadowy room.

"Damn you, Maudley. What have you been tampering with?"

Their faces are grim in the fading light. An entire day of searching has yielded no result. Dr. Maudley has simply vanished. Rapley, Roan, Cage, and Andrew sit together in the kitchen. Jenny potters about handing them bowls of broth from a steaming pot on the stove. Roan would rather have Seamus sitting by her side, for she likes his calm company, but he is with Emma upstairs, and she will not ask for them.

"He might have fallen where I could not see," Rapley says, his arms folded. He is wrapped in a thick fur blanket, his hair still dripping. "The storms have never been this bad, nor persisted this long. And now we have a rolling fog like a velvet curtain during the day. To attempt a descent in order to seek the constable would be a death sentence. It is nothing but mire and jagged rock with hidden crevices and steep stops."

"So, what?" Cage says. "We stay here until spring? What of the stores of food? Will they last some four months?"

"There will be no supplies reaching us in conditions like this," Rapley agrees, "but we've survived through storms before."

"*Has* there been a series of storms like this before?" Cage asks, and Roan shudders when his eyes flicker to her and then away again so fast she can't tell if she saw it at all.

Rapley hesitates. "No. Not like this."

Cage folds his arms. "When was the last time we saw blue skies? Or the sun?"

"Not since I arrived," Roan says. "I don't think I've ever seen a blue sky here. So…three weeks."

"Unnatural," Cage murmurs.

"It is winter," Rapley snaps. "The weather will break."

"And if it doesn't? We die?"

Rapley shoots him a furious look. "No, we do not simply lie down and die."

"Like dogs on their bellies," Roan adds, her distaste evident.

Rapley's eyes meet hers and there is a spark of warmth there.

"We survive. I hunt—I do it well. I will have to go to the high ground where it is less barren and less dangerous. There is no game here, but there will be rats, mice, snakes. We will kill them and eat them if it comes to that."

Jenny crosses herself. "We cannot partake of snakes, Master Rapley. They are the Devil's creatures."

"Trust me," Roan says, stirring her broth, "when you get hungry enough, you'll eat anything."

"It won't come to that," Rapley says. "In the meantime, we need to check when the next delivery is coming. Jenny, do you know?"

"Mrs. Goode keeps all that information to herself. She does not even share the schedule with Andrew. But she's not well, again. Said she was feeling tired yesterday and did not come down this morning."

"Well or no, we need to know where every last store of food in this house is kept and when the deliveries are scheduled to arrive."

Roan cannot suppress her grin. His voice is…pleasant. And to see him so animated, rather than still like the rocks out there on the mountain, reminds her of spring.

"She will have my hide for waking her," Jenny says softly, her blue eyes so wide they almost tremble.

"Then we all go," Rapley says. "She can't very well get angry with everyone."

He smiles. How transformative! His teeth, still canine in shape, no longer make him a wolf on the prowl, but a *man*. A man who had once, as a boy, perhaps, even laughed.

When it disappears, Roan is surprisingly crestfallen.

"Up, then," Cage grumbles, turning to Jenny, who must lead the way.

What a comic company they seem, walking through the entrance hall, up two flights of stairs, and then trudging up the narrow attic stairs in single file, each wrapped and draped in blankets, furs, and soft coverings to wake the housekeeper from her sickbed. Banded together purely for fear of her wrath.

Jenny pauses at the door with a fearful look at Rapley, who nods with another smile.

Roan again finds it unexpected. How different he looks with it upon his face.

"Mrs. Goode? Are you decent?" Jenny knocks again. "It is Jenny. I am come with some…visitors."

Nothing.

"Be damned with it and open the door," Cage snaps. He is wedged between Rapley and Andrew.

Jenny glances uncertainly at Roan, who gives a small nod.

After sticking for a moment, the door gives way suddenly, and they tumble in one after the other. Cage and Andrew remain upon the stair.

Jenny's scream rends the air before everything goes utterly still.

Chapter 18
COLD AS WAX

The corpse of Mrs. Goode lies like a waxwork on the bed. Roan's candle does little to make her seem more lifelike. Death is always empty. The men have departed, leaving Jenny and Roan to wrap the body respectfully before they return.

"I cannot," Jenny whispers, hanging behind Roan in the hallway.

"We have to wrap the body before it begins to smell."

"God almighty—mistress, I can't."

"Wait here, then. I will call you if needed."

In honesty, Roan wants to do this alone. She had not seen her father's corpse, though she had begged to. She wants the chance now. Needs it.

She closes the door on Jenny's startled face and advances to the bed, her candle turning the grim scene even more macabre. Mrs. Goode's body is athwart the bed. Robbed of life, it is now but an object, no different from the bed or the chair or the bedside table.

The door creaks open and Jenny slips inside. She gasps in horror—it is almost comical—and scurries into a corner, looking away, as far from the body as she can get without trespassing the wall. Jenny's breathless prayers are a strange memorial to the moment. Like a song.

The garments appear as before, but Mrs. Goode's skin looks like a sheet of paper that has been crumpled into a ball. Besides colorless, she is dry; no moisture here. No elasticity. She is near yellow with it. The contrast with the rain-soaked air in the room, blowing through the open window, which slams rhythmically against its frame, couldn't be greater.

Roan leans closer, her candle hand steady, and examines Mrs. Goode's face; it's the impossible look of someone who's fallen asleep while startled. Before Jenny came in, the room felt peculiarly empty.

Mrs. Goode is no longer here.

Roan reaches out a finger and pokes at Mrs. Goode's face, feeling the strange texture of the devoid flesh.

"You old hag," Roan whispers, leaning close to Mrs. Goode's ear. "You look as dried up and bitter as you were in life. For all your venomous words, look at you now." She sniggers. "Still. No one deserves to die alone in a cold room. For that, I am sorry. Perhaps we'll meet in hell, you and I. Or…in heaven."

She gets to her feet, reaching over the corpse to grab the sheet. Something catches her eye. The plain wooden cross that hangs over Mrs. Goode's bed has fallen and landed upside down on the headrest. Roan reaches for it, but a gust of wind disturbs the room, rumbling as the window slams violently against the frame once more. Roan moves to close it, but struggles as the wind blows the window frame away from her hand. At last she grabs it and, looking down as she pulls it closed, notices something far below in the grass. A book, pages fluttering in the wind, possibly a Bible, soaked beyond use.

She closes the window, dread slinking down her spine, only to find that Jenny has fled the room, leaving Roan alone with the dead once more.

The mist hangs in the air; it is so dense that it is only from the sound of Emma breathing that Roan knows the girl is still standing a pace away. The cold bites bitterly and they all shiver into their warmest coats and cloaks. Roan doesn't see Cage approaching; only his footsteps and panting pierce the gray. There is a faint *thud* as he unburdens himself of Mrs. Goode's body, and Emma mutters, "Lord almighty," and steps closer to Roan.

Roan listens as Cage lowers himself into the hole, which he's spent the morning digging, and then drags the body into it, before climbing back out. He is a vague shadow.

He speaks briefly of the love of God, of Mrs. Goode's Christian character—of which he knew little—and then bows his head and makes the sign of the cross.

"*In nomine Patris,*" his voice booms, "*et Filii, et Spiritus Sancti.*"

Minutes pass, featureless but for his verses and four moribund lanterns on the ground, marking her position, Emma's, Cage's, and Jenny's. Andrew waits inside with Seamus, keeping the boy plied with warm ale. Rapley is nowhere to be found.

"Well, that's that," Cage says. "Jenny, please be so good as to make us some tea. We'll take it in the Red Room."

"Yes, master." She recedes back toward the house.

Roan arches an eyebrow, but says nothing.

Emma hesitates for a moment, and says, "God invented whiskey to keep the Irish from ruling the world, and I'm content with that."

She nods her head toward Mrs. Goode's final resting place, and then turns back toward the house. Roan watches her shadow as it fades.

Cage remains motionless, bolted to the ground. Roan can sense that he is staring at her, as she is at him, a duel of sorts, but neither can see the other's visage, let alone their eyes.

The duel is inconclusive, and both quit the scene with deliberate slowness, almost at the same time.

Chapter 19
HOWL

The storm rattles the windows and hammers at the walls, a symphony of chaos. Roan no longer sleeps at night. Since Mrs. Goode's death, she has been unsettled. Rapley has not returned, and Dr. Maudley is still missing. She lights candle after candle, placing each in the window seat, hoping that the light will guide Rapley back, but as the days pass with no sign of him, everyone feels the strain. With nothing to do but wait, Roan wanders the house at night, wrapped in a blanket that cannot warm the cold thoughts in her mind.

Roan's candle burns low, but the lightning, what little of it bursts through the small windows in the corridor, is enough to burn the stairs white.

She doesn't see him right away. But the second shock of lightning illuminates his small frame on the cold floor below her.

"Seamus?"

Another slash of light and a roll of thunder. He is pale. Small.

She hurries down the stairs two at a time and falls to her knees beside him.

"Seamus!" She heaves him up, but he is a deadweight. "Come on!"

A faint heartbeat whispers through his icy skin. She shakes his body, slaps him hard, yelling into his face.

No response.

A horrible thought: Is he going to die, like Mrs. Goode? A small, boy-size grave beside the crone's?

Getting to her feet, she jerks him up, but only manages to lift his torso. "Someone!" she yells. "Someone, help!"

The house is still and dark.

Lowering him again, Roan does the only thing she can think of; she runs across the entrance hall and out through the main doors into the storm.

Somehow, she knows where he will be.

"Rapley!" she yells through the ruckus, which buffets her from all sides. She's blinded by debris and lanced by rain; her memory guiding her across the courtyard. The winds howl.

For a moment, she is lost, surrounded by slate and shale and bombarded by flying pieces of heather and detritus from all sides. They slice at her face and hands, tangling in her hair.

The sigils flare in her mind quicker than anything from the English language, and then are on her fingers. A mix of symbols for Parting and Revealing and Urgency. Her fingers dance and she mutters beneath her breath, the taste of ash rising up, and then the storm parts like a seam in the fabric of the sky, finding a figure on the mountain, stumbling through the pitiless storm.

Rapley looks up, sees directly, impossibly to the house, where Roan stands, hands curved like claws.

Roan staggers. An overwhelming weight presses against her. One she does not expect.

are

you

here?

I you feel...

"Rapley!" Roan screams his name, or she thinks she does, but perhaps she only thinks it.

His eyes meet hers through the tunnel she has made. He doesn't hesitate, running toward the house, the storm around but no longer buffeting him.

"I found him here," Roan says, after she's closed the doors behind them. "He's so cold, Rapley..."

Without a word, Rapley hauls the boy into his arms and heads for the Red Room, placing him down on the sanguine sofa on the far side near the piano.

"Blankets," he instructs. "Quickly. As many as you can find."

Roan runs from the room and into the kitchen, grabbing every blanket, table covering, and sheepskin rug she finds. When she returns, Rapley is shaking Seamus roughly.

"Nothing?" she asks, piling the blankets on top of him.

"No."

She lifts the blankets off his legs and pulls off his socks, rubbing furiously at his small, shriveled feet but to no avail. She covers them again, tucking the sheepskin rug tightly around them.

Rapley stands, his eyes flitting to the windows in the room, jaw clenched. "I must go."

Roan opens her mouth to reply, but at that moment, Seamus begins to shake, a convulsion overtaking his entire body.

"He's seizing! Grab his face, make sure he doesn't bite his tongue!"

Rapley does as commanded, but his eyes dart continually to the window and the door.

"Your mountain can wait!" Roan yells. "Hold him steady and don't let go. I need you to watch us both."

"What?"

"Just do it!"

Roan lies down on the floor and closes her eyes, letting her mind drift.

Up, she breathes. *And out.*

She is in the air, near the ceiling, watching Rapley as he restrains the seizing Seamus. They are moving slowly. So slowly.

Movement in the room startles her. Not slow movement, like the movement of the living—like Seamus and Rapley, but movement in speed with her own floating spirit.

Dark shapes are gathering around Seamus and Rapley, inching closer and closer.

Roan cries out, but there is no sound here. The figures do not even sense her.

Roan looks around the room, searching for some sign of Seamus, but it's too crowded. She is about to fly farther when a cold, chilling sensation runs through her.

There. Down in the crowd…someone is slicing at her cord. The small silver cord, no thicker than a spider's web. There. She can see it. And she can see the person slicing at it. He, for she's certain it is a male, lifts his hand, a scalpel glinting in the strange other-light of this place, and comes down to strike again. It is like a slice to her heart, which blanches inside her.

She screams, waking herself up with a violent movement, hitting out with both arms and both legs and then clutching at her heart.

"Oh, God," she says, "Rapley—"

But it is not Rapley who stares down at her.

It's Cage.

"What…" Roan blinks hard, trying to catch her breath, her heart still stuttering inside her.

"Rapley asked me to watch over Seamus. And you, of course." His eyes are appraising. "What on earth were you doing?"

"I…must have fallen asleep."

"This boy is an innocent," Cage says, glancing at Seamus, whose color is much improved. "A child, still."

"Where did Rapley go?" Roan asks, getting gingerly to her feet.

"Innocents need protecting."

"Did he go back out?"

Cage turns his cold eyes on her. "I know you're up to something. You aren't right. Aren't…normal."

She wants to be indignant. She wants to protest. She wants to be angry.

But she knows he's right. She isn't normal. She chose to use those base skills tonight. She felt the storm yielding to her, felt the power in it.

She had relished it.

And now, doped up with power, she is satisfied. Horribly, terribly satisfied.

"You know as much," Cage adds.

Roan finally finds her voice. "You don't know anything—" she begins, but is cut off by thumping from the windows.

Cage stands, eyeing her sharply, and goes to inspect, drawing back with a hiss when he sees that a grotesque, curling mess of snakes, scorpions, bugs, and spiders are twisting and writhing against the glass.

"Monstrous!" he yells, looking at her.

He strides forward in four long paces and grabs her by her arms, shaking her roughly.

"You're doing this!"

"Let me go," she snaps, and the residue of the power flickers in her voice. *"Now."*

He releases her at once, and steps back, a sheen of sweat upon his cheeks.

"There is something wrong," she agrees. "With this *place.*"

PART 3

With the Mountain

Fools that will laugh on earth,
most weep in hell.

—CHRISTOPHER MARLOWE,
DR. FAUSTUS

ZOEY

NOW

Chapter 20

THE NOTEBOOK

October 23

    I have to get out of this tent. I have to investigate. I keep wondering if this is the kind of thing that sent Dad over the edge. Spent yesterday sleeping mostly and doing self-checks. Am I scratching myself? Am I twitching? Am I grinding my teeth? I count from one to ten and ten to one. These checks are to make sure I'm still...well, sane. I think I'll do them every day.

    Then it started storming so I went back into the green room and set up the tent in there. But I couldn't bring myself to get out of it. Ate cold canned soup. Miserable.

    OH MY GOD. POLE IS HERE!!! Chat later!

Zoey Camera Footage

Date: October 23

Poulton stands in the green room, beside the hole in the wall where the daylight is strongest, rummaging through his backpack. He pulls free a packet.

"Brought sausages," he says.

"Nice one."

"We'll have to eat them tonight."

"How many d'you bring?"

"Twelve."

"Blimey."

"I can do seven."

"Bet you can't."

He looks at Zoey and pushes up his glasses. "You're on. Loser has to..."

He leaves his sentence hanging, raising his eyebrows at Zoey.

She folds her hands in her lap. "Loser has to go first when we explore upstairs," she obliges.

He scoffs. "Yeah, *okay*."

"Fine," she says. "Loser has to cook meals for the next two days."

He groans at that. "Yeah, all right." Zoey puts the camera down so that she and Pole are both in the frame. They sit down on the floor, backs to the wall.

"Brought my Trangia cooker, gas, and a small generator," Poulton says. "And lights. And cameras. And batteries. And food. We'll probably not stay more than a week, but I brought enough for two."

Zoey snuggles into his side. "You're the best."

"Yeah, yeah, I know."

"Pole?"

"Hm?"

"Do you hear that noise?"

His reply is slurred with sleep. "What noise?"

"It's like...a whirring noise. Like air-conditioning or something."

"You're mad," he mumbles. "It's quiet as the dead in here."

[Footage sped up X20. Both Zoey and Poulton fall asleep and the light fades into darkness.]

Poulton stirs. "God, I'm freezing my balls off."

Zoey groans. "We fell asleep."

"Your camera's still rolling. So weird. I must have arrived later than I thought. But seriously," he adds, getting to his feet stiffly. "My balls are frozen."

"Ditto. My balls seem to have fallen off already. Oh. Wait. I'm a girl."

"What a shame," he gibes, helping Zoey to her feet.

"You said something about lights?"

"Yeah, hang tight. Climb into your sleeping bag or something."

It takes a good while to get the generator going, but then, as if by magic—light! Zoey walks over to her camera. "Ten percent battery and thirteen minutes left on this memory card. Shit." She looks up, over the camera. "Photography box lights?"

She turns the camera to reveal the tall lamps Poulton has set up. Brilliant white boxes that diffuse the light so it looks like a bright and sunny day in the gloomy house.

"You take photos, don't you?"

"They're for my photos?"

"Why else would I bring them?"

"Pole!" She turns his name into two syllables. "Po-*ole!*"

"It's no warmer, but it somehow feels like it is. Besides, like I said, I brought my cameras too. Can't trust the results of someone who *believes* in ghosts. I need verifiable data."

"We're not ghost hunting," Zoey says, turning the camera on him. "We're looking for information about my dad. Trying to follow in his footsteps. See what he saw. Investigate what he would have investigated. Working what he might have—"

"Are you fucking *crazy?*" Poulton stares at her.

The camera drops ever so slightly. "Pole, I have to think like he would have...otherwise it's pointless."

Poulton looks very much like he wants to tell Zoey that it *is* pointless.

"We'll do everything he might have done, but no spells."

"Pole—"

"I swear to God, Zoey, if you start Working, I'm leaving."

"Would you just listen to reason?"

Poulton waves his hand, shaking his head, and climbs out of the hole, away from the light.

"Poulton, *listen* to me—"

[End of clip]

October 24

We pulled out my floor plans and had a look. Most of the house is exactly the same, but we've marked up the damages and changes. I teased Poulton about marking up the original floor plans and he gave me one of those looks of his that he gives me when he thinks I'm being needlessly dense. It was his idea to go through the house, room by room, following the plans, and to mark up any unsafe zones.

"Very logical," I said, thinking: <u>Yeah, yeah, Mr. Spock.</u>

"East Wing first?" I suggested.

He nodded and got to his feet, still studying the floor plans. "Looks like we broke into the...here," he said, pointing at the map. "Green Room. So we're already in the East Wing. I suggest we go back to the gatehouse and follow on logically until we reach the end of this wing and then turn around and do the same for the West Wing."

"Okay, Spock."

"You may think that's an insult, Zo-Zo, but I take it as a compliment. Now, engage."

"Wrong series, you poser geek. That was Picard."

"Same difference," he said, grinning at me for a reaction. "May the Force allow you to live long and prosper."

UGH! I rolled my eyes. "Pompous ass."

October 24

I took photos of as much as I could, but I only brought two rolls of film. The instant paper is expensive and I don't exactly have parental support on this trip. I was planning to ask Mum for some cash so I could buy more, but I left in a bit of a hurry. I do feel a little twinge of guilt. Maybe she's worried about me. But then, she did say I was crazy like Dad, and I can't forget that. I'm not ready to.

The gatehouse was locked and boarded up from the inside, which was weird. I figure that the last owner wanted to keep intruders out. But I've never seen an abandoned house that was boarded up from within before. Almost like they wanted to keep something inside <u>with</u> whoever put the boards there.

"Don't you think it's weird that there aren't any spiders?" I asked Poulton. "Like, no spiderwebs or anything? Or, like, bird nests? Don't they love places like this?"

Pole just shrugged.

We walked along the circumference of the entrance hall, noting how there were cracks in the slate here and there, and at one point, a huge dent as though something had fallen from above and smashed into the floor. Whatever it had been was gone now. We went right back into the Green Room.

Poulton noted the hole in the wall on the floor plans and then we moved on. If the previous room was the Green Room, then this for sure was the Red Room. Everything was either a faded wine color or a version of pink that would clearly have been a richer red back in the day. The piano still looked beautiful, but when I sat down to play, there was no sound.

Across from the Red Room stood the kitchen. It was larger than I was expecting, the fireplace big enough for me to climb inside. A large table and bench ran along one side of the room, while the rest was dedicated to the fireplace and racks along the walls, which displayed an impressive array of goblets and plates, pots and pans. It was like walking into the past, that's how new everything felt.

"Creepy," I murmured.

"Very," Pole agreed.

There was a door in the kitchen leading outside, which would not open, but we could see the mountain beyond through the fogged window. Connected to the kitchen was a scullery of sorts. It was a room with a huge basin, which Pole told me was likely for washing linens, and then racks and racks of jars, bottles—some of them still full!—and then large, ominous hooks.

"For hanging the meat," Pole added.

Across from the scullery and the kitchen stood the dining room. The dining table was a beast of a thing, heavily carved, thick legs and a smooth, rich tabletop. I ran my hand along it in wonder.

"My mother would flip her lid to get hold of something like this."

"I think you're touching a small fortune right now."

I removed my hand and Poulton laughed. "Touch it. I guess it's up for grabs."

My stomach dropped. No. Nothing must be removed.

Poulton placed both hands on the table and inspected the wood grain, his eyes an inch from the surface.

"What next?" I asked, needing him to stop touching it.

"Two more rooms," he said, consulting the floor plans.

One of the last two rooms in the East Wing turned out to be the best of all. A library! When I saw it I could have cried. Okay, I cried a little. Poulton laughed and told me that was why I was his best friend and why he loved me.

We completely forgot about the floor plans and spent the rest of the day exploring the tomes.

Mostly esoteric in nature, a lot of the books looked at the occult, at secret languages and the like, while the others were scientific papers and research. Guess where Poulton spent his time? Guess where I spent my time?

Eventually we got around to checking the final room, but it was locked. It's listed as a small study on the plans, so we're going to try to jimmy the lock tomorrow, as well as the one on the other kitchen door.

I can hardly believe that the whole first day is gone already. We'll have to break into the West Wing at some point, because the whole thing is locked.

Roan Eddington c. 1849

Meddwyn "Mill" House
C.1851

The ruins, today.

Poulton was already up when I rolled over. He once told me that my high-pitched squeak when I stretch in the morning sounds like a mouse giving birth. So now every time I do it, I burst out laughing. Every. Single. Time.

"Good delivery?" he asked. He was standing by the box lights, examining them. "Healthy babies?"

I nodded, rubbing my eyes. "Very healthy. They're hungry, and so is their mama. What's for breakfast?"

"You eat a lot for such a small thing," he noted, as he does every time I ask about food.

"Well, you lost the bet. You couldn't eat seven sausages, so you cook for the next two days."

"I don't trust your cooking anyway."

I sat up, huddling under the sleeping bag. "What's going on with the lights?"

"Not sure yet. They were off when I woke up."

"Did the generator die?"

"No. Looks like they were switched off."

"Wasn't me."

He didn't say anything else, but his mouth kept twisting as he examined the wires, the bulbs, and the generator, like he was chewing on something sour.

Zoey Camera Footage
Date: October 25

The first floor of the East Wing contains another parlor, although this one is much more masculine than those downstairs, and of no definite color, except perhaps beige and brown. Along the corridor on the right, a bedroom with what appear to be wooden aids. Rails along the side of the bed, rails along the wall, while everything else is set quite low.

"An invalid's room," Poulton says, nodding. "I'm sure of it."

"Pole! Don't say *invalid*."

He gives Zoey a look.

"Say 'differently abled person.' It's better. Nicer."

"It means the same thing."

Zoey turns her face into the camera and whispers, "Seriously. Poulton is *definitely* on the autism spectrum. His lack of understanding social cues and empathy is a true skill. I think I should study *him* one of these days."

"I heard that," Poulton calls.

"You were meant to," she says, turning the camera back on him.

They move on, entering a room across the hall.

"Hunting Room, according to the floor plans," Poulton says.

It's not hard to see why. Every wall is lined with weapons. Spears, arrows, knives, swords, axes, and several types of old guns. Zoey turns and films the wall adjacent. This one is covered with horns...animal horns of every kind, mounted flat against the wall in a sinister display. Some of the horns and skulls lie on the ground as if piled there, discarded. The room itself has two large chaises and a drink stand between them. Nothing more.

"Men and their toys," Zoey mutters, leaving it to move on. "Surprise, surprise, Poulton lingers behind."

The room beside the one with the rails is another bedroom.

"I can't read anything from this room in terms of the visual," Zoey murmurs. It is a plain room with one chest of drawers and a small desk with nothing on it. "But the *feeling* in the room...that's something else." Zoey pauses in the doorway. "Hello?"

"Coming," Pole calls from the Hunting Room.

Zoey takes a step inside. "There's...a particular kind of coolness that interests me. It's as though someone just opened the window." A pause. "Hello?" Another pause. "Who's there?"

The silence of the room grows heavy, like someone holding their breath.

Zoey films the floor plans, focusing on the word written in small letters under the outline of the room she is currently in. "Andrew."

Another pause, and then Zoey says, tentatively, "Andrew?" Another pause. "Is the ghost of Andrew in this room?"

After a moment, Zoey leaves, heading farther down the corridor.

Next to the Hunting Room are two smaller rooms: a Games Room with a table, round bats, billiards equipment, and more, then another nondescript bedroom. After a brief glance inside, Zoey heads back to the Hunting Room to find Poulton holding one of the daggers.

"Poulton!"

He jumps and puts it into its scabbard.

"We said not to touch anything!"

"I..." He puts it back on the wall and turns a sheepish smile on her. "I couldn't help myself."

Zoey grabs his arm and marches them both out of the room. She rounds on him in the corridor. "Why did you write on the floor plans?"

"What are you talking about?"

"Look!" She thrusts the plans at him. "There. See? Someone wrote *Andrew* there."

"Well, not me. Weren't these your dad's? Maybe he wrote it."

"He never mentioned anyone called Andrew."

Poulton turns the plans sideways. "There's more. The writing is minuscule. This one says...*Goord? Goode?* And here. *Jenny.*"

Zoey passes the camera to Poulton and takes the floor plans back, squinting down at them. "You're right. *Emma... Seamus...Roan.*" Zoey looks up. "Roan Eddington. She lived here in the 1850s—it was in Dad's notes."

"So maybe the other names are contemporaneous. Maybe your dad found out which room belonged to which person."

Zoey looks up, her eyes wide. "I can't believe I missed these."

"Well, your dad didn't exactly advertise the names, did he? I don't even know how you spotted them."

Zoey shudders. "Let's do the West Wing—*fast*—and then enough for the day. I need to think and read through Dad's notes. Come on."

They march across the landing, which looks down upon the entrance hall, and cross to the West Wing side.

"Oh, yay," Zoey mutters. "Another parlor. I suppose this one is the ladies' private parlor and the one on the other side was the men's one. Such sexism."

"I don't know," Poulton says, lifting a frilly lace doily

from the table. "I think most men would like this, don't you?"

Zoey snorts. "Most girls I know would vomit."

"No, *you* would vomit. But please hold it in until we get outside, m'kay?"

"Bugger off."

They follow the same pattern checking each of the rooms along the corridor, consulting the floor plans.

On the left: a blue bedroom that looks like something exploded in it. The label beneath it: *Blue Room.* There is a large black stain on the floor and another on the bed, and Zoey flinches, almost as though she intends to run back downstairs, but Pole takes her hand and they continue on.

Across from the blue bedroom, a locked room. Then two more locked rooms, then another locked room, and a small bedroom with two single beds in it.

"Well," Poulton says. "Enlightening. I suppose they had a lot of guests." Poulton walks to the window. "Oh, look! This is the side built into the mountain. Why bother to have a window if the mountain blocks half the light."

He looks across the room at her. A pause. "Zoey?"

He turns the camera on her, but she is frozen, staring into the twin bedroom, eyes darting all over the place. The tendons in her neck strain and her lip twitches.

Poulton is beside her in a single stride, camera forgotten. His muffled voice. "What is it?"

Silence.

"Zoey, what is it?"

"Nothing. Let's go. I'm done. I'm—hungry. Switch the camera off. It's enough for today."

[End of clip]

October 25

I know Poulton didn't see what I saw or feel what I felt, but I had to get out of that room. We hurried downstairs and he got to work putting on some lunch. But that room...It was covered in little crosses and markings. Tiny. Scratched into the walls. Like for protection or something. And I felt it. As soon as I was in that room, it felt safer than out here. But that's just in my head. It has to be. Maybe Dad slept in there. Maybe he made the marks.

Or maybe she did.

Roan.

Because according to the floor plans, that was Roan Eddington's bedroom.

My notebook is missing. I'm writing in my school planner.

I blamed Poulton and he's not speaking to me.

But who else?

My stuff's been riffled through.

Chapter 21

UNDER SIDE

October 26

Pole didn't come back last night, but when I woke up he was making breakfast. I found my notebook over by the fireplace. He didn't exactly rub it in, but I could tell he was thinking, <u>I told you so</u>. I shouldn't have thought he took it. I don't know what came over me. I tried to apologize, but he just told me to eat so we did, in silence.

I've sprayed a bucket load of dry shampoo in my hair and put on some deodorant. Feeling more human.

Eventually, I worked up the nerve. This is our usual thing. I mess up, and then I apologize, and he acts like he forgave me ages ago. It didn't go like that this time.

"I'm sorry," I said. "For thinking you took it."

"And for going through my stuff like a thief. Like someone who doesn't believe a thing I say."

"Poulton—"

"No. How long have you known me? You think I'd stoop that low?"

"No, but I—"

"And you know what's worse? That you threw it in my face. The fact that you have <u>private thoughts</u> in that thing that I couldn't understand."

We stared at each other, and I couldn't think of a single thing to say.

"It just shows me what you really think of me. And how little you tell me."

He dumped his bowl down and stalked out of the room, and then I heard his footfalls on the stairs.

Zoey Camera Footage

Date: October 26

Zoey holds the camera on herself. Behind her, a narrow door stands open, revealing a black space beyond. The camera shakes as she holds it.

"This door was locked yesterday," she says, glancing behind her twice. "And now it's open. I found it like this when I walked past this morning. I don't have a key and neither does Poulton. He swears he never touched it and I believe him." She swallows. "I'm about to take you guys in there with me.

"On the floor plans this is listed as the study." She nods. "Right. Let's go."

October 26

   We've found something—I don't really know what.
Papers. Drawings. Letters. Even daguerreotypes and
old photographs. Weird stuff. And a book. I'm going to
photograph as much as I can on my instant camera
and put it in here for reference in the order I
found it.
   It's so weird. My biggest question at the moment
is—did Dad see this stuff too? Did he get into that
room as well? What did he make of it? Did he even get
this far?
   I've left the papers pretty much how I found
them. I'll catalogue them in my notebook and see
if there's anything of interest. Obviously, I'll
photograph them all, but honestly, they look pretty
confused. The writing is hard to make out, but the
pages with drawings are easier. The book is something
else entirely and asks way more questions than it
solves. It's a diary. And if it's genuine, then it's old.
Like, fucking <u>OLD</u>; 1500s old, and written by a girl
called Hermione Smith. There's so much to read.
   Poulton is still upstairs in the Hunting Room. I
think it's become his favorite. All the weapons, all
those skulls and pelts and horns. I think he's trying
to catalogue them the way I'm cataloguing the
papers.
   I'm glad he's here with me. Even if he's not talking
to me.

My John is fervent and excited with the work continuing. The wheel is a magnificent thing! Much larger than I had thought, and the supporting spokes have been installed. It is mostly underneath the ground, which I had not expected, with less than half the height peeking above the hole into which it has been built. Now the men quarry and gather rocks for the surrounding walls, and soon the wheel will not be seen at all. I cannot help thinking that once it is covered, the men will feel better, and that my John is not the fool they continue to jest he is.

I dreamed ill last night. My belly was full with child, so high that I could not see my feet. It moved with life, yet I did not feel a motherly joy. Instead, a red sky rose and I was filled with terror as a black ram looked down upon me. And as the birth pain began, I could hear myself shout and cry with fear—"Baptize the babe! Baptize him!"—and thought my heart would break with fear that my child, my son, would be born damned. The ram watched with hungry eyes and I felt myself damned.

I have not been able to settle since my dream, nor can I speak aloud of it. I continue to pray to the Lord, our God, but I would feel better could we only attend church, or could I speak with a priest.

FROM THE DIARY OF
HERMIONE SMITH,
13 JANUARY 1584

October 26

Something drew me to that bedroom at the end
of the second floor corridor in the West Wing again.
The twin room with the two narrow beds. I just
found myself wandering in there without knowing why.
When I blinked, I was standing in front of the Narnia
wardrobe. I opened the doors and discovered dresses
inside.

Two different sizes, so I guess two people did
sleep in this room. Maybe servants? I couldn't really
tell. The larger dresses are all black, and the other
ones are faded grays and browns. I was tempted to
put one on, because it looked like they might fit, but
then I remembered that these people are dead now
and the moment passed.

But the real find was the box under the lower
shelf; a pretty little thing inlaid with mother-of-
pearl and closed by a delicate brass clasp. I opened
it, expecting jewelry, but instead I found letters.
Letters upon letters.

FROM ROAN EDDINGTON HERSELF.

I nearly peed myself. They're all still perfectly
intact. This room is like a vacuum, and locked away
in the cupboard, the paper hasn't even yellowed that
much at all. It's surreal. I could have written them,
they look so new.

They look foreign, the script spidery and slanted,
written in some other language I couldn't recognize.
Not Welsh, not Latin.

And then I realized. They are written in reverse

script. Like Da Vinci! She wrote them to be kept secret, I think. But, why?

I used the silvered mirror on the wall to read some of them, looking for an insight into this girl from a hundred or more years ago. Looking for a clue as to how she might be related to my father, or me.

My God. Touching them is like touching her. I'm going to photograph every single one and put the images in here, but for now, I'm going to transcribe one (right way around, of course!).

FATHER,

RAPLEY AND I TALK NOW, OUT IN THE COURTYARD MOSTLY, WHERE THE LOW WALL MARKS THE BARRIER BEFORE THE MOUNTAIN'S WILDNESS. HE DOES NOT SAY MUCH, BUT I HAVE LEARNED THAT HE HAS BEEN HERE A LONG TIME. HOW LONG, HE HAS NOT SAID, BUT THE RARE PIECES OF INFORMATION HE PROVIDES ME LEAD ME TO THINK HE KNOWS THIS MOUNTAIN BACKWARD AND FORWARD, UP AND DOWN.

TO THINK OF REMAINING HERE FOR ANY LENGTH OF TIME THAT SHOULD ALLOW ME TO KNOW THE PLACE SO WELL WEIGHS ON ME LIKE A PRISON SENTENCE. THE WEATHER HAS NOT ALLOWED THE POST TO COME THROUGH, AND THOUGH RAPLEY DOES INDEED SOMETIMES GO INTO TOWN, AND ANDREW ALSO, I HAVE NO ONE TO WRITE TO.

EMMA, SEAMUS, RAPLEY, AND ANDREW ARE ALL THE FRIENDS I HAVE IN THE WORLD NOW. EMMA

BEGINS TO FEEL ALMOST AS I WOULD EXPECT A
SISTER TO FEEL. HER INJURED LEG CAN NOW BEAR
HER WEIGHT, THOUGH I SEE HER WINCE NOW AND
AGAIN WHEN SHE THINKS NO ONE IS LOOKING.

UNTIL MY NEXT LETTER, FATHER.
YOUR LOVING DAUGHTER,
ROAN EVELYN EDDINGTON

Isn't that weird? She wrote the letters, but
never sent them. None of the letters are dated, so
I can't make out any real order, but at least I now
know that this room, this <u>exact</u> room, was hers! Dad
was right. And a girl called Emma. I supposed they
were having a country visit, or taking the country
air. Except Roan speaks of her time like a prison
sentence. Maybe she had to come here. Maybe she
had no choice.

So, Roan was real. And a girl called Hermione was
real.

How are they connected to my dad?

And how is this place connected to it all?

Chapter 22

THE NOTE

October 27

Poulton made breakfast again. It smelled amazing. After days of beans and canned soup, it was just what the doctor ordered.

"I kept the bacon outside," he said. "It was cold enough. And they're powdered eggs."

I eventually told him that I lost something yesterday.

"I didn't take it," he said, jerking upright. "I didn't, Zoey, I swear."

I couldn't help but smile. In that one gesture he looked a bit more like my Pole again. "I know you didn't. It's just gone."

"What was it?"

"My heirloom ring. The one that's been in my family for hundreds and hundreds of years."

"<u>What?</u> But you never take that thing off."

"Yeah, I know. I noticed last night that it was... gone."

I was trying not to cry, but it got harder the more we talked about it. Dad gave it to me before he... well. Before. It was too small for him to wear, but it fit me perfectly. I've never taken it off since that day. But it's just....gone.

"Zoey, I'm not sure we're alone."

A shiver of ice ran through me.

"When I woke up this morning, the lights were off again. They had been switched off. The bulbs were cool and the generator was fine—it was switched off too."

I looked around the room. Could the shape at the foot of my bed be doing this? Taking my stuff too? Had it followed me here?

I told him I'd sensed something in the house. Some kind of presence. Fucking idiot I am. He laughed.

Hard.

For ages.

"Zoey! I'm not talking about ghosts here! I think someone might be in the house with us—a real, corporeal human being."

I pretended to joke along with him, but honestly I'm hurt. He never believes these things about me. I know he's a scientist and super-rational, but it makes me feel crazy, and given that my genes <u>might</u> lead me there someday, I'd rather not be treated like I'm crazy now.

He tried to swallow his smile. "You weren't joking. I'm sorry. But look, I've done this thing. It's what I was working on yesterday."

"With the wires."

He grinned and moved closer to me, then talked low into my ear as though he didn't want to be overheard. "I've set up three cameras in the room. Tonight, I'm going to leave them recording and catch our little meddler in the act."

"That's...actually really clever. How'd you do it?"

He pulled a face. "Do you _really_ want to know?"

I did not.

I should have known it was a stupid idea when Pole pulled out a bottle of vodka. And on top of that, he got out a bottle of red wine too.

"I suppose the trashy vodka is for me?" I said.

He laughed and pulled out a six-pack of Pepsi. "And these?"

I grabbed the Pepsi cans and took one out, popping it open and taking several long gulps.

"Oh yeah," I said through a burp. "S'good."

He offered me the vodka. "It's five o'clock somewhere."

"It's like, what, nine a.m. here?"

"Noon," he corrected. Apparently I slept big-time.

So I took the stupid bottle and poured a little vodka into my Pepsi can. I don't need to justify myself. _I don't._

I was on edge. Someone took my notebook, someone took my heirloom ring, my dad doesn't know who I am, and my mom thinks I'm just as crazy as him. Oh, yeah, and my best friend keeps telling me I'm nutso.

I drank my vodka and Pepsi and ate the now-cold food he'd prepared and I let the alcohol slowly warm away my worries.

Dangerous.

My conscience told me that over and over. I drank more to ignore it.

Night-Camera Footage

"Okay, okay," Poulton slurs. "My turn. Did you hear the one about the red-eyed goat?"

"No, probably because it's so bad no one ever tells it except dorks like you!" Zoey and Poulton roll over laughing, Pole's face turning blue. Eventually he gasps in a breath like a drowning victim and laughs raucously again.

"Bitch!"

"The *goat* with *red eyes*," Zoey says, mimicking his tone and affecting the Queen's English. "I am *terrified*, darling, *terrified*. For my *mortal soul*."

"Shutupshrutup! Listen." He takes a theatrical breath, closing his eyes, and then quickly adds, "Pregnant mouse," while peeping one eye open at me. "The tale of the red-eyed goat goes like this. Once upon a time, this dude decided it would be a great idea to buy a goat to put in his apartment. He figures, hey, free milk, man, and goat milk is extra creamy, so I get more bang for my buck. I'll bring in buckets of grass and shit from the park, take the thing for walks in the park, pick up its poop—or not—in the park, and essentially be self-sufficient in the milk department."

"Too bad he didn't think of getting a chicken and a pig. Then he'd have breakfast sorted."

"Shh! *Anyway*, so he goes and buys this cute-ass little baby goat from some dodgy farmer somewhere and brings it home. Needless to say, the goat was a little traumatized at first, but then quickly got used to the cushy environment and made himself quite at home, especially loving the plush carpet and electric fireplace.

"Every day the bloke would get home from work, hang out with his goat friend, and every morning he'd try to milk the thing before breakfast. Well, no milk, because the goat was a baby. Clearly, duh, so the guy decides to wait. If, he thinks, no milk comes, I can always kill little goat friend and eat the meat. Save the money he spent in that way."

"Not cool, Poulton!" Zoey snaps, slapping his arm. "Killing a baby fucking goat? To *eat*?"

"It's not me, it's this guy! *Anyway*. So every day he hangs out with his goat, whom he names Go-tee, and they get closer and closer. The guy is sleeping better than he ever has, and he's less lonely, less grumpy, less of a git, basically. Clearly, right? I mean, he has a goat-friend. Who wouldn't be delighted by that?

"*Anyway*, the goat grows up. And the guy still can't get any milk out of Go-tee. So, with a heavy heart, he decides that tomorrow, he's just going to do it. It's the hunter versus the hunted, blah, blah, blah, circle of life, all that jazz. He's going to do it.

"Only, he decides he needs to do it earlier than he would normally get up, because he doesn't want to frighten Go-tee, and thinks he can just, you know"—Poulton makes a sound as he mimes cutting his throat—"before the little guy even wakes up."

"Ew."

"So he wakes up at three in the morning and gets out of bed, only to discover that he seems to have killed Go-tee in his sleep. He is *covered* in blood. He's so shocked that he actually did it, that he has to find the proof, so he stumbles into the living room, only to see Go-tee sitting in the middle of the floor with the guy's severed dick in his mouth."

"What the fuck, Pole!"

Poulton can barely contain his laughter, which erupts after every second word. "The goat—looks up—drops—the guy's dick—and says—'Sorry, mate, but you stopped producing milk!'"

"That's fucking gross!!! *Ew!*"

Poulton rolls on the floor, clutching his stomach, roaring with laughter while Zoey gags.

"You're so fucking gross. Only a guy would make that shit up."

"Thank you," he says, "thank you very much."

"We were supposed to be telling ghost stories."

"Well, I figured this one was scary. I mean, imagine a goat biting your dick off and you don't even know it. Or—or—worse! Imagine a goat sucking your—"

"THANK YOU."

"—with those goat teeth—"

"Pole! And you totally spaced on the red-eye thing."

"Oh. Well, he was evil, wasn't he?"

"It had no place in the story. Fail."

"You loved it," he says.

"Really not," Zoey argues, though her smile is barely contained. "Dickhead."

"See if you can do better, then."

"I would, but I'm too drunk to think. I'm going to sleep."

She climbs into her sleeping bag and faces away from him.

"A challenge refused?"

"Good night, Poulton."

"By Zoey *Root*?"

"Good. Night."

He tuts.

She rolls over to look at him. "Don't pout. You look like a girl."

"Budidwassomushfun."

"Poulton, the room is literally spinning. And you're slurring. Big-time."

"Can I comin fer cuddles atleas?"

Zoey unzips her sleeping bag and holds a flap open. He stumbles over, stepping on her foot, and clumsily wiggles himself in.

"Cheers. Ooh, niceanwarm."

"Night, night, sleep tight."

And then he leans forward and kisses Zoey. His tongue slips into her mouth, his hand slips around her waist and she stiffens. Then the kiss is over and he's snoring into her face.

Zoey stares at him wide-eyed for a moment, and then wipes her mouth and turns over. She stares into the dark for a long time as he snores behind her, then she wiggles herself out of the sleeping bag and walks to the other end of the room. She sits down, hugging herself, still wiping her mouth.

She reaches for her notebook, but then stops. Instead, she crawls into his sleeping bag and faces away from him. It is many long minutes before she seems to sleep.

"No loud words," Poulton whispered, crawling out of my sleeping bag.

I was too stunned about what happened last night to speak at all, let alone speak loudly.

"I think...that was...a mistake."

"Yeah, it definitely was," I said, glad he was getting to the point right away. "I mean...what the hell was that?"

He turned and grinned sheepishly at me. "I take no responsibility for Go-tee. It was the wine."

I laughed uncomfortably. "Go-tee. Right. Yeah. And after?"

"I have no idea why I was in your sleeping bag, but I take no responsibility for that either. You were more sober than I was."

"I guess so."

"Did you bring aspirin? I forgot to pack medicine. And I could really use some."

I shook my head. "Wasn't planning on getting drunk, to be honest."

Poulton rooted around in his bag, pulling out clothes, cans, and more in a Zoey-like manner. "Maybe I have some in here."

He stood up with his bag, pulling items free as he walked, discarding them behind him in a quasi-Hansel and Gretel trail. He stopped beside the fireplace and knelt on his haunches.

"I don't think I brought any."

Hungover Poulton is completely useless.

"Come on, I'll boil us some porridge—" I broke off.
"Poulton?"

"Yep."

"Do you see what I'm seeing?"

"Yyyyyep."

A note. Written in the ashy hearth of the fireplace. It read:

GET OUT.
WHILE YOU STILL CAN.

ROAN

❦

1851

Chapter 23
RAGE

Rapley walks over to the long window in the entrance hall, staring out into the fog.

"There is no choice now. I'll go out onto the mountain today."

"That's suicide," Cage says.

"Not for me."

Cage folds his arms and paces the hall. "What if they're empty? Your *snares.*"

"As I said, I'll hunt. I've done it before, I'll do it again."

"In these conditions?" Cage snorts. "Impossible."

Rapley heads for the stairs, commenting over his shoulder, "Even if I catch rats and scorpions, we'll eat." He pauses. "Unless you'd like to die when the stores run out?"

Cage watches him warily.

"Well, then," Rapley says, and climbs the stairs two at a time.

"Remember what I said," Cage calls, but Rapley does not reply.

In the safety of her room, Roan slips into the window seat and draws the curtains closed around her. She glances out the window, hoping in vain to see something of Rapley—a light, a fire—any sign that he is alive and well. That he is close by. But there is nothing but the blackness and the rain. Endless, despondent, rain.

Tentatively, she allows her body to settle into that low place required for any kind of Conjure. The deep, still Nothing where even breath is too low to hear or heed.

And her fingers begin to dance.

A sigil drawn between forefinger and thumb. *Reveal.*

Another looped into it with the ring finger. *Enemy.*

A whisper from her lips. Her fingers tingle with warmth.

And then—

stop.

Something

big

presses

back.

Feelers in the dark.

where

are

you,

little

girl

?

Roan opens her eyes.
Something is out there.

i

feel

you

Pressing in.

where

are

you

?

Like someone standing too close. She clenches her fist and holds her breath, breaking the Conjure, like cutting a rope. The presence keeps searching, but is now looking elsewhere.

When all is still again, she leans back.

Who are you? she thinks.

Cage's face leers from her imagination, all stark lines and contempt. She allows herself to focus on the air around her, the particulates and dust motes of the watery scent of the house, and the strange persistent hum. It is barely there, the sound, like the *buzz* of something insectile. Like bees. Or wasps. But pulsing too.

Wump…wump…wump…

And then something else pricks at her awareness, like a sewing needle in her finger. It is not quite a smell, nor a touch, nor a sound…but it is there. A heaviness. A magnet. Drawing her senses toward it like gravity.

Someone is Conjuring.

Got you, she thinks, pulling off her blankets without opening her eyes. She does not need to see to follow the pull.

She feels the change in the air when she opens her door and steps into the corridor. Colder. But more vibrant. The pull is stronger. Whatever fool is Conjuring, she can find them as easily as they found her.

Down the corridor.

Across the first-floor landing.

Down another corridor—

Crash!

—Her eyes snap open. She is standing before Seamus's room. There is a strangulated sound and then a familiar roar. She flings the door open, knowing what she will see before she does.

Fire.

A broken lantern on the floor, the oil alight—flames licking the floor, spreading fast across to the bed, where Seamus lies convulsing.

Roan doesn't think. She raises her hands, fingers dancing, drawing the symbols for Quenching, Control, Banishing—a multitude of signs she herself cannot fully grasp before her fingers have drawn them and cast them outward.

"*Egk ti*," she growls. The words are out before she can stop them, slipping from her tongue as easily as silk on smooth skin.

The fire blinks away, the smoke curling in upon itself like it never was, only the broken lantern showing any sign of what might have been. Only Roan's nightdress is smoking. At the hem.

Her hands still tingle when Emma rushes in.

"Seamus! By God, what's happened?"

"I heard a crash—" Roan mutters, hurrying to Seamus's side. He is still twitching, but the convulsions are over.

Emma wipes away the froth at his mouth. "No," she whispers. "Not again."

Roan grips her wrist. "What do you mean? This has happened before?"

"What is that smell?" Cage strides into the room looking about.

"Seamus is unwell," Roan says, her heart squeezing tightly in her chest. *Be gone*, she wills him. *Leave us be!*

But he steps purposefully into the room, sniffing the air. "Burning. Something was burning."

"He used to have these…spells," Emma murmurs to Roan. "But he has not had one since our mother passed. I thought we were done with it."

Roan says nothing, but watches Seamus carefully.

"What have you been doing?" Cage says, turning his eyes upon Roan only.

"I heard a crash. The lantern there, it fell. When I entered, Seamus was convulsing. He is ill."

Cage narrows his eyes, but does not reply.

"I had a bad feeling tonight," Emma murmurs, eyes swimming.

Roan reaches for Seamus's room bell, ringing it urgently, and holds Seamus down when he begins to twitch once more. He is sweating, but cold to the touch. Or perhaps he only feels cold to Roan because her hands are still smarting with the Conjure. Her mouth, too, tastes of ashes.

A hurried *clatter* of steps on the corridor.

"Jenny, come. Seamus is unwell. Could you bring some water and some mugwort, meadowsweet—anything you have for fever."

"Oh, Master Seamus," Jenny moans, but she does as Roan commands.

Emma stares on, her eyes strange and glassy, and then she stands suddenly, stumbling toward the door.

"Emma, where—"

But Emma faints clear away, a little red-haired pile on the floor before Roan can finish her sentence.

Andrew hurries in a moment later. "By God." He sets his jaw. "What do you need?"

"Fetch smelling salts," Roan says. "Dr. Maudley would have kept a supply somewhere."

Andrew nods, bending down and lifting Emma into his arms as though she is a feather pillow. "She's burning up," he says, frowning.

"Put her here beside her brother," Roan says, gesturing. "They may have caught some illness. Jenny has gone to fetch some mugwort and water."

"I have some birthwort and peppermint," Andrew says. "They may help."

"Fetch them, quickly."

Through it all, Cage stands in the corner, eyes dark and watchful. Roan dislikes being alone in a room with him, but what can she do? He insists on watching her, following her, frowning at her. Roan untwists Seamus's blankets and covers him, tucking them around his arms lest he begin to thrash again.

What is going on? Was *Seamus* Conjuring? Or was someone—or something—attacking him? Her eyes flutter over to Cage and away.

"Must you stare at me?" she says.

He says nothing, but continues to watch her.

"You will not alarm me."

Roan's thoughts race and whir. She had known someone was Conjuring in the house…had sensed it like another's breath. But…*Seamus*? She glances at Emma.

How much do you know?

Roan and Cage remain in silence until Jenny returns, and soon after: Andrew.

"We have to make a new attempt to find Dr. Maudley," Roan tells him.

Andrew nods. "I will find Rapley and we'll search again tonight."

Roan strokes Emma's hair. "There has to be a place we've over-looked."

This search is as fruitless as the previous.

They are alone.

Chapter 24
SOLACE

They are congealing together in the house. Emma and Seamus both woke the following evening, complaining of empty stomachs. Jenny, delighted to have a new purpose, had rushed to the kitchen, promising bread and jam, but returned to the Green Room, where they had all gathered, pale-faced and trembling.

"The flour has mold. Almost all of it is turned and useless."

"Could that have been the cause of the convulsions and fever?" Roan asked. She herself had taken no bread in many days.

"If so, I would be sick, as would Mr. Cage and Andrew." Jenny covered her mouth. "We shall starve!"

"Calm yourself," Cage snaped.

"Calm ourselves?" Roan asked. "We have a man missing, a woman dead, and two others sick—or have you forgotten?"

"I have not forgotten. We will find a way to send for the constable."

But after less than half a day, Rapley dragged Andrew into the house, coughing up half of the mountain and rain with it, both of them slick with mud.

"Mud slide," Rapley yelled, hauling Andrew over the threshold. "Saw him trying to get down the mountain on my way back when I saw it happen." The storm howled and screamed beyond the gatehouse like a demon, heather and bracken and stones all flying past like some hellish hailstorm.

Roan hurried forward with Cage to shut the door. Only with Rapley's help did they manage, and they bolted it into place where it rattled and complained. Roan stared at Rapley, her heart hammering as she leaned against the door.

"You're back," she breathed, her eyes searching his body.

He's unharmed. He's back. Alive. Safe. Well.

She had no idea why she cared. But she was immensely glad to have him safely back in the house.

"Fool," Rapley muttered, looking at Andrew and wiping mud from his face.

"How long will it last?" Roan asked Rapley, breathless.

"I don't know," he said, wiping the mud from his own face. "This one is uncanny. Months without letting up."

Roan felt herself pale.

Cage's lips tightened and he turned away. "Come. Let us read a while from the Bible and rekindle the fire. The Lord, our God, shall save us from our tribulations."

Rapley gave Roan a look as Cage passed them, but what else was there to do? And so she followed.

Roan can only stand the stifling air of the Green Room for so long. No, she thinks. Not the air. It is the people. So many of them in one place. Emma, Seamus, Cage, Andrew, Rapley, *and* Jenny. All of them together, gathered on the sofa, the rug, huddled by the fire—all of them listening with deepest hope to Cage's drawling sermon. For that is what it has turned into.

She's had enough. The barren, hollow hallways of the empty house appeal more. She is burning with questions. Where is Dr. Maudley? Did he run away? Did he fall on the mountain? Is he dead? Or merely hiding? And if so, why? Who is Conjuring? Surely it was not Seamus. But someone was…something drew her to his room. Perhaps she was led there on purpose, to see him convulsing. To save him? Or perhaps as a warning…

More questions—many more. But Roan cannot think. What is she seeking? Solace? Walking without much purpose, she finds herself at the threshold of Maudley's study.

She can feel the ghost of Mrs. Goode, watching them all with her sour face and disapproving eyes. Twice, she thought she had seen the woman, walking solemnly down the hallway, and watching from the shadows.

The master won't take kindly to nosy young ladies traipsing through his possessions!

She can almost hear the old crone.

Still. What does it matter now? She isn't expecting to find him; she wants only to feel closer to him and, if she is lucky, to get some answers. This man who knew both of her parents before she was even a thought in their minds. This strange, eccentric doctor who had saved Emma's life and taken them all in.

But the niggling doubt remains. He hadn't known Roan's father very well if he thought him a loving father. And of Emma's mother? That he was a school friend when they were young? How can it be proven?

Stop it. What point is there, now, of questions?

She sighs as her fingers brush the bookshelves that hold Maudley's favorite, most-used books. Mostly scientific journals, anatomical studies, medical papers, and some novels. Her eyebrows arch.

"*Novels*, Doctor?" she murmurs. Well. It seems he still has the ability to surprise her.

"Did you just leave?" she whispers. "Did you sense the oncoming gloom? Did you go out looking for some aid, and get caught in one of the mountain's tricks, as Rapley suggests?" She looks around at all his knickknacks, his candles and jars and crude little sculptures. "Did you die trying to save us? Or have you simply vanished, as Jenny claims? Like those poor workers in the tale of the miller?" She smiles, and then laughs at herself, walking around his desk and sitting in his chair. "You would grin at that, I think. A man of science vanishes without a trace, and it all comes down to a legend of a mountain—what—*eating* people?" She allows herself to play out the comical scenario in her mind before the joviality sinks into a low, still despondency.

"Please," she whispers. "Come back. Explain all this away."

Absentmindedly, she toys with the pages on his desk until something catches her eye.

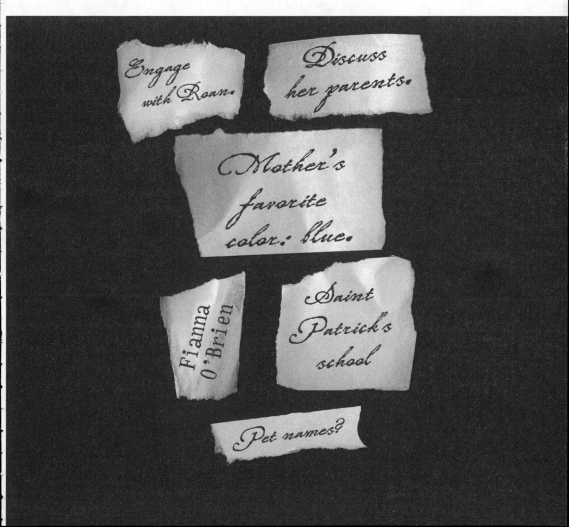

She lifts another sheet from the scattered mess.

Onwards Onwards Onwards
Onwards Onwards Onwards Onwards
Onwards Onwards Onwards Onwards
Onwards Onwards Onwards Onwards
Onwards Onwards Onwards
Onwards Onwards Onwards Onwards
Onwards Onwards Onwards Onwards
Onwards Onwards Onwards Onwards
Onwards Onwards Onwards Onwards
Onwards Onwards Onwards
Onwards Onwards Onwards Onwards
Onwards Onwards Onwards Onwards
Onwards Onwards Onwards

Three pages continue like that.

Rapley is asking questions.
Questions always!

Emma and Seamus go their own way.
GOOD.

Roan seems happy to also—

MUST ENGAGE.

MUST ENGAGE.

TAKE THE STAGE,

MUST ENGAGE.

And then some kind of journal. The book lies open and is covered with the same scrawl.

Roan is...beautiful.

But cold. Like me.

She would be soft to touch.

But who would dare?

I AM VITAL.

I AM
VITAL.

Choose me—

I can prove
my worth.

CHOOSE ME!

232

The writing goes on and on like that, pages of nonsense notes and scribbles. Those of a man coming undone. Losing himself.

Bile rises in Roan's throat as she stares down at the mess in front of her. What is this? She riffles through the pages—so many of them! Who is Dr. Maudley? These notes read like...like memos. Like an actor trying to remember lines to a part he is playing.

"Who are you?"

She recalls their last, eerie conversation with a shudder.

Could he have gone mad and...and...

No. A man of science would not do such a thing. A man of science would never end his life. He would continue on and seek answers. If that is truly who he was. Now, in this moment, she does not know.

Unless the presence she had felt when she Conjured a Revealing had been working on *him* as well. A man of science would, no doubt, try to find a logical explanation. He would have investigated. But what if science provided no satisfactory answer besides madness? Would he have turned to God? To faith?

Somehow, she knows it is unlikely.

Or...perhaps the Revealing Conjure had revealed the truth...about *him*.

Fake, a little voice says inside. *Fraud...*

Roan clenches her fists upon the table. "No. No, I refuse to believe it. I had nowhere else to go...He took me in. He knew Father was ill... Perhaps he *did* think he was going mad." The pages before her certainly suggest it. A sudden and terrible guilt begins to rise within her.

"Oh, Doctor," she whispers. "Why did you not seek help from us?"

Even as she says it, she knows it is impossible. Seek help from an adopted son who detests him, his hired servants, or his wards? Excellent options.

She leans her head on her hands.

By God. He had brought them here to give them a new life. Instead he vanished into an impossible, but likely, death. Now they are alone.

Stores running low, an unrelenting storm, and something…inhuman… wandering the halls.

For all Roan is uncertain of, she most certainly is certain that there is an evil presence within these walls.

Chapter 25

IN SICKNESS AND IN HELL

Roan kneels over Seamus, clutching his face.

"Please…please, Seamus. Please, wake up."

"What's happening?" Emma mumbles, still feverish. She is rocking on her knees beside Roan and her brother. They are in the entrance hall, where they found him, unconscious, his wheelchair a few feet away.

"He's cold," Roan says, getting to her feet and running to the Red Room for a blanket. She wraps him in it, pulling his head onto her lap and rubbing one of his hands. "Come on," she mutters. "Come on, please."

Emma covers her mouth. "What's wrong with him?"

"What's going on?" Andrew says, coming from the kitchen. His arms bear the weight of a dozen logs.

"I can't get him to wake," Roan says desperately. "He's cold, Andrew…"

The logs clatter to the floor.

He is kneeling on the floor next to Roan in less than a moment. "Move over."

She slips out from underneath Seamus, allowing Andrew to take over.

"I learned a few tricks from Dr. Maudley," he murmurs, lifting Seamus's eyelids, one after the other. "He's not seizing. It's like he's asleep."

"But he won't wake," Emma cries. "He's not waking up!"

Andrew lifts the boy with ease and they follow him into the Green Room where Andrew lays him down on a leather sofa. The red blanket is an ugly contrast.

blood on the mountain

dripping

on

the

moss

this is your fault

murderess

Roan clenches her jaw and steps away from Seamus. Andrew wets one of the napkins from breakfast in a vase and wipes Seamus's head. Roan can smell the brackish water even from her distance.

Emma sits, with a heavy sigh, on the sofa beside her brother.

"They're everywhere," she murmurs, and closes her eyes.

Andrew feels her face. "She's burning up. One hot, one cold." He shakes his head. "I don't know what's happening."

Roan backs away, the voice still ringing in her head.

This is your fault.

Murderess.

Father,
I've seen Seamus's ghost wandering the
house at night. His rotten ghost.

He turns hollow eyes upon me as if to say,
Why do you not save me?

Dr. Maudley has not returned, and I do
not believe any of us think he will.

He has vanished, just like the miller and his
workers in the story—

The story! What if it is no mere folktale?

What if there is truth in the legend?

I must find Jenny and persuade her to tell
me all she has heard.

Perhaps there is some key detail I have
missed. Perhaps I can save Seamus after all!

And if this is mere madness, then let me
lose myself entirely in trying to save my
friends.

My friends…

Oh, let me be able to save him!

R.E.E.

"Close off the entrance hall!" Cage yells through the tumult. One of the large paintings smashes as it falls from the wall, splinters flying in all directions.

The storm has blown in most of the windows and the house is now a small hurricane in monsoon season.

"We must search for Rapley," Roan cries. "He's out there!"

"Help me with the door or back away," Cage growls.

Andrew obliges and the two men finally get the doors shut and barred.

"The rain is cold as knives," Andrew murmurs. "I hope Rapley has some shelter." He glances at Roan and smiles. "He will be well. He knows the mountain. I am certain—"

"That ought to keep us safe and warm," Cage interrupts briskly, rubbing his hands. "And we have access to the kitchen here. Good. Good." He turns to Jenny. "Have we supplies enough for some warm tea?"

Jenny nods and hurries away.

"Let us sing a ballad," Emma says, though Roan does not much like the glassy sheen of her eyes. "'Miss Bailey's Ghost.' Come, now. It will rouse Seamus. It was...it *is* his favorite." She leans over her brother, still unconscious, and whispers, "Ye'll help me sing it, won't ye, brother mine?"

Seamus, huddled beneath one of the thickest blankets in the Red Room, does not respond.

"Do you know it, Roan?" Emma asks, and Roan almost chokes on the sadness in her voice.

"I do," she concedes. "Though it has been a long time since I had occasion to sing."

"Well," Emma says, attempting a grin. "We shall butcher it together. Come. One, two, three—"

The words come easily to Roan, as does the memory of her mother singing the same song to her and her father on cold nights. She would play the pianoforte in accompaniment.

A Captain bold in Halifax,
Who dwelt in country quarters,
Seduced a maid who hanged herself
One morning in her garters,
His wicked conscience smited him,
He lost his stomach daily,
He took to drinking turpentine
And thought upon Miss Bailey.
Oh, Miss Bailey, unfortunate Miss Bailey,
Oh, Miss Bailey, unfortunate Miss Bailey—

Cage does not sing, but Andrew joins in at the chorus, lending a deep baritone to their tune. Roan hopes that Rapley can hear them all the way outside, wherever he is.

When it is done, they clap merrily, and almost forget their woes.

"What a voice you have, Miss Roan," Jenny says, bringing in the tea. "I heard it all the way from the kitchen. And you, Miss Emma! You sing like a lark."

"Well, we shall have to coax a song from you next, Jenny," Emma says, taking her tea with both hands and walking to stand by the window, even though it is shuttered. "Soon we won't even have candles to see by," she says, staring at nothing.

Something drops inside Roan's stomach, and she looks up just as it happens. The teacup shakes as Emma lifts it to her lips, and then falls.

It seems to happen unnaturally slowly. The cup slipping from her fingers, the tea spilling down her dress, the china shattering on the floor as Emma falls.

It is Andrew who catches her.

Roan is by her side within a moment. "She's even more feverish. I don't understand."

"Look at this," Andrew says, turning her head so that her neck is visible. "A rash."

Cage grips his Bible as he speaks. "This is the work of the Devil."

Roan would scold him, but a chill runs through her and she cannot argue.

Andrew peers closer. "It looks like a burn."

Emma moans and thrashes out feebly. "Don't…"

She blinks, but her eyes roll and she does not focus on any of them.

"I can help her," Roan says, getting up.

"I used the last of the mugwort," Jenny says as Roan approaches.

"I have something else. Bring water. Hot."

"But miss, the wood…"

"Would you see Emma die?" Roan snaps. "Bring it!"

She rushes to the door, ready to unbar it, but Cage steps into her path. "Where are you going?"

"I can help her—move aside!"

He does so, but upon her return, there he is again, staring down at her with hawk eyes.

Roan hurries to Emma and opens the little box she has brought with her. From within, she pulls free a vial of milky liquid.

"She must drink this. It is a kind of herbal tea, it—"

The vial smashes as it hits the floor, the sound almost drowned out by Cage's loud roar.

"No witchcraft here!"

Roan has hit him before she can think. "You stupid fool! You might have just killed her!"

He grabs her wrist. "I think I just prevented you from doing so."

Chapter 26
A ROTTEN GHOST

Roan leaves her body that night without meaning to. The taste of the mountain settles in her mouth like the bitter after-bite of strong liquor. All about her are tangible shadows that arch and dance, alluring. She avoids them, resisting the pull of the Universe at her back as well. She can hear something rhythmic in the background—a continual *whoosh.*

The mountain is breathing.

Below her, Seamus lies still as death, small as a babe, and Roan chokes out a little sob. Beside him, Emma lies in her fever, tossing like the storm beyond the windows, kicking the blanket free of both of them.

And then…

…something else.

They are not alone.

The walls shiver, wriggling on their foundations as though to squirm away from something repellent. The windows too—the glass moves and bends, contracting outward, even as Roan herself feels a huge presence enter the room.

It is tall. A dark, near-shapeless form. Human-like, yet…

Two large curled horns stand upon the head, like the ram.

That is all Roan can say about it.

The shape moves toward her friends where they slumber, and a clawed hand reaches out…

No. No!

Roan struggles to regain her body, to wake from this terrible night-walk, or nightmare—anything to get to Seamus before…

But the thing has the boy in its arms. Dark masses curl and snake about his small, helpless form, and his glasses fall to the floor.

With a magnificent burst of will, Roan wrenches herself out of the ether and blinks awake. For a moment she is confused— What is happening? Where is she? And then she remembers. She fell asleep in the armchair watching over Emma and Seamus last night—

Seamus.

She stands, staggers sideways when her vision wavers, and then stares around.

Seamus is not there.

But something is. Something large…she can *feel* it, if not see it. The room bends and wobbles around her, taunting her.

What is *the thing pressing in?*

Man?

Witch?

Creature?

Satan himself?

Or, simply…me?

She closes her eyes.

Do not think of the ram out there, his proud, gnarled, ancient horns, his bloodred eyes.

"Come on," she growls, raging at her body for taking so long to adjust to her soul returning.

She reaches for the Conjure with both hands, drawing the symbols for Protection, Revelation, and Pain all at once. She throws them out, draws more, muttering the foul words in her mouth, which tastes of ashes as soon as she speaks them.

"*Egk ti*," she growls, the sounds guttural and beastly. *"Arok shi!"*

Come out. Reveal yourself.

And with the Cursèd language of Conjures, each word contains more than the meaning, for the room bursts with the smell of burning.

"What are you doing?"

"Devil woman!"

Emma's voice.

Cage's voice.

Both raised in alarm and at the precise moment when the presence vanishes. Roan stumbles, the Conjures burning out of her mind and out of the air. She wants to spit them from her mouth—the fetid taste of the mountain was a better alternative by a margin.

She looks through her hair to see Emma sitting up rigidly on the sofa, staring at her with wide, terrified eyes, and Cage looming in the doorway.

"Where is he?" Emma cries, her hands searching the blanket she kicked aside during the night. "Where is my brother?"

She turns her jade eyes on Roan, and screams.

"Where is he? **Witch!**"

PART 4

Upon the Mountain

Hell hath no limits, nor is circumscribed
In one self-place; for where we are is hell,
And where hell is, there must we ever be.

—CHRISTOPHER MARLOWE,
DR. FAUSTUS

Daylight Shadows

The little girl crawled out of bed before the sun had risen over the garden. It was frosty, but she was too excited to stay in bed. She even forgot to put on her slippers. She ran across the hall to Adam's room, and poked her head around the side.

He was still asleep, curled into a tight ball under his covers, his particular way of sleeping.

You can relax, you know, she had told him. But he never ever listened to her. He just nodded, but then in the morning she would find him in a ball, curled up like a snail or a hedgehog.

She suppressed a laugh, worried that she might wake Mother, Father, Cook, or Betty. With care, she tiptoed across the floor.

Adam was a light sleeper. Once, she had just breathed too loudly and he woke up with his hands out, ready to fight. She had learned her lesson since then.

Besides. She was good at being quiet. She always snuck around the house without Father ever knowing. She was like a shadow, a whisper—even less. She was nothing.

She paused when Adam flinched in his sleep, and then continued on her perilous journey when his ball tightened up some more. She lifted herself up in her special way, her little feet dangling above the floor, and lifted the covers without touching them. Then she let her weight fall gently, and ever so slowly, onto the bed beside him.

By the time the sun was peeking over the windowsill, she had curled around him in her own warm little ball, his body stowed in front of hers.

Don't worry, she thought. *I'll keep you safe.*

His reply was hard to catch, as it always was. Evie...

She smiled and closed her eyes.

She had broken one of her rules, and now everything was wrong. Father was upset, and Mother stood behind him wringing her hands.

"You cannot sleep in the same bed as a boy. What have I told you? It is indecent! You are getting older and you must learn. What am I to do with you?"

His face grew red. "And you," he said, turning on Adam.

"But it wasn't Adam, Father! I crawled into bed with him because he was having nightmares. I was protecting him!"

"Enough of this tosh! I swear, you are not my daughter!"

Mother flinched, and began to cry, and Father looked like he wanted to hurt himself. He turned to her, his shoulders slumped.

"Oh, darling, I didn't mean it. You know I didn't." He gestured helplessly. "But the two of them in a bed, it's unsightly. It's dangerous."

Mother wiped her eyes with her kerchief and nodded. "Go easy on them, Arthur. They are children. God's innocent children."

Eve remembered seeing her father's face then. The way he flinched and grew pale. They were God's children, were they not? God was the keeper of all children, wasn't that true?

Eve had looked at Adam, felt his terror at those words and the reaction he too had seen, and smiled.

We are special, *she reminded him.* We have the magic.

When the man in black came to take Adam away, Eve clung to him with all her strength. When her father ripped her away, she wept bitterly.

She never forgot.

And she never forgave.

Chapter 27
AIR, WATER, FIRE

"WITCH!"

The word rings in the air.

Emma covers her mouth as though to take it back, but it spreads like a plague to everyone within earshot and echoes on and on. Roan stumbles back, both from the look on Emma's face and from the shock of the word itself.

Witchwitchwitchyouareawitchevilwicked WICKED!

"How could you?" Emma whispers through her fingers. "You were my *friend*!" She begins to sob. "You did it. Seamus is gone because of your witchery!"

Defending the house has left Roan exhausted, but through the horror of discovery, she cannot help trembling from a deep, unshakable satiation.

You did it.

> *You did it.*

>> *You did it.*

—*What have I done?*

Cage steps forward, hands clasped before him. Emma, tearful, shakes her head, looking from Roan to Cage and back. No one moves.

Until Andrew comes running in. "He's gone. Seamus—he's gone."

Roan points weakly to the wall. "Someone...took him. I was..."

"Restrain her," Cage says suddenly. "Now. Do it now."

Andrew hesitates, glancing from Cage to Emma and Jenny and then Roan. It would almost be funny if Roan weren't so exhausted, nor so terrified.

Finally, Cage strides forward himself and takes Roan by the wrist, pulling her closer to him. She allows herself to be manhandled, her head and heart full of turmoil and confusion.

Has she brought this on them? Is it her fault?

Seamus is gone. Has all she witnessed *really* happened, or is it in her mind? Maybe she is confused. Maybe she has been Conjuring longer than she realizes and can no longer trust her own mind...

Roiling inside, she allows Cage to lead her upstairs and into the Blue Room. His grip is firm. So firm that her hand begins to ache. The others follow, confused.

In the Blue Room, Cage turns to Jenny, ignoring Emma and Andrew. "Get rope. Now, girl."

Jenny curtsies without a glance at Roan and hurries away.

"Restraining her?" Emma says, her voice wholly unlike her own. "Must you?"

"Yes." Cage gives her a sharp look. "Lest she bewitch us all."

Emma, openly weeping, looks at Roan. "Witch..." She whispers it so softly that the word almost doesn't exist at all. It sounds like a question. An almost-question. Roan turns away, unable and unwilling to see her.

Emma is thin, pale, blotched in the cheeks. But her fever seems to have passed, for which Roan is thankful. Emma's once-wild hair hangs limp around her, and she still jumps at the sight of nothing. Bewitched, Cage had said. Maybe it is true. Maybe Roan is simply cursed to bring suffering wherever she goes.

"Perhaps another room," Andrew says. "This one still bears the brunt of the first storm."

Cage ignores him, instead pondering his captive. "How long have you been practicing dark magicks?"

Roan sinks to the floor, heedless of Cage's grip, so that she is sitting with her arm bent up at an awkward angle. She draws up her knees and hugs them with her free arm.

Cage relents and releases her, but steps closer and bends over.

"Tell me," he says, as though coaxing some private trust between them. Some secret confidence. "Tell me all."

"Where is Rapley? Bring Rapley."

Cage sneers. "I see your hold on him. I sent him to check his traps at the summit of the mountain again. He left before your trickery began."

Roan hunches into herself, willing his awful, awful voice to stop. She cannot speak; if she were to open her mouth, she would spill forth a vile string of curses in his deformed face.

"No matter," he says, straightening up. "I will have all from you. In time."

Jenny hurries into the room. "I have the…rope." She swallows at the sight of Roan in a heap on the floor. "Sir."

Cage takes it and offers a rare half smile. "Good girl. Now go to the kitchen and make us all some tea. I will be down shortly."

Jenny curtsies awkwardly, then hurries away. Emma, who sways in the doorway, no doubt seeing very little, collapses to the side, but Andrew is quick and holds her up.

"She isn't well," he says to Cage.

"Take her to the Yellow Room. Let her rest awhile. It is not easy learning your friend is working with Satan and has stolen your brother away." He says all of this without glancing at Emma, nor at Andrew, only staring down at Roan.

251

She can *feel* his gaze like the touch of an unwanted courter, and yearns to protect herself, but she must not—*will not*—Conjure again.

Tricks. It had been tricks.

No doubt whatever was working against her had pushed for just such a conclusion.

Cage unravels what is cooking string, rather than rope, discolored in places, the product, no doubt, of inventive sauces and the blood of carcasses that adorned dinner tables long ago.

Roan allows Cage to tie her wrists to the posts at the bottom of the bed that was meant to be hers, because the longing is coming back. The itch, the yearning, the desire—and she has to stop before she can no longer make that choice.

Emma's words haunt her.

How could you? You were my friend*! You did it. Seamus is gone because of your witchery!*

She was so unlike Emma when she said it, her face contorted by rage, fear—and the pallor of the dying. Her eyes were little more than black bruises, her skin more blue than white. Yet…was that real? What can Roan trust in her own senses? And a treacherous thought that sticks like lichen:

Maybe…maybe I have caused this?

  Maybe I have caused this?

  I have caused this?

  I have caused this.

Did Roan not Conjure on the mountain on the very first night she arrived? Did she not feel the rush of something responding? Was it not she who Conjured up the thing pressing in?

But this image is replaced with the memory of the beast, hooves stomping slowly, echoing as they drew near; she cowered in her bed. His breath as he snorted, his eyes, also red. The same shocking red.

Stop.

It won't stop.

Stop!

Roan opens her eyes, instinctively twisting to rub her face, but the string, twice-wrapped, tugs into her wrists. Cage is watching. How long has he been staring? What has he seen?

His lips open torturously slow. "Your tricks will not work on me."

She looks away. She is too tired for this.

"I vowed, long ago, to find abominations like you. I am well protected."

That gets her weary attention and she notes, through the fog of her mind, that he clasps a hand to his chest.

"Half-breed, vile—unnatural!" He takes a breath, nostrils curling. "You revolt me."

A pause. "And yet, how can I fully blame you? You did not ask to be made. Yet here you are. *Wicked, blasphemous creature!*" The last, spat with such venom!

"Why do you hate me?" she manages, though she wants to hold up her hand, to block his words from her ears. The string pulls tight when she tries.

Stop.

Please, stop.

He walks to the window and considers the boards nailed in place.

"You are hateful," he mutters, but Roan can see there is more. Much more.

Then, with surprising speed, he wrenches each board from the walls until the broken window is exposed, and the rising storm beyond it.

"I want you bathed in the water of the Lord," he murmurs. "I want you to be cleansed of your filth and vile baseness. I will extract answers from you yet."

He turns back to her, retrieving a book from the inside pocket of his jacket, and begins to read. "'The Lord is nigh unto them that are of a broken heart; and saveth such as be of a contrite spirit.'"

Roan's muscles relax.

"'Many are the afflictions of the righteous: but the Lord delivereth him out of them all.'"

Cage pauses, and when he speaks, his words are soft. "Would I could save that half of you that is innocent." Then his face changes again, the skin turning rigid. "Alas, evil runneth over. You are corrupted through and through. And so, I must exorcise you…or destroy you."

The light slices at her retinas as Cage pulls off her makeshift blindfold. He is rough, and she winces. As her vision adjusts to the sudden light, she can see black spiderwebs hanging from between his fingers. Her hair.

He kneels before her, and she smells him—he is potent and unpleasant and she wrinkles her nose, turning her face away. He yanks it back.

"Tell me the secrets of your dark magick," he whispers, his voice tender yet pinched, as though he restrains some great emotion. His hand lingers on her cheek, hot and moist. "Confess."

Ah. There it is. He is holding back rage. And disgust. She recognizes it like the scent of home.

She smiles.

And he hits her.

The blow is not sharp, as would be an open-palmed slap. She knows that pain well. No. This is a punch—the kind he would use on a man. Something within her shrieks a laugh, followed by the high squeal of metal. Inside, somewhere deep, a bolt that had been slid shut through years of suppression, releasing mere smoke around the edges, has moved toward opening.

Anger is exhilaration. A long-lost friend.

The bolt slides some more.

Open up, wake up, rebirth.

Why should men be allowed to express their rage, and not she? Has

254

she not three times—*ten* times the violence of any man? Has not Emma? She yearns to bite his hand like a wolf, for wolf she is.

So she does.

His howl of surprise and pain invigorates her, and she bites harder, feeling the skin crack and break, the sudden taste of blood.

It's the taste that makes her let go, and she spits it from her mouth, baring her teeth at him.

I dare you, she thinks, willing him to challenge her.

But he shuffles back on his buttocks and scrambles away from her, clutching his hand to his chest, eyes two white orbs in the darkening room.

She grins. How men like to show their power. Well, let him see hers.

She laughs as he flees the room.

It is late when he returns.

She has gotten used to the thing in the corner of the room, the rotted ghost. It lingers like a bad smell. She stares at it instead of at Cage, who yanks at her chin so that her neck cricks and aches. Still, he does not move. Seamus.

Cage's shoes hammer the floor; his confidence could not be so easily shaken. He places something heavy on the table beside the ghost.

"I have been in prayer," he says, as though he owes her an explanation.

"Water," she croaks.

"Be you devil or victim," he continues, "it is in your interest to resist me." She is bothered by his back to her, a thick black wall, hiding his face. She needs to see his face.

"Water..."

"Resistance is natural. The body will fight the process, the demon will fight the banishing. And if you are, as I suspect, a witch—a creature of eternal night—then you will lead me well."

His words tumble one over the other and Roan shakes her head trying to straighten them out. He is weaving a tapestry, a pattern, with his words and actions. If she could have some water, then she could make sense of it. Could use it to free herself.

When he turns, he is wearing a minister's collar. He fades in and out of focus, but the thing behind him, in the corner, is in sharp focus.

She squints. "Go away."

Cage smiles, and opens a book. Was he holding a book before? It's a Bible. She knows it well. She studied for hours at her father's behest when she was small, right after Adam left her. She thought it was his way of giving her comfort, of distracting her, but she soon realized it was to try to contain her. He had given up when it made no difference, and the episodes still came, but she kept studying. She enjoyed it. The words, the parables, the thin, crisp pages crinkling as they turned.

Cage's Bible crinkles too, and she smiles.

"'Be not overcome of evil—'"

"'—but overcome evil with good,'" Roan finishes. "Romans 12:21."

"'Woe unto them that call evil good, and good evil—'"

"'—that put darkness for light, and light for darkness; that put bitter for sweet, and sweet for bitter!' Isaiah 5:20."

"And so," Cage says, closing the book and smiling slowly, "the devil shows himself."

Roan frowns. *"What?"*

"And the devil shall have knowledge of scripture..." He turns briskly. *"Jenny!"*

The door opens slowly and Jenny hurries in carrying a bucket.

"Shall I wash her?" Her voice is small.

Roan licks her lips. "Jenny..."

She flinches. "Shall I, Mr. Cage? She doesn't look well. I could bring some broth. Please—"

"No. Leave."

Jenny hesitates, eyes dashing to Roan and away. Her worry has thinned her face some, and Roan cannot stand to see it. So she smiles, and the smile says so many things.

Don't worry.

I'm all right.

Please smile.

Be happy.

Jenny's face contorts and she is sobbing before she leaves the room.

"How you beguile the innocent," Cage says, bringing the bucket closer.

The water inside sloshes over the edge and Roan's relief is so profound that she leans forward, straining against her bonds, head lolling toward it.

"Thank you," she whispers.

Cage is gentle as he releases her arm. It falls to the floor with a dead *thump*. When did the terrible pain go away? She can't move it. How long has she been here, like this?

She leans closer to the bucket, she can almost smell the water, when a hand clamps around her neck and forces her face downward.

She gasps, but there is no air, and water cuts like glass as it enters her. She has taken it in. The choke is profound, her body fighting to get it out, to gasp in air, but all she takes in is more water.

She fights. She thinks she does.

But the black at the edge of her vision is closing in and the pain has become pleasant—*it is so warm*—and she drifts.

Life is painful.

A rib snaps as the water purges from her lungs.

He is kneeling over her—his knee is on her chest.

There is no thought, only breath.

And then *his* breath, hot in her face. "You didn't die." His face floats into focus. *"Witch."*

You deserve this
  Is it not what you sought by coming here?
  Your father knew what would happen
  It was a trap
  To contain you
  To cleanse you
  To save you
  To destroy you

She drifts.

It gets cold, then colder. Dark, then light.

Dark again.

Cage comes, reads, hits her, leaves.

Seamus watches her and cries. Roan tells him it's all right.

This is what she wants. Purity. Innocence.

He leaves. Lost.

Her jaw has stopped opening, she has clenched so hard that her teeth have grown together, intertwining like roots.

Sometimes she fancies she has wings on her back. Black wings—like a rook. Or a raven.

He comes with the water again, unsure, and once again she does not die. She feels as if she has, though.

Chapter 28
A HISS,
A SCREAM...

He's here again.

She has learned his scent, the sound of his footfalls, the way he stands so silent as if not breathing, only to take a deep breath and sigh. She has learned the way he considers her, perhaps wondering how such a young, pretty girl could be the witch he knows she is.

But today is different, because he doesn't stand long. Instead, he sits in the blue chair in the corner.

Something catches at her senses, like an alluring scent, and her head snaps in his direction. Though blindfolded, she knows that something is different...and wrong. Very, very wrong.

"What is that?" she croaks.

He does not answer right away, and she leans forward as though she might sniff out the thing.

"Nothing but a book, my dear," he says at last.

The sound of the cover opening drifts across the room and she jerks back, for the scent—or, the *feeling*—is so strong.

"*Close it*," she whispers, the familiar tingle of desire—hopeless desire—and need rising within her core. "Close it!"

Instead, he turns another leaf, and the paper sounds old and thick.

She can hear everything with the clarity of crystal now.

Cage licks his lips.

His fingers tremble on the page.

He takes a breath.

And begins to read. The language is guttural, belly deep and harsh as a dryad's cry.

"'*Ta Gerott limba, verogk...*'" he murmurs, clumsy with words that should be used with such care—or not at all. *In Divine darkness, begin.* Roan shuts her eyes beneath the blindfold, but her ears are wide open. She struggles against her bonds, the string biting in.

"'*Arok sho glimbok.*'" *Open your mind.* "'*Arok shi...*'" *Reveal yourself.* She tries to scream in her mind, to drown out the words, but they are like fleas seeking warmth. Like rats, fleeing fire. They scratch and scratch at her skull, burrowing deeper and deeper until she can feel them intimately, beating to the rhythm of her heart.

On and on he reads, and she can *feel* the sweat gathering upon his brow, running down his face and neck.

When Roan's mouth opens, her voice is changed, utterly.

"*Foolish child,*" she says, the language fully formed and fluid in her mouth. "*How disgraceful your pronunciation.*"

"*And so,*" he says, in the same language—a language no mortal speaks without cost. "*The Devil's Tongue is natural upon your accursed lips.*"

"*And yet you speak it also.*" She laughs. "*Tempt a girl to evil using evil. How quaint your faith must seem to you. To bend it so.*"

She knows his face blazes scarlet with indignation and she laughs again.

Silence follows, and he closes the book. The moment he does so, she slumps against her bonds, breathing hard.

He looks down on her for a long, eerie moment, and then he is gone, storming from the room with purpose and drive. Roan shrinks into herself, terrified of what will happen when he returns.

The words form, and then choke themselves free. *"Please...don't."*

He is holding a branding iron in his hand, the symbol of the cross burning a brilliant red, smoking comfortably. It puts her in mind of the ram. The ram. Its—*his*—burning red eyes, the smoky breath fogging the night until she could no longer make out his form, only those eyes. Those red, knowing eyes.

The book is in the room somewhere. She can feel it, whispering—

Come to me...

...open my ivory pages...

...feel the flesh of my bonds...

...speak Me.

Cage advances.

"Don't..."

He smiles and she knows that nothing she says can, nor will, make him stop. This is no longer about saving her, or cleansing her.

He is *enjoying* it.

Cursed words upon his tongue have spread like poison to his veins.

He releases her bonds and drags her off the bed by her hair. She lands hard, and sharp pain cracks in her elbow and hip.

Where are her friends? How can they allow this?

She tries to scream; this has gone too far. But her voice has died, a mere croak of a thing. A frog. A bat, lost in the night.

"Emma...Rapley...Andrew..."

He is on her then, ripping the shift off her shoulder. She curls up to protect herself lest he expose her completely. She is almost too cold to move. Days of exposure have rendered her weak, hard as rock, fragile as a newborn sparrow.

And then

her skin screams,

it hissssssssses,

burns and

m

e

l

t

s

And she does have her voice after all, for the room is filled with it. No man has ever rent the air with such a cry, such pain, sorrow, and humiliation. Roan sees it all in one defining moment—her eyes blinded by white-hot agony, but her mind suddenly open, seeing far, far back, long, long ago.

...A sorrowful woman on a dark mountain, tied to a post atop a pile of wood. Her eyes fixed solidly and brightly upon another woman, held back by savage men who jeer and spit. A woman screaming, begging the men to stop, to hold, to have mercy. Two women, both restrained, one held by ropes, the other by hands. Men light the wood beneath the pyre; the sticks catch quickly—too quickly. Flames lick at her skirt, her skin, her hair.

And who screamed louder? Which woman?

A man hisses, "Witch woman!"

Something inside Roan, something that she secured away long ago with an iron lock crested in complex inhuman symbols—a lock she closed when she was but a child—now slides fully open.

The ropes that hold her feet begin to smoke—and then melt as she speaks the Cursèd words, throwing them back at the man who tempted her with the very same.

They are guttural, inhuman, spitting things. They plague the air with their signs and spines.

Her ebony hair hides her face, but could Cage see it, he would flee the room, soiled.

He would be too late.

Her body, doll-like, rises by inches, humming in the air like an earthquake. Cage stares as she rises, the pulsing air quivering through skin and muscle and bone until his very soul must quake.

Her joints crack as she unfolds, up, up, until her feet hang in the air, higher than his head. Her arms unfurl, spread wide, her fingers straining, curling in like claws as though she is still, *still*, trying to contain the Thing.

Her darkness.

Then her hands are quaking too, and the windows quake, and the walls quake; dust dislodges itself from fissures that run like veins through the stone, filling the room with fog.

Cage stumbles back, crashes into the chair, and drops the branding iron. It melts into the wood. The chair splinters beneath him and he is thrown to the floor amongst the debris. The entire room is lifting up around him: curtains, carpets, bottles, vials, and the Cursèd Book with it. All but him.

When she lifts her head, Roan can see his terror, can see herself reflected there.

She is the nexus of all things.

She is the heart of the volcano.

She screams, the world hums, Cage freezes, shakes, rises into the air.

"P-please—"

She laughs. She screams. She

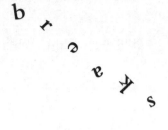

Cage is dead by the time he hits the floor.

Roan stares at his body for only a second before she grabs the book and throws herself out the window.

PART 5

Within the Mountain

Within the bowels of these elements,
Where we are tortured and remain forever.

— CHRISTOPHER MARLOWE,
DR. FAUSTUS

ZOEY

NOW

Chapter 29
MY WORKING

October 29

    I've decided to cast a spell to reveal the entity. Pole has been searching the house all day, and he just left to search the grounds and courtyard. He won't find anything, but he's too logical and practical to admit that there is something supernatural going on.

    I have lavender, dragon's-blood incense, some thyme, a sprig of lemongrass, and some cowslip. I can use the cowslip for the finding element of the spell, but I'm not sure what to use for potency. Lavender, I guess.

    All I can do is try.

Pole finished searching the house. He didn't find anything. He's pissed off with me now and doesn't want to talk. He's gone up to that room with the skulls in it. Suits me. I can't work a spell with him around. Let him be angry.

Suits me fine.

It's done. I've done it.

Now, I wait.

⌒

Zoey Camera Footage
Date: October 29

The girl is standing in the doorway for a full minute before Zoey notices. Her hair, a brilliant copper, hangs loose and long, down to her hips, and though her face is beautiful, her expression is terrible.

When Zoey finally sees her, she screams.

Roan's letters, which Zoey has been photographing, slip off her lap and pour all over the floor like spilled milk.

"Holy shit!"

The girl stares, steely eyes unnervingly strange.

Zoey steps closer, eyes narrowing. "Are you...a ghost?"

The girl frowns. "Fuck, no."

Zoey's arms, which had been raised in surprise, fall to her sides. "Oh." She shakes her head. "Who are you? What are you doing here?"

"I was compelled to come," the girl says with a scowl, "by your Conjure."

It's Zoey's turn to stare. "By my..." Her sentence falls

away as her eyes drop to the chain around Copper Girl's neck.

"That's my heirloom ring. You're the one who's been stealing from us!"

The girl steps into the room and closes the door, shushing Zoey. "All right, calm down."

Zoey holds out her hand. "Give it back."

The girl hesitates for only a moment, and then removes the chain and hands it over. Zoey clutches it to her lips.

The girl turns to go, but Zoey catches her arm. "Hey, no you don't, you little klepto! Why the hell did you take this? And how did you know about Conjuring?"

"Klepto?"

"Thief? Burglar? *Crook?*"

"Oh. Well. Yes."

Zoey shakes her head. "Who *are* you?"

"Can you let go of me, please? I really don't want to hurt you."

Zoey snorts. "You. *You* don't want to hurt *me*? Dude, I took karate lessons. Tell me who the hell you are!"

The girl wrenches her arm from Zoey's grip. "Calm down, Zoey."

Zoey steps back, her finger raised. "How the hell do you know who I am? What is this?"

"I stole your notebook."

Zoey's eyes narrow. "And you *read* it."

"I had to know who you were and why you were here. This place only attracts the worst kind of humanity."

"That's it, I'm calling the police." Zoey strides past her, but the girl jumps in front of the door holding out her hands.

"Wait a second—I'm"—she swallows—"I'm sorry. Please just...sit down. I'll explain myself."

Zoey looks her up and down, and folds her arms, but remains standing.

"My name is Len. I come here a lot." She looks around at the dark green walls. "My own private obsession."

Zoey unfolds her arms. "Me too."

Len smiles. "I noticed. I just wanted to see what you were like. I...I wanted you to leave."

"The note in the fireplace ash. It was you."

"Yes. I thought you'd be scared off. But you weren't. You're different from the kids that find their way up here now and then."

Len turns into the room with a sort of sigh, and then her eyes travel down to the letters on the floor.

"W-what are those?"

Zoey hurries over and crouches down, attempting to gather the sheets into a pile. "Shit. I can't believe I just dropped them. They're really old."

Len goes very still. *What are they?*

"Just letters."

Her eyes stray over to the wardrobe. "Where did you find them?" Her voice is soft.

Zoey nods to the closet. "In there."

"In a box?"

Zoey stands, the letters piled up in her hands. "You know about them?"

"I found them ages ago. But the pages—they're blank." Len turns to look at her, almost desperate. "They're blank."

"No. Look."

Len bares her teeth and growls, "You're lying."

Zoey holds one up. "See?"

Len looks away and holds up her hand as though shielding herself from sunlight. Zoey reads it out, instead.

"'Father, I'm lost in this place. Dr. Maudley is a stranger. Why could you not tell me of him or of his other wards...' It goes on like that mostly. There are dozens and dozens of them."

Len slides down the closed door until she is sitting, head bowed. Zoey waits, her eyes roaming over Len's form, waiting. Several times, she opens her mouth to say something, but then closes it again.

"How is it," Len says softly, "that you can read them, and I can't?"

"Maybe because you refuse to look at them?"

Len shakes her head. "I found them...They were just blank pages. All I see are blank pages."

"Well, I'm not lying," Zoey says, placing the letters back into their box.

"I know."

Zoey pauses. "How long have you been here? How long have you been watching me and Pole?"

"It doesn't matter."

"Poulton was right..." Zoey says suddenly. "There was no ghost. Only you. I accused him of stealing from me... Shit. He was right all along. There are no ghosts here. Only you."

"There are ghosts here," Len says through her hands, which are now over her face.

"No, there aren't. There's only you. You, who steal my things, you who caused the worst argument I've had with my best friend, and you, who left that stupid fucking note in the ashes!"

Len is on her feet in an impossibly fluid movement. "I'm telling you, there are ghosts here. I've seen them."

271

"I'm taking you to Poulton so he can see that he was right all along."

"Listen," Len says, holding up her hands as though she wants a truce. "I'm sorry if I scared you, but I was only trying to get you to leave."

"Yeah," Zoey says wryly. "'Get out. While you still can.' Very original."

"I wanted to protect you."

"Forgive my skepticism," Zoey snaps. "Move."

"Let me just explain."

"Fine," Zoey says. "But I'm taking notes."

October 30

Len came here looking for signs of the Roan girl. That's what she said initially, before she said she was looking for "evidence" of Roan. Signs, as in, signs she had been here. Apparently Len knows all about Mill House, more than I do, even, but she won't tell me any of it until we agree to leave. Except, she said that when she tried to leave, she found she couldn't. She also wouldn't explain what she meant by that. Sounds kind of mental.

She doesn't know why I can read the letters when she can't, and it turns out that Poulton can't either. So, yay for me. Either I'm crazy and making up the letters in my delusional brain (Mum would totally agree) or there's some cosmic reason that only I can read them. And maybe Dad could too.

And get this. Not only does she know that I can

Work/Conjure/Cast—whatever. Turns out I've been doing it wrong the whole time. Dad too. Apparently we don't need any of the herbs, candles—none of that crap.

It's just something in my blood. Like, literally something I was born with.

She calls it Unclosed. It sounds so...insane, but...it also makes so much sense. She said that the Unclosed are people born with access to death. She said that people are born with a doorway inside them. That for most people the doorway only opens twice (at birth and at death), but that for people like me—and like her—after we're born the door stays slightly open—Unclosed. Mediums, psychics, ghost experts...the <u>real</u> ones are Unclosed. Gifted.

Well. She didn't exactly say <u>gifted</u>. She said <u>cursed</u>, but she's more of a glass-half-empty kind of person.

Anyway, she said she's come across Unclosed people before, but never one as strong as me. Usually the person just has a sixth sense or strong intuition. Sometimes it's a person who can sense a presence or know it's going to rain before it does. But with me... it's much stronger.

I told her about Dad. I told her about how he could do it too...until he lost it all. How it must have been a huge Conjure for him to lose himself so fully.

She had no idea what I was talking about. The price we pay...She says it doesn't work like that. She said there's no price. It's like our eyesight or our taste buds. Part of us. She thinks that it must have been something else—something biological, like Alzheimer's. But she doesn't know. She hasn't seen.

But that's not the hardest part. Because now I have to take her to meet Poulton. And I doubt he'll be as forgiving as me.

~~

October 30

We talked for a couple of hours until she got sleepy. I said she could go back to wherever she sleeps, but she said she'd rather stay with me so I didn't get into trouble with "that guy."

I let her have my sleeping bag. She's asleep in there right now, but I'm too wired. I have to get down everything she said. It's like this whole other world exists that I should be a part of, and I never even knew.

I want to learn as much as I can, but I don't know how much to believe. And yet...she said so many things that make sense.

That the "original" Unclosed lived hundreds of years ago, but that I am the descendant of someone who was once an Original. We all come from one place. She wouldn't say more there. But she did say that each Unclosed person has a particular Conjure. There are six of them, and each has a symbol associated with it. (She gave me the names but I forgot them. NOTE: GET THE NAMES OF ALL THE CONJURES FOR MY NOTEBOOK AND BEGIN STUDYING WHAT IS KNOWN.)

Also, the ~~symbols~~—she called them <u>sigils</u>, or Conjures—are all important, but she warned me that they're dangerous and shouldn't be read aloud (are these symbols, these...Conjures...some kind of alphabet, then?). She was hesitant to show them to me but said maybe she would in the future. (She said she would never teach me to speak them. NOTE: FIND OUT WHY SPEAKING THE SIGILS IS DANGEROUS.)

Another thing: her mother was also Unclosed, but she's dead. She asked me to describe my Conjure. I've never really thought about it, and I didn't know what to say, so she told me to just tell her about some of the Workings I've done.

"They're all about finding something," she said. Then she looked at me.

She said I'm a Finder/Revealer. I find what's lost. I compel the hidden to be seen and come forward. <u>Of course</u>. She said she felt my Conjure like a pull, and that she can resist most spell work. She said I'm strong.

I'm good at something.

I'm a strong mothafuckin' witch.

I feel cooler than I ever have in my whole life.

And then she said something that made my stomach churn.

"Watch out for that guy."

"Who? Poulton?"

Her expression darkened. "Yeah."

I laughed. "Why?"

"He's started to feel it. The house."

My smile fell off in a hurry. "What do you mean?"

"This house. It affects them. Normal people, I mean. They don't know what they're feeling. With us, it makes our Conjures stronger. It tries to tempt us to use our power."

"Is that a bad thing?"

Her head snapped at me, her hair flying. "Yes! Don't you understand where this stuff comes from? I guess you wouldn't." She took a breath. "Being Unclosed is being cursed. We were...bred. In an evil, ritualistic way. With sigils inviting Lucifer to touch us, each and every one. Even though you're a descended Unclosed, your power comes from a dark place. I try not to use my Conjure unless I have no choice." She broke off, peering around. "But this house tempts me. It's always tempting me."

"I'm...evil?"

"By nature. But we have a choice. Each and every one of us."

I told her that I don't feel evil. Not at all.

She shrugged. "Maybe it's different for someone so far away from the Original. Or maybe it's because you don't speak—" She broke off and convulsed in the funniest way, as though she had just come close to the lip of a precipice and had held herself back at the last moment.

"Don't speak..." I prompted her.

She looked at me sideways and shook her head.

"Fine. But explain what you mean by Poulton being affected."

"Like I said. The house affects normal people. This whole mountain is infected by darkness. It's insidious. Like poison slowly seeping in. Nothing survives here. Not anymore."

"It compels us to use our Conjure..." And I realized

that she had handed me the answer. Dad. He came to this place and he Conjured. It was that simple. It _is_ that simple. My father is lost forever because he was drawn here and he couldn't help himself, and he paid the ultimate price.

And now I've gone and followed right in his footsteps.

"Watch it with him," Len said again. "With your friend. I'm not joking about this place. If it compels us to Conjure, it will do much worse to a normal person like him."

"Maybe Pole's Unclosed too and doesn't know it."

She shook her head. "You know he isn't."

"Well, I haven't noticed anything off. He's just angry with me about accusing him of taking my notebook."

She shrugged. "He's scratching."

That got my attention. She said it starts with scratching and irritability. I couldn't say anything then, because that's exactly what Dad does. He scratches, as though there is something in his skin he's desperate to claw out.

So I'm sitting here, writing down everything that's happened, hoping I can escape the one fact that eluded me and that now haunts me.

While I've been doing checks on myself every day, I forgot to notice what was happening to Poulton.

Here he is, in my arms. My son. He is small, and blue, with strange little black eyes, and he is beautiful. I have named him John, for his father. He is so small that I can comfortably write while rocking him. One little fist lies upon my finger, tiny and blue. I sing him lullabies.

I have rebuked both John and Nebula, and told them to stay away. I need no cleaning! I need no assistance! I am with my son, and that is all that matters. He is no bigger than the side of my hand and is of such a vivid red when he came out that I almost mistook him for the son of Satan before my eyes cleared.

I am a mother. I am mother.

FROM THE DIARY OF
HERMIONE SMITH,
30 JANUARY 1584

ROAN

1851

Chapter 30
AN OFFER

She should be dead.

Instead, she's moving.

Or...the ground is moving.

Above, the sky churns like an upset belly, clouds fighting one another in endless, unceasing layers of gloom. There is no sense of day, or time, or hour. She simply is.

The movement continues, steady paced, bumpy, and she almost falls, yet doesn't. Why should the ground move so?

Time passes, she supposes, and eventually the movement beneath her back stops, but the clouds above continue their petty argument. Warm turns to cold with a slide and a *thud*, and she knows suddenly that she is lying on the mountain. She can feel its cool awareness beneath her like a corpse.

Her future looms in gloom.

Time has ceased to have meaning.

Her mind spins and whirls and the thoughts are chaotic and frag-
mented. She sees a shape move away from her, but not too far. It stops
and stands, watching. Waiting.

She recognizes his proud horns.

She can see, through the fog, a glimmer of sharp red, and she rolls over
to vomit. His smell is more toxic, more noxious than the slums of London.

Get away, she wants to say.

But he stands unmoving.

She begins to shiver even though the heat pulses through her skin.
Everything hurts, everything is sharp and intense—like fire ants crawling and biting from toe to chin. Fleas scamper over her lungs, worms
writhe in her brain.

And then, his voice.

Daughter, mine.

She turns to look at the ram, and one word forms.

"No."

*Abandoned, abused, admonished. Would I treat such
a jewel so poorly? I should burn them in their sleep.*

She is tempted to say it, one little word. *Yes.* Instead, she closes her
eyes and begins to pray.

Kill me. Let me die.

Suddenly the ram is at her face, lips pulled back on long yellow teeth,
blazing red eyes with their inhuman pupils not two inches from her face.

I will never let you go. You are mine.

She screams.

And screams.

Yet the mountain remains, insistently silent.

"Roan—"

Go away.

"Roan."

No...She wishes to be left alone. To sink into the mire beneath her, to feel the cool turn to cold and then to nothing as she decays. But the voice calls her name again, urgently, and there is pain on her cheek. Someone is shaking her. Or perhaps the mountain is shaking her.

Time passes. Darkness becomes light becomes darkness again.

At some point, Roan becomes aware that she no longer feels the damp air on her face and that a warm glowing light is nearby. Warm... so warm. And hot. Too hot.

She struggles against some kind of confine—a blanket, maybe? Groans when fluid seeps over her lips.

"You must drink this," says a voice.

"Rapley?" she murmurs, and the liquid slips in. She swallows, gags on the bitterness of it.

"Drink, fey girl. Drink."

She opens her mouth and obeys before the darkness swallows her once more.

The book is rough in her hands, paper crinkled like old skin, heavy as stone. She steels herself before she lifts the cover, straining with the effort. She turns the next page, and the next, and keeps turning, not allowing herself to read the words that were forbidden long ago by the one who taught her.

I forbid it!

—But Father—

Never again! Do you hear me?

Never again will these Cursèd

words be read or spoken in this

dwelling. By God, heed you not?

—Why then teach me at all?—

Heed my words, child, or be

it on your head. And mine.

We tamper with much worse

than fire. Speak no more.

Less than a fortnight hence, he was dead.

Something compels her to keep turning, as though searching for a favorite page or passage. At last she finds it.

Not ten pages in, Cage has left scrawled notes in the margin beside a text written in Latin. In places the writing is tidy, controlled, neat. In others, however, the writing is chaotic, scrawled across the text heedless of what it obscures.

DISTINCT CONJURES.

I soother? Attraction, giver, weakest, last Conjure. Dispensable?

SICKNESS WITH USE—DANGER.

Fever.

Seizures.   MANIFESTATION

Confusion.   UNCLEAR.

Proliferation snakes, scorpions, spiders, bats.

She reads it three times, but her brain is full of cottonweed and thoughts run vaguely into the wind of her mind. One phrase sticks, though: *Sickness with use.*

Seamus and his snakes. Her snakes. The spiders, the scorpions, the bats...Had Seamus made himself sick somehow? But use—use of what? She squints and reads the scrawl again. *Distinct Conjures.* As in, magic. As in, what she was doing...what she and her father had always been doing simply referred to as "Conjuring."

Seamus was making himself sick by using—what? His gift with snakes? His—his...Conjure.

She finds another note and leans close to read it.

Seamus. Emma? Roan. Rapley? Dr. Maudley?
Which Conjures? If any?

She thinks back to every conversation she and Seamus ever had. Conversations about his snakes—the way they came to him when he wanted them. Sometimes when he needed them most. How they kept coming, more and more snakes, as he grew weaker. And when he lost consciousness, they had left without warning. Had his call been cut off?

She remembers how they had been a kind of barrier to his body, letting only her near. Yet why her? Why did they not let Emma near, though she loved her brother best of all?

Whatever meaning there was, one thing is confirmed: Seamus *was* Conjuring. He was like her, as she had sensed from the beginning. And he *had* been Conjuring the night of his first seizure.

And Cage had been watching them the whole time. But then why not give Roan lessons too? Why not keep her close? Nothing makes sense.

A persistent thought racks her: Perhaps the things that slithered, crawled, and skittered had been placing their trust in her. Trusting her to look after Seamus, as they could not do. If so, she had failed them. Seamus had been taken in the night by…*something.*

The ram. It was the ram.

She had seen it. Ram-*like.*

Even now, sitting in the dark, knowing that something is wrong with the house—with the whole mountain—she cannot abide it. Is it not more likely that she, the girl who had been taught to Conjure, is the reason such tragedy has befallen her new friends? Is it not more likely that Cage, a man of God, had simply sensed the evil within her? For would not a man of God, working against evil, appear evil to the girl he worked against?

"That was real," she whispers to herself. "Seamus is gone. He was taken. It was *real*. I saw it."

She knows he is there before she turns.

The ram stands eerily still in the raging winds. She can see his nostrils flaring as he scents her on the air. He is waiting. The beast is patient, as God knows well.

She stumbles from their shelter, leaving Rapley exhausted and asleep on the pile of furs and blankets, and moves forward as one swimming toward the shore.

She is exhausted, drained, empty—and he knows it. This trial will be hers alone. Even now, the fever, which had burned her skin for near on a week, begins to fade in the cruel winds, which lift her hair from her neck and wash her clean.

Come, daughter, she hears him say. *Come.*

She is ten paces away, can smell his hide; when he turns away, she sees his horns curled and proud and magnificent.

"*Wait,*" she calls, but it is not even a whisper. She stumbles, and carries on.

The ram walks steadily upward, heading for the concealed darkness of the caves at the summit of this Cursèd mountain. At the edge of the blackness, he turns back to look down on her, judging, disapproving.

"I am not weak!" she calls, her voice carried away on the wind. "*I am not weak!*" Spittle flies from her chapped lips, landing cold and sticky on her chin.

The beast stares for one moment and then is gone, disappearing into the dark spaces as if he had never been.

A blanket comes around her shoulders. "*What are you doing?*"

Rapley's voice, hot in her ear.

"Do you *want* to die?"

"*Yes*," she spits. "Yes, I want to *die*."

His lips thin, he gathers the blanket around her roughly, yanking her as he wraps her like a package for the postmaster.

"I will never let that happen," he says, his voice low as he trusses her up. Once he is finished, he pulls her closer by her shoulders, his teeth bared. *"Never."*

She stares at him, black eyes meeting gray in a searing battle. Then she spits in his face.

He yanks her up over his shoulder and lugs her back to the shelter before unceremoniously dumping her beside the embers of the rapidly cooling fire.

"You're a fool," she says, her mouth contorted into an ugly scowl. "You're an oaf and a *fool!*"

He ignores her and builds the fire up again, strong and steady against the wind.

Roan's body gives out after a few moments and she collapses back onto the furs where his body has just lain. She tries not to think about that, but finds that it is *all* she can think about.

His face, in slumber, had been softer. Lax with exhaustion, and free of the harsh tension that angles his jaw and digs a line deep into the space between his thick brows.

"You disgust me," she says, when she means to say, *You're beautiful.*

"Good," he mutters. "You'll stay to tell me so, then."

She laughs, bitter and harsh like the winds beyond the slate. "Never. I shall leave this mountain. I shall leave this island. I shall leave this life and I shall leave *you!*"

She is satisfied when his hand clenches into a fist and she sees his jaw work beneath the skin.

"Oh, yes, *fool.* I shall leave you behind."

And she allows herself to relax. If he would force her back to health, she will be damned if she lets him do it with any ease. Damn him! Damn his will to save her. Damn him all the way to hell!

Later, when the fire had once again cooled to glowing embers and Rapley was somewhere out on the mountain, Roan tries to wriggle herself
free of the blanket and Rapley's damned knots. He had done well, but
the blanket is soft and supple, and after much effort and biting with her
teeth, she gets an arm free. From there, the rest is simple.

She pushes the blanket aside and hunches on her haunches, searching
the night beyond the opening of the shelter for signs of movement. For signs
of the ram. Her eyes are wolfish, her sight good—she has always known
this. Nothing stirs but the heavy mists as she pushes off the ground with
all her might and races through the opening and into the night like a wolf.

She has a moment's delirious freedom before she hits a barrier and
flies backward, landing hard on her back. It knocks the wind out of
her, paralyzes her, and she can only lie there staring at the sky, mouth
wide, willing the air to come. And then his face appears above her, one
eyebrow raised.

"Really?"

She wheezes in a garbled breath and manages to roll to her side.
"Pigeon-livered, gibfaced *fool!*" she manages.

He kneels beside her. "I am not above dueling with a girl. If you
wish to insult me, then accept the consequences."

She leans closer. "Gib. Faced. *Fool.*"

He looks down his nose at her. "You're a child."

The last of Roan's fever blows away with the storms and she regains her
appetite. She eats to spite Rapley, knowing that without her strength,
she will never get close enough to stab him in the neck. But really, she
eats because her hunger is profound, and though she wants to die, her
un-willed instinct for self-preservation is fierce. It sickens her.

Daily, she watches him, observing how he moves, what he eats, where he goes. She sits in the shadows of the shelter each morning before the sun rises and watches him practice with his knives and his small axes. He is precise and strong, but she would be quick, and that is all she needs. He aims high and is a fair bit taller than her. Maybe she would be able to undercut and get him in the armpit. Cut down, deep down, to his heart.

When he finishes practicing, he always goes hunting or to check his traps, whatever it is he does to bring them the rabbits and small game he has been keeping them alive on. When he is gone, she climbs from the shadows, stretches, and watches for the ram.

Where did you go?

There is no reply.

I am not weak, she thinks again. And she runs over the mountain, back and forth, strengthening her muscles, regaining what has been lost, prepping her lungs for the task ahead.

Before he returns around sunset, Roan climbs back into the shadows, stacks the fire, and reads the Unbound Book. She has discovered a clasp at the opening of the tome with a small hole for a lock. Since it is unlocked, it is unbound, and so she calls it thus.

The more she reads, the less she wants to live. The book itself drains her energy, something she realizes on the fourth day of reading it. It is as though the book itself were breathing something out of her. As though reading these cursed pages demands a price. She ought to stop altogether, but finds she cannot. In all her years of asking, or wondering, and of blindly training with her father in dark arts and alchemy, she has never once been given answers.

Yet here is a book. A living, diseased book that seems to know all about her. She bends low and studies it until she can no longer stand it, and then she closes it, burying it beneath the furs, and collapses into fitful sleep until Rapley wakes her with some new thing to eat.

Tonight, though…she feels her need for answers outweighing her fatigue. She bends closer, squinting to follow the small, peculiar writing.

The Unclosed Conjures, she reads, *number six. Six unhallowed, unholy gifts for his children, those cursed in this life and the next. Poor, damned souls. Conjure, Rapture, Soother, Corder, Sighter. And the sixth, one that binds them all: Breaker—the most cursed amongst those Unclosed few.*

She looks away and shuts her eyes. Seamus is a Soother. She knows it now. The way he had called the serpents and calmed them so. How scorpions slumbered on his arms and never once stung—how spiders nested in his hair, contented as little kittens.

And she is now certain Emma is Unclosed as well. Her vague unease in the house and the way Roan had seen her hide inside the wardrobe on one occasion—and how she often flinched when nothing was there. She had thought the behavior odd and superstitious, but now she has to wonder. What had Emma seen—or sensed? Being Unclosed is the only connection she can find among them all, and it fills her with dread.

Connected by cursed Conjures. Children of devils, indeed.

Had this been the reason they were chosen? Had Dr. Maudley known? How? Why then had he vanished like those mill workers in the tale? Why then had Seamus been snatched away?

Who is the grand orchestrator?

She closes the book, trying to unsee the sigils and symbols that had accompanied the six Conjures—tries not to think about what her Conjure might be—but they seem to be burned into her memory. Indeed, she sees echoes of them hovering before her as though branded in the air the same way she had been branded.

Crawling forward, she pokes her head around the slate and up toward the caves, now nothing but darkness above. If the ram is there, she cannot see him, but she feels that she is beginning to understand what he was waiting for.

Chapter 31

ADAM

With her returning strength comes a desire to provoke the man who had rescued her. He'd had no right, and she couldn't help sniping at him until one day he withdraws a long knife. She anticipated that he might try to scare her. He had been using his knives to cut up roots and butcher the rats he caught in his snares for their meals, and she had stolen one two days ago, anticipating this very moment.

She does not wait for him to attack. Instead she strikes out with her knife, as if to stab him in the chest. He is fast—faster than she expected—and dances out of the way, smacking her knife with his own as he would slap the hand of a naughty child caught stealing. Gritting her teeth, she circles him, then attacks again, faster this time.

Again, he dances away and slaps her knife down.

"Fight!" she yells. "Damned coward."

He laughs. *Laughs.*

She circles, then changes direction and attacks again, this time keeping her knife low and going for the only part a man considers valuable. He dances away again, but she anticipates it and sticks up in a skyward jab, but he moves away again, spinning and tapping her knife twice.

"Fight me!"

He seems to still, but doesn't, and his eyes focus. Then he is at her, spinning his blade around and behind her so fast she can't keep up. She feels her anger rise—he is playing with her! She is nothing but a toy. She moves as fast as she can with the knife, but he is always there to counter her. In one move that sends her over the edge of her restrained anger, he spins away from her and taps her on the bottom with the knife as he passes by.

She feels it happening in the same way she did before, with Cage. The power unclenching in her body like a fist opening, like those ropes melting away. She feels the energy rising and knows that she will lift from the ground as before and that, in that moment, she will lose control.

And as she realizes it, she no longer wants it.

Oh no...Rapley, no!

But it is too late.

She manages to drop the knife and push away, but the power is strong and all consuming. It devours thought, empathy, reasoning, and all emotion except rage. One word pulses in her mind before she loses control completely: *Breaker. Breaker. Breaker.* The worst of the six and also the culmination and combination of the six.

As her heels begin to rise from the ground and her arms begin to open and strain against the power, Rapley rushes forward, his eyes full of something unspoken. He grips her arms, and then—she can't say what happens first. His arms come around her, his eyes blaze, his lips are on hers, and then—the power flees, engulfed and drowned by something much more powerful.

Their kiss is wild and desperate, something that Roan had been long-ing for without knowing it. Something she *needed*, but had denied herself. And Rapley...He kisses her like someone insane, desperately, uncontrol-lably insane. Then he breaks the kiss and holds her to his chest fiercely, trembling, his hands tangled in her hair. Roan can feel his heart pounding behind the muscles of his chest, and her own is no slower.

But then something else happens.

It is no more than a moment. No more than part of a second, and yet it lasts hours. Rapley pushes her away, makes as if to turn, and then stumbles as though about to collapse. She sees him falling, as if time has slowed almost to a halt, and then, to the side of her, he appears, faint as a rippled reflection on water, as indistinct as mist, but quite definitely *him*, touches her hand—it is cold and shocking and...disarming—before vanishing into the air.

By the time he hits the ground, Rapley is back, awake, and staring at her where she has also fallen, now crouched on the ground.

She looks at him, and she sees. She really, truly *sees*.

The name rushes out of her on a breath. *"Adam..."*

And then she flings herself at him, into his arms, clinging so tight she thinks she will lose feeling in her limbs before she ever lets go.

Rapley has gone rigid, no longer burning with passion as he had a moment before, but cold as ice.

"How do you know that name?"

She chokes on her laughter and tears. It is him! It is! Adam. Her Adam. Oh, God, could it be? After all these years?

Dear God...Adam is alive and has been with her all this time.

She begins to sob, the first tears she has shed since the moment he was taken. "Adam," she sobs, clinging tighter, even as he grows yet more rigid.

He pushes her roughly away.

"Who are you?" he demands, his eyes wide and wild.

"Oh, Adam! Don't you recognize your old friend?" Roan cries, tears and dirt and his kiss all over her face all at once.

He blinks, and his shoulders begin to drop. And then she is holding him again, sobbing his name, *"Adam, oh, Adam…"*

And slowly his arms come around her and he shuts his eyes and tries to squeeze the years back into himself, to find that person Adam, who he lost so long ago.

But she is here…his Eve, his Roan Eve is here…and it is all coming back.

It takes a long time for sense to return. Roan cries herself into exhaustion on top of him, and he has to roll out from underneath her. She lies weakened and small amongst the heather in the clearing, where he intended to teach her a lesson earlier—the spoiled brat he knew her to be. And yet, she is that other…that girl he had so loved and been so cruelly torn from. His first and only friend. His Eve.

How could he not have seen?

But she is different now. So angry. So hateful. So dangerous. It is a startling contrast to the beautiful child he had loved so dearly. The child who had helped him discover his magic. The magic that now curses him so. Maybe it is the same for her.

Still…he is different too. And he doesn't want her to see that. Doesn't want her to see the thing he has decayed into. She is his dark mirror, always has been, and he fears her gaze.

He should have known. Fool, indeed.

From the moment he saw her on the mountain—here—he knew something about her was different. Her eyes have no walls. He has seen inside her and he should have known.

No. No, he will not allow her to see him thus.

He takes the knife from the ground where he dropped it, but leaves the other for her. She has won it from him.

Then he leaves, not once looking back.

He is gone when she wakes, and the terror in her gut rents a choke from her.

"No," she whispers. "No! Adam! *Adam!*" She gets to her feet in a daze. It is past dawn, and he is nowhere to be seen. She aches all over, can feel her own heartbeat in her lips, and her head throbs like it has before with the oncoming fever.

"No, please. Adam…"

She looks around but knows it is useless. He is gone. She may have known him as her dearest friend and gift, Adam, but he is Rapley now. Rapley, who vanishes into the shadows of the mountain at a moment's notice, as if he never were.

She sits down on the ground again and stares around her with a profound sense of loss. She wraps her arms around her legs and waits, with no sense of hope but with the memory of a little boy who always came when she needed him.

He does return. It is dark. She has lit small fires all the way along the ridge, lighting the way home. She is half-asleep under the furs, watching the flames dance as they warm the little space she had once so feared, but which they had made a kind of home.

She hears his footsteps; she is learning his sounds. He crouches by the opening, hands resting on his thighs, staring at the ground rather than at her.

"A man," he says, his voice so low she has to strain to hear. "A man in black brought me here when I was a child. Eight. Nine, maybe. It was a long journey, and he never once lifted his hood. I was left on the doorstep by the kitchen and taken inside by Mrs. Goode. I was inconsolable. He had torn me away from a warm place, a place where I felt whole and loved. A place where I had the truest of friends who knew my very self before I knew it myself. He ripped me away and left me"—he gestures blindly—"here." She lets him talk.

"I saw no one for three years, excepting Mrs. Goode and her staff. Then Andrew was hired, and a tutor, Mr. Firth, and, one day, Dr. Maudley came home. He explained the situation. For years I had waited to find out what was happening. By then I had come to know the mountain and its tricks intimately and was no longer the boy he had stolen away.

"So you see...I am not just a selfish brute of a son, a cretin who disrespects his adoptive father. I am a captive with no power or means to flee. Since...where could I find that warm, safe place again? Where could I find her?"

She budges over and opens the fur to invite him in.

Like a boy long neglected, he crawls inside and lies with his back against her, smaller than she had ever seen him, this man who is also a boy, and her dearest friend.

She closes the fur around him and her arm with it. He begins to shiver, and she rubs his arm, his back, kisses his beautiful neck.

How could she ever have called him those awful things? She hates herself.

And he weeps. She knows it is the boy, deep inside, who had been locked away, grieving for all the years lost, abandoned, alone, and hurting. And she will see him through the storm of tonight, and all the nights to come.

She isn't sure when the caressing becomes something more, what time of night it is when his lips find hers. She loses all senses completely when his lips part and his body relaxes beside hers and then grows firm.

All she knows is that she needs him; she needs him as she always has, and his hands are golden warmth on her skin and she doesn't want him to stop.

She gasps as he kisses and touches hidden places, and again when his naked torso presses against her breasts. And when he enters her, pain and terror and beauty all at once, she cries out and clings to him harder. He tries to stop, to pull away, but she makes a sound of protest and holds him like her life depends on it. He moves with her and in her, and she feels a burning she has never felt give way to a rising warmth that chokes her with its power.

His breathing intensifies, and he stares down at her with an expression of shock and wonder and she smiles. He makes a sound and leans into her, moving faster, until the thing inside her builds and builds like a wave waiting to fall, until all at once it crashes upon the shore of her body, and she cries out again. He moves for a little longer, and then he too stiffens, jerks, holds her closer, and then lies shivering on top of her.

She hugs his head, his sweaty hair, and she kisses it.

"Adam," she breathes. "Where have you been?"

"He came for me. Came back for me." Rapley's eyes are expressionless as he looks up at the slate above them.

Roan rolls onto her side and rests her head on her palm. "The man in black. I remember he took you."

Rapley nods stiffly. "Yes. He brought me here."

Something hits her low down inside, like a cold stone dropping dully into a despondent pond.

"Maudley was the man in black?"

"I don't know. He never showed his face. All I know is that the man in the black cloak brought me here. And here I've been, ever since."

Roan sits up and stares down at him. "I cannot fathom that you have been here for ten years. Here? On the mountain? In this…place?"

He looks at her then. "Yes."

She closes her eyes. "My God, Rapley."

He flinches; she feels it. She touches his cheek. "Adam."

"No, you're right. I'm Rapley now."

"Who gave you that name?"

"I gave it to myself. Adam was gone."

She leans down and kisses him full on the lips. "Not gone, just lost."

He responds to her touch with one of his own. "Eve."

Her smile lights up the space they share, and his heart aches with longing. So does his body.

She feels it and her eyebrows quirk up. "Again?"

He reaches for her, drawing her close over him. He presses his face between her breasts. "I could never get enough of you." She barely hears his words, muffled as they are by her flesh, and she laughs as he runs a cheeky tongue over her skin there.

And soon they are moving together again, joined in passion, in love, in long years separated.

Who knows what might have been had he remained with them. Perhaps her father would not have grown so odd and fearful. Perhaps he would never have begun her schooling in symbols, sigils, and dark practices. Perhaps her mother would still be alive.

They might have been betrothed, married already, perhaps. What might he have been? A lawyer? A teacher? Banker? Doctor?

She cannot imagine him as any of those things, can only see him as he is now, here, her wild, untamed man with his knives and his axes, challenging women to duels and brooding in the night.

Brood no longer, she thinks. *I shall light your days. Damned I might be, but you are not. And I shall live for you.*

Chapter 32

A MEMORY
IN BLUE

When it is done, they rise together and wash in the morning
dew. Rapley marvels at her naked form, marvels at what they had
done—what he couldn't have imagined doing before. He marvels at
the change in her, how he had missed the signs of her suffering. He
marvels, too, that on some level, he had loved her. His unwillingness
to let her die. His steadfast vigil night after night since she arrived at
Mill House.

She calls to him.

His soul answers.

"You need to tell me what's going on," Rapley says later as they
stand in the moonlight. "You need to tell me what happened."

Once again, the mists have given them reprieve, as though sensing the importance of the moment. Roan does not want to taint it,
hates that he even uttered words belonging to that world of before—
before they found each other again. But she knows that she cannot
linger in this perfect limbo forever. The ram will be waiting, it will
return. And she owes Seamus more than that. Emma, even, despite
what she has done.

And she has a crime to face. A murder to claim.

She takes his hands, knowing it might be the last time he offers them so freely.

"I will tell you, but you will hate me."

He squeezes her hands tight. "Never. Impossible."

"Let me tell it straight, then. I killed. I killed...Cage."

His jaw clenches at the mention of the name. "He branded you."

"Does that deserve death?"

His eyes blaze. *"Yes."*

Despite herself, she is relieved. "Still...there's more. I need to show you something."

She leads him to the foot of the shelter and crawls in to get the book. She sits beside him and the fire, and reads to him in the morning light.

When she is done, he whispers, "Unclosed...is that what it's called?"

And despite the fact that she has suspected, or known all along, his words turn her deathly cold.

"No. No, *you* are not Unclosed," Roan says. "You're perfect. Pure. Good."

He shakes his head. "No. No, I'm not, Eve. And you know it. You've known it since back then, the night it happened."

She frowns. "What are you talking about?"

He looks away. "You don't remember? My God, no wonder you held me to you so close." He holds his head between two fists. "I'm a monster."

"Stop it," she says sharply. "You're alarming me. Tell it straight, Rapley."

He looks at her. "The night your mother...the night she...jumped."

Everything goes still. "I...I was alone. My mother saw me lose control, like I almost did tonight, like I did with Cage—she saw, she saw my evil, and she—she couldn't handle it—she—she—I was alone! I was alone, Rapley."

He shakes his head. "No. We were together. We were Conjuring *together.*"

And like a burst of fire in the sky, she remembers the night in all its painful detail.

It was easy. The magic came now without the faintest glimmer of thought. The long summer days they had spent in the flower garden, hidden amongst the trees, coaxing the magic from their fingers and minds, had reaped glorious results. It had been like learning to walk—they did it now without thinking.

Eve was always faster than Adam, and he was continually delighted by her tricks and performances. She was patient with his attempts and soothing when it proved impossible for him to mimic some of the games.

Still, he had skills of his own.

They were hiding in Father's library, waiting for the moment of quiet when they could steal a book from the wide bookcase. Adam was playing his tricks, appearing in one corner of the room before disappearing and reappearing in another. The game was simple: Eve had to predict where he might pop up next.

Their father was away at a meeting in the center of town; it was safe to be less careful. Eve, in a rare show of her skill, and a desire to win the game, let all the barriers fall.

She felt her hands tingle first, and then her eyes. She felt herself rising up into the air, and—for lack of a better word—"sniffing" Adam out.

She found him hovering above her, his back to the ceiling, looking down.

"Got you," she said, grinning, but then she stopped.

Her voice was all wrong.

Adam was looking at her funny—

Her arms were getting warmer, getting harder to hold down.

Her eyes were burning like fire, but she couldn't rub them.

She didn't like this game anymore.

She wanted to stop.

The magic built and built, consuming her, until one moment hit her like falling into a frozen lake.

Her mother walked in the door and stopped dead, her mouth opening into a slow, terrible grimace. Her whole body shrank into itself as she stared up at her daughter floating in the air—those hands, those eyes—

Eve saw something break inside her mother's eyes. She would spend years trying to explain it to herself—that knowledge that she had done irreparable damage.

Her mother shook her head, back and forth, slowly at first, then gaining speed and violence.

"No, no, no, no, no—"

She said it over and over, backing away, backing farther even when Eve collapsed onto the floor, a beautiful, normal little girl once more. Eve felt her heart thumping inside her. This was bad. Very, very bad. She hadn't meant for her mother to find out about the magic.

"Mama," she said, reaching for the shaking woman, but her mother jumped back, holding out her palms.

"Get back! Do not touch me!"

Eve began to cry. "Mama, I'm sorry!"

"Demon," her mother whispered. "Demon child!"

"Mama, no! It's just a game. See, Adam is playing too!" She gestured to Adam, who was getting to his feet behind her. He nodded earnestly, but the woman didn't seem to notice.

"Look," Adam said, hoping to explain. He closed his eyes and then, a moment later, was standing beside Eve's mother, who was ethereal and beautiful.

Her mother screamed, and would not stop screaming, and then she ran from the room, her shoes stomping on the hardwood floor. She ran to the top of the house, into the attic, where she had a small desk and chair and where she read her Bible each day.

Eve, sobbing, collapsed onto the floor, and Adam came to sit beside her.

"It's okay, Eve. She'll be fine. Maybe she was surprised, like I was when I first saw the magic."

Eve nodded, but could not be consoled. She yearned to take it all back. She *yearned to go up to her mother's room, beg forgiveness, and never do any of the magic ever again.*

She got to her feet, brushed her skirts down, and headed for the stairs.

What was it that made her turn to the flower garden? Had it been a sound? Or had she simply sensed it?

She had left her body behind without thought, appearing in the flower garden a moment before her mother hit the stone paving, her head exploding like a melon, her body unusually flat.

Adam was beside her, in astral form, and he took her hand.

Roan hands Rapley the book. "You can feel it, can't you? The wrongness of the book."

He nods. "It feels like poison. Something I should be wary of."

"It is. But you must read it. I've realized that it's not just about me, but about Seamus, and you—and maybe Emma, too."

"Roan…" He touches her face, eyes darting all over her. "Eve," he breathes, as if in disbelief. "Eve…" He leans forward and kisses her so gently she almost doesn't feel it.

She pulls back. "I want you to read it."

He looks down at it and hesitates.

He opens the clasp and opens the book, allowing it to fall flat at whatever page it likes. As if the book has wants and desires. It is the page she expected. The same page that it opened to for her.

He says nothing, just stares at the symbols and the text without moving.

"Read it aloud."

"I can't."

She frowns. "Why not? Oh—" She takes the book from him when she realizes her mistake. "You're not schooled in Latin. Why would you need to be, here, on a mountain? Yet Maudley should have schooled you nonetheless—"

"Eve, stop."

"What is it?"

"I can't read. Not just Latin. I can't read at all." When she says nothing, he pulls away, makes to get up.

She grabs his arm. "No! Do not leave!"

"I cannot stand your judgments—"

"I do not judge you, I only feel—"

"I will not bear your pity either!"

"I feel angry, Adam. I feel angry that so much was taken from you. Please, love. Stay."

His breathing remains rigid and fast, but his muscles relax.

"Listen to me," she says, taking his hand. "I will never judge, nor pity you. I shall rage beside you. And I shall love you. No more and no less."

His eyes flash with something she cannot name, but which is familiar in the way that her own spirit is, and then he kisses her—hard.

She pulls away once more and pushes him back. "Now, practice stoicism and let me read you this book, you knave!"

He grins, eyes narrow and piercing. "I prefer the other option."

"I'm certain you do."

"As do you."

She laughs. "Yes, I do."

His grin is wide and wolfish, and he nods for her to proceed.

She takes the book from him. "After I jumped out the window, when I woke on the mountain, I had this book with me. I have no memory of taking it. Seamus was there."

"Seamus? But you said he had been taken."

"I know. When I was in the house and Cage was…He was trying to cleanse me."

Rapley jerks violently.

"In the moments afterward, when he left me alone, I saw Seamus. I mean, I saw his essence, his spirit—I don't know what to call it. He was lost. But he would talk to me."

Rapley blinks several times. "Why didn't you tell me this before?"

"Do you really want to know why? Isn't it obvious? I didn't trust you."

"What did he say?"

Roan lifts the book. "He was reading this."

"I think you'd better tell me what it says now."

Roan nods. "It tells of how one man, a man named Fostos, made a deal with the Devil himself, and how, in exchange for long life, he sold his soul."

"Fostos…The Faustian legend? Maudley told me the story once. It's true?"

"And there are a list of dates, written in by hand. They're sightings. Sightings of Fostos himself."

"Pant Tywyll?" Rapley says, frowning. "Is that what it says?"

"Yes."

"But that's here. It's the folk name for the mountain, before it was renamed Meddwyn. It means Devil's Peak."

It rings a bell. Roan gives a mirthless chuckle. "I do love subtlety. So these catacombs—we're sitting on top of them?"

Rapley pales. "I have a feeling we are. It would explain a few things."

Roan gives him a pointed look.

"In there. It talked about Conjures. I'm almost certain I'm this one." He points to the symbol for Sighter. "What did you say when you pointed to it? Visions? Seeing things. Seeing things that were once alive?" He nods. "Me."

"Adam…"

"You were right. It does concern me. I first saw one when I was a child. It was my mother, Daphne. She was standing in the kitchen, smiling at me. I pointed to her, called her. My father said she was asleep upstairs. I just remember the look on his face when I shook my head and pointed, insisting she was in the kitchen."

"She had…passed?"

Rapley nods. "I saw another when I was older. Then again at eight." He looks at her. "With you. You helped me to find them. You showed me not to be afraid."

"I never saw anything."

"But you believed me."

"Of course I did."

"When I came here, there were more sightings. One every few months. It was like that for ten years."

"And then the three of us showed up."

He nods. "*You* showed up. Then I saw them every day, all day. They would gather under your window."

Roan's spine runs cold as ice. "My window? God help me."

"Always there. Standing. Looking up. I tried to keep them at bay. It worked."

"Your vigils."

Rapley looks at her sharply. "You knew?"

"Of course. You sat under my window almost every night. There's a window seat that I hid on every night. I would watch you."

His jawline and neck flush, and it is the prettiest thing she has ever seen on a man.

"Thank you."

He nods, silent. "They gather around you," he says at last, "hundreds of them. But they're not all. There are other things. Darker things."

She nods. "I know. But hundreds? Why are there so many? There is nothing here. We are the only people for miles."

"The tale of the miller must have some truth to it."

"Oh, I agree. The way Seamus was taken…Maudley's disappearance."

He looks at the book again, at the crudely drawn map, which they had found hidden in the back of the Unbound Book. "We need to find this place. This hidden cloister within the catacombs."

Roan takes the book from his hands. "It says the entrance is hidden in rock and air."

"How can an entrance be hidden thus?"

Roan shakes her head, and then closes her eyes. Perhaps she may sense something, the way she had known someone was Conjuring in Mill House. Her senses snake outward like the mists on the mountain, and she is surprised when they do not go far.

Her eyes snap open. "It's here."

Rapley leans closer. "Where?"

"Here, in this cave. Hidden in rock and air. Rapley, we're sitting on it."

Rapley hesitates only a moment, and then he is on his feet, searching. Roan finds it first. At the back of Rapley's small cave, a boulder stands unnaturally tall in the corner. A blanket is folded in front of it. Roan can feel something here. Old magick.

She doesn't need to speak. Rapley removes the blanket and rolls away the boulder to reveal a narrow corridor, crudely made, leading farther into the mountain. It is blacker than the blackest night and reeks of clay, magick, and mildew.

She sees a shudder run the length of Rapley's spine as he takes it all in.

"I've been sitting on this for years. And I never saw."

Roan shakes her head. "You were drawn to it. This cave. That much seems clear."

He spits a laugh. "Drawn to it indeed. Like a moth to hellfire."

She puts a hand on his arm, still thrilling at the contact of her flesh on his. "We are what we are," she reminds him. "Now we find out why."

Rapley gives her a stiff nod, but there is a warmth in his eyes that was never there before, and she takes it. Each and every sign of life within him as their days together pass, she devours with a hungry relish. But gently, oh so gently.

Come out, dearest. I am waiting for you.

He gives her hand a squeeze before he lets go and steps back.

"We'll need supplies," he says pragmatically, "if we're going to go down there." He reaches for the cloth map. "If this is anything to go by, it could take time. It's…labyrinthine. And this map is old. We don't know what we'll find down there." He pauses. "Are you certain you want to go? I could go alone, see if—"

She snatches the map from his hand and begins to roll it up.

He grimaces. "I thought not."

"One can dream," she says, grinning sweetly.

That cracks his exterior, and she sees a small smile appear on his unyielding lips.

"Ah!" she gasps, leaning close and squinting. "I saw it! Not much of it, but I'm sure…yes. I'm certain. A smile."

He raises his brows and fixes his lips firmly. "You must still have fever."

She laughs and hands him the map. "If we're to go, the map goes too."

"And much else, besides."

By the time the pack is ready, it contains canisters of water, dried meats, bread, candles, spare clothing, and—

"Matches," Rapley says, packing them securely in their own little pouch. "Without light, we're dead."

The temperature drops as soon as they cross the threshold and the moist, telling air of deep compression wafts up to greet them. Rapley glances back at Roan again.

"No going back?"

She steps around him to lead the way. "No."

At first the lanterns reveal little besides the rocky walls of the mountain, the cave stretching thinly in a narrow, jagged pathway deep into the heart of darkness. Roan can scarcely believe it herself; that Rapley has lived on the mountain all of ten years and never once knew upon what he wandered.

"Go carefully," he warns from behind her, and Roan nods. Beneath their feet, the rocks lie twisted and fallen, misshapen by years of corrosion and movement. Here and there slick patches of lichen and moss drape themselves artfully over hidden boulders so that they slip and have to touch the walls close by on either side to maintain balance.

Then, gradually, the ceiling begins to shrink. Lower and lower they have to bend, until Roan is forced to lie down upon her stomach to get through a small space, leaving her lantern for Rapley, who hands it across to her with his own lantern before he himself follows.

Deeper and deeper and the ground slants down at a noticeable angle, so that they both cling to rocks to keep from going too fast. Every now and then they stop to consult the map, and choose left-leading tunnels, Roan's instincts telling her to move before the map confirms it, always careful to mark their progress on the map itself and with strips of material tied to rocks upon the floor.

At one moment, both of the candles gutter alarmingly, and simultaneously a sound far ahead and below moans, a low kind of rain.

"Nothing is stable," Rapley says, his voice tight.

Roan avoids adding that she does not think they're very welcome, pushing away the thought, once more, that the mountain is very much aware of them. And is hungry.

Devour us not, she wills it, grabbing her knife and poking the side of the rock walls. *I will give you indigestion!*

Rapley is behind her in moments. "What is it?"

"Just having a chat with the mountain." Roan eyes the wall. "We understand each other."

Roan feels his grin in the air behind her. "Fey witch," he mutters, and kisses the top of her head.

They continue on.

"Here," Roan says after a long, winding walk. She points to the part in the map where the tunnel indicates a shaft going directly downward.

She lifts her lantern and spies a stairway cut like a ladder into the rock wall.

She steps up to the rim.

"Don't," Rapley says, touching her arm.

"There are answers down there. There must be."

"I won't fit. I can't follow you."

Roan nods. "I know. Pass down the lantern when I'm in. I'll be fine."

He hesitates a moment and then, knowing her resolve will not be challenged, nods stiffly.

And so she goes

D
O
W
N

DEEP

IN

THE

BELLY

OF

THE

MOUNTAIN

AMID

THE

RUMBLING

WALLS

SHE

FINDS

THE

PLACE

WHERE

THE

DEVIL'S

TONGUE

WAS

FIRST

SPOKEN

AND THE ROCKS GROAN IN THEIR WAKING
AND BEGIN TO RAIN DOWN
LIKE THE END OF THE WORLD UPON HER.

My belly swells with the passing months and I delight. Nothing has been found of the missing men excepting some torn cloth and a great pool of blood. Huw and the others believe they did not light their fire high enough and were found by wolves in the night. I cannot fathom that to be the truth, since we heard no howls, nor screams, nor massacre.

I have been watching the ram amongst the goats. He has been watching me also with a preternatural gaze. It is a strange kind of creature to stare at me so! I wish there were two, so we might put this one to death and eat of its flesh. Then I could be rid of its ever-watchful gaze.

I dream strangely of late. I sleep long, strange hours, and wake crying out. I dream of my babe suckling at my breast, and I am filled with a wonder so strong I praise God for it. But then I look down upon her, and she is a goat, not a child, and her teeth are those of a wolf, and my breast is half-eaten.

What a thing to dream! If it is not the devil himself putting such images in my head then I must be well and truly mad.

FROM THE DIARY OF
HERMIONE SMITH,
SEPTEMBER 1584

ZOEY

—————

NOW

Chapter 33
. . . AND I LIKED IT

I didn't sleep well. Len was awake before me, sitting
in the hole in the wall, staring out at the foggy
morning.

She doesn't understand why I have to pay a blood
price for my Conjures.

I told her it was more than a blood price. "If I lie
after I Conjure, then I bleed. The price is honesty.
So I add my blood to my spells as a kind of...sacrifice.
To show that I mean what I do and don't do it
lightly."

"Don't," she said. "Don't use your blood again.
The Conjure can be easily corrupted. Like with
me. You didn't mean to call me out, but you did.

You might have called out something much, much worse. Using your blood is a way for the Conjure to trick and hurt you." She stops. "Honesty is a price?"

I nod. "My father was the same. His price was memory."

"Memory?"

"Every time he...Conjured, he'd lose a memory. Usually one of me."

"That's...harsh. But you see, that's exactly what I mean about blood."

"What?"

"Conjuring doesn't have a price. It's as natural to an Unclosed as it would be for a normal person to have a drink or take a drug. Addictive, but not costly like that. The only way this could have happened is if someone in your line, someone among your ancestors, cast a blood curse."

"You think this was done to us?"

She nodded. "I don't pay that kind of price." She paused, and then said: "Show me."

I told her it was a bad idea. She had no idea what would happen...none.

"Maybe it's something you're doing," she told me. "Maybe I can fix it."

She took my hands. "Show me."

And I found that I was powerless to resist.

What do I do if I don't use blood?
     Focus. Think about something specific that you've

lost. Something small. An object. Close your eyes, and see it. And then call for it.

I did exactly what she said, picturing a green pin that I lost when I was six. It was my first merit badge and I lost it on the way home from school before I could show Dad. Then I open my eyes.

That's it?

Should be. So what now? You have to be honest?

Yes. For a few hours. Especially about what I've just done.

What did you Conjure?

A photo. A photo I lost.

She smiles at me. **Good. Now we wait.**

I bite my lip for the **lie** I have told. <u>Now we wait.</u>

⌐⌐

Everything is
                    dark.
Everything hurts.

Oh God.

It hurts.

There's something in my
                    eyes.

I
   s
       t
         u
           m
             b
               l
                 e

where am i?
  i can't see

        i can't

                        it hurts

        ⌒

Len found me sometime in the night. I was shaking, shivering—wet. I was so wet all over. And cold. It hurt everywhere.

It was dark and I couldn't see. When would the sun rise? I needed to get warm, but I couldn't move. I was standing in a corner of a room somewhere.

I heard footsteps. Thought it was Poulton come to save/comfort/help me like old times. Was I in my bed? Was I dreaming? I reached out as though he'd be next to me, but there was only cold, dark, empty space.

Then a flashlight in my face; I cringed back. So bright. So brilliant.

The light fell. There was a <u>crack</u>.

"Lord preserve me," Len whispered in a choked kind of way. "Oh, Zoey."

And then there was a lot of movement. I was aware of being covered, of being wrapped tightly, and then she was hugging me. She was hugging me, and she was—was she crying? No. No, but she was speaking.

Her hug was so painful...but I didn't want her to let go either.

"I should never have asked," she said softly, tears in her voice.

<u>Be okay</u>. I wanted her to be okay.

"It's fine," I told her, trying to make it all better.

And then she was crying, holding me so tight I hoped she would never let me go, but it was painful. It was so, so painful, and though I tried not to, I cried out a little, and suddenly her arms were gone.

She led me back to the Green Room and stoked the fire. I sat huddled in front of it, wondering why I couldn't get warm. And the whole time I kept thinking—where is Poulton?

"I might go to sleep," I said. "You don't have to worry. I'm feeling much better."

She brought over bottles of water and one of Poulton's towels. "No. You're going to tell me about your father."

"My dad?"

She let me talk for a while, and I told her about the rabbits I make because I'm his little Rabbit. I told her a million other little stories, while she washed me down with a damp towel. She got up several times to get more water, or change the towel, but I couldn't stop talking.

When I finally ran out of things to say, I was wrapped in blankets and there were three bloody towels in a pile by the fire.

Len was rubbing her hands.

"What did it look like?" I whispered. My hair was cold and damp, but I felt cleaner.

She shook her head and wiped her nose. "It's been a long time," she said vaguely, "since I cried. You have no idea how long."

"I cry every day. Takes practice to get it right."

A hint of a smile appeared in the twitch of her mouth.

"The snot needs <u>real</u> practice though."

The twitch turned into a crack, and her teeth showed. Then a laugh!

"It was horrible. I've seen some things, Zoey. Some terrible things. Worse things, even. But seeing you like...that. Knowing I caused it." She shook her head. "Don't do that again. Ever. Not for anyone." She looked at me. "Always be honest. Don't tell a lie. No matter who gets hurt. And if you can manage it, don't Conjure again. Not ever."

I remembered the pain, which still lingers in my nerve endings even now, and I nodded. "Okay."

"Good."

"But what did it look—"

"Blood. You were bleeding from every single pore in your body. "It was trypophobic. The more I wiped, the more these little spots of blood would grow and grow until they rained down your body. It was in your eyes, your hair. When you spoke, your tongue bled. I'll never forget your skin with those red dots growing bigger and bigger, like some kind of acid attack, erasing you. Making you part of the darkness of the room. Like hundreds of little pinpricks." She swallowed.

"That's what it felt like. Like thousands of little pinpricks. But...inside of me as well. Through my heart, my lungs, my stomach, intestines..."

She took my hand abruptly. "Stop," she whispered. "Please, I can't hear any more."

Her hands were still covered with smears of my blood.

I closed my eyes. "I'm sorry."

"I'm the sorry one," she said, her voice so close to my face. "Shit!"

I opened my eyes, and Len was sucking her finger. Before I could ask what had happened, she lifted a small shining object from the ground. My pin.

I was burning inside, fiercely, but not with pain as much as an <u>ache</u>. This girl...She was like the wind. Unobtainable. Free. Mysterious. The light of the fire splayed over her face, her lips, her hair. She smelled like autumn.

She was completely beyond me.

And I kissed her anyway.

She pulled back, and we stared at each other. Her eyes roamed my face, looking for the trick or the lie, but if she was looking for malice she didn't find it.

She released her breath and then she kissed me back, and I was alive for the first time in my whole life.

I lifted my phone and took a photo of her. She was serene with her loose hair, her eyes closed, lips just-kissed. I never wanted to forget that moment.

Her eyes snapped open. "What did you do?"

"Pull back your hair," I said, and watched as she did. I aimed my phone again and took another photo. "So beautiful."

She blinked at me like a curious bird, and then smiled. She kissed me again.

We broke apart at the sense of movement in the doorway, but when we looked, no one was there.

ROAN

❦

1851

Chapter 34
THE DARK

light

is

gone   and

the

earthquake

is

stones,

rubble,

rocks,

and screaming   dust.

and

Roan
falls
long
and
far,
and
lands
in
a
heap
in
a

deep

dark

place.

There

is

Nothing.

There

is

no one.

I'm going to die in here.

325

Roan bites down upon her lips to keep herself from speaking. She blocks her ears to keep from hearing. She stops all breathing and hopes that for one small moment, the niggling, itching, clawing thoughts, which work upon her mind like rats scratch, scratch, *scratching*, will leave.

When the quiet comes, Roan sits wrapped in it. At
last, she lifts her head and allows herself to listen. She
can feel the rocks collapsed behind and above her and
knows that all is lost.

Still, she says it. "Rapley?"

No reply.

She tries again, this time louder. *"Rapley?"*

Her voice echoes back from a long space before her.

Reaching with her hands, she finds the walls beside
her. A little farther away than what her arm span
reaches. She coughs the dirt and dust from her lungs
and her mouth as she attempts to get to her feet.

Her pulse quickens when she moves and the world,
black though it is, tilts unnaturally so that she is
leaning against the last wall without knowing how she
got there. Hot wetness running over her scalp lets her
know, dimly, that she is injured.

She stumbles forward, feeling and falling, onward,
downward, not knowing where she is going or why.

There are no longer any *whys.*

She is dead already.

The tunnel narrows as she goes, until she is crouching, her head skimming jagged stone, shoulder to shoulder with rock harder than bone.

I am walking into my grave.

The thought seems almost delightful and she laughs.

Onward she walks, forcing her eyes wide, as though some light may penetrate if only she could open her lids enough.

She closes them sometimes, wondering if she has eyes at all, but when she touches them, there they are.

The world dips and sways and she is on her feet, then on her back, and things keep hitting her in the chin, in the cheeks, on her knees and on her back.

And then, all at once

a glimmer of light.

She takes one of the candles from the wall, ignoring the molten wax that drips down her hands, and follows the room from one tunnel to another. Candles have been lit in sconces all along the walls, but she doesn't trust them or herself. The tunnel

which

narrows

so

much

as

she

walks

that

she

has

to

slide

forward

sideways

to

make

any

progress

at

all.

And then

it all

widens

up

so

Roan's

candle

flame

touches

Nothing.

It is a flickering ball of light in a room, the cold air of which would suggest is more than magnificently large.

**She is aware, now more than ever,
of how much mountain is above her head.**

And of how very small she is.

The tunnel continues on and then narrows once again, whereupon it becomes a narrow stairway.

There is no choice but to climb.

And so she does.

The wax has pooled in her hand, dripped onto her borrowed trousers, and scuffed her boots. The flame is burning low.

Up she climbs.

Round it bends.

Up, always up.

It occurs to her to keep count.

But 677 steps later, she forgets what number she was on and starts again.

Did I come down this far? She senses that the mountain is moving and playing tricks on her.

⚟˥˦˧

And there, as though waiting for her, the room appears, and breathes a sigh. There is no door, but thick nails hanging from two bolts in the wall suggest that at some point there would have been.

She stumbles across the threshold and falls to her knees at the sight of it.

Candles sit in every nook and niche in the walls, wax flooding the stones around and below like white seaweed, dripping slowly to the rhythm of the mountain. The candles illuminate the walls, every inch of them scrawled with symbols and words. Thin lines of rope are strung about in haphazard zigzags, bloodred with wax and blood, tendrils of flesh hanging from them like garish garlands.

She tries to close her eyes, to see the blinding nothing of the tunnels from before, but she can't move. Her breath, jagged and raw, sears her throat. Everything in this room burns like acid upon her skin and mind.

The first thought is this:

Someone was here recently.

The second:

This is the place.

She gets to her feet, steadying herself against the left wall, but then flinches and pulls back her arm when the heat of the candle below burns her. The room has numerous holes in the walls—pigeonholes that perhaps once contained scrolls and letters. All are ash and dust now. Except one.

She walks over to it and reaches out a shaking hand.

She feels the thing before she touches it. It is clothed in foul magic—it reeks of evil. Her fingers want to recoil rather than touch its oily surface. Still, she unfurls it carefully, like it is a snake, and stares.

She drops the scroll when she is done and flings it away; it is a vile, cursed, rotten thing, and though she wipes her hands she cannot feel clean. *Tainted. Unholy. Evil.*

The scroll tells it plain. The symbols, the linguistics—the *language…* of Satan. Evil incarnate. Every foul, dark, inhuman thing that is in this world and the next, laid out in harsh script for any to learn.

Here, *confirmed*, laid down in a cursed scroll.

Her native tongue.

She lifts her lantern and gasps.

An entire wall is covered with the devil's script. That forbidden language Cage used, which her father taught her, which she had taken to so very easily as a child.

The addiction within her raises its head, sniffing the air.

Speak, it calls. *Taste me.*

She steps forward, reaching for the words, which seem to glow in hues of red. So *beautiful*.

"Roan, stop."

Rapley's voice shatters the spell. He is in the room behind her.

"Thank God," he mutters, and then he is by her side, holding her to him. He pulls back and examines her face. "You're hurt. Your head…"

"How did you get down?"

"I went back and found another way down. There are more rooms. At least—" He breaks off, taking in the wall of solid writing. "…twelve. What is this?"

"It's the same script as in the book."

He hesitates. "Can you read it?"

Roan tries not to look, but she has already taken in more than half of it. She nods stiffly.

"Is it important? For us, I mean. For the…Unclosed?"

She nods again, swallows, and begins to read, translating as she goes.

"*Here I knelt upon the rocky ground and unraveled a scroll of scar-made flesh, and upon there writ were words profane, cut like knives and sewn back closed to keep within the secret power. And I spake the words and struck my head and they did burn me coming out. And then abound the rocks did roar and a voice declared WHO DARES SPEAK MY TONGUE? And the devil and I spake Unholy, Ungodly pacts and life was giv'd, yet soul was tak'd and now I shall live by others until my due comes again. And then to hell I must go.*"

Roan swallows, closing her eyes. The words were so smooth in her mind, yet their pronunciation was harsh, crude, and guttural. It was no matter. Her mind swallowed the words down like a fine wine, or sweetest honey.

"It is signed with a name. There. *Fvstvs.*"

Rapley's lips harden. "Fostos."

"There's more," Roan says, taking a breath before turning to the richer brown writing beneath the first section of wall writing. "He's talking about time. About time running out." Her fingers follow along the symbols. "A search for more time. A new sort of bargain. He's…My God, Rapley. It's just like the stories my father used to tell me…He's seeking a way to harvest souls. To barter back his own…or for more time." Roan exhales slowly. "My father was trying to warn me…My father knew that Faustus…Fostos…was real."

"This must have been added long after the first text," Rapley says.

Roan's stomach contracts. "Yes. Much later. Rapley…this…this is my *name*. And here, Emma's…Seamus…you…my God. We're all here. And here, another. Dylan." She steps back. "My God, it's real."

"And if it's real…then the tale is true. Fostos is immortal…and he's here. Somewhere."

He knew…He was warning me. Her thoughts race like ants all over, crisscrossing and weaving through one another.

Roan turns toward the entrance through which Rapley had come and heads swiftly out. She discovers that he is correct: There are more rooms. More than that: These tunnels are different. They are carved carefully, cleanly. Deliberately. And there are sconces for candles built into the walls every few feet. Roan follows the corridor onward, discovering sections where pieces of stained-glass windows have been inset with space for candles behind.

"This must be the cloister," Roan murmurs as she passes a silver cross inlaid in the wall.

Rapley nods. "There was a monastery here, perhaps."

They follow the new series of tunnels onward until they've come full circle.

"If these corridors existed, then why dig out the other way?" Roan says. "Look, here are stairs that seem to spiral straight up to the surface. Why go to the trouble to dig those crude paths if this is right here?"

"Perhaps because there is another reason for the tunnels. When we came in, you took the left-hand path on each branch. Why?"

"I don't know. I was following my instinct."

"I have an instinct of my own. Come."

They head to the crude tunnels and make their way back, but instead of branching left as they had done coming in the first time, they now take the other path, to the right. After more turns and stairs than Roan can follow, they come to a corridor with glass panels placed in the walls at intervals.

Roan steps close to the wall where a pinprick of luminescence tunnels into the gloom. She presses her eye to the hole—

and shudders.

There it is. The Blue Room.

The room that was meant to be hers.

The room where Emma was…hurt.

The room where she was imprisoned.

Exorcised.

Drowned.

The room where she…murdered Cage.

All of it, right here, at the end of a peephole in the depths of the earth.

Chapter 35

HIDING FROM THE LIGHT

Drowning.

That is much what Roan feels is happening to her. Drowning, right in the dank air dozens and dozens of feet beneath the surface of the mountain. All of this...all of it...had been so thought out. Giving Roan the Blue Room, blue, which had been her mother's favorite color, the storm that almost cost Emma her life, Cage, Seamus's ghost...all of it could have been witnessed.

She follows the rudimentary stairway farther up, then along a corridor, knowing that she will soon find...yes: another horizontal strip of light cutting the darkness in two. Another peephole. This one looks into a room of...yellow. It's the locked room along the hall.

The mountainside has been cut to pieces, like some kind of horrific circulatory system. Here, a stairway cuts down again; there it cuts away from the house, which seems to lie parallel to it. The West Wing. Of course.

No wonder it was always forbidden, Roan thinks bitterly.

Corridors follow other corridors and it is clear, suddenly, that this is not a mere lifespan's work. This must have taken a hundred years or more. How vast is it? How intricate?

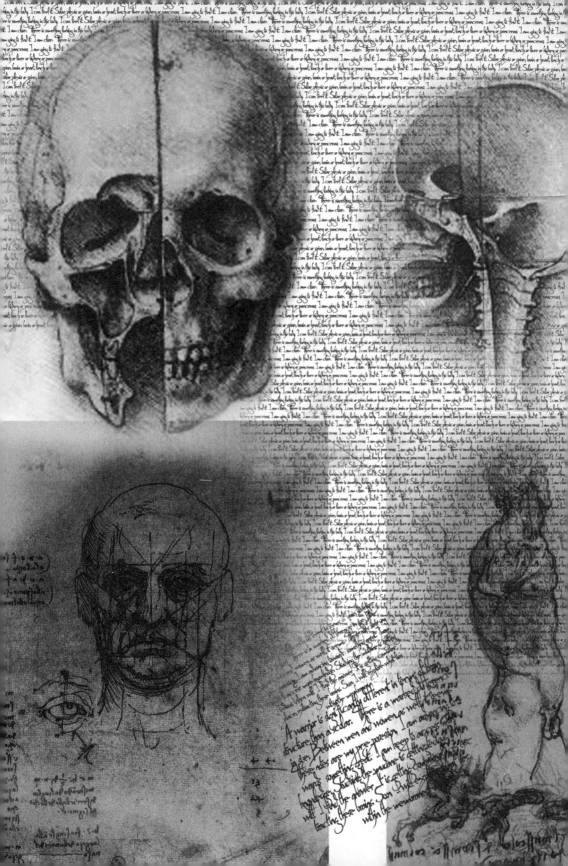

I have found a subject for study. A miller, young and strong, and oft by himself. His brain was a unique and marvelous thing, although to cut it from the casing which is harder than any bone in the body, I fear, was a trial. I had to saw very carefully with a circular saw and even then the bone splintered and caused minor damage to the brain. I must create a more sturdy cutting tool, one that works on a rotating pin perhaps. There is much to study in the human brain. I have not even begun to comprehend the membrane, let alone the delicate grey-pink tissue beneath it. All I know is that the brain is a jelly like texture with a connecting cord. It is divided into two, just like the human body is divided into two with the spinal column, and just as human nature is split into the good and divine, and the evil and perverse. I feel I am on a path to discover thus far unexplored.

The mandibular area where the mastication of food takes place seems like an unlikely area to explore. However, for the purposes of completion and thoroughness, I have studied the jaw line at death. When dissecting the human skull, the jaw bone and teeth left intact, a foul odour, close to that of wet gummy and rot. I is an curious smell. I wonder if the evil side of the human nature is tied to smell. Bitter foul smells for the evil within us, and pleasant beauteous smells for the goodness. If this theory could be proven correct, then it would not be far to speculate that the teeth, most especially the mandibles, are formed of the evil half of the body. And if a thought occurs to me. If we are made of two sides, good and evil, then surely God could not have created us wholly. For God is good, perhaps then we are created by both sides, the side of God, which angels sit upon, and the side of evil, where the beast lies in wait.

The skull is a casing, like an egg, keeping the soft brain matter safe?

The socket of the eye is much like the skull, only a half container for the fleshy eyeball inside. I could scoop out the eye without having to remove an outer casing. It is worth noting that the eyeballs cloud after death had been present for a while, and I speculate that this is either a chemical reaction or the soul leaving the body.

How recently used?

She follows the sigils and symbols cut into the walls, which direct her upward toward light, eventually staggering out into the open air where a gathering storm rumbles above. Rapley follows, brushing himself off and coughing up the wretched dust. Roan looks around, disoriented, and realizes how far they have walked, for Mill House is far away.

Rapley gathers Roan into his arms fiercely, growling in his throat as he lifts her up and presses her against him.

"By God and the Devil, I thought I would go mad when I was separated from you."

"I did, as well," she admits, once she is back on her feet. And then all words are lost to their furious, dusty kiss. At last, they break apart, gasping.

"I can't believe it," she says. "We found the place where the monk Fostos made his deal with the Prince of Darkness. With Lucifer himself."

He curses under his breath.

"And more. He's here. Fostos has been with us all along. I felt someone Conjuring…someone powerful. My father knew—he told me tales about Fostos when I was young. As though to warn me. To prepare me. Fostos is still there. In the house. Now. One of our own."

"Who?"

"I don't know."

Rapley steps away from her, shaking his head. "No. No, we should leave. Put this behind us."

"I…can't." She releases her breath in a rush now that it is said. "I have to go back. I can't leave Seamus somewhere in there…and despite what Emma did…I can't leave her either. Nor Jenny, nor Andrew…And we still don't know what happened to Maudley."

"Damn you, Roan Eddington," he snaps, turning back to her. Then he steps closer and puts his forehead down upon hers. "Damn you for your goodness."

She almost laughs at that.

The walk back to the house is the longest Roan has ever taken. Every inch of her wants to flee in the opposite direction. Instead, she grits her teeth and plants her feet more forcefully.

Until at last, she can walk no more.

"I cannot do it," Roan says, bending to rest her palms on her knees.

Rapley does not turn back. "You can. You must."

"Rapley, I—"

He faces her abruptly. "Everything you have done was nothing more than anyone would. You defended yourself."

"I *killed* a man."

"A man that branded you." His teeth clench. "He hurt you."

"And Emma, my friend? She who condemned me?"

He takes hold of her hands. "You are the torch in my night, my Eve. You will be so for her, also."

Roan closes her eyes. "I am angry."

"And a little afraid."

"Yes," she whispers, "and a little afraid."

"Be a beacon for her lost soul, and let her see that she was wrong, so very wrong, to condemn you."

Roan's voice is low. "And she delivered me into his hands. He who scalded me. He who burned me with water."

Rapley's eyes flash. "And we shall save her, nonetheless, for Fostos is within those walls, and she is not safe. We can be good, Roan. We can resist Fostos by doing something good, even if you are angry with Emma. We must try."

Roan stands upon the mountain, which so resembles the Yorkshire moors this far up, and looks down upon the terrible Mill House embedded within the mountain, and feels a vile spite and hatred welling up.

Why should I? a rebellious voice whispers in her ear. *Why should I save them at all?*

And then…there he stands. So suddenly that Roan jumps back, a cry on her lips.

Seamus.

His rotted ghost stands looking mournfully up.

Will you not save me? Will you not come?

"What is it?" Rapley asks, by her side. "What do you see?"

Roan's air rushes out of her and with it, the rage within. "Seamus…"

She blinks and he is gone. So quickly. As if he had not been there at all.

"My rage tricks me," Roan says, swallowing. "I will return to Mill House. And I will find the heir of all this sorrow."

Rapley smiles. "Good."

"And I will kill him."

Mill House. Roan steels herself, glancing at the space where, only moments before, Seamus's rotten ghost had reappeared.

Rapley looks at her, his gaze once more the gaze of the gruff Mountain Man she had met all those weeks ago.

She nods, and together, they fling wide the doors of Mill House—

and freeze where they stand.

He is standing halfway down the grand stairway, a nightmare personified.

He is clothed in the black cassock of a priest.

Cage.

PART 6

Beyond the Mountain

FAUSTUS: Where are you damn'd?
MEPHISTOPHELES: In hell.
FAUSTUS: How comes it, then, that thou art out of hell?
MEPHISTOPHELES: Why, this is hell, nor am I out of it.

—CHRISTOPHER MARLOWE,
        DR. FAUSTUS

*P*raise be to God for my daughter is here!

She is dead and blue and I cannot stop laughing!

"Raise her up!" I cried. "Raise her up so God may see!"

I held her to me for some days, but when she gave off an odor most foul, John pried her away from me.

"Babies will smell, John!" I cried. "I must change her dressings! Babies will smell!"

I have not seen her since.

Perhaps the wolves took her also.

I cannot stop laughing!

FROM THE DIARY OF

HERMIONE SMITH

ZOEY

NOW

Chapter 36

COME ONE,
COME ALL

I was busy showing Len the photos and video footage
we've compiled when Poulton finally came down.

"We're having beans," I said. "I'm warming them
now. Want some?"

He ignored me.

"I'm showing Len the photos I've taken, and your
video footage too."

Again, nothing. He just sat down and stirred the
beans in the pot.

"Pole...Len's a friend, okay?"

Finally, he looked up. "Friends would come out,
introduce themselves, and ask questions, not spy on

us for more than a week and steal notebooks and personal jewelry."

Len half smiled. "Point taken."

"Why did you spy?" he asked. "And what else did you steal?"

"I wanted you gone," Len said simply. "And some toilet paper."

I couldn't help laughing. I like this girl. Like, I <u>like</u> her. She's fucking awesome. I like the way she lets her hair do its own thing. She never combs it. I love how she doesn't wear any makeup. She has this completely natural, innocent look, and then she pulls lines like that out of her ass.

"And what's your excuse?" Pole said, looking at me.

I had never seen him look at me with such suspicion before.

"Pole, when was the last time you had some water? Or food?" I asked.

"I asked you a question," he said sharply. "What. Is. Your. Excuse?"

"Excuse for what?"

"Acting like a disgusting fucking slut?"

I couldn't speak. Eventually I said, "What?" at the same time that Len said, "Shut your mouth."

Pole began to stir the beans faster so that the sauce dripped over the sides and hissed in the gaslit flames. "A disgusting slut
who kisses perfect strangers right after kissing their best friends?"

"Poulton!"

Len was on her feet. "Take that back."

"I suppose you want to lick her disgusting—"

Len was on him in a second. I literally didn't even see her move. She hit him in the face, but he was tall and shook her off. She got up, panting, and said, "Go for a walk."

Neither of us was expecting that. Len looked like she regretted getting angry.

Pole stared at her, his fists clenched.

"Go for a goddamn walk before you do something you'll regret."

He looked at me for a long while before he spun around and walked out of the room.

"He's been spending all his time in that room with all the skulls and weapons."

"Leave him there for a while," Len said. "We have to leave soon. Pack up everything you have. We'll go in the morning. He needs to get away from this house as soon as possible."

Pole won't leave with us.

He insists that he wants to stay. I point out that his cans of food won't last forever. The bacon and the bread are gone, and so is the milk. He tells me he doesn't care.

Len insists we go, even if only to town for a couple of days, to wash the effects of the house out of us.

I feel horrible, but I think she's right.

We have to get out of here.

We're getting out in five.

Leaving Pole here feels wrong.

She was right and still, we left too late.

We set out at around eight this morning. I pleaded with Poulton through the door to the Hunting Room, but he told me to get out. I left crying. Len took my hand and we climbed out the hole in the Green Room wall together, me looking back and stumbling, her leading the way.

It was such a dark morning that it felt like a solar eclipse. You know, that eerie, weird light that feels like you're standing on another planet. Everything felt breezy and alien, and the wind picked up the farther from the house we got.

And then the mists rolled in.

They were like waves. Huge plumes of mist so thick they were like clouds tumbling down on us, and Len grabbed my hand and yelled, "Don't let go!"

We stumbled over the rocks and the lichen, through heather that was barely alive—and then I fell.

It felt like something grabbed my jeans, low down near my ankle, and pulled. I lost Len's hand, heard her scream, and then I was tumbling, falling—

I don't remember landing.

But I remember waking up in this foggy half day and hearing Len calling me. It was like she was in a wind tunnel. I couldn't hear her properly.

And then the pain.

I yelled, I think. Well, I mean I must have. Len found me somehow, but I don't remember that.

The next thing I knew, I was back in the house and Len was pulling a jagged piece of slate from my calf. She threw it away from us like it was poisonous and it landed with a <u>clank</u> in a corner of the room.

It looked like a giant wolf's canine tooth.

"I'm bleeding again," I said, and my head swam in and out.
I kept waking up and Len was doing something different

holding something on my leg

calling for Poulton

cursing under her breath

running from the room

alone

POULTON!

She's hurt!

Poulton arriving...my heart swelling.

Thick tongue. "Pole..."

heavy head

"stupid idiot"

don't touch her!

something cold
sticky

I woke up about an hour ago. Len and Pole were both sitting near me, determinedly not looking at each other. My leg's been superglued together. Trusty Pole with his knowledge of first aid. It looks gross, honestly, and it hurts like nothing I've ever felt before.

I licked my lips. "Too bad we drank all the alcohol already."

They both jumped like I'd electrocuted them.

Len was at my side at once. "Zoey—"

Pole inched closer too. His eyes looked dark—not his eyes, really. The shadows around his eyes.

His lips thinned and he frowned. "Idiot."

I managed a smile. "Thanks."

He smiled back, but then he said something that made my insides freeze. "Did you really think he'd let you go?"

Len's head turned toward him really, really slowly. "What did you just say?"

"Oh, please." He rolled his eyes. "Did you really think you'd get very far in this weather?"

I tried to sit up, but the pain in my leg was intense. "That's not what you said..."

He frowned. "What?"

"You said..." I shook my head. "You said _he_ would never let us go. Who?"

Poulton licked his lips. "I said...I said..." He frowned. "The weather is bad. You didn't think you'd get far like this, did you?"

Len and I exchanged looks and Poulton caught it.

"What?"

"Never mind."

The storm pounded against the front doors and they rattled on their hinges. I was thankful they had brought me into the Red Room, rather than the Green Room, or we would have been sitting inside a mini-hurricane.

"I don't feel so good," I murmured, the ache returning to my leg and my head at the same time.

"You need sleep," Len said. She put her hand on my forehead and I closed my eyes.

"We'll leave you in peace," Pole said stiffly, and then they both left.

I felt my eyelids grow heavy.

I've been awake for a while now, and neither of them have come back. They left me with the space heater and the generator, though. My leg feels a bit better. Think I'll go look for them.

I'm writing this as fast as I can. I saw it with my own eyes. I _saw_ it. I need to get it down before I stop believing that it happened.

I heard them whispering in the hall outside. I didn't think anything of it right away, but then Len said, "Step away." It was such an odd thing to say, and her tone was dangerous. So I peeked through the gap in the door until I saw them a little way down the hall. Len was standing against the wall and Pole was towering over her—too close.

He was standing so close to her that they might have been kissing, except his body language was all wrong. He was aggressive.

"I know what you're doing," he hissed in her face. "Trickster, vile impersonator, whore!"

I opened my mouth to speak, but Len beat me to it.

"Do you speak to Zoey like that?"

And then he shoved her into the wall, his forearm pressed fully against her neck. I was so shocked I stood there gaping like a fucking fish and I didn't do anything.

"You're a liar," he said quietly. "I'm watching you. I'm _fucking_ watching you."

Len stared for a moment, and then she was pressing back as though his arm wasn't hurting her neck at all.

"Fight it," she whispered. "Fight this house. Fight _Him_."

Pole sort of shook, like he was vibrating, and then he roared into her face, shoved her hard into the wall, and ran away as though someone had thrown acid on him, screaming the whole way up the stairs.

Len didn't even rub her neck, she just looked after him and shook her head like she was disappointed.

ROAN

❖❈❖

1851

Chapter 37

UPSIDE DOWN

Roan cannot understand what is happening.

Cage, dressed in a long black cassock, and leaning heavily on a wooden stick. Cage, staring down at her with a sneer on his face. But… Cage is dead. She killed him.

She shakes her head, mouth gaping, when finally, something clicks into place.

"You," she breathes. "It's you…"

And it all makes sense. Everything had turned so badly wrong after Cage's arrival. Everything had suddenly felt claustrophobic, dangerous…

She growls, sure she will kill him this time, but before she can do anything, Rapley is charging up the stairs at Cage himself. Clearly, he has deduced what she has: Cage is Fostos.

He has been watching them all along.

Rapley hits Cage with his entire body and the two of them go sprawling. Roan loses sight of them, but their grunts and the muffled *thumps* tell her everything she needs to know.

She hurries up the stairs after them, ready to add her own fists, nails, and teeth to the fight. In the back of her head, she is mildly surprised that Cage has not used any kind of Conjure on them—hasn't muttered a single syllable of the Devil's Tongue since they returned. She pushes the thought aside and kicks at Cage, who is laid flat out on the floor beneath Rapley, who delivers blow after blow with his fists.

"*Stop!*" rings a shrill voice.

Emma stands at the bottom of the stairs, Jenny clutched in her arms. The poor servant girl is shaking, but Emma looks fierce and irritated, much like she had before the fever got her—something like the Emma she had been when Roan had liked her best.

"Stop it," she says again, "all of ye! Just stop!"

Roan lowers her arms and turns to face her once-friend, waiting. Beside her, Rapley grunts and lets go of Cage, getting to his feet. Cage himself coughs and rolls over, breathing heavily. He spits blood from his mouth, but does not get up.

"Help him up," Emma demands, gesturing to Cage's legs, which are lolling about.

"He's evil," Rapley says, scowling.

"No, he isn't. But I'd be tempted to think *you* are. If you would come and sit down and *listen*, then I can explain a few things to ye."

Roan glances at Rapley and then nods at Emma, feeling, all of a sudden, quite ashamed of herself. "I will listen if you will give me the same accord."

Emma nods once, stiffly, and then helps Jenny into the Red Room.

Roan looks down at Cage grimly, watching as Rapley hauls him up.

"You'll have to do some of the work yourself," he growls at the man leaning heavily on him.

Cage nods in the most cooperative manner Roan has ever seen, and the three of them make their way down the stairs and into the Red Room as well.

An awkward silence falls after Rapley dumps Cage onto one of the red chairs and then sits down beside Roan on the sofa. Emma is sitting in the armchair, while Jenny stands silent in a corner.

"Jenny," Roan begins, leaning toward the girl, who rocks back and forth on her heels. "What has happened?"

Emma exhales. "Much. So please listen."

She looks pointedly over at Cage and folds her hands in her skirt.

Cage clears his throat. "I know what you suspected when you attacked me," he croaks. "It gives me some heart." He pauses and looks at Rapley. "I did not come here by accident, but by design. I am part of an…order, you might call it. A group of watchers and hunters. We aim, above all else, to find and destroy the one called Fostos. No, I am not Fostos," he adds with a glance at Roan, "though I believe he is here."

"He is," Roan says simply.

"For a time, I believed you to be his vessel. His witch. His spy."

Roan laughs mirthlessly. "And so I suffered by his design, and by yours."

"For that, I apologize. I cannot make it right."

"No." Rapley's voice is low and dangerously quiet. "You cannot. But continue."

"I was sent here by the command and request of my father. He and I, by birth, are members of the order called Crucisvigil. We keep eyes open for the cursed man, that we might one day discover and destroy him. We were formed of his brethren, when he was a holy monk in the tenth century, here. On this very mountain. There were those who had seen what he did, the deal he made with Satani, and they formed

Crucisvigil with a solemn oath to stop him. No matter how long it took." He pauses. "No matter how long it *takes*."

"So this...*order*..." Roan says, her voice harsh. "They charge you with exorcism as well?"

"Yes. And much, besides. Though I came here seeking out Fostos, to bring him to justice and rid the world of his evil, I had another purpose also." He glances at Rapley as he says this. "To find my little brother, and return him to us."

Roan glances between the two. "Your brother?"

"My half brother by my mother, Daphne Maurier. He was taken from us by his father when he was a small child—stolen. Taken far away so we could not find him. I will admit that it took some dark Conjuring to locate him. I regret nothing, for I found him."

Rapley shakes his head, but says nothing.

Cage nods once. "It is true. You are he."

"Impossible," Rapley scoffs. "I have no brother."

"How do you know?" Emma snaps. "Were you not brought to this mountain as a small child by Dr. Maudley?"

"I was...I was taken from a good place," Rapley says, glancing at Roan. "I was delivered here when I was a boy of eight, but not by Maudley. I only met Maudley three years ago. I know nothing of my mother," Rapley adds, turning back to Cage. "The place I was taken from was not a place with a mother and a brother."

"Then you were stowed away somewhere else, first. My father searched London high and low for you in the name of our mother."

"I know nothing of that."

"She was a beautiful, kind woman. She fell in love too quickly, and was tempted away by another. She died when you were young. Out of guilt, I think."

"Are you saying I am a bastard son of the woman who is your mother?"

Cage looks grim. "Yes."

Rapley rubs at his mouth. "Who is my father, then?"

"You know who he is," Cage says. "You know."

"No, I don't," Rapley snaps. "Speak plain if you wish to speak at all!"

"Fostos! Fostos is your father, brother. He tempted my mother and you came of the union. And by his foul Conjuring, by the laying out of those bedeviled symbols, you were conceived in the foulest, darkest manner—and so you are Unclosed. Cursed." Cage pauses. "Do you know what you are, brother?"

Rapley's voice is barely audible. "Yes."

"How are the Unclosed made?" Roan asks, leaning forward. A horrible pulsing runs through her body. She does not want to hear this... yet she must.

"I don't know precisely," Cage says, hesitating. "Only that...Fostos uses the forbidden tongue and his own seed to do it."

"His own seed..." She swallows, a sick feeling rising within her.

Cage looks at her pointedly. "Yes."

She gets to her feet. "No."

"*Yes*," Emma says, leaning forward. "It is so for Seamus and myself as well."

Rapley stares at her. "It cannot be..."

"Half siblings," Cage confirms. "All."

Roan closes her eyes, and the world turns more than dark. Every hope she has newly acquired: shattered. All the color, gone.

"To what end?" Rapley says. "For a mere experiment?"

"The Crucisvigil believe that Fostos breeds the Unclosed as a means to extract human souls. To barter them to the Devil for more time on his contract."

"Or to bargain to get his own soul back," Emma adds, helpfully.

Had not Roan's own father...the man who *pretended* to be her father... said as much? But...why? Why raise a child that was cursed and not his own? Had her father been there during the cursed coupling between her mother and Fostos?

Cage nods. "The Unclosed are linked to whatever comes after this life. They must have access to knowledge Fostos wants. Or their souls must be easily obtained, through that doorway." He pauses. "We do not know the mechanics of it all. For that, we need Fostos himself, and I doubt he would offer up his secrets."

There is a long silence.

"But there is worse," Cage adds softly. "For you, Roan."

She almost does not need to hear it.

His words seem to bend and warp, to fade and *boom* so that they are not a steady stream, as words tend to be, but trickles and tickles, music and discord, and they come to her in a sort of cavern, void of meaning. She has to piece them together before she can understand.

...wondered why you...

special

...a darkness

more than Unclosed...

Satani

Devil

Lucifer

You are more than cursed

Potential for good, but...

                              born of evil

      Lucifer
            in
                  the
                        body
                        of
                        man

                        inside Fostos

                                                dark ritual

                  daughter.

All his words *boom* and bind together until she can hear nothing but noise.

f. How could God forgive me? Father ent me aw
se he does not trust me in society. I am an anim
: savage his good reputation, and justly so he fea

M IN EXILE DO NOT L

ome I could call friend. Not a sou
ild care to hear my cries. To be a
world so soon, I had not known i
ld be suffered, and in such unbear
ince. If I should deliver a prayer,

o listens to the mount

ire conveyed to the last place on hell

not speak, girl, I deserve this. Cold shall be my h
shall be my bed. Everything I break and everythin
turn sour in my mouth! Foolish! Foolish little g
k I could be free I hate myself I'm sorry! Silence
ice and be damned!

I shall no want, l
step then another. One more step *he leadet*
me in the paths of
Yea, though I wal
no evil: for the

STOP IT STOP IT

If I were to kill this evil in self, would God then ag
to his kingdom. If were to rid the world of ungrtten
in my huge hungry fleshy wuldnt it be a mortal sin, and
run for the world, and I mourn for my good father wh

e me for my sins one step after the o
one prayer after an
: nothing on the mountain but mists

he who casts the first ston

t me to this place beca

The air rushes out of her lungs and everything shrinks, until at last, only the meaningful words remain.

Daughter

of

evil.

Daughter

of

Satan.

I am the daughter of Lucifer.

She longs, more than anything, to return to her room and write her father a letter, and beg him to contradict Cage. But all his warnings, his strange looks...it all made sense.

And she thought he had never loved her, but maybe...maybe he *had*, despite knowing. And that was why he had armed her with exactly what she needed to defeat this evil. To defeat Fostos.

"Kill me," she says suddenly, the fog in her brain sweeping away like the mists after a storm, because it is too much. Being this...*thing* that she is. She is defiled, she is cursed, she is unnatural.

She is dangerous.

Cage's lips part. "What?"

She turns her eyes on him. "I cannot live knowing this," she says urgently. "*Kill me.* It's what you wanted. Do it! Do it, now."

Rapley takes her hands roughly in his own. "I won't allow it! We don't know anything for sure. We don't know whether this is true or—or just another trick."

Roan shakes her head. "I know it's true. I feel it. It explains... everything." She turns her eyes on Cage once more, pleading. "Since I arrived here, I have seen him. I have seen the likeness of a ram out on the mountain. I have heard the hoofbeats of an animal. Horse, mule, ram... Nothing lives out there except...Him. My...my father. The Devil." She swallows heavily. "I hear him," she whispers. "In my mind sometimes. Tempting me to do great and terrible things..."

Cage shakes his head. "You may be born of evil, but you were born of a woman too. Woman, beloved of God. You have a choice. You can choose to fight the darkness within."

"What could you know of it?" Roan snaps. "Your father is a mortal man, not Fostos. Not the Great Deceiver. You don't know what it is to be Unclosed!"

"I do. Though I was not born from this Conjuring of Fostos, am not of his terrible seed...my father, Damon, was." He glances at Rapley. "I am your brother. And I am your nephew. And all this pain, this unnatural evil, this terrible contamination of natural law...it is all due to one man. Fostos." Cage looks at Roan. "He must be stopped. Fight your darkness, and I shall fight mine."

Emma leans forward on her elbows. "We all must fight the darkness. And if we stay together, *work* together, then we can—" Her voice breaks, and she swallows. "We can find Seamus."

Roan wipes her mouth, then nods. "We *will* find Seamus, and Dr. Maudley too," she says, voice hardening like steel. "For I wish to know *his* part in this too, and why he brought us here. They'll be wherever Fostos is. Get Andrew, he can help us search. And we will destroy Fostos."

Emma's face falls.

"What? What is it?"

"Andrew...he...he was taken. Shortly after you left. He's missing too."

Roan fills them all in on what they found in the catacombs, and as she expected, they are as horrified as she had been to learn of the peepholes.

"He's been watchin'," Emma says. "All along."

Roan nods. "The Blue Room was the worst."

"I undressed in there!" Emma cries, cheeks flushing.

Much to Roan's and Rapley's surprise, Cage takes Emma's hand and gives it a squeeze. Her cheeks flush even deeper, and Roan raises her brows. It seems that she and Rapley have not been the only ones to find love in the darkness.

Her stomach turns when she thinks of it.

They are half siblings...for the Devil had been in the body of Fostos at her conception...did that not make it so?

Such evil. Such cruelty.

And yet she loves him more than ever.

Wrong. Cruel, and wrong...

They have not touched since they learned the truth, but it cannot undo what has already been done. They can barely look at each other. Yet...Roan feels herself stirring for him, even now.

Cage, meanwhile, teaches them all what he knows of the Conjures themselves, and of their perilous gifts.

"The Crucisvigil have been documenting the Conjures. Ever since Fostos began...breeding."

Jenny has not said much since they arrived, but she watches them with wide eyes in her pale face. This, Roan knows, is the thing she feared most. Who knows what she is thinking or feeling.

And though Emma has grown stronger with the knowledge of what they face, and a grim determination has hardened her eyes, Jenny has fallen apart.

"This one," Cage says, pointing to a symbol that Roan knows, "depicts Soother."

"The Unclosed with the Soother gift can calm, heal, and manipulate. Those drawn to the Soother Conjure get what they want without stirring even a ripple of suspicion. They can pull thoughts from minds, money from hands, and memories from children and leave their victims soothed as babes. They can make someone forget a hate, or remember one that had never been there.

"This one depicts Sighter. The Sighter can see what others cannot. The departed. Spirits, energies, demonic elements."

"That's me," Rapley says simply. "Sighter. But there is more. A kind of shield. A way to keep darkness away. To keep the ghosts from… hurting."

Roan frowns. "They…try to hurt you?"

His lips thin. It is enough of an answer.

"This one," Cage says, pointing to another symbol, "depicts Breaker. The darkest of the Conjures."

Roan knows the symbol well. It had been cut into the cellar walls by the man she had thought was her father, and she also saw it in the West Wing when she had gone searching for Maudley. It was inked into the skin below her hairline, at the base of her skull, done painfully with needles and ink by that same man when she was a mere seven years old.

"If we want to stand a chance," Roan says abruptly, "we need to learn to use our Conjures. Properly."

Emma squares her shoulders and looks at Roan. "Teach me."

She is the only one to notice. The rest sleep on.

A small, slate-gray snake slinking over the floor. It is tiny. No longer than the length of her hand, and no thicker than her smallest finger. She watches it absentmindedly, the sadness inside so strong that it pulls down the edges of her mouth as though they were attached directly to the weight in her heart by invisible string.

She is thinking about Rapley.

She is thinking about good.

And evil.

About right.

And wrong.

Another snake, a darker gray, slithers past the Red Room door.

No other room seemed fitting to sleep in. They searched the entire house. Again. They even broke into the West Wing—nothing. Nothing but a deep surety that Roan has, in fact, been brought to this house before, as a little girl, by her father. The man she had *thought* was her father. The man who had lied to her. But no sign of Seamus, nor of Maudley, nor of Andrew.

She closes her eyes. *"Rapley..."* His name is a whisper. A prayer. A plea.

She opens her eyes, and a third snake slides over the floor. A balmy green.

She blinks and sits up straighter, then pushes herself from the chair. It rocks behind her, rapping the wall.

Tap, tap, tap.

She follows the green snake in the wake of the two grays, and sees now that there are more—dozens of them—slinking over the floor toward the kitchen. She dares not breathe.

Seamus...

They slither through the kitchen and down the stairs to the cellar door. She grabs a lit candle from the wall sconce and follows them down, careful not to tread on them.

They are congregated against a back wall of the cellar, which has been painted in a complex Romanesque fresco. She walks over and places her hand against the stone—and freezes.

She runs.

Back up the short staircase out of the cellar, through the kitchen, and to the entrance hall.

"Rapley!" she yells. "Emma, Cage! Come quickly!"

When they are gathered before the painting, standing amongst churning snakes, Roan points.

"It's a trompe l'oeil. An illusion." When they all look confused, she adds, "A false wall."

She knocks on the wall, and a hollow echo replies. "Wood," Rapley murmurs.

Roan nods. "It's been painted to look like artwork on a stone wall."

Cage smiles slowly. "Let's break it down, shall we?"

It is flimsy wood, and a few good kicks drive a hole in it deep enough to climb through. The men go first, and Roan and Emma pass through flaming torches and candlesticks in firm holders and then climb through as well.

A small corridor leads to a short flight of stairs going down, and then opens up into a grand room. They all raise their lights high, and no one says a thing.

The room in which they stand is a replica of the entrance hall. The tapestries, the grand staircase, the floor and the chandelier—all of it, identical.

Except inverted.

Every detail replicated...

Upside down.

Chapter 38
AN ITCH

"My God," Cage whispers, crossing himself. "What is this place?"

"The unclean one is upside down of God," Rapley murmurs. "So I have a pretty good idea."

They are a silent company as they walk on what feels like the ceiling of the entrance hall, except for the brief moment when Emma touches the chandelier beside her, hanging upward, and it tinkles softly.

She looks at Roan. "But how?"

Roan has no answer, but she squares her shoulders and walks on, past the inverted paintings and crosses, past the strangely burning wall sconces and over to the stairs.

"We have to go up—I mean, down. Look at the snakes."

"I have a bad feeling about this," Cage mutters, looking back.

"Leave, if you want," Roan tells him, "but I am going on. Seamus needs us."

"You can't really believe he's still alive after all this time?"

"I do. I believe it and I will prove it. Go back, if you must, coward."

Cage sneers and grabs her arm, his face close to her own. Rapley steps nearer, fists clenched.

"Speak not, little witch, for I have seen more than you can imagine. You think you know the dangers we may encounter, but you are a child in the face of such horrors."

Roan pulls her arm free. "Why do men think they may grab at a woman when they choose? Is my body yours to command? No. So molest me not!" And she spits at his feet before venturing forward alone.

Rapley cannot hide his smile when he turns to follow her. Emma, for her part, pauses beside Cage and looks after her friends.

"She is correct," Emma says mildly, "in that regard." Then she looks up at Cage and smiles, patting his arm. "You are too forceful, and so come off as a little ridiculous. Can you not stay calm and not behave as a—what did you call it? 'Hysterical female'?"

She departs with her own grin, leaving the giant man looking for all the world like a sulking pup. At last, he too follows on.

A shudder runs down Roan's spine, and she hates that it is not all revulsion. Some small part is...*delight*. How inventive. How crafty. How peculiar.

The room they now stand in would have been the upside-down attic, had the pattern of the last two floors continued. But it didn't. No, this room is something else entirely. Part workroom, part surgeon's house, and part dungeon. None of them speak—*can* speak—for the stench rises like a noxious acid and they gag where they stand.

Every inch of the crude stone walls is covered. Scripts, diagrams, pages torn from books—mostly, it seems, medical—and...flesh. Roan approaches one of the macabre models, only to discover that it is a human heart, cut open and spread wide, then nailed into the stone as if for admiration or study. She has never seen a human heart outside a book before, and wonders that such a gruesome aspect should contain all human emotion.

More parts. Lungs, intestines, what appears to be a spinal column and a rib cage. More diagrams. Some blood.

Rapley is inspecting the jars, his lips curled. Most contain liquids he would not dare guess at. But others…others contain brains of various sizes. He wants to believe they are goat, sheep, or pig brains, but senses deep within that he is looking at men, women, and children. He lifts one of the bottles. An eyeball rolls to peer at him and he scrambles back, placing the thing quickly down.

How old they are, he can only guess at.

"We must leave," Emma breathes. She flaps her hands and shakes her head, her voice rising to an almost-shriek. "We must leave!"

Roan hurries over. "Emma, what is it? What's wrong?"

"We have to leave. Now."

"But we haven't found Seamus yet—"

"The snakes have vanished," Rapley says, looking around. "Do you see them?"

"*Please*," Emma whispers, grabbing Roan's hand. Her grip is crushing. "We must go. Now!"

"Tell us why!"

"The rips…the tears…they are everywhere. We must not touch them!" And she jerks to the left with a shriek as though burned and rushes from the room without them.

"Curses," Roan says, wiping her mouth. "What now? Do we continue on?"

Cage is the only one who has not spoken. He turns slowly to face them, his face drained of all color. "I must…" he begins, and then stumbles. "I must leave also." He takes a few steadying breaths. "We should come back in the daylight hours. Do not ask me why I think so."

"It seems obvious," Rapley says. "Everything that's happened occurred in the dark hours." He looks to Roan, who stares into the gloom with a fixed gaze. She reminds him of a wolf on the hunt, and he smiles. "Roan. What do you think?"

She flinches at the sound of her name, then grumbles, "Very well."

She turns and hurries for the stairs and the two men follow behind her.

"She is wild," Cage mutters, staggering on the steps.

Rapley slips a shoulder under his arm and helps him up. "She is. The wildest thing I did ever see." Rapley grins, and when he sees the look of bewilderment on his half brother's face, he bursts into a peal of laughter that can be heard all throughout the dank, grisly room.

The entrance hall—the *real* entrance hall—is a sight for sore eyes. Even the feeling within the room is markedly different from the upside-down version beneath them.

"Better," Emma says as she sits on the slate floor, heedless of her skirts or of propriety. Roan half smiles and sits beside her, noting with pleasure that some things never change.

"Tell me what you meant when you spoke of the tears. What did you see? What do you flinch away from?"

"I see...rips. Rips in the fabric of things. They look like tears in a tapestry, only the tapestry is the world. When they touch, they burn. They appear where there has been death. I do not know why."

"And now?" Roan asks. "Do you see any of these tears now?"

"Some," Emma says, glancing to her left. "But far off. Small."

"What is taking the men so long?" Roan mutters. "Tell me again of male courage and women's fear?"

Emma laughs hollowly. "Should we go back?"

Roan is getting to her feet when Rapley and Cage stagger out of the hole.

"Something's wrong," Rapley says, sagging under Cage's weight.

Cage falls from his grasp and would have collapsed bodily onto the slate floor, only Roan's hand flies out and Cage's fall halts entirely.

Then, his body is lowered to the ground gently. Rapley sees it then. The black of her eyes. The way they truly have no walls. Her Unclosed abilities pour forth as easily as water from a glass. Not like his. Not like the rest of them, whose abilities are a toil and a struggle and—somehow limited. He knows what he is, he found the symbol for what describes him...Sighter. But her? No one symbol can contain what she possesses within herself.

He shudders.

Cage looses a low groan and begins to shake where he lies. His eyes roll back and the shaking intensifies; his mouth froths, first white, and then pink.

"He's turning blue!" Emma cries, crawling over.

Rapley tears his eyes away from Roan, but not before hearing her thought at that moment.

He knows. He fears me.

Emma cups Cage's face. "Cage! *Cage!*" She heaves his shoulders up enough that his head rests on her lap, and she strokes his forehead until a long, long time later, when he lies still, his breathing normal.

"Just like Seamus," Emma says, her eyes wet. "Just the same!"

Roan watches them with a deeper shock than she felt at finding the dungeon below. Emma. Little sprightly Emma...truly harboring feelings for this brutish man? The man who fought her at every turn and called her every name under the sun...The man who tortured and branded her?

"Will wonders never cease," she mutters beneath her breath.

Rapley paces up and down the floor, his breathing fast. Roan desperately wants to know, *needs* to know, that he is all right. That he does not think less of her. But of course he does, and she cannot bring herself to speak. A prickling feeling at the corners of her eyes angers her. She does not cry. She should have expected this. Her father told her that no one could ever love her. No one could ever understand.

How wrong she had been about him. He had not hated her. He had loved her enough to teach her about her nature, loved her enough to teach her to control it and to control herself.

How badly she had misjudged him.

Her ruminations are broken by a **BANG** on the front door.

They stare at it as one.

BANG

It is Rapley who turns to face the door, as though he is expecting it to shatter or cave in. She is enthralled by him.

BANG

The way he curls his hands slowly into fists that look strong enough to punch a hole in the world, should it be necessary.

BANG

The way his hair has come partly loose from the leather thong he ties it back with, and the curious color of it—like oak and coal. How his shoulders tense, and how his back responds, as though he is leaning into something.

BANG

The sweat building up on his roped neck as he strains and fights. The effort of his will and the way she can see his use of his ability. Like a shield, how he keeps them all safe. How he keeps *her* safe.

He loves me, she realizes. *He knows it. Knows my easy corruption. And he loves me anyway.*

BANG

She can *feel* it. His love for her. And how wondrous it is! How overwhelming. She is crying now because she finally, finally, has felt what she thought impossible. Because *she* loves *him* also. And she loves Emma and she loves Seamus.

And the thing beyond the door wants her. Only her.

⚡ ⚡

Emma is asleep, slumped over Cage, when Roan slips away silently to the kitchen and out the scullery door.

Inside the house, Rapley breathes a small sigh of relief as his battle gets marginally easier.

⚡ ⚡

Roan feels the change in the air the moment she steps outside. The pressure changes, the air thickens, and the wind picks up. All around, low-lying heather and moss break under the strain of the wind, which thrashes with a force the mountain has not seen.

Onward she walks, feeling the wind grow stronger, stronger, until the rocks themselves begin to blow away, tumbling down the hillside or into the air where they circle her, deadly and sharp.

Her steps are easy, for the winds, now swirling defiantly as a tornado, carry her in the eye of the storm, which she is, up and up and up to the place revealed in her dreams.

Rocks collapse under her feet as she steps, higher, higher.

When she reaches the mouth of the great cave, which sits beyond and above the circle of slate teeth, where she saw the earth devouring all in her delirious dream, she finds that the ram—that He—is waiting for her already.

And as quickly as the storm came, it is gone.

Girl and Devil converse.

ZOEY

NOW

Chapter 39

MORTAL

We've run out of food.
  We have enough water for another week.
  After that—

I'm too tired to write.

∽

Zoey Camera Footage
Date: November 4
  Zoey sits in front of the camera on the floor of the kitchen.
  "Len got the fire working. The chimney is fine. Didn't need cleaning. It's nicer in here than anywhere else in the house. I can pretend we're just preparing a big meal."

She looks around, then turns back to the camera with a sleepy sigh.

"I'm sorry, Mum," she says, and then she breaks down. "I—I—" She swallows and takes a few breaths. "I'm sorry. You were right. Coming here was a mistake." Wiping her nose, she looks up at the ceiling. "I thought I was risking my sanity, not my life. I was so *sure* that I was meant to come here, find some magical fix or explanation, and come home to find Dad fixed. Cured."

She laughs derisively, then sits staring into the camera for a while.

At last, she shakes her head and turns it off.

Camera Footage

Zoey holds the camera in her hand, which shakes. She is sitting outside on a slate surface, the sky a darkening gray behind her.

"Still too tired to write. But I feel a compulsion to record everything. Maybe someone will find it. Pass it on—"

She looks behind her and the camera picks up the red hair of Len.

"What are you doing on the roof?" Len calls.

"Thinking!"

"Couldn't you think closer to the ground?"

Zoey laughs and turns back toward the camera. "She's worried about me." A roll of her eyes. "She thinks I'll fall."

A moment later, Len has slid in behind Zoey, putting her chin on her shoulder. "You haven't had your share of the water."

"I know. I just felt like talking."

Len looks into the lens. "Who are you talking to?"

"Sometimes my mum. Sometimes my dad. Other times, to whoever finds this."

Zoey lifts the camera so that they are both in view. "My name is Zoey. Pleased to meet you. This is Len. We're trapped in a house in the middle of nowhere and are probably going to die." She gives a falsely cheery grin. "We've tried to leave a few times now. But it's always the same. We can't."

"Don't," Len says softly. She gets to her feet. "Let's go inside. It's freezing out here."

Camera Footage

Zoey and Len are sitting in the kitchen talking to the camera about what has happened, when Poulton stalks into the room. He is carrying a long ancient-looking knife in his hands.

"Look," he whispers, scratching his neck with the point.

Zoey jumps up. "Pole!"

Len stands as well. "Poulton, put the misericorde down."

"Please, Pole."

Pole smiles. "It's a rondel," he says, looking at Len. "But close. You know something about the weapons in my room, then?"

"Poulton!" Zoey snaps. "Stop it! You're scaring me."

"I know everything about them," Len says calmly. "Now put it back."

Pole cocks his head. "Nnnnnnnnno."

He advances on them. Zoey jumps up, but Len stands slowly. She walks around the table to face Pole.

"Give it to me," she says, holding out her hand.

He sneers. "I know what you are, little witch."

"We're both little witches, Poulton," Zoey says, inching closer. "Len, be careful. I have a bad feeling about this."

Len holds out her arm. "Stay back."

Pole mimics her voice. "*Stay back.*"

His lips are ringed in white gunge.

Len steps forward. Pole steps back.

And then, unexpectedly, he lunges forward, plunging the rounded dagger into Len's chest before running from the room.

Zoey's scream is earsplitting as Len hits the floor.

ROAN

1851

Chapter 40

HIS SEED

When dawn peeks through the front window, Rapley collapses from his long vigil, his shield having kept whatever evil was outside at bay, and Emma starts awake. The light is a surreal reminder that the world is still here. They are still alive.

"Thank the Lord!" Emma cries when Cage opens his eyes.

He blinks several times, frowning up at her. "Did you just say... 'thank the Lord'?"

Emma rolls her eyes. "Pf! Get off me, you oaf of a man and don't you dare accuse me of such foolishness. You banged your head, is all."

Cage gets up onto his elbows and grins as Emma stands and rubs her legs, muttering about his fat head and how she'll never walk again.

Rapley grins despite himself, and Cage shrugs at him. "Women are strange creatures. Where is Jenny? She might have come to see that we are still living and thought to offer refreshments, if there are any to be had."

"She was hiding in her room when last I saw her. Perhaps she has gone home, as she ought to." Emma looks around. "Where's Roan?"

There is no sign of her.

Rapley's face pales. "You let her leave?"

"How could I have stopped her? I didn't hear her go!"

Rapley attempts to stand. "We have to find her—" Cage grabs his arm as his legs buckle beneath him.

"Wait, brother. Please. I must tell you what I've seen—"

"Let me go, I have to find her!"

Cage's grip tightens. "I must tell you something first! Listen—Do not struggle so! Listen to me!"

Rapley wrenches himself free and half runs, half stumbles to the front doors, where he collapses, panting, hanging on to the handles as though to a life raft.

Emma hurries over to him. "Listen to Cage, you fool! Roan's life may depend on it. Curse you!"

Rapley releases the handles. "Speak quickly, then. Brother."

"My seizure…they happen from time to time. When they do, I…I…"

"You see things," Emma finishes. "Like Seamus."

Cage nods stiffly. "Yes. Like Seamus, and like Rapley, I see things. I am Unclosed also. And Rapley too."

Rapley's fury could not be more complete. "You fiend—you hurt Roan! You hurt her for being Unclosed, yet here you stand. Snake!"

Cage places his palms together as though in prayer. "It is difficult to take in, but you must. I think that perhaps Dr. Maudley is Fostos."

"Maudley is gone."

"Conveniently, yes. He was the first to disappear, and we have seen no body, no blood—nothing. Maudley brought you all to this place, he owns it—how, I do not know. But he is connected. *You* have lived here with him for some years, have you not?"

Rapley covers his face. "Yes."

"And did you not think him peculiar?"

"I avoided him."

"He brought us together for some purpose," Emma says. "I have been thinking, myself, about the root of it all. Why did he come to Ireland and collect my brother and me? Why us? It felt too convenient for me. It always did."

"He was a father bringing home his children," Cage says.

"To what end?" Rapley says through clenched teeth. "To play happy family?"

Cage looks away. "You know why. Like I said before—he needs souls to barter with—"

"And did he summon you, as well?" Emma asks.

"No. I came looking for Fostos on my own."

"It makes no difference to me," Rapley says. "Roan is out there and I'm going to find her. Damn anyone who tries to stop me."

"But don't you see? Those organs we found—that's his work. Who knows how many people have been dissected in his quest for yet more time. And Roan—she is everything he has been trying to create!"

Rapley storms over and shakes him. "How? Why?"

"She has more than one ability. Can you not sense her before she even enters a room? She *is* the Conjure, she *is* the Devil's Tongue. A culmination of all his power. She is a storm, Rapley. She is *evil*."

Rapley laughs harshly. "So those words before, about fighting her dark side...they were lies. They were mere manipulations."

"She needs to have hope, even if there is none. She would not have left to deal with—" Cage breaks off.

Rapley goes very still and his voice is as dangerous as a scorpion sting. "You best be straight with me, brother. Where has she gone? To deal with *what*?"

Cage glances at Emma who frowns. "What have you done?"

"She would never have left if she thought she was evil. If she had hope, she would go. I knew she would. Go and barter her own deal."

"Her own…" Emma's voice is strangled. "By God, Cage…she's gone to deal with the Devil…"

Rapley hits Cage. Hard.

The bulky man staggers back, clutching his jaw.

"You blaggard!" Rapley roars. "She was bait!"

"She's a vessel for great evil," Cage corrects, wiping blood from his lip.

"You knew this all along," Rapley says, his wolfish teeth on full display. "And you did nothing to warn us. You did nothing to save Seamus from being taken. You took Roan prisoner, you tortured her. And you knew this all along."

"I thought…I thought her in league with the Foul One. I thought her a witch."

And Rapley would have hit him again if Emma had not rushed between them. *"You are Unclosed yourself! We are all witches!"*

"I made a terrible mistake before with her. But do not let it lead you astray."

Rapley shakes out his fist and Emma covers her mouth.

"I need to find her," Rapley snaps.

"Fostos is *here*, Rapley. He never really left, I don't think."

Emma uncovers her mouth. "What do you mean? Speak plain."

"The man who built this house. The miller. He was Fostos. He built this house atop the desecrated caverns where he made his deal. He has been here for generations. We need to stop him before he gets to Roan. And the best way to do that is to go find *him*, not race after *her*."

Emma's scream cuts through their talk. *"Seamus!"*

Cage is beside her at once, but she is stumbling back, away from him.

"Seamus, oh God, Seamus!"

"Tell us what you see," Rapley demands.

"A t-t-tear! A rip in the world." Her eyes are huge in her haunted face, her lips quivering with raw fear. "It is so big...It is so black." She sobs, her chest heaving. "It is Seamus! I know it is!"

Cage looks at Rapley and their eyes connect.

"We have to go back down," Rapley says.

Cage pauses. "The Underneath."

The only light is dim and red, and it glows low by the ground like some small revelation of the fires that burn far below. It reveals in silhouette the shape of a man…and of a beast. Tall, proud horns, larger than any she has seen on any animal, seem to grow from his head, twisted, gnarled, and old.

This is an ancient creature.

Roan stands before it, considering the darkness, considering herself, and then she sits down, getting comfortable.

Across from her, the man sits as well.

"AND SO I HAVE COME," she says at last, but these words are not human. They are harsh, guttural sounds deep in her throat. They are teeth and hisses and growls. She looks about her, as if curious.

YOU HAVE COME AND I REJOICE.
"WHY DO YOU WANT ME HERE?"

The thing, man or beast, never moves. She cannot see any form of mouth. Only the shape of him, stiller than the night.

I WANT YOU. ANYWHERE.
"WHAT FOR?"
TO BE MY OWN. TO BE MY CREATURE. TO SERVE ME.
"AND MY SOUL. YOU WANT THAT ALSO?"
I WANT IT ALL.
"I AM HERE TO BARTER."

Something like laughter ripples through the cavern, and then the shadow moves with unexpected suddenness. He leans on his elbow, the proud horns tilting to the left as he considers her.

KNOW YOU WHAT I AM? KNOW TO WHAT YOU SPEAK?
"I KNOW. I AM HERE."

SING A SONG, LITTLE THING.

Roan does not hesitate. She opens her mouth and sings. She sings a song her mother once sang to her.

SHE IS MINE, THIS WOMAN OF WHOM YOU THINK.
"I HAVE LITTLE DOUBT."

Again, the strange laughter.

AND IT IS YOUR DOING.
"AM I NOT EVIL INCARNATE, AS YOU INTENDED?"
SPEAK WHAT YOU WILL, AND MAKE YOUR OFFER.
"I HAVE QUESTIONS. I WANT THE ANSWERS. THE FACTUAL ANSWERS. I WANT THEM CLEAR AND PRECISE. AND IF YOU LIE, I THINK I WILL KNOW IT. AND AFTER THAT, I WANT SOMETHING MORE."

The man smiles, and his grin is sharp and white and horrible.

ASK, AND OFFER. I WILL DECIDE.
"I WILL NOT OFFER MY SOUL. THAT IS MINE ALONE. BUT WHEN YOU CALL, AND FOR WHATEVER YOU ASK, I WILL ANSWER AND I WILL GIVE."
I WILL TAKE IT.
"ANSWER ME THIS. AM I BORN CURSED?"
YOU KNOW IT.
"AND RAPLEY? EMMA. SEAMUS. WHO ELSE?"
ALL. YES. THAT MAN YOU CALL CAGE AND TWO OTHERS.
"TWO MORE UNCLOSED?"
TWO MORE CURSED LIVES.
"NOT UNCLOSED?"
NOT UNCLOSED.

Roan takes a moment to think.

"WILL RAPLEY AND I EVER BE FREE OF THIS?"

A moment of silence.

HE TOLD YOU TRUE ON THE MOUNTAIN THAT DAY.
"I DON'T BELIEVE IT."
HE WILL DIE ON THIS MOUNTAIN. AND BE CURSED EVERMORE.
"LIES!"

Again, that terrible white grin.

"HE IS MY ADAM, YES?"
YES.
"TELL ME WHAT HAPPENED."
A CLOAKED MAN BROUGHT HIM TO YOU THAT YEAR. IT WAS A SPECIAL YEAR.
THE YEAR YOU DISCOVERED YOUR UNCLOSED NATURE. AND HIS. YOU CONJURED
TOGETHER. YOU LOVED HIM. AND HE LOVED YOU MORE. AND THEN HE WAS TAKEN
AWAY BY THE MAN IN THE CLOAK, BROUGHT TO THE MOUNTAIN WHERE HIS LOVE,
HIS SOUL, AND HIS SELF WITHERED TO A PIP AND NO MORE.
    "WHO IS THE MAN?"
    THE ONE WHO BROUGHT YOU HERE. THE ONE YOUR LOVE IS GOING, RIGHT
NOW, TO CONFRONT. ALAS, HE IS TOO STRONG FOR A PIP.
    "TELL ME WHY YOU WANT ME. WHY THE MAN WANTS ME. TELL ME NOW!
QUICKLY!"

The thing shifts again in the cave, somehow growing bigger and
closer all at once.

YOUR POWER IS PURE, MY DAUGHTER. THROUGH YOU, HE WILL SURELY GAIN
A THOUSAND YEARS THRICE UPON HIM. IF HE WERE TO CAPTURE YOUR SOUL...HE

MIGHT HAVE ENOUGH CURRENCY TO BARTER BACK...HIS OWN. OFFER YOUR SOUL TO ME NOW, AND YOU ARE NO USE TO HIM.

"IT WILL NOT HAPPEN."

YOU, MY CHILD, WERE CONCEIVED UPON THIS VERY MOUNTAIN. AND YOU LIVED HERE FOR A TIME. DO YOU NOT REMEMBER THE INTOXICATING TIME OF YOUR EARLY CHILDHOOD. WE WOULD SPEAK OFTEN, YOU AND I. MY HAND IN YOUR CONCEPTION WAS GREAT.

Unbidden, an image flashes into Roan's mind, of a time before she existed. A brown-haired man, naked, lying with her mother. The bestial quality of it as she saw man merge with horns and out again. An unholy union.

"ENOUGH—"

HE WILL CARVE THE HEARTS FROM MANY MEN AND WOMEN AND CHILDREN LOOKING FOR THAT PRECIOUS SOUL...

"GIVE ME WHAT I NEED TO DEFEAT HIM. GIVE IT TO ME NOW."

GIVE YOURSELF OVER TO MY DARKNESS, TO MY WILL, AND I WILL KEEP YOU SAFE.

"I WILL KEEP MY FREE WILL UNTIL I DIE. YET I WANT THE STRENGTH— WHATEVER IT IS I NEED—TO DEFEAT HIM. I FREELY OFFER ONE FAVOR IN RETURN. ANYTHING, AT ANY TIME."

DO YOU KNOW WHAT YOU ARE DOING, LITTLE GIRL?

"ENOUGH. DO IT. DO IT NOW."

When the laughter comes this time, it does not stop. Even when Roan is screaming.

The light, dim when Roan walked willingly into the cave, is now a hot, white, throbbing orb. She cries out, shielding her eyes, and shies back into the dark.

Behind her, the cave is cold and empty. She is alone.

Blinking back tears, she looks out into the late afternoon again. She can see the piercing white mists and the jagged shapes of the slate protruding from the veil. She cannot see the house. She cannot see much else besides.

The light is a knife in her head.

She stumbles out of the safety of the dark, moving as fast as she can, opening her eyes as little as possible, heading for Mill House and her friends.

Hurry, something inside whispers. *Do not tarry.*

A gust of wind throws itself unexpectedly against her and she falters. The mists coil and part, and there in the vacuum stands Rapley. He is indistinct, faded around the edges like he is becoming part of the mists themselves. He does not see her. He is somewhere else.

"You," he whispers, and Roan reaches out her hand, calling his name.

Rapley bares his teeth. *"You!"*

Hovering over his head...a crow, wings beating furiously as it squawks, the eyes as red as the ram's.

She blinks, the mists rush in like a tidal wave, the crow screams— and Rapley is gone.

Her heart drops to her feet like a cold stone. *"Rapley!"*

He is waiting for them in the lowest part of the house. The dungeon.

Rapley, Cage, and Emma freeze when they see him. Robed in black, face hidden from view, the man they know is Fostos.

"Corrupt," Cage murmurs. "Vile destroyer."

The man opens his mouth to speak, but it is not Maudley's voice that issues forth.

"Devil-Talker, Deal-Maker, Hell-Fated...so many names. And only one that was truly ever mine."

Rapley's lips curl. "Fostos."

The man raises his head, the shadows flee from his features, and he smiles.

"You," Rapley breathes. *"You."*

"My God," Emma whispers. "It cannot be...*Andrew*. But why?"

Andrew...Fostos...removes his hood, folding it back. His beloved cassock had seemed the most fitting attire for this moment. Behind him, the waterwheel stands stationary, and yet...it also spins slowly. Like some kind of strange mirage on top of reality, there are somehow *two* wheels. One in this world still as stone, and another in that other strange world that he and the others have access to—and *this* one is spinning.

Seamus is strapped to the wheel.

ZOEY

NOW

Chapter 41
SO. . .

Camera Footage

Zoey runs to Len's side, screaming her name. Len coughs, grimaces, and then reaches for the hilt of the weapon. She pulls it free and rolls over, coughing blood.

"Len? Oh, God! Len!"

Len coughs again, and then grunts. "Hate it when that happens."

She sits up, and Zoey screams again, but this time for a very different reason. Len's chest is closing up in front of her eyes.

Len wipes her mouth. "We...we should talk."

⌁

Diary,

I...hardly know what to write. So much has happened. So, first: Len's immortal. Ha. Go figure. That shit's real.

My best friend tried to murder her—<u>did</u> murder her, actually, only she didn't die. Yeeeah. I can't wait to read this back when I GET THE HELL OUT OF HERE.

This is crazy.

I couldn't look at Len for the whole day. I just...I couldn't stop seeing her there, the knife in her chest, the blood in her mouth. I thought she was dead. Gone. And then...she pops up like a daisy.

I'm so...<u>grateful</u>. But my head is a mess.

I've been mulling over an idea ever since we read about the waterwheel in Roan's letters. I'm going to propose something to Len, but I know she's going to refuse. I'll record it. Tonight.

"No," Len said, pacing up and down. She swept her hands apart. "Absolutely not."

She wouldn't listen and she was making me dizzy. I was sitting on the sofa in the Red Room perfectly calm, but as the morning wore on she had become more and more nervous. We ate the last can of chicken curry this morning. I took half and left the rest for Pole outside the Hunting Room, which is now his bedroom apparently. Even knowing this, Len wasn't willing to risk me Conjuring. I asked her what she suggested. As far as I can see, we have three options:

1. Pole and I starve to death.
2. Pole kills me in this—whatever madness this is.
3. We Conjure one last time to find the wheel and break it.

At least with option three we have a chance.

"I don't want you to Conjure again," she said. "Look what happened last time."

"I told you, there's a price. But the injuries heal."

"Your anemia hasn't."

I hesitated. "Maybe it has."

Len turned a sharp look on me. "It hasn't."

"You don't know that."

She blinked hard. "Yes, I do."

"How?"

"I just do."

I insisted she tell me how.

She turned away from me. "Zoey, leave it. Please."

"You don't know—"

"I can smell it!" she yelled, facing me abruptly.

I have no idea what reaction I had, only that Len turned away again, her skin suddenly more sallow than I had noticed before. There had been an odd flash in her eyes when she'd said it.

I opened my mouth to ask her what she meant and found that I didn't really want to know.

<u>Later, though. I'm going to ask her later. (Note to self: DO IT.)</u>

"I just think that it's too much of a risk," Len said eventually, her voice calmer and softer.

I took her hands as she passed me and pulled her

to the sofa beside me. She couldn't meet my gaze. "If we do nothing, I'll die. Pole will die."

I tried to turn her face toward me by nudging her chin. She didn't budge, so instead I hooked my finger into her ear and used it as a lever to turn her head my way.

She laughed and faced me. And then she kissed me and we didn't speak for a while. We just sat and looked at each other. She touched my cheek, touched my hair, touched the hollow of my neck.

"Zoey…" she said softly, her fingers roaming lower.

"I don't want to die here," I whispered.

"But what if you lose something vital. Your sight, your mind—"

"I don't intend to lie."

"I think Conjuring damages you whether you lie or not. At least, Conjures of this size."

"There's no choice."

She closed her eyes and her answer was more an exhale than words. "Okay."

I swallowed and closed my eyes too. "Thank you."

"This one," she said, kissing my neck, "last," her breath sweet on my skin, "time," her tongue on my collarbone.

I shuddered.

She opened her eyes and got up. Then she went over to the door and closed it, pushing a chair up beneath the handle.

"I want to show you something," she said, and my heart beat once, stopped, and then thudded erratically.

Then she was on her knees in front of me, her

396

hands sliding up my top, and each bit of skin she revealed, she adorned with kisses.

She touched my breasts, and then removed my bra, and I found myself touching and kissing her as well.

When she reached for the laces on my track pants, she looked up into my face and smiled.

"Beautiful," she said, and went lower.

~~

We hear Poulton upstairs, but never see him. He's most active at night, when we hear him grunting, banging, and running, his footfalls loud and unnerving. During the day, we don't hear a thing.

Len wants to tie him up, but I won't do that.

But I do worry about him hurting himself.

Is this what my father went through?

It's seven in the morning. Len is still asleep and upstairs is quiet. I'm going to go and check on Pole, but I'm going to take the camera. I'll talk to him, without Len nearby, and ask him what he's experiencing. I'll try to get him back to himself. I want my best friend back.

~~

Camera Footage

A hand knocks on a door, and a voice calls, "Pole?"

Zoey knocks again, but turns her camera on herself to say, "No reply."

She waits a few more seconds, and then there is a sharp **bang** on the door.

"Poulton, please, can I come in?"

Silence.

She turns the door handle, but the door doesn't budge. She rattles the handle—nothing.

"I'll be in the twin bedroom. Please come and talk to me. I'll be alone."

She turns away from the door, the camera on her face. She opens her mouth to say something, but then the distinctive sound of a door creaking stops her. She turns around, camera still on her face, and screams.

The camera hits the floor.

The door is standing open.

The room beyond black as night.

Zoey stands still, breathing in, out, in, out...

Then, slowly, she bends down and picks up the camera.

"Pole?" she calls, her voice shaky. "Please don't mess around."

She steps slowly into the room and gasps.

The room has been decimated.

The camera shakes as Zoey looks around. The animal skulls, which before had been arranged in a pile along one wall, some mounted on the wall itself, have all been hung.

Upside down.

The weapons, which had been on the other three walls, have been removed.

None of them are in the room now.

The eye sockets of each of the skulls are dark and menacing, and when Zoey focuses the camera in their direction, she takes a step back. The eyeless black spaces glare with a kind of cunning; the long teeth almost make them look as though they are grinning.

Zoey backs away and then, with a little sob, runs from the room.

Poulton was not there.

〜〜

Dear Diary,

I haven't been able to find Poulton since I went looking in the Hunting Room yesterday morning. At night, we hear him, though. We've searched everywhere for both him and the wheel.

Nothing.

We hear crashes. Then long stretches of silence. The floors creak.

Len sits still, her lips thin, and when I ask her what she thinks, she doesn't answer. Tonight, we Conjure. We find the wheel Roan talks about in her letters. We find our way out.

〜〜

Poulton:

I don't know

        there were voices.

                sounds.
              movement.
              sensations.

yes, the room was altered.
the skulls were inverted, yes.
hung upside down.
no, not by me.

I don't know who
something evil.

demonic

I had horns, yes
they grew
right out
of
my skull

yes, okay?
yes. I was a

beast

an animal.

I was lost in the dark.

why did I do it?
Is that your question?

I don't remember.

Where is Zoey?
I told you.
I don't know.

No I did not kill her.

〜

We found the wheel. At first, I thought nothing
was wrong.
It was one of the snakes that led us there. I

saw it move first. It seemed to crack and move, each twitch just a little too fast.

And then it began to glide over the floor in jagged, strange movements, unlike a living snake altogether. It was more like some strange stop-motion puppet show.

"Your food is slithering away," Len murmured. "You can see that, right?"

I nodded. "Mm-hm." And we released each other's hands.

I got unsteadily to my feet; Len was already following, a small bag clutched in her fist.

The snake led us through to the blocked wing and slid beneath the door. Len removed a piece of chalk and drew some symbols on the door, spoke some guttural sounds, and the door burst open.

I opened my mouth to ask her what she'd just done—was that the language she had spoken of? The one made of all the symbols she knew? The one she had refused, point-blank, to teach me?

I looked at the wreckage of the door as I passed and could see why. She was...powerful.

Len left her little bag behind but slipped her chalk into the zipped pocket of her jacket, and we followed the snake. It led us into a church, but unlike any church I've ever seen. It was the opposite of holy, with a large, black inverted cross on the altar. After that, another set of stairs. The snake descended very slowly.

It was pitch-black.

"Wait here," Len said, and ran from the church.

The cold coming up from that doorway and those stairs was intense. Like opening a freezer door.

Something moved in the blackness. It sounded strange and rippled. More than the snake was waiting for us.

Len returned with two flashlights.

"If Poulton wasn't a risk, or if we knew where he was," she said, "I would ask you to wait here for me."

"You should know better by now," I told her, and she grinned.

It was hard to make head or tail of what came next. Most of it was just rocky, broken passages, blackened and old. The smell of moss and neglect was rife and made us choke.

There were stairs and passages and what looked like rooms. There were many, many inverted crosses and I stuck close to Len, holding on to her arm.

On and on the snake went, down and down it took us.

There were holes in the floor that we had to jump across, and then one large section of the floor entirely missing. The snake slid across the sliver of space that was left, a kind of ledge where the rocks had not quite fallen away. We could shimmy across, but it was precarious.

Len turned to me. "Wait—"

"No. I will not wait here."

Len grinned, and nodded. We peered over the ledge, her flashlight trying to find anything but blackness. And it did—

the wheel.

A spoke, a wooden frame...

"My God," I said.

From where we peered down at it, into the huge cavernous space, we saw that the wheel was at least forty feet high, and half-submerged in water black as tar. A giant.

Len went first. She edged along the tiny little bit of floor that was left. The snake had stopped moving in the shadows. I kept my flashlight on it and on Len in turns.

My heart was in my throat. I don't think I've ever been more scared in my life.

"Now you," Len said from the other side.

My heart was thumping slow and hard in my chest. I could feel the truth of Len's declaration that I was still deeply anemic. My arms shook as they tried to bear some of my weight, holding on to the rocky wall. It was so cold and slick that I worried I might not make it.

I was almost with Len, her hand a mere inch or two from mine, when that fear became reality. My legs gave out with no warning and I fell, down into the inky, icy blackness below.

I didn't hear her scream.

The shock of the water drove the air from me, and I couldn't move my limbs. I went down like a rock, my flashlight still gripped in my rigid fingers.

All around me there was green water, horrible, horrible green water, and beneath me, a seemingly endless blackness.

I thought of the Titanic.

My lungs screamed for air.

Move, I told myself.

But I couldn't.

Len reached me some time after. She pulled me up and onto a landing that sat halfway up the height of the wheel, just out of the water. I was frigid, too cold to shiver.

"F-f-found it."

Len was panting hard. She pulled off my jacket and shirt, tossed them aside, took off her own jacket, and wrapped me in it.

"Y-y-you're j-just t-t-trying to get me n-naked," I said feebly, trying to grin.

"Your gums are blue. Fuck."

"One of these d-days," I told her, some warmth returning now that I was out of the water and in her fleece-lined jacket, the outside of which was waterproof, "you're going to have to tell me how old you are. You have a foul way of speaking." I tried to wink, but only succeeded in closing one of my eyes.

She swore again, then reached into one of the zip pockets in her jacket and pulled out the chalk. Once again, she drew some symbols, muttered under her breath (I noticed her shudder and grimace), and the edges of the platform lit up with fire.

We sat like that for a while, and the wooden platform didn't seem to burn beyond the very edges.

"I can destroy this without you," she told me. "I just need to rest and prepare. Lie down. Get warm."

I did as she said, wishing that the feeling would return to my legs, but I was still wearing my sodden jeans. I inched closer to the fire, feeling weird about lying so close to open flame, but knowing Len would protect me.

The heat ran through me like a warm summer, and I had never felt this good.

There was no sign of the snake.

When I woke, the fire was still going, though less intensely. The flames were simmering, rather than roaring.

Len was gone.

I called her name, panic rising wildly inside me.

"Up here," she murmured.

She was on the top of the wheel, twenty or more feet above me. The entire surface of the wheel had been covered in little chalk symbols.

"My God," I whispered.

"This thing will blow like dynamite."

"How will we get out?"

"Behind you," she said. "That doorway. It looks like it leads right up. Straight into and out of the mountain. I went up a few stories. It's our exit."

I wiggled my toes—they were cold and tingling, but fine.

"There's something else," she said, nodding toward the shadowy ruins behind me.

I looked, but saw nothing. "What?"

"He's in there, watching us. Keep a lookout."

I stared at the shadows, and as I looked, my eyes adjusting to the dark beyond the fire, a pale figure appeared, crouched in the darkness. It was watching us.

I gasped, and the figure scrambled away.

"Was that—is it—"

"Yeah," she said, without turning away from her

furious scratching. "We found where Poulton's been hiding out."

I wanted to go to him. To run over and hold him and tell him everything was going to be fine, but I knew he would only attack me.

"But those <u>bangs</u> in the house," I said, trailing off. If they weren't Pole...

"I don't think those were him," Len said, confirming my thoughts.

"Who else?"

She looked down at me. "I think you mean <u>what</u> else."

Suddenly I felt very exposed. I looked at the darkness that surrounded my little flaming platform like a cage. It was like the darkness contained many eyes, all of them watching me, all of them waiting for the fire to burn out.

Len lured Pole out with the snake, as though it were a tasty treat for him to enjoy. She found it floating in the water beneath the surface near the wheel when she was climbing down. I was feeling more sick than I ever had, my legs shaking with fatigue. She told me to go ahead of her through the doorway and I didn't argue. Poulton was slow to advance, distrusting as a feral cat.

We only had the one flashlight left, so I took it, leading the way. Occasionally I shone it back, wanting to see what was happening, but Len would tell me not to. Poulton, it seemed, was scared of the light. But his hunger overran his fear, because eventually, as the stairs narrowed and the meager light seemed more bountiful with the reflection from the water, he crept out and I saw with a shock that he was skin and bones—and naked as the day he was born.

Len hushed me and told me to keep going; we couldn't stop to rest, since Poulton might snatch the snake and run back down. I wept all the way up, partly from the pain in my body and my legs, but mostly for my friend.

Poulton.

I kept thinking: What the hell have I brought him to? This is my fault. My stupid quest to save my father has cost me the dearest thing in my life. If we survive, how will he ever be the same again? Even now, he's tied to the piano like a dog and he howls all night as though in agony. We've had to strap his head to it too, since he kept trying to ram it with his head. We've used some of our clothes for rope.

He's not my intelligent, logical friend.

He's not even human.

We came out onto the mountain into a dull, gray morning. We had been under the earth for more than twelve hours. The exit was nothing more than an opening in a shallow cave, but the walk back to the house was long.

The light was a balm, but I could barely carry myself.

I told Len to go on. Poulton had tried to back away near the top, and Len had seized him by the arms and dragged him the rest of the way. Then she had muttered her guttural speech and we heard, far below, a great rumble, and felt it beneath our feet.

There was a growing sound, like an approaching wave, and then the exit puffed with noxious-smelling smoke and the mountain shuddered and collapsed a little beneath our feet.

I screamed and fell as the earthquake shook our bones, but when I looked up, Len was still standing— and still holding Poulton.

The sound died away. A few <u>bangs, crashes</u>, and the dull, tinkling sound of dirt falling, and then nothing.

"Go on ahead," I told Len, coughing. "I'll follow right behind. I can't go that fast again."

She opened her mouth to refuse, but Poulton broke away and made a mad dash through the mists and Len shot after him. I hadn't seen mist this thick before. It was only three feet before I lost sight of them entirely.

"I'm taking him to the house," she called. "Stay put—I'll be back soon."

I called out my agreement and lay my head down on the rocks.

Beneath me, I thought I could feel the slowing heartbeat of the mountain, and then I fell asleep.

Len came back for me a little while later. She woke me with a kiss.

"I'm so tired," I breathed.

I didn't know if I had the energy to lift my head, but of course I did. Len helped me up and we half walked, half stumbled back to the house.

And that's when I knew something was wrong.

I was grinning as I entered—she had put on the space heater, even though we were conserving the last of the fuel for really bad nights.

I took one step, another—

everything was looking a little brighter. We had done it. We had done it! We had destroyed the wheel that was keeping all things bound to the house, and

we could leave! We could leave! The mists would clear,
the storms would pass, and we would be able to walk
out of here.

—and then I hit the floor.

⌒⌒

I haven't been able to get up since.

Len caught us some snakes while we waited for
the healing to begin. At first, we thought it was fine.
Like before, my injuries would heal. A few hours and I
would be fine. Okay, yes. I was still anemic, but that
was because you can't grow red blood cells overnight.
In a few hours—it would be fine. Like always.

Hours turned into a day. I still believed. Len
paced, ashen, but I smiled at her and let her cook us
rats on a fire she lit with her strange words. I asked
her to tell me stories, but she couldn't. She was
feeling sick, she said.

⌒⌒

The day after, I was worried. What if it was forever?

⌒⌒

Today is the third day. And I know it is. I can't move
my legs. I can't walk.

⌒⌒

And the mists remain fixedly in place.

*W*e have a son! Living, breathing, alive! We are delirious with joy! John cannot stop kissing my face. He now insists we bed upon the mountain! For was not our boy conceived under the stars on the far side of the mountain? John says it is fated, and what am I to think? It must be true! We have named our son Nicholas, and may he have a long life!

FROM THE DIARY OF
HERMIONE SMITH

I watch John speak to that ram at night, whispering into its ear. I watch the ram stare at me and I know it talks to John in turn. It is a fiend, it is the Prince of Darkness, slanderer, spoiler, the Great Dragon, Lucifer! I shall cut out the heart of the beast and burn it to ash! John speaks with Lucifer and so my babes have been stolen like John's men!

I curse all that live! I curse all who bear children! I curse my own self! Let not me suffer this pain again! May there be a price!

My babes, oh Lord, my babes!

FROM THE DIARY OF
HERMIONE SMITH

ROAN

✦⟡✦

1851

Chapter 42

FOSTOS

Emma rushes forward with a cry, but a dance of Andrew's fingers and she is flung away.

He clucks his tongue. "Naughty, saucy girl."

"Give him to me," Emma cries. *"Give him to me!"*

It is difficult to tell if Seamus is alive. His hair has been shaved away so that he looks like a strange baby, though the rough stitching along his skull almost shouts with its ghastly savagery. He has been cut open from ear to ear and sewn shut again.

Emma retches, her eyes and nose streaming.

Both of Seamus's legs are gone below the knee, and there are more stitches on his torso.

"What have you done," Emma chokes. "Seamus! *Seamus!*"

Cage holds out the crucifix from around his neck, his eyes fixed on Andrew. He mutters constantly beneath his breath.

"Save your breath, priest," Andrew says, and in the darkness of the Underneath, his eyes glow like a cat's.

"Back, demon," Cage spits with a savage force. "Back!"

Andrew skips back, laughing. "Oh, this *is* fun. It's been such a long time since I've had fun."

Rapley eyes the wheel, a beast of a thing, wondering what purpose it serves, and how he will be able to get to it before Andrew stops him.

Andrew, distracted by Cage, allows his hands to fall, so that Emma is released. She glances at him, then inches forward, all the while avoiding pockets of empty air as though they are wasps no one can see.

Rapley steps forward to further distract Andrew, and Emma reaches her brother, but once she lays a hand on him, she cries out.

"*Seamus!* Oh, no! *No!*" Her scream echoes through the Underneath, an earthquake of grief.

"I'm close now," Andrew says. He gestures with his arm to the wall to his left where new organs have appeared, nailed into the wall. "His heart, his lungs, his spleen…"

Emma retches twice, then vomits.

Andrew grins and licks a finger. "His blood was particularly sweet. Tell me," Andrew says, turning to Emma, "did you enjoy the boy, Dylan? He was another of my wards, but sadly…we needed supplies. You had to eat. And then my son, Maudley, was of no more use to me… and you devoured him also. I saw how famished you and Seamus were, stuffing your little faces with his meat."

Emma's eyes are glassy as she stares at the thing that bred her. "We… ate…Dr. Maudley…"

"Foul beast," Cage says, raising his crucifix higher. "Back with you!"

Andrew smiles. "Crucisvigil, we meet again. You all have a certain stench about you, did you know? I remember it well from the catacombs." He pretends to retch, then glances at Emma, grinning. "Where is my daughter, Roan?"

"She's been sent away," Rapley says. "Far from you and your evil."

"Do you not fear the wrath of God?" Cage asks.

As the candles and torches burn and smoke, Andrew's face shifts ever so subtly, until he looks more beast than man. His eyes, Rapley realizes, at this moment, look just like Roan's—no walls. No barriers. Unclosed and open to the evil beyond the doorway. But no thoughts spill out. Only the deepest malevolence Rapley has ever felt.

Rapley strikes out, but Andrew is fast.

"Do you think you can kill me?" Andrew bellows. "I am older than this house—older than your conception of time."

Cage joins the fight, but Andrew's strength is uncanny, his speed doubly so. His eyes are darker than the night now, and his skin is pale as ice.

Andrew roars as Cage and Rapley rush at him. "I am Fostos! I taught Da Vinci, directed John Dee, and I am the miller, John Smith, who built this house! I made you, one and all."

Emma hurries to the wheel again, climbing up upon the spokes to free her brother from the restraints. She pulls him from the stone and he lands with a dull, wet *thunk*. She drags him across the room, heading for the stairs.

Andrew slams Cage and Rapley to the ground and then jumps several dozen feet to where Emma stands, pulling Seamus.

He lifts her by the hair. "Do you see my rips, daughter?" he asks, his grin a little too wide for a human face, his teeth a little too sharp.

Terror shines from her eyes like beacons in a foggy night. The rips are everywhere. Blacker and wider here than anywhere else.

"Do you know where they lead?" Andrew asks. Emma soils herself.

Andrew leans close and whispers in her ear, "To hell," and he throws her away like a bit of rubbish. She hits a rip in the air, screaming. And then everything goes silent. She looks at Cage, her mouth open in a little O, and then a series of loud *cracks* rend the air. Her legs break outward at the knees and she is sucked through. The rip seals behind her.

"Emma!" Cage screams, and he tries to run after her, but all he knows is that she hit the air like it was a solid wall, and vanished into nothing. There is nowhere to go. He scrabbles at the air as though trying to find the place where she disappeared and drag her back—but there is nothing.

With a growl, Cage runs at Andrew, his heart beating with a deeper hate than he knew was possible. But he is too weak for Fostos.

"You have passing abilities, boy. Who are you?" Cage tries to hit out, but fails. Andrew smells him, his nostrils wide, and then rips his shirt. "Strange…You are Crucisvigil…but you are also *mine*."

"Yes, Grandfather, I am yours!" says Cage, and hits him hard.

"Intriguing," Andrew says, reacting to Cage's blow as though he is nothing but a fly. "You are born of a failure. I thought I had destroyed them all. I will take that into account."

Cage reaches into his pocket, pulling out a small vial. He thumbs away the cork and throws the water over Andrew, who laughs. "Do you think you can hold me down with your holy water and fists?"

He throws Cage away with a flick of his arm. Cage flies twenty feet, lands, and is still.

Rapley's Unclosed abilities are straining against his flesh, but he rejects using the evil he was given at birth. He is a man, a mortal, born of a good woman who loved him. Andrew avoids his blows, delivering his own like a strange, bloody dance. He toys with Rapley on the blood-soaked floor.

At last, seeming to grow bored, Andrew drags Rapley to the waterwheel. It is turning again, carrying nothing. Nothing Rapley can see, at any rate, but he is overcome with the presence of evil. He senses that if Emma were here to see it, the rip would be so wide that it would swallow all light. The burning light from the cressets on the wall cannot pierce the darkness.

Andrew talks to Rapley in the Devil's Tongue as he straps him into place, but Rapley cannot understand, grateful that he does not have this knowledge. He lets the monster talk, and closes his eyes.

She is running fast.

Come on, Roan urges herself. *Come on!* Though she knows it must be late afternoon, the light is terrible—she is choking on it.

Rapley appears before her on the mountain. Only...not Rapley, exactly. His nightwalking form.

"Rapley!" she cries, stumbling. "What have you done?"

He shakes his head. "I'm at the bottom of the Underneath with Andrew." He smiles at her, and she goes cold. "I need to finish it."

Roan reaches for him, but her hand passes straight through as it would the mist itself. "Wait for me. We can do it together."

But Rapley shakes his head. "He wants you. If he gets you...You're too powerful." He reaches out for her. "I love you."

Roan screams when Rapley vanishes in a hole of fire that isn't there, and it echoes through the mountain. The ram watches.

Roan closes her eyes and speaks words she has not dared to before. When she opens them, she is in the Underneath.

Andrew's head snaps in her direction, and his grin widens. "Ah..."

Rapley is half-strapped to the enormous wheel, which pulses with vile energy. As Andrew focuses on Roan, advancing, Rapley unties himself.

"I've been waiting for this," Andrew says, spreading his arms. "I knew the moment I saw you. You write those silly letters backward... just as I taught Da Vinci to...upside down and backward of God. You are *unique*."

"I have nothing to say to you," Roan snaps, "except good-bye."

They lunge for each other, a burst of uncanny speed and strength, mere blurs to Rapley's eyes. He hurries to the shelves, throwing down the medical jars that crowd them, spilling embalming fluid and alcohol everywhere. He reaches for his torch, some feet away, and then throws it at the liquid.

Roan!

He thinks her name with all his might.

She looks at him, smiles, and then—faster than Rapley can see—forces Andrew into the flames.

She grabs Rapley's hand and they run for the stairs to get out of the cavern.

"Cage," Rapley says urgently, turning back. And there...eerie and still in the roiling smoke...stands Seamus, his eyes moist with rotten tears.

"No time!" Roan yells, pulling him on.

They take the stairs three at a time, Roan pulling Rapley fast and hard.

We've done it, her mind screams. *We've done it!*

But as they are clearing the stairs, a pale hand emerges out of the flames and grabs Rapley's leg. Rapley looks up at Roan, his eyes wide and terrified, and reaches out a hand.

She grabs it, remembering her vision. Remembering his wide, pleading eyes, which now stare up at her, the palest gray she has yet seen.

He will die on this mountain.

I've got you, she thinks—

and they are all pulled into the flames.

ZOEY

NOW

Chapter 43
MY LULLABY

I wonder what our bones will look like when someone finally comes looking.

Bones are all I can think about.

We've been saying how weird it is that nothing lives on this mountain. But it does. The snakes, the rats...Those things seem just fine. And it will be those things that finally have a decent meal with our bodies.

Of course, not Len. How long can she live on rats? What about water? We blew up what I guess was the only source on this poisoned mountain.

Eventually, I'll need to ask her.

It comforts me to imagine our bones, though. Picked absolutely clean.

When I talk to Pole, I don't expect a reply. He spits vile words in my direction, sticks out his tongue, leers, and makes sexual sounds. It has no effect on me. I don't seem to care about very much. It was all a waste anyway.

~~

Len and I don't discuss the future anymore. We've run out of water. I'll die soon.

I can't believe I've done this to my mum and Greg. I won't get to see Dexter grow up. I hated having a half brother, but now I think it could be kind of fun. Except he'll never get to know me.

And my dad...he won't even know I'm not there. Ha-ha-fucking-ha! I did this all to save him, and he won't even know he's lost me. He doesn't know. And I lied about texting Dexter my location and now I've killed Pole too.

What have I done?

Arms are getting stronger.
Writing.
Dragging myself around.
Almost freed Pole.
Len stopped me.
Who cares if he kills me?
He'll get to eat.

Camera Footage

"How long have you been here?"

Zoey is slumped next to a sleeping Poulton, leaning

against the piano in the Red Room. Poulton's head is not tied to the piano, but the rest of him is. Arms, torso, and his legs tied together.

Len, sitting on the floor some way off, has been staring at a tapestry. She turns her head.

"Drop it, Zoey."

"You don't die. How old are you? Where are you from? What do you like? I don't know you at all."

Len closes her eyes. "Please, Zoey..."

"You're a fucking stranger," Zoey spits. She picks up a piece of cloth, the debris clearly from Pole's "ropes," and throws it fiercely at Len, then collapses back, panting. "I don't know you at all."

Len wipes away a tear. "Don't say that."

Zoey's eyes narrow. *"How. Long. Have. You. Been. Here."*

Len inhales shakily, more tears falling. "I don't want to hurt you."

"HOW LONG?" Zoey yells, waking Pole, who looks blearily around before starting to roar and shake his head, banging it back against the piano over and over. The piano gives off-key protests each time.

Len hurries over and secures his head so that he can no longer move it; he spits at her and says something in a guttural language. Len replies, her words even more venomous and savage.

"Tarvok arra" she growls, and he falls silent, but continues to smile manically, his eyes bright with madness and fever.

"Give me a fucking answer! I'm going to die, so give me that at least," Zoey says, her voice harsh and dry.

"Five years," Len says, turning away and returning to her spot on the floor. "I've been here five years."

Zoey, it seems, had not expected that answer. Her

mouth falls open and she blinks slowly, dumbly, trying to speak. Eventually, she chokes out, "Five...years?"

Len looks away. "I didn't want to hurt you."

"Oh, Len..."

It is Zoey's turn to cry.

Weird thing about dying: It's much slower than you think it'll be. I was convinced I wouldn't wake this morning. I couldn't eat yesterday. I thought: this is it. Over. I could barely hold this pen.

And yet, here I am, munching on rat and snake, hungrier than I've ever felt.

Len's feeding Pole like an animal. Tearing off bits and using the old iron fireplace poker to get it to his mouth. He broke a couple of teeth trying to chew the iron itself in the beginning.

Now he's learned.

The other weird thing about dying: remembering stuff. Stuff about your life, and things you've done and not done. It all ends up seeming so pointless. Like, what did I add to the world? What have I given that makes things better or worse? Have I made a difference? And for me: No. Aside from killing myself and dragging Pole with me, I haven't done anything.

I'm a blip.

Here in a moment, gone in a blink.

And we think we're so important, don't we? We think we're so special, convinced of our own uniqueness, our own destiny. I was destined to come here, find some great revelation and take it back to free my father.

And why?

For a noble reason? HA! I did it because <u>I</u> wanted <u>him</u> back. Not because <u>he</u> needs <u>me</u> back. He doesn't know who I am. He's happy in his little care home with the nurses checking in on him twice a week. He doesn't need what he doesn't remember.

And I rejected Greg and my half brother and I left my mum...

For a dream.

A wish.

An illusion.

I remember when Mum took me to the park near our flat in Finchley when Dad was still...Dad. I jumped on the roundabout next to the seesaw, my favorite thing ever, and Mum started spinning me. I was lying down on it, looking up at the sky, watching the autumn leaves falling. I remember the feeling so clearly...like I'm spinning on it right now. I can hear Mum laughing! And then, when she couldn't make it go any faster, she'd jump on it next to me and we'd lie together, watching the sky spin until eventually we stopped. We would lie there, panting and grinning, and then I'd beg her to do it again, just the same.

Nothing could make me leave, nothing. Not even bribes of ice cream. The only way she got me home was when she started to walk home without me. I would fill with terror of losing her, and I'd jump up and chase her all the way back to the flat.

She would ask me, later at night, what I was

thinking and I would tell her how scared I was when she walked away. I was scared she would disappear. She said she would always be there. That she was only a bedroom away and that whenever I felt scared, I could come and talk to her. No matter the hour.

And I did. For years.

When we lost Dad, I did it less. And then, when I turned eight and saw the black form at the foot of my bed, I stopped telling her anything.

I'm sorry, Mum. I'm so, so sorry.

Camera Footage

Zoey's face is drawn, thin and haunted.

"Mum," she says, her voice breathless like a sigh. "I wanted you to know that I'm sorry. I'm so sorry for coming here, for running away, for the last things we said to each other. I want you to know that I know, in my heart, that you didn't mean what you said. You were angry. I understand that. I got your temper." She laughs. "Anyway. I hope that someone finds this and gives it to you so that you know I was thinking of you the whole time. And also because I wanted to remind you of the park days in Finchley, and that one day I told you I was afraid you'd disappear. You told me that night I could tell you everything."

She pauses to wipe away a tear.

"There's something I never told you. No, it's not my coming out," she jokes. "I'm pretty sure you knew that already. I never felt like I had to say it, despite your jokes about Pole and me. I think…it was your way of trying to get me to tell you. But you knew. What I wanted to tell you was a secret I've been carrying for a long time." She sobs, and it takes a moment for her to continue. "So, so long. I've been...seeing something. Since I was seven or eight. Right after Dad left to go to the hospital. For years, I've been haunted. I don't why I didn't tell you...Maybe because I was scared you'd think I was like Dad...that it was a sign I was going mad. And maybe it was. But...see, that's the reason I came here."

She wipes her face, then grunts as though wanting to shake away her emotions.

"I came here because of Dad's obsession, his trip here when I was little, his madness and forgetting...but also because of the black figure. At night, it would sit there in the corner of my room on your old rocking chair, rocking back and forth, this...horrible presence. And it would whisper...'*Mill House...Mill House...*' over and over.

"That horrible voice, that croaking whisper—those words...they were my lullaby for years. So I had to come. And I regret it. I regret everything. But I had to tell you. You said I always could, and I'm so sorry it took me this long."

She rests the camera on her legs so that her chin and torso are in the shot with part of the ceiling.

"I'm sorry," comes a voice from far off. "I came to check on you...I wasn't prying."

Zoey shrugs and the camera shakes on her lap.

"What you said...about the form..." She comes closer so that part of her leg is in the shot along with the edges of long, red hair. "Have you seen it since we came here?"

Zoey shakes her head.

"I never told you what my Unclosed ability is. I didn't want to scare you away." Len sits down beside Zoey, but

Zoey doesn't move. "But I've learned to trust you. I don't want to hide anything from you."

"Because I'm dead anyway."

"No," Len says fiercely, taking one of Zoey's hands so that the camera falls, angling so that Len's face is also now fully in the frame from beneath. "Because I care about you. I...I love you, Zoey. So much. More than anything. And I know it's true, because the thought of losing you has had me thinking about how to kill myself. Fire, drowning— how can I escape this life?"

Zoey reacts for the first time. "No, Len! I don't want that. I want to stay here. I want to live. I want to spend a lifetime with you. More if I could."

Len grabs her face and then they are kissing, the camera forgotten. When they pull away, both are crying. The moment is ruined slightly by the cackling of Pole nearby. He is not in the shot.

"Cccccccccyyyyeeeeeeewwwwt," he drawls, his voice high and ragged. *"Burn in hell with me, you lesbian whores!"* he mutters.

The girls ignore him as though his heckling has become so normal that it doesn't faze them. They don't even break their gaze to look at him.

Len licks her lips and Zoey waits. "Necromancy. My Conjure. I commune with the dead...among other things."

Zoey looks at her for a moment, and then looks down at the camera on her lap.

"Mom, Greg, I want you to meet my girlfriend."

Len's eyes widen and then she bursts out laughing. Zoey laughs too, in a tired, alarming way.

"She's a necromancer," she adds. "Hot, right?"

"What if...what if I could call your ghost, if that's what

it was...What if this is all about that black form? What if it's the key?"

"What if it was a delusion?"

"Then no harm done. It could be something darker though, which is why I want your permission before I try."

"Darker..."

"Something...sinister. Demonic."

"It never hurt me. If anything, it always seemed... desperate. And when it was with me, I was terrified, yes, but also sad."

"Let me try to call it."

"I tried once," Zoey said. "And you turned up."

"You're not a necromancer. You're a beautiful, wonderful Finder. Leave the dead to me."

Len gives Zoey a kiss on the cheek, then gets up and walks out of the shot.

Zoey looks back down at the camera. "She's a keeper, eh?"

I am sickened in body and soul and mind. John and what men remain took my Nebula, my sweet, dear friend. Nebula's head did roll across the mountain, down, down, down, and I saw whence it landed; her mouth opened and closed and she frowned most heartily, blinking as though indignant. It took so long, so long for that head to stop moving, and when it did, I loosed a cry as a wolf and fled, my book and flint and candle in hand.

I must hide. I must escape. For what can happen now that has not already happened?

A dreadful night.

THE LAST DIARY ENTRY FROM
HERMIONE SMITH,
NOVEMBER 1588

ZOEY

———

NOW

Chapter 44

HERMIONE

Camera Footage

Len places the camera down on a surface. "Here?" she asks, turning back to Zoey, who sits in the middle of the floor. They appear to be in the kitchen in front of the large fireplace, which is lit without any logs. Symbols have been etched into the fireplace in chalk.

"Yes," Zoey says. "That's fine. I want to record this."

Len joins Zoey on the floor. Zoey has been zipped into her sleeping bag, her arms free.

"Don't be alarmed by what you see," Len says. "Remember what I am, and trust me."

Zoey nods.

"And most importantly—do *not* speak. Not a sound. No matter what happens. It's important."

Another nod from Zoey, though now she looks a little afraid.

Len cricks her neck left, right, then closes her eyes. She might be meditating. Beside her lies a fresh supply of chalk, as well as Pole's penknife, a pad of paper, and a pen.

Len begins to speak. Her words are not human. Not English, not French—but the same guttural sounds as before. They are quiet at first, rising in volume as she continues.

She begins to breathe heavily, taking great breaths between the sounds, until she is shouting, her neck taut, her fists clenched and arms straining. The sounds reach a magnitude of volume, then as quick as wildfire, Len snatches up the penknife, flicks it open, and slits her flesh from forearm to wrist.

The blood pours from her and coats the floor. Zoey inhales, covers her mouth, and seems to inhale her scream.

Len's voice changes all of a sudden—it is no longer her voice. It is inhumanly loud, deep, and raw as gravel, her teeth bared in an animalistic snarl. She whips forward, her torso bending like rubber, until she laps at her own blood pooled on the floor.

She continues to growl the words, her teeth still bared like a wolf's, only bloodied now, the spray hitting Zoey in the face.

Even through all this horror, Len remains preternaturally glorious. She is an awesome, terrifying specter of savage beauty. Her hair begins to move on its own, as though there is static in the air, then at long, long last, Len throws her arms wide in the mimicry of a crucifixion, spraying blood across the room—

And then she slumps, her hair falling forward over her face.

Zoey opens her mouth to speak, but then hesitates. She lifts her hand as though to touch Len's head, but at the very point that Len sprayed her own blood, something moves.

Zoey flinches when the movement becomes more rhythmic, until even the camera can make out a dark shape sitting on a rocking chair, moving back and forth, back and forth.

Zoey's shoulders come up and she pulls her sleeping bag higher so that only her face peeks out. She glances between the shape in the chair and Len.

And then the shape begins to stand.

Zoey flinches again. Her lips part, and she whispers, "Not again...I don't want to see this. I've seen this thing for years in my bedroom. I can't...Len..."

Len lifts her head, ignoring Zoey. "Come into the light."

The figure moves with unnatural stiffness, sometimes slow and languid, other times jerky and forced. But come, it does. The thing hesitates at the border between the shadows of the room and the dancing ring of light from the fire.

"I will guard you," Len says, her eyes still closed. "Come into the light and reveal yourself."

It moves its arm first, almost hesitant, and as it touches the light, the blackness falls away from it, upward like falling ashes in reverse, to reveal a slim, young hand.

Zoey sees the ring right away and she covers her mouth with both hands. It is an exact replica of the one she wears on her own finger. Her heirloom ring.

The figure steps forward and the ashes rise off her as she does, until Zoey is staring up at a young woman in a white dress with pale hair. She has a glow about her, and she isn't quite corporeal.

She looks around in wonder, then at her own hands, and then, at last, at Zoey. She opens her mouth, but there is no sound. She looks to Len.

"She cannot hear you speak," Len says to her. "It's not within my power. But I hear you."

There is silence as the woman sinks to the floor to kneel by Zoey. She makes to touch Zoey's cheek, smiling, but stops mere inches away.

"She says 'daughter,'" Len says. "She's calling you daughter. Zoey, you can speak now."

Zoey licks her lips. "D-daughter?"

"She says that she is your ancestor."

Zoey laughs. "Really?"

"She says her name is...slower please. It's too much. Okay, yes. Hermione."

Zoey looks at the woman. "Hermione...I've read your journals. You've been watching me for a long time."

"She has watched as many of you as she could over the years. She says you are one of the last. She watched your father as well."

Zoey's face falls. "Did you send him here too?"

Hermione nods.

"*Why?*" cries Zoey. "He went mad. Forgot everything!"

"Slow down," Len mutters. "She's showing me things. I can't...Slow down, please."

Len falls silent and Hermione stares.

"She wants to show us something. I...I don't know how."

Hermione draws an invisible picture in the air.

"Okay," Len says. "Zoey, give me your hand." Zoey does as instructed and Len picks up the piece of chalk. She draws something on Zoey's palm, her eyes still firmly shut, and then takes Zoey's hand in her own. The blood-soaked arm is still outstretched, dripping slowly. Hermione stands in the blood, touching nothing else.

"Close your eyes," Len says, and Zoey does.

And each woman, mortal, immortal, and dead, goes still.

⌁

When I closed my eyes, I was on the mountain. I saw Hermione, as she is now, but somehow I knew she was alive. She looked pale, thin, and small. She seemed beaten. She was standing in a patch of darkness, looking all around, holding in her arms a torch, the flames of which illuminated the other cargo there.

A small infant.

Hermione kissed the child, her eyes red and swollen from long weeping, and she muttered, "I love you, my boy. Love you enough to give you away. But by God, I pray that you'll never suffer as I have suffered. Never fall into the Devil's hands." She closed her eyes. "I curse you never to work the magic of your father. But if you do, I curse you to suffer for it, forever."

Something moved in the distance and Hermione hesitated, but did not turn away.

"Huw?" she called. "By God, is that you?"

A boy hurried toward her. "It is I, lady. Well met. Where be your husband tonight?"

"Conjuring," Hermione said darkly. "He works the Devil's magic even now. Take him, Huw, and hurry. Begone, and safe away."

She handed over the child, her whole body trembling, and then Huw backed away.

"Keep him safe!" she whispered as the two vanished into the night. "Take him far away...my little boy."

And then she was racked with sobs that overcame her entire body, until she curled herself into a tiny ball in the dirt.

After a while, she got to her feet. Len and I followed her along the mountain, which was crystal clear in the night, nothing like the misty view we had known for so long. She approached a large tent, peered inside. It was empty.

Then she headed for the jagged part of the mountain, for the same little cave that Len and had I crawled out of days ago.

A small fire burned inside. Hermione crouched low as she approached and peeked around. I could <u>feel</u> the uncleanness of the air, not so much the smell of the fire, but the spiritual stink of foul magic.

Two men, one young and one old, sat before a tall mirror, conversing in a language that I couldn't understand, but somehow recognized. Polish, or Russian, maybe.

"Dee, be not a fool," the young man said. "Persist in the face of persecution. Continue to speak to your angels. And let them guide you to the language of God."

The old man grunted, and nodded. "I must return to Jane and the children. She cannot sleep until I am with her." He stood, but then looked back at the mirror. "You have shown me much, John," Dee said.

"There is more to be discovered," said the young man. "Good night, John."

Two Johns. John Smith, and the Queen's most famous Conjurer...John Dee.

The older John walked past Hermione without seeing her, heading for his tent, his wife, and his children, and Hermione looked in again.

"You are out of bounds, wife," the younger John said.

"And you," she said, stepping into the light of the cave, "have been working with the Devil. Tell me, husband. Have you signed over your soul? Is that how you work such evil?"

John smiled and turned to Hermione. "Yes."

Though she had, perhaps, expected this answer, she still shook her head and backed away.

"How can you, John? Do you have no fear of God?"

He smiled. "I spit on your God."

"Damned," she said, still shaking her head. "You are damned!"

He sighed. "I know."

Hermione spun around, and tried to run, but with a few words and a dance of his fingers, she was caught in midair, as though by a spider's web.

"Shh," he whispered. "You'll wake what's left of my workers. And I need them. I'm still looking."

After that we melted away and I thought it was over, but there was worse yet to come. Hermione was being dragged over the mountain, pulled along by a group of men and women who had tied her hands.

John stood silent at the crest of the rocky part of the mountain, where a pyre had been constructed.

I went cold.

I couldn't look away as they tied her to the stake. She was beaten and bloody.

"Tell us, witch!" one of the women yelled. "Where is the child? Where?"

Hermione looked up to heaven and began to pray.

"She is witching us," John said.

The hysteria was intense. "She is in league with the Lancashire witch!" someone cried.

"Let not her speak!" yelled another.

And then someone threw a torch.

In the movies, they make it seem so fast. The fire erupts, the body screams for a second or two, and the person vanishes.

This was not that.

The fire took a long time. More torches were thrown. Hermione's eyes bugged out in terror and she was screaming long before the first lick of flame touched her.

The hem of her dress finally caught, and her screams became something else entirely. I never want to hear that sound again.

The burning took a long time. The fire remained low, never reaching her head, the wind blowing away the smoke.

It took hours.

We saw it all. We couldn't leave.

She kept moving even after she stopped screaming.

We heard it all.

The crowd cheered long after the end of it, and then they went back to their beds and fell asleep feeling satiated and safe, while Hermione's body still simmered in the dregs of the fire.

And then we were back in the room. The camera had died already.

Hermione was gone.

"She told me how to do it," Len said, smiling faintly when she finally opened her eyes. Her arm was already healed. "I know how to get us out."

You learn something new every day, I guess. Len said that we hadn't destroyed the wheel. Not in the way that counts. We have to go back down there. HA-HA-HA. Len's working on a way to do it from here. She's studying this great fat book she never told me she had. It's got the language in it. After hearing some of it and seeing her using it, I'm not so sure I want to learn anymore.

The new thing I learned is: nightwalking. Astral projection, seems like. Apparently we have to destroy the wheel in the nightwalking plane. The physical wheel was just an anchor—blah, blah.

And now I know that the shape at the foot of my bed was Hermione all along. My ancestor. Except now it doesn't seem too important anymore.

I'm so tired. I've been sleeping a lot.

Len keeps waking me up.

ROAN

1851

Roan stirs.

It is a foggy morning. The sun has not yet risen.

It is raining.

No.

Snowing.

No…

Ashes are falling from the sky.

She smells like fire, and is blackened with soot. She has no clothes, no hair. But her skin is whole. She sees the ruins around her, and then she screams. Rapley is gone. She looks at the sky. Is he falling down around her, she wonders through her red tears. She can see the rips in reality now too. They float around her like so many eels.

He awaits her on the mountain. The ram.

She stumbles to her feet, and goes to meet him. A warm blanket lies beside him. He looks at her with a penetrating gaze, and she hears the Devil's language in her mind.

And then he turns and walks slowly on.

Roan stares at the house, which looks so untouched from this distance, and feels nothing. Her rage is gone. Her love is gone. Everything is gone.

Fostos—is gone.

And then.

A carriage on the road far below her, speeding away.

Fostos.

Alive. Alive after all.

The nothing inside her bursts into a feeling…Her rage is limitless.

She must hide, she knows, before dawn brings the sun. She is now a creature of the night, just like Fostos. No more sun. No more food. No more life. Centuries before her.

She vows revenge.

There is time. Too much time. Already her teeth are growing sharp.

She turns and stumbles away, and as her new heartbeat echoes through the mountain, a smaller heartbeat echoes inside her.

ZOEY

NOW

My name is Poulton. I'm writing this for Zoey.

There are parts that I don't remember. She's telling me those. After that, I'll take up what I remember.

<u>From Zoey</u>:

Learning about nightwalking was like remembering a forgotten recurring dream. Everything was vaguely familiar. Len told me how she did it—what she saw when she did it, and how she had learned the sigils to make it happen. Now she was going to teach me.

We spent hours going over the symbols in chalk. I was slow and clumsy, thick-headed and thick-tongued. But by that night, I had it. She told me I would see something different. She warned me. It might not look, as it did for her, like a carousel that she had to climb onto while it spun before her.

I drew the symbols with a level of concentration I had never before exerted. Len told me that if I got even the smallest thing wrong, I could end up somewhere else. Sure, I'd wake up in a few hours, but who could tell where I would have to spend those hours.

I lay back and went to sleep.

For me, the nightwalking access vision was a black mountain, not a carousel; a sheer face towered before me. And halfway up: a spot of red.

I touched my legs—I was standing. I gave a laugh—it was loud, harsh. I could <u>walk</u>. I started climbing right away, my hands finding the right niches and dents, the rocks they needed to find. Up, up—I felt like I was flying. I was half tempted to let go to see if I could, but the thought of losing my legs again sobered me up pretty fast.

The spot of red became, at last, a door. It was open just a crack.

I climbed up beside it, pushed, and it creaked open onto a dark nothing. I looked out at the landscape below me, rocky and barren, but beautiful, then up at the gray, rolling clouds above; I tumbled through the doorway.

I was hovering over my body. Len was beside me, her arm slung over me as though for protection. I smiled. And then Len, the noncorporeal Len, was beside me.

She grinned.

Unreal.

We didn't move, as such. We didn't really fly. We just sort of thought of where we needed to be, and were there.

The second wheel—the spiritual wheel—stood perfect and unbroken, superimposed upon the destruction we had wrought in the waking world upon the physical wheel. We had destroyed the wheel made of wood and iron, but in the nightwalking world, the wheel turned, slow and proud. Every inch of it...was covered in people. Dusty white, the wheel was a teeming mass of heads, arms, hands, legs—contorted together—and the cries were so loud and so pained, it was agony to hear it.

Now and then, one of the people would break away from the wheel and move beyond it, as though straining against an elastic, only to be pulled back again and jumbled in with the others.

This was why, I suddenly knew, there had been no ghosts in the house. These were them…They were trapped.

It was far simpler to draw the symbols in the nightwalking plane. I watched Len draw right onto the bodies of these men and women. I watched glassy-eyed, and spotted, for a moment, Hermione among them. Then she was swallowed up by the limbs and faces around her.

When Len used the words as we floated there, she whispered them.

I opened my eyes. Back in the Red Room.

And I knew it was over.

I came to at that moment, tied to the red piano. I had never felt so cold, so hungry, nor so sick in my life. My stomach rolled over and I vomited. I heard her say my name, tentatively.

I answered that it was me. Poulton. I was Poulton again.

And I remembered everything.

Len untied me and brought over a sleeping bag. I thanked her. Moving was agony. Knives in every joint. Worse. I crawled over to Zoey, wanting to hug her, to say how sorry I was—but she just lay there on the ground, crying. Her tears fell, but she didn't sob.

And I guess Len realized why before I did.

She cried, "No!" But I didn't yet understand. Not until Len pulled Zoey onto her lap and began to sob.

So that's why I'm writing this for her. Because she can't. Zoey hasn't moved more than her chest or her head since that day. She's quadriplegic.

After a while, she kept saying, "I can't live like this." Over and over she said it, and over and over Len said she could. That she would learn. I was numb with shock. I couldn't take it.

I remember the way Len said, "They're gone. The ghosts are

gone," and she looked around as though she could see them walking away. Then, without another word, she got to her feet.

"Get dressed," she told me.

I didn't need telling twice.

I clothed myself, as best I could. Got on my boots. She had to tie my laces.

Then she hauled Zoey onto her back, still in her sleeping bag, and walked right out of the house.

We walked back to town and beyond it. I followed. We stopped a lot at first, but after a couple of nights with warm food, water, and a bed, I was able to keep up much better.

I won't say where we went, or where we are.

Zoey kept asking why. What the point was.

Until one night Len finally answered.

"I'm taking you to my mother. She can help you." Then she looked at Zoey and said, "Her name is Roan."

Len—Raplen—was born in 1852 to Roan Evelyn Eddington and Rapley Setters.

So we go on. A new journey begins.

ACKNOWLEDGMENTS

First, big congratulations to the two lovely readers who won my Instagram giveaway, the prize of which was a character in my next novel named after them. So, Emma Petfield and Hermione Simpson, these girls are for you. Hope you like them!

Books are never made in isolation, and I had an amazing team of people who brought *Teeth in the Mist* into the world. Huge and heartfelt thanks to Alvina Ling, my editor from the start, who saw my weird found-footage book (and loved it), who loved my creepy tree novel, and who allowed me the time and mental space for *Teeth* to form. Thank you for always bringing out the very best in my writing, and for understanding my unusual methods and unconventional stories. It's an amazing thing to feel like you've come home.

Thanks to Kheryn Callender for answering all my questions, for keeping me in the loop, and for being the kindest soul; thank you to Ruqayyah Daud (also the kindest human being) for the contact, jokes, and smiles. To my badass agents, Sarah Davies and Polly Nolan, who always do the very best for me, and whom, I am convinced, are actual badass witches. You'll have to tell me what your Conjure is one of these days....

Thank you to the team at Little, Brown Books for Young Readers for such an incredible cover, beautiful interiors, eagle-eyed copyedits, and for endless support and love; as well as Natali and Valerie, the trade marketing and digital marketing interns at NOVL, for fun and games, and for always having a shout-out to hand. You keep books fun and relevant on social media, for which I am definitely thankful. Thank you, Alvina et al., for allowing me the space to use my art in a book like this too.

My early readers, Kat Ellis, Ashley Hartzell, Patti Rossier, and my family for their continued support; to Lindzi for writing sessions, the weirdest (and best) conversations ever, and for the spooky tales. Shout-out and thank you to Jennifer Faughnan (@jennielyreads) for endless enthusiasm and for always having an ear. I love you!

To the bloggers and booktubers who have shown such love for my books, I couldn't have reached so many readers without you. Special thanks to Cameron Chaney for your love of horror and absolutely brilliant horror book reviews! To the close community of bookish fiends on Instagram, including @ladiesofhorrorfiction, I adore you and am grateful for your enthusiasm in spreading the word about the female horror writers who are too often overlooked. What a great community we have.

And to my readers—thank you. You make this possible. Very special thank you to those readers who take the time to read, review, comment, and rate my books on Amazon, Goodreads, and other social media outlets and for spreading the word. Your Instagram accounts are devilishly gorgeous and I can't wait to see what you do with them next!

Finally, a request: If you are depressed, alone, suffering, or just need an ear, please call someone. Anyone. You are not alone. But if all else fails, send me a tweet, email, or message and I will do my best to reply.

Teeth in the Mist came out of a very dark, lonely time in my life, and no one should suffer alone. So for those of you who scream in silence, look for the light.

PHOTO CREDITS

Dawn Kurtagich

Dawn Kurtagich

is a writer of psychologically sinister fiction, and she has a dark and twisted imagination! She lives in Wales, an ancient and mountainous country within the UK (go to England's Midlands and turn left toward the sea). However, she grew up all over the world, predominantly in Africa. She is the author of *The Dead House, And the Trees Crept In,* and *Teeth in the Mist.*